PRAISE FOR

DRAGON BOUND

"Black Dagger Brotherhood readers will love *Dragon Bound* . . .
I'm hooked!"

—J. R. Ward, #1 *New York Times* bestselling author

"I loved this book so much I didn't want it to end. Smoldering
sensuality, fascinating characters and an intriguing world—
Dragon Bound kept me glued to the pages. Thea Harrison has
a new fan in me!"

—Nalini Singh, *New York Times* bestselling author

"Thea Harrison has created a truly original urban fantasy
romance . . . When the shapeshifting dragon locks horns with
his very special heroine, sparks fly that any reader will enjoy.
Buy yourself an extra-large cappuccino, sit back and enjoy the
decadent fun!"

—Angela Knight, *New York Times* bestselling author

"*Dragon Bound* is full of tense action, toe-curling love scenes
and intriguing characters that will stay with you long after the
story is over. All that is wrapped inside a colorful, compelling
world with magic so real, the reader can feel it. Thea Harrison
is a fantastic new talent who will soon be taking the world of
paranormal romance by storm."

—Shannon K. Butcher, national bestselling author

"Thea Harrison is definitely an author to watch. Sexy and
action packed, *Dragon Bound* features a strong, likable heroine, a white-hot luscious hero and an original and intriguing
world that swallowed me whole. This novel held me transfixed
from beginning to end! I'll definitely be keeping my eyes open
for the next book in this series."

—Anya Bast, *New York Times* bestselling author

"Fun, feral and fiercely exciting—I can't get enough! Thea Harrison supplies deliciously addictive paranormal romance, and
I'm already jonesing for the next hit."

—Ann Aguirre, national bestselling author

STORM'S HEART

Thea Harrison

Thea Harrison

BERKLEY SENSATION, NEW YORK

THE BERKLEY PUBLISHING GROUP
Published by the Penguin Group
Penguin Group (USA) Inc.
375 Hudson Street, New York, New York 10014, USA
Penguin Group (Canada), 90 Eglinton Avenue East, Suite 700, Toronto, Ontario M4P 2Y3, Canada
(a division of Pearson Penguin Canada Inc.)
Penguin Books Ltd., 80 Strand, London WC2R 0RL, England
Penguin Group Ireland, 25 St. Stephen's Green, Dublin 2, Ireland (a division of Penguin Books Ltd.)
Penguin Group (Australia), 250 Camberwell Road, Camberwell, Victoria 3124, Australia
(a division of Pearson Australia Group Pty. Ltd.)
Penguin Books India Pvt. Ltd., 11 Community Centre, Panchsheel Park, New Delhi—110 017, India
Penguin Group (NZ), 67 Apollo Drive, Rosedale, Auckland 0632, New Zealand
(a division of Pearson New Zealand Ltd.)
Penguin Books (South Africa) (Pty.) Ltd., 24 Sturdee Avenue, Rosebank, Johannesburg 2196,
South Africa

Penguin Books Ltd., Registered Offices: 80 Strand, London WC2R 0RL, England

This is a work of fiction. Names, characters, places, and incidents either are the product of the author's imagination or are used fictitiously, and any resemblance to actual persons, living or dead, business establishments, events, or locales is entirely coincidental. The publisher does not have any control over and does not assume any responsibility for author or third-party websites or their content.

STORM'S HEART

A Berkley Sensation Book / published by arrangement with the author

PRINTING HISTORY
Berkley Sensation mass-market edition / August 2011

ISBN: 978-0-425-24266-7

BERKLEY® SENSATION
Berkley Sensation Books are published by The Berkley Publishing Group,
a division of Penguin Group (USA) Inc.,
375 Hudson Street, New York, New York 10014.
BERKLEY® SENSATION and the "B" design are trademarks of Penguin Group (USA) Inc.

PRINTED IN THE UNITED STATES OF AMERICA

10   9   8   7   6   5   4   3   2   1

ACKNOWLEDGMENTS

I owe a big debt of gratitude to all the usual suspects, but a few bear special mention.

To my agent, Amy, and my editor, Cindy, thank you for everything you do. I will never take either of you for granted.

To Lorene and Carol, your support continues to be miraculous.

To Matt, my generous and patient rock-star web designer. You are totally made of angel material, and you created a classy, beautiful site.

And to Kristin, who came along at a very late date to join the beta reading. Your enthusiasm, prompt replies and fine eye for detail were a total pleasure. You, Shawn, Anne and Fran have made my work much classier than it would otherwise have been.

queen, n:

1. the wife or widow of a king
2. a female monarch
3. a woman eminent in rank, power or attractions, such as a beauty contest winner <a movie queen>

queen, n:

4. a royal pain in my ass

—NINIANE LORELLE, DARK FAE QUEEN

≈ ONE ≈

You didn't ignore a summons roared from the Lord of the Wyr in New York, since it usually heralded a disaster of some proportion. You especially didn't ignore it if you were one of his sentinels.

Tiago strode out of the Starbucks located on the ground floor in Cuelebre Tower. He jogged up the north stairwell to the seventy-ninth floor. He could have taken the elevator, but he was feeling trapped and restless. He could have pushed out the coffee shop's street exit, shifted into his Wyr form and flown to the roof of the Tower then gone down two flights, but frustration gnawed at his insides and he wanted to feel the burn of the climb in his muscles and lungs.

He didn't like modern urban spaces. He was counting the minutes until he could get out of New York. A rainy, wet spring-time had evaporated to sultry ninety-degree weather, bypassing mild early summer temps like they never existed. Now June felt like August. Exhaust fumes, construction detritus, trash, restaurant odors, dry cleaner chemicals and all the various other scents of modern humanity sizzled in the heat. The smells burned the back of his throat, leaving him feeling irritable and out of place.

He was one of the ancient Wyr who were so long-lived they were known as immortal. The old ones had either been formed in the creative fire from the birth of the solar system or had been born so long ago their origins were a mystery even to them. They had existed in their animal forms for millennia, but when the new species of humans burgeoned, the old Wyr learned how to shapeshift so they could walk in secret among humankind.

Civilization was a dance, and the ancient Wyr were late to the ball. They donned masks and slipped with silent predatory grace into the ballroom. They watched with sharp eyes that glittered deep in the shadows behind their assumed facades, recording and learning the twist and rhythm of the dance, the social mores, when to bow and press their lips to the back of the hand, how to smile and say good evening, please and thank you and yes, I shall take more sugar with my tea.

All the while they noted the pulse that fluttered at the base of the dancers' necks, the scents of sweat and the quickened breath. They noted these things because they remembered they were animals playing a role. *Primal* was the first word they understood when they learned language, for that was what they were. Despite their smiling human masks, they were feral creatures who knew how to survive by the slash of tooth and claw. They remembered the gush of blood from the jugular as they crushed the life from their prey.

The ancients settled into their guises and grew comfortable with them, some with more charm, skill and enjoyment than others. But all of them carried that feral wildness at their core, the certain knowledge that they needed to roam the secret uncultivated magic places of the world.

Time and space had buckled when the Earth was formed. The buckling created dimensional pockets of Other land where magic pooled, time moved differently, modern technologies didn't work and the sun shone with a different light. What came to be known as the Elder Races, the Wyrkind and the Elves, the Light and Dark Fae, the Demonkind, the Nightkind, human witches and all manner of monstrous creatures, tended to cluster in or around the Other lands.

Those of the ancient Wyr that chose to adapt to human civilization were driven from time to time to slip away from modern cities and towns. They would shake loose from their human facades and drench themselves in archaic argent sunlight as they lost themselves in flight, or in plunging deep into the magic-saturated green of the oldest of untamed forests. There was a fundamental difference between the old ones and the younger Wyr. The younger Wyr were born into civilization. They arrived at the ball already tamed.

Tiago was not tame. He was more feral than the majority of even the most ancient Wyr. He needed to be worked hard, to face tough challenges and to be let loose to roam free. It was not wise to hold him too long in a city.

Two and a half weeks had passed since Rune had called him back from South America. Dragos Cuelebre, Lord of the Wyrkind demesne, had been missing at the time. Tiago had just arrived back in the States when Dragos had reappeared with a strange woman. The tale they told was one of thievery, kidnapping, magic and murder.

A lot had happened since Tiago's return and Dragos's reappearance. Some of it had been fun, like tracking Dragos's new mate when she had been kidnapped—again—and being in on the kill when Dragos had finally taken down his old enemy Urien, the Dark Fae King.

Vengeance, served hot. That had been Tiago's kind of party.

Since then all he had been doing was cleanup and busywork. Make sure all involved Goblins were dead, check. Chase down and slaughter any Dark Fae that had been part of Urien's party, check. Go to sleep with his thumb up his ass, check.

He smacked open the door that had the number 79 painted in a circle. His long legs ate up the distance as he strode down the marble-floored hall.

Cuelebre Enterprises was a multinational corporation that made an ungodly amount of money. Corporate employees and those involved in the governance of the Wyr demesne were compensated extremely well. Wyr sentinels had expense accounts that took care of clothes (the violent aspect to the sentinels' lives made this a substantial perk), travel, food and weapons. What else did a guy need? Once in a while Tiago would doublecheck his escalating bank balance to make sure all the numbers added up, but otherwise, for the most part he ignored it.

He remembered when Cuelebre Tower had been built. The 1970s had seen the invention of the neutron bomb, the Three Mile Island disaster, the terrorist attack at Munich's Olympic Games and the construction of Cuelebre Tower.

Yeah, staying far away from that project had been a good

thing. He had been quite content to travel across the world to hunt down, depose and kill a dusty little sorcerer in South Africa who had acquired his own army and a penchant for the Power he could gain through human and Wyr sacrificial rites. When Tiago returned to New York—and he had been sure to take his own sweet time in doing so—Cuelebre Tower had erupted onto the landscape and forever changed the skyline of the city.

The outer surface of the Tower was sleek and gleaming, reflecting the changeable sky, while the interior had been decorated with an extravagance of gold-veined Turkish marble flooring, gleaming frosted glass lights and polished brass fixtures, along with strategically displayed, priceless works of art and sculpture. The entire skyscraper was a proclamation of the Wyr Lord Dragos Cuelebre's wealth and power.

The achievement had more than architectural or economic significance. It made more than a political statement to the other Elder Races. The year of the Tower's construction went down in recent Wyr folklore as a miracle of collective cooperation, personal dominance and merciless rule. Just as Dragos had dragged the recalcitrant, volatile Wyrkind under his reign so many centuries before, he bludgeoned them into modernity and forced them into compliance.

Although some of the Wyr bloodied each other during the highest-stress points of the Tower's construction and the subsequent move of corporate and administrative offices, nobody actually dared to commit murder. They had been in the final stages of settling in when an amused Tiago had taken a tour of the skyscraper. All Wyr had been sent to their respective corners to settle ruffled fur or feathers, lick literal and metaphorical wounds, furnish their offices and unpack files. Now, without exception, anyone who had been involved in the creation of the Tower spoke of that time with pride and without the slightest comprehension of irony.

Tiago reached the conference room. It was a large executive boardroom with all the perks: black leather seats, a large polished oak table, state-of-the-art teleconferencing equipment and mysterious black metal contraptions that Tiago had been told were designer cappuccino and espresso machines. He couldn't remember the instructions for how to operate them. As soon as he had realized they weren't some kind of newfangled weapon the sentinels would be trained to use, he had lost interest in the conversation.

Dragos and all the other Wyr sentinels were already in the boardroom. Tiago almost twitched when he saw that Dragos's new mate, Pia, was also present. She had come out of nowhere and now all of a sudden she played a major role in Dragos's decision making.

When Wyr mated, they did so for life. It was a rare occurrence, especially in their exceptionally long lives, and it was an irrevocable one, so the change was here to stay. Dragos's mating had sent shock waves through the Wyr demesne, and no doubt through all the other demesnes as well. It wasn't a change Tiago liked, but he, along with the rest of the world, had to suck it up and start getting used to it. Dragos, a massive dark man with gold dragon's eyes, paced at one end of the room.

"About time," the Wyr Lord snapped.

Tiago stalked to his customary corner where he held up the wall during their sentinel meetings. "I'm here now, aren't I?"

Tiago's sharp hearing caught Dragos's mate, Pia, as she whispered to the gryphon Graydon at her side, "Are you sure he's housebroken?"

Tiago chose to ignore her. Instead he took his first good look around at those in the room. All the usual suspects were present, minus one. The four gryphons, Bayne, Constantine, Graydon and Dragos's First sentinel, Rune, were all tawny, suntanned and muscled. They kept the peace in the Wyr demesne. The harpy Aryal, who was in charge of investigations, sat with her arms and legs folded, jiggling a foot. That chick didn't do well with the concept of sitting still. Cuelebre Enterprises' head of security, the gargoyle Grym, sat by Aryal as usual, half of his attention on the harpy. More often than not, when Aryal's impetuous temper got her into trouble, Grym was there to haul her ass out of it.

Tiago scowled as he acknowledged the one person who had not joined them, and who would never join them again. Tricks, the faerie who used to head the PR department for Cuelebre Enterprises, had been an integral part of their group for a long time. Odd, how the absence of one cute little faerie could cause such a big hole in the room.

Then there was yours truly. While his Wyr form was known to the American Indian nations as the gigantic thunderbird, most just saw his human form, a six-foot-four, two-hundred-fifty pound male with barbed wire tattoos circling thick muscled biceps and swirls shaven into his short black hair. His face looked like it had been hewn with a hatchet, and he didn't often remember to smile. When he did, he seemed to cause alarm more often than not.

Here was the central dynamic of his life: while he went about the business of war, the usual tenor of his days was surprisingly peaceful. The reason why was simple. People tended not to argue with him.

Several hundred years ago he had become head of Dragos's private army, most of which was currently traveling back from a canceled engagement in South America. He should be traveling with his troops and preparing for their next assignment instead of sitting in New York with his thumb up his ass. Fuck.

The upset in the room finally registered. Tiago's eyes narrowed. Everybody had some kind of unhappy vibe going on. He said, "What's up?"

Dragos spun at the end of the room and paced another lap. "Tricks is missing. She's not answering her cell either."

Tiago straightened from the wall and planted his hands on his hips. "She's only been gone four days. What happened?"

Dragos turned to the huge flat-screen on the other side of the room and aimed a remote at it. "Some people have already seen this."

Tiago turned. The flat-screen came alive to MSNBC morning news. The running ticker tape across the bottom of the screen indicated it was from this morning. The recording was only a couple hours old.

An unsmiling female reporter faced the camera. "It's a story that could have come straight from a faerie tale—a fictional one, that is. It has captured the imagination just as Marilyn Monroe once captured hearts all around the world. For many years Thistle Periwinkle has been America's sweetheart and one of the most famous public personages of the Elder Races. She has acted as PR spokesperson for Cuelebre Enterprises since the early 1970s. Both the paparazzi and the public love her. She has graced international magazine covers, made regular TV appearances, and was once a guest on Johnny Carson's *Tonight Show . . .*"

Tiago's brows lowered in a scowl as photos and film clips of

Tricks were shown while the reporter spoke. Taken from a wide variety of sources, they showed the petite faerie in different styles over the years. He learned more about her in just a few minutes than he had ever known before.

In one film clip she wore her hair in a Mary Tyler Moore flip. In another, her dark hair was teased and bouffant, à la Monroe, as she winked at the camera. In a third clip from the 1960s, she wore long braids, platform shoes and a tie-dyed minidress. The braids clearly showed delicately pointed ears, long dark gray Fae eyes that were larger than most humans', high-cheekbones, a snub nose and angular face and a full mouth that was more often than not beaming a wide smile.

This was not going in a good direction. His stomach clenched. He demanded, "Why are they talking about her in the past tense?"

He got shushed by several of the other sentinels who were focused on the screen, their expressions tense. His scowl deepened, but he turned his attention back to the film clip. It cut back to the reporter, who said, "Then just days ago America was shocked when Dark Fae King Urien Lorelle was killed in a freak riding accident . . ."

"Freak riding accident," Graydon snorted. "Yeah. He accidentally got torn apart by an angry dragon. Oopsie."

This time Tiago joined in shushing the gryphon. The news segment was just getting relevant.

". . . and it was revealed that Thistle Periwinkle was in actuality Niniane Lorelle, the long-lost daughter of deceased Dark Fae King Rhian and his Queen Shaylee. Niniane Lorelle had long been assumed dead, but both DNA and magical tests confirmed Thistle Periwinkle's claim. She was indeed the heir to the Dark Fae throne." The reporter paused dramatically. "After the break we'll show the already infamous footage captured last night on a bystander's cell phone. The clip shows an incident that has left three Dark Fae dead and the heir apparent missing. Posted to YouTube late last night, the video has quickly gone viral. It has taken the Internet by storm and left the Chicago police and Fae authorities asking serious questions. What really happened in that dark Chicago alley last night? Is Niniane Lorelle responsible for the Dark Fae deaths? Where is the heir apparent to the Dark Fae throne? Stay with us."

Violence fulminated in the room as the scene cut to a toilet paper commercial. "Shit," said Dragos as he looked at the remote. "Just a sec."

The commercial went into fast-forward.

Rune said, "She was right about what she said before she left. We need to change how we think of her. We should remember to call her Niniane now."

Pia said, "She must be so scared."

The Dark Fae society had been under Urien's iron-fisted rule for the last two hundred years and had for the most part become closed off from the rest of the world. Tricks—or Niniane, whatever—had gone alone to meet representatives of their government, individuals who had unknown allegiances and motivations.

Tiago shook his head, anger roiling inside. He wrestled it under control before it could slip loose. "I told you some of us should have gone with her!"

"There's no point in rehashing an old argument," said Dragos, shooting a glare at him. "Tr—Niniane and I both decided nobody from the Wyr demesne would go with her. Otherwise it would look like the Wyr were making a power play for the Dark Fae demesne."

There were seven demesnes of Elder Races that overlaid the human geography of the continental United States. The Wyr demesne, which Dragos had ruled for centuries, was based in New York. The seat of Elven power was based in Charleston, South Carolina.

The Dark Fae's demesne was centered in Chicago, and the Light Fae in Los Angeles. Aside from discrete geographical and political differences, the Dark Fae and the Light Fae were also different in coloring and in manifestations of Power. The Light Fae was a blond, charismatic race, with either blue or green eyes, and they had an aversion to iron. The Dark Fae were black haired with pale skin and gray eyes, and they often had a gift for metallurgy.

The Nightkind, which included all Vampyric forms, controlled the San Francisco Bay Area along with the Pacific Northwest, and the human witches, considered part of the Elder Races due to their command of magical Power, were based in Louisville. Demonkind, like the Wyr and the Nightkind, consisted of several different types that included Goblins and Djinn, and their seat was based in Houston.

Dragos and the faerie had good reason for coming to the decision they had made. All of the Elder Races were jealous of their territories and the current balance of Power. They would take violent exception to one demesne attempting the takeover or control of another.

However.

"That was then, this is now," said Tiago.

Dragos nodded, expelling a breath in an explosive sigh. "Agreed."

Tiago rubbed the back of his head. Unfamiliar emotions cascaded through him. Niniane had escaped when her uncle Urien had taken the Dark Fae throne in a bloody coup and killed off her family. She had run straight to Dragos for sanctuary and had been part of the Wyrkind inner circle for almost two hundred years.

For all that, Tiago hardly knew her. Most of the time he was off with Dragos's army, embroiled in distant conflicts. He had met her maybe twenty times over the years, usually in meetings such as this one during his rare visits to New York. He had spoken with her one-on-one maybe a dozen times.

Still, she was one of theirs. He had gotten used to her infectious grin and that sexy wriggle she did with her cute little ass when she was flirting either with the camera or with someone in person. Anger burned that someone would dare try to harm her. She was so small and delicate, maybe all of five-foot-nothing and a hundred pounds, soaking wet. And now she was missing.

His hands fisted.

Dragos grunted and pushed a button. "There."

Tiago looked back at the flat-screen along with everybody else.

The female reporter came back, speaking more news babble. Blah-fucking-blah. More sexy footage of Niniane, winking at the camera and blowing a kiss. Damn, that mouth of hers was made for Playboy TV. He clamped down on the thought and concentrated on being relevant.

She had arrived in Chicago with an escort of Dark Fae that had been made up of some second cousin or other and assorted guards. She had met with a small delegation that was headed by one of the Dark Fae's most powerful governmental figures, Chancellor Aubrey Riordan. She and the delegation stayed in the penthouse suite at the Regent, preparatory to crossing over to the Dark Fae Other land for her coronation. She had, by all accounts, left the hotel last night for dinner with her cousin and a small escort.

The usual swarm of paparazzi had bayed in pursuit. The Dark Fae lost the paparazzi after a high-speed chase. What happened for the next couple of hours was unknown.

Tiago gritted his teeth as he glared at the screen. Get to the fucking point already.

And there it was, the fucking point, sprayed all over a fifty-six-inch plasma flat-screen and, apparently, all over the Internet as well. One million, seven hundred and fifty thousand hits and counting, as of 1:30 A.M.

The grainy, badly shot footage showed a dirty alley that could have been anywhere, in any city in the world. The scene jerked. Whoever had recorded the footage couldn't have done a worse job if they'd tried.

Still, Niniane was unmistakable in a red halter dress that accentuated her compact hourglass figure. Two Dark Fae were already on the ground. She was locked in some sort of struggle with the third.

The Dark Fae struck her hard in the ribs. The breath left Tiago in a growl as if he had been the one who had taken the blow. The asshole with the cell phone kept *filming* this shit and did nothing to help her? The scene jostled. Shit!

Then it came clear again. The last Dark Fae was down.

Niniane stood over her attacker, gasping and disheveled, one hand pressed to her side. She started to kick the body. "I hate my family!" she shouted. "I hate my family! I hate my family!"

The scene cut back to the MSNBC reporter, but Tiago had seen more than enough. He pivoted on one heel toward Dragos and growled, "Leave of absence."

The dragon looked at him, no less furious than he. Dragos said, "Go."

Rune followed Tiago out into the hall. He turned to face the gryphon as the door settled into place.

All of the immortal sentinels carried an intense furnace of energy that boiled the air around them. Dragos's First sentinel was as tall as Tiago but not quite as bulky. Rune was the most handsome of the four gryphons. He looked like a Greek god masquerading as a Grateful Dead fan. He wore a Jerry Garcia T-shirt that strained across the chest and at the biceps, faded jeans with the knees torn out and steel-toed boots, the treads of which had been imprinted on more than one Wyr ass. He had sun-bronzed, fine-grained skin with laugh lines at the corners of lion-colored eyes. Both the camera and females seemed to adore his even features and rakish white smile, and the tawny mane of sun-streaked hair that fell to broad shoulders held glints of pale gold, chestnut and burnished copper.

Tiago regarded the other sentinel with a warrior's assessment that never fully went to sleep. He had seen Rune fight in his gryphon form many times. Rune's gryphon shape was the size of an SUV, with a lion's heavy muscular body. He had a feline agility in both of his forms and projected an aura of lazy easygoing indolence that could, when he was provoked, vaporize in an instant into a roaring attack. In his human form, Rune had the lean hard muscles of a swordsman. He was built for both power and speed, whereas Tiago sometimes fought with his feet planted wide apart, a battle-axe gripped in one hand and a war hammer in the other. Tiago had been known to chop his enemies into pieces, or just smash them into the ground through strength and sheer dogged endurance. He had been called many things over the centuries. *Subtle* wasn't one of them.

Tiago said, "Talk to either Riehl or Jamar about stepping in for me until—"

"T-bird," Rune said. "Don't worry about the troops. I got it covered, man. I'll call Tucker in Chicago, so that you've got transportation and supplies waiting for you when you get there."

"Thanks." Tiago gave him a grim look, which Rune returned.

Neither male said what they were thinking. There were a whole host of reasons why they may not have heard from the faerie since the incident, and most of those reasons were not good ones.

"Tricks is okay," Tiago said. She'd better be okay, or he would make sure there was hell to pay.

"Niniane," Rune said.

Impatient, Tiago shrugged. "Whatever."

Rune clapped Tiago on the shoulder. "Well, go find her and make sure she stays okay."

"You know I will."

Tiago jogged up the stairs to the Tower rooftop. He turned his face upward to look full upon the bright orb of the sun. With a sense of unutterable relief he let his human form fall away, along with the shackles of the city. He lunged upward. Massive wings hammered down as he climbed into the air, and a thunderclap tore through the sky.

He slipped into the oldest, truest part of his soul.

He did not know his actual age, but he remembered soaring high above the Great Plains as vast herds of bison covered miles upon miles of land. The bison had once been his favorite prey. He would plummet from a great height, a murderous juggernaut that would slam down on the beast he had chosen and shatter its spine. The rest of the bison herd would stampede in a panic, leaving him to gorge in solitary peace as the wind undulated through an endless sea of prairie grasses under a colossal turquoise basin of sky.

He was known to many of the American Indian nations as the creature that commanded thunder and lightning, quick to stir to wrath and war, but his true identity was as a sojourner of the Earth. He would take flight for days on end, slipping into a fugue state as he watched oceans and lands scroll by underneath the glimmering shadow of his giant outspread wings.

When curiosity brought him to ground at last, he shape-shifted for the first time to walk among humans in a land filled with golden desert temples and palatial burial tombs of kings surrounded by cities of the dead. The humans clustered in a vibrant green fertile strip of land that followed the snaking path of a river like the folds of a silken dress molding to the curves of a voluptuous woman.

He mingled for a brief time with a small, dark, intelligent people who wrote of him in the Pyramid Texts, from the time of the Old Kingdom in Egypt. The people worshipped his winged form and called him a god of the wind. They claimed he brought with him the breath of life.

The people of Egypt had offered him everything a human being could desire, but he was not human. They tried to hold on to him with offerings of gold, and chains of worship, sex and dynasty, but he would not be chained or held. Only when the great winged serpent Cuelebre hunted him down, pinned him to the ground and spoke to him with patient beguilement and cunning intellect of a vision of a nation of united Wyr did he consent to listen.

Cuelebre had faced a formidable challenge with the oldest and strongest of the ancient Wyr. He could not bludgeon them into submitting to his rule and then hope to trust them in any kind of high-functioning level of governance afterward. Instead, he had to use persuasion to bring them to his side, to ask them to partner with him in the creation of a Wyr nation. Cuelebre coaxed Tiago into realizing that growth was inevitable for both humankind and the Elder Races. Civilization's dance had begun an inexorable waltz across the world.

Tiago must participate in the waltz. He must change as the world changed or become irrelevant. He refused to be reduced or set aside in the new formation of the world.

Thus, long ago, he agreed to work in a sometimes fractious collective partnership. He grew to admit it did not lessen who he was but enhanced him and used him to their best mutual benefit.

He was a warlord. To an ancient people he was a god of storm and lightning, a prince of the sky.

He was Wyr.

⇒ TWO ⇐

Motel 6 wasn't so bad. In fact it was kind of cute in a polyester sort of way.

Sure, it wasn't the Regent, or the Renaissance, or the Ritz-Carlton. But the desk attendant had been cheerfully disinterested when Niniane had checked in, the prices were affordable and, most important, they had smoking rooms. Score.

On the one hand, there wasn't any room service or those darling little liquor bottles in a small refrigerator. On the other hand, there weren't any assassination attempts or a pending coronation. *Hmm.* Niniane wondered if they offered a twelve-month lease.

She limped into the room. She pulled her new sunglasses down her nose and took a long, careful look over the rim at the surrounding scene. The warm afternoon sun toasted the asphalt of the motel parking lot, and a fitful wind swirled dirt and exhaust fumes into a toxic soup. The motel was located near some interstate exit, along with several fast-food restaurants, gas stations, and a Walgreens. The sound of traffic was a constant in the background, but it shouldn't be too disruptive once she had the door closed.

She couldn't see or hear anything unusual in the motel's immediate vicinity, and her sight and hearing, along with her sensitivity to magic, were inhumanly acute. She wasn't up to a more strenuous inspection. A visual scan from the doorway would have to be good enough.

After she shut the door and put on the security chain, the first thing she did was kick off her stylish four-inch heels. Ah, thank you, god of feet. She set her sunglasses on the TV. The double room was either painted or wallpapered beige. It had bright bedspreads patterned with an insistent orange, a window covered with short heavy curtains that hung over a long thin wall air-conditioner unit, and a plain table and chair that were pushed against the wall. She dropped her shopping bags on the nearest bed, limped to the air conditioner and turned it on full blast.

Life had sure gone to hell since Dragos had killed her uncle. Oh, Urien had to die, without a doubt. She was *glad* he was dead. She just wished it could have happened in a couple of decades or so. This business about her becoming the Dark Fae Queen? She was so not in the mood.

She dumped out the contents of the shopping bags. The items chronicled a long, busy day.

She'd had a lot to do once she had killed her second cousin Geril and his two cohorts. First item on her agenda was to run away. The second item was to get stuff and keep running. She had walked into a twenty-four-hour pharmacy, bought bandages, a pair of sweatpants, sunglasses and a T-shirt, changed in their bathroom and walked out.

Sunglasses at midnight. *Huh*. Idiot.

Those had gone into her first shopping bag until daybreak. Then she stole a car and drove in aimless circles while she tried to think past the frozen tundra in her head. She stopped at a superstore and bought more stuff, left the stolen car in the parking lot and got a cab, took the cab to the airport where she got another cab, and here she was.

Her path had been so random, so erratic, made up as it was by stress-induced on-the-spot decisions, that she defied anybody to figure out where "here" was. Hell, even she didn't know where "here" was, just that she was still somewhere in the greater Chicago area. Neither ride had been long enough to get her anywhere else, more's the pity. She hadn't wanted to imprint herself too deeply in the memory of either cab driver, so she had tried to keep both trips as normal as possible. She could always steal a car again and drive away from the area, but first she needed a few hours to recuperate while she considered what her next moves should be. At the moment she was too awash with conflicting impulses, pain and exhaustion to be sure of anything.

One shopping bag held her crumpled red halter dress and the matching evening bag that carried a compact powder, a lipstick, her wallet and two small stiletto knives. She kept the tips touched with poison and had a variety of places she could wear or carry them, in the side pocket of a purse, strapped to her arms, or underneath her dress and strapped to her thighs.

Good thing the red color of the dress hid the bloodstains, or she might have occasioned more attention at the pharmacy. She set that bag aside. Another bag held an unopened bottle of vodka, a bag of Cheetos, three packs of Marlboro reds and a lighter.

Say hello to tonight's hot date. Why did she always want to smoke when she was stressed? She sighed and set it all on the bedside table near the head of the second bed.

The third bag held a first aid kit, extra bandages, toiletries and underwear. The last bag had jeans, flip-flop sandals, a pair of shorts and a couple of tops.

She sat on the edge of the bed and inspected the blisters on her heels. Should have changed into the flip-flops as soon as she bought them. Should have bought the flip-flops at the first store and the sunglasses later, but all she could think after the attack was, oh gods, I can't be recognized.

Shoulda, woulda, coulda. They were the Three Stooges of regret. All they were good for was saying *whoop-whoop-whoop* and smacking each other over the head.

She gritted her teeth. She had slapped a temporary bandage on herself when she had changed in the pharmacy bathroom, but she needed to clean and bandage her knife wound properly.

She showered first. It was harder and more exhausting than she had counted on. Afterward she sat on the toilet and hissed as she blotted the knife wound with fresh cotton pads. She poked it to see if there were any cloth fibers from her dress or any other kind of dirt still in the wound. Gray stars bloomed in front of her eyes. Damn, that hurt. A deep puncture, it kept seeping a slow, steady stream of crimson.

She put antibacterial goop on it, doubled up on the padding and taped it in place as best she could. She smeared more goop on the blisters on her heels and put Hello Kitty Band-Aids on them. Then she put on her new underwear. Teeny-tiny little camo boxer shorty-shorts that rode low on the hips.

The next bit wasn't so easy. She grunted as she worked her way as carefully as she could into a sports bra. Structurally she may not be very big, but her perky pair of puppies made her a C-cup. Shoulda bought a bra with a front clasp, but today hadn't been a shining example of her best thinking. *Whoop-whoop-whoop,* smack. After she managed to get the bra on, she eased on a matching camo spaghetti strap T-shirt that stopped above her pierced navel.

Then she put her hair in pigtails. Because it was layered to fall in an outward flipping bob, the pigtails stood up on her head like twin black starbursts. She pouted at herself in the mirror, wrinkled her nose and said, "Sowwy."

Didn't she look cute? Looking cute and helpless could get you a long way sometimes. It had gotten her out of a whole lot of trouble in the past. You never know. The way things were going, she might need to rely on it again.

And now it was past time for that hot date. She limped to the bed and eased her sore, bruised body onto it, lit a cigarette and flipped on the TV. She tore open the bag of Cheetos and popped a bright orange puff into her mouth.

Then what was playing on the television registered in her tired brain.

She stared. Put the cigarette in the ashtray. Picked up the vodka bottle, opened it and took a stiff drink.

That was the first time she saw the cell phone video footage of the attack in the alleyway, where she had kicked the crap out of her second cousin Geril's dead body.

It wasn't going to be the last time. Not by a long shot.

Tiago believed in giving credit where credit was due. The little shit had tried like hell to avoid being tracked down.

By the time he had reached Chicago, the SUV Rune had requisitioned was waiting for him, along with a detailed list of supplies, including cash, a couple changes of clothes, a laptop and an assortment of his preferred types of weapons. Tiago picked up the vehicle in Lakeview from their Wyr contact, Tucker, who had already stashed the supplies in a large duffle bag in the backseat.

Tucker was, like his Wyr badger nature, a short, powerful, stocky and antisocial male. He did well living in relative isolation outside the social structure of the Wyr demesne. The badger was content with a job that had sporadic, often strange duties and irregular hours, as long as he could live within walking distance of his beloved Wrigley Field.

Although Tiago hadn't thought to ask for one, there was also a cell phone tucked into a side pocket of the heavy canvas duffle bag. He discovered it when it rang as he climbed into the driver's seat.

He clicked it on. "What."

Dragos said, "Preliminary autopsy report is in on the three dead Dark Fae males."

Tiago's eyebrows rose. "That was fast."

"With the next ruler of the Dark Fae demesne missing, the authorities put a rush on the job," Dragos said. "All the Dark Fae males died of the same kind of poison T—Niniane favors on her stilettos."

Tiago adjusted the seat and pulled into traffic. He grunted, "At least she kept her weapons poisoned when she left New York. Good for her."

"The fucker who filmed the footage is cooperating with police," Dragos said. "He's claiming he didn't see anybody else in the vicinity when she took off down the street."

"I want to know where he lives," said Tiago. He drove fast and aggressively as he glared at the other vehicles on the road.

"Later. Check out the airport. Security footage shows someone that looks like it could have been her climbing out of a cab."

Dragos hung up without saying good-bye. Tiago turned off the phone and tossed it into the passenger's seat.

When Urien had assumed control of the Dark Fae government, Niniane had taken sanctuary with Dragos in 1809. While young, she had already reached her adult size. She was small and delicate even for one of the Fae. She had a mere fraction of the strength the Wyrs had. She also had her uncle Urien, one of the nastiest and most Powerful men in the world, who had been determined to see her dead.

The Wyr sentinels had proceeded to teach her every dirty trick they could think of in order to help keep her alive, which was how she had gotten her nickname. Nothing was off-limits, or so Tiago had heard. He had been busy elsewhere, helping to keep the peace in Missouri when the Osage signed the Treaty of Fort Clark and ceded their land to the U.S. government.

Everything added up. She had left the hotel with three males, and three males were dead. She had either been taken from the site of the attack, or she was on the run. Logic said she had gotten away and was on the run.

But if so, why hadn't she called New York for backup? She was family. Any of them would gladly have rushed to help her, but she still hadn't tried to call anybody, and she hadn't replied to any of the phone messages left on her cell.

Tiago planned on asking her that very question when he caught up with her. She might be hell to track down, but he was old and steeped in Power and most of his talents were concentrated on the hunt. There wasn't anything on this Earth he couldn't track once he put his mind to the task. He recovered lost scent trails, made intuitive leaps no one else would think of and shit, more often than not, luck just fell his way. It might take him a while, but in the end he always brought down his prey.

His prey, in the end, appeared to be holed up in a motel room off the I-294 Tri-State Tollway.

He paused for a moment outside a door and listened. Her scent was all around on the surrounding sidewalk, but it was close to midnight and he didn't want to knock on the wrong door by mistake.

He heard her inside. She was singing in a clear, sweet voice. His eyebrows rose.

"'*Down in the valley, the valley so low, hang your head over, and hear the wind blow . . .*'" The singing stopped. He heard her mumble, "Can't remember what comes next, something, something . . ."

He grinned as he relaxed and leaned against the doorpost. If she was singing and talking to herself, she wasn't dead in a ditch. It was all good.

She said, "Oh, that's right . . . No, wait, that's another song. Crap, I'm too drunk."

That sounded like his cue. He knocked.

Silence. He imagined there was a startled quality to it.

He knocked again. "Tricks, it's Tiago. Open up."

She said with the slow incredulity of the inebriated, "Is that you, Dr. Death? There isn't anybody named Tricks here."

Dr. Death? He rolled his eyes. "Come on, Niniane. Open the door."

"Wait, I'm in hiding. Don't use that name either."

He put his hands on his hips. "Then what the hell do you want me to call you?"

"Nothing. Thank you for stopping by and go away. I'm okay. Everything's okay. It's all taken care of now. Just don't watch any TV for a while, okay? You can go back to New York, or wherever it is you lair when you're not killing things."

He scowled. No, thank you and don't watch any TV? What the hell did she mean by that? He muttered, "I do not live in a lair."

He settled his shoulder against the heavy metal door that was constructed to meet fire-safety codes and keep thieves out. After pushing with a steady increase of pressure, the lock and chain broke.

Cigarette smoke billowed as the door opened. He coughed, waved a hand in front of his face and stared at the scene inside.

The motel room was a pigsty. Shopping bags were piled on the bed nearest the door, with clothes and other items spilling out. Clothes tags littered the floor. Niniane lay on her back on the other bed, which was rumpled. She had kicked off the pillows, and they were on the floor too. She was dressed in some kind of porno version of camouflage, in very short shorts and a tiny stretchy T-shirt that left her narrow waist bare. Her head was hanging off the end of the bed. She held a bottle of vodka in one small hand. It was significantly low in liquid. She clutched a remote control in the other hand. A cigarette smoldered in a half-full ashtray and an open bag of Cheetos lay on the bed beside her.

Her compact, curvaceous body was laid out like some kind of offering to a pagan god. As someone who had once been a pagan god, he knew what he was talking about, and he definitely appreciated the view. As her head hung over the end of the bed, it accentuated the thrust of round luscious breasts that curved over a contrasting narrow waist. A gold ring glinted at her navel, just begging to be licked. Her graceful hip bones and the arc of her pelvis were outlined by shorts that Congress ought to make illegal. Slender, shapely bare legs tipped with toes painted a saucy pink completed the package, and his appreciative cock swelled to salute every visible succulent inch of her.

He glowered, thrown off balance by his own intense, unwelcome reaction. Rein it in, stud. Under the reek of smoke he could smell feminine perfume and—was that the scent of blood?

"Oh, you shouldn'ta done that," Niniane said. Large upside-down Fae eyes tried to focus on him. "Breaking and entering. That's against the law." She sniggered.

Tiago took refuge from his strange feelings in the much more familiar emotion of aggression. "What are you doing?" he demanded. "What do you mean 'go back to New York'? Do I smell blood?"

"I can only answer one question at a time, you know," she said. With remarkable dignity, considering. "I am hanging my head over to hear the wind blow. I never did get that bit in the lyrics. Who hears the wind blow when they hang their head over? Hang their head over what? What does that even mean? Do you know?"

He had no idea what she was babbling about. Something about the stupid song she had been trying to sing. He pushed the door shut with a foot and strode over to stub out the smoldering cigarette. "This is disgusting," he snapped. "Why haven't you called? We've been worried sick about you."

"Whoa," she said. She looked up—or down, as it were—at Tiago's crotch, which had stopped right in front of her. He was one scary, mean-looking oversized barbarian, in black jeans, black boots and black leather vest. He bristled with weapons and anger, and muscles bulged everywhere. His crotch sported a significant bulge too. A very significant bulge. She licked her lips. She might be drunk, but she wasn't dead. She wouldn't be forgetting this sight in a hurry.

Obsidian eyes glittered. "Tricks, what the hell? Seriously."

"I'm gonna be Queen, you know," she said. "You gotta stop calling me Tricks. It makes me sound like a circus clown. And I don't think I'll be a highness for long, so you should practice calling me your majesty." She hiccuped and waved a hand in the air. "You may begin."

"I notice how you're ignoring the important part of what I said," Tiago told her. He squatted and suddenly his upside-down face was in front of hers. "So I'll repeat: what the hell?"

She tried to track where that mouthwatering bulge in his crotch had gone, couldn't and focused instead on his face. Brown skin, strong hawkish features and a sensually shaped mouth that more often than not looked like it could cut through concrete. She had always thought he was a proud, aloof man with the longest legs and the sexiest moves she had ever seen. He walked everywhere with a quick ground-eating, lean-hipped stride.

She asked, "Has anybody ever told you, you look a lot like Dwayne Johnson?"

He scowled. "Who the hell is Dwayne Johnson?"

He tried to take the vodka bottle away from her. She clung to it.

"You know, The Rock? Hot, sexy football player–wrestling guy turned movie actor? Only . . . you're a whole lot meaner." She concentrated very hard, tongue between her teeth, and touched the tip of her forefinger to his scowl. The vodka bottle bumped his nose. He jerked his head out of the way.

His eyes narrowed on her. Was that male interest in his dark, glittering gaze? She didn't trust her powers of observation at the moment.

"Hot se—" he stopped dead. When he spoke again, his normal growl had dropped to a husky murmur. "You're comparing me to a movie actor? Fuck yeah, of course I'm a whole lot meaner."

Huh. Wasn't he the cock of the walk?

"Whatever, don't let it go to your head," she said with scorn. "You're not as sexy as I think you are." She squinted. Wait. That hadn't come out right. She tried to sort it all out in her vodka-befuddled head. It didn't help that he gave her a swift white grin that scrambled her brain even further.

All too soon that grin disappeared. Then Dr. Death was back and scowling again.

Ooh. Sexy. No, scary. No, sexy. Oh phooey.

He grabbed her hand. He could feel how delicately formed the bones were. He could crush her so easily. Any one of those Dark Fae males could have snapped her neck effortlessly if they had gotten her in the right hold. He took care to keep his touch gentle, even as he said, "Goddammit, faerie, you'd better start answering some questions."

"Or what?" She pointed the remote at him and pushed the mute button. "*Pleh.* I'm gonna get someone to make me a magical mute that really works."

A kind of desperation came over his harsh features. He snatched the vodka bottle from her and took a swig. She watched with acute interest as shock shot across his face. He gagged and spat the mouthful out on the carpet. He glared at the bottle. "Bubble gum–flavored vodka? *Bubble gum*?"

"What? It's good." She reached for the bottle.

He held it out of her reach. "No way."

She scowled. "That's my dinner. You give it back."

"Oh no, young lady. You've had more than enough."

Only a gazillion-thousand-year-old Wyr could get away with calling a two-hundred-year-old faerie "young lady." Holy cow, he was one devastatingly good-looking barbarian, upside down or not. But so preachy! She remembered the vodka. She reached for it again.

He stood, grabbed the ashtray and strode for the bathroom. She could just barely see what happened in the corner of the bathroom mirror as he turned the bottle upside down in the sink. There went the rest of her hot date.

"Screw you," she called after him. There was a thought. She scoped out his lean, tight ass with interest. Bow chica wow wow.

Tiago ignored her and dumped the ashtray in the bathroom trash. He paused, looking down in the trashcan. If anything, he looked even angrier than he had before. He looked fit to murder somebody. The strong, proud bones of his face clenched like a fist.

Her eyelids closed in a slow blink as she tried to process. If he was that mad at her, she should give some serious thought to running. And she would too, just as soon as she found her feet again.

A shiver rippled down her spine. She rolled onto her side, tucked her knees against her chest and wrapped her arms around them. She didn't want him that mad at her. She didn't want anybody that mad at her.

Tiago walked back to the bed. She could have sworn she heard a rumble of thunder in the distance. He squatted by the bed and rubbed her shoulder with a giant calloused hand. "Where are you hurt, faerie?"

His gentleness was so unexpected, coming as it did from such a wrathful clenched-fist face, that it almost did her in. Her eyes filled with tears. She gestured to her side.

Icy shock ran over his skin, followed by a blast of heat. Tiago didn't know where to put his rage. That bastard Fae hadn't punched her in the alley. He had *knifed* her.

"Let me have a look." He tried to raise her T-shirt.

She resisted. "I already cleaned and bandaged it."

He exploded. "Goddammit, woman! I said let me have a fucking look!"

Her eyes went wide and she froze. The force of his anger was palpable. It beat against her skin. Thunder rolled, this time closer. It was almost overhead.

She had heard the stories about Tiago. The thunder and lightning came when he really lost it. Cautiously she uncurled. She made herself lie passive as she stared up at him. Sometimes with dominant Wyr warriors the best thing you could do was stay quiet and get out of their way—or in this case, acquiesce. Sooner or later their rampaging always ground to a halt, and then they could listen to reason again.

He put one knee on the bed and leaned his weight on it as he lifted up her T-shirt. The bandage covered her ribs under her left breast. She winced as he peeled back the bandage to look at what was underneath.

"Do you know how irritating you are?" she said. "Because if you don't, I've got time."

"This looks deep," he said in a quiet voice. Lightning flashed outside. Thunder exploded with a boom. She jumped and shivered. He put his hand briefly against her narrow waist. "*Shh* now, be easy. The dressing is soaked. I'll change the bandage."

She knuckled her eyes. Damn it. She hadn't slept in two days. She was starting to come down from the singing part of the drunk. He was acting far too serious and concerned, a storm was brewing outside, and all the fun was packing its bags and ditching the party. She tried to hold on to it.

"You know, technology in the twenty-first century is pretty cool," she told him. "I'm going to DVR my own meltdown and email it to my therapist."

He didn't so much as crack a smile.

She drooped. She uncurled as he urged her to lie flat. He removed the soiled bandage, and with a careful, velvet-light touch he cleaned the wound and covered it with cotton padding again. At one point he bent down close to her skin and sniffed the wound. Okay, so that looked a little weird, but she knew what he was doing; he was checking with his Wyr sense of smell to see if he could detect poison. He caught her eye afterward and gave her a tight, quick smile that was probably meant to be reassuring, but he didn't speak. He seemed busy with his own internal issues. Lightning struck the parking lot. Her shivering deepened. That was just downright sexy. No, spooky. No, sexy. DAMN IT!

"All right, I'm all done for now," he said. His soft, even voice was somehow so much worse than his yelling voice. He taped the bandage in place. Then he looked at her, and the fury in his dark eyes stabbed her. "We know everything that matters."

She rubbed the pointed tip of one ear, which was burning in embarrassment. "Apparently the whole world does," she muttered. "I never even saw the guy with the cell phone."

"That asshole is going to be lucky to live out the week if I have anything to say about it. I can't fucking believe he didn't call 911 soon as he realized someone was being attacked." He took her hand and held it. "Now I want you to tell me, why didn't you call, and why do you want me to go home?"

She pulled her hand away and tucked it against her chest. "Don't be nice to me."

"I'll be whatever the hell I want to be," he snapped. "Why didn't you call?"

She muttered, "I'm supposed to do this on my own. No Wyr allowed."

"That's old news," Tiago said. "Plans have changed."

Just like that? Plans have changed? She scowled at him. "Hey, cowboy, remember what I said. I'm gonna be Queen. I don't think you get to boss me around like that."

He rubbed the back of his head and raised his eyebrows at her. "How are you going to stop me?"

"Screw you," she said.

"You've said that already," he pointed out. "I'm getting bored now."

"Yeah, well, it's the only thing I can think of at the moment," she muttered. With a Herculean effort she managed to keep from looking at his crotch again.

"The game's changed. Deal with it."

Her gaze bounced around his dark saturnine features. The force of his presence was such that the tiny hairs on her arms rose. It cremated the numb state she had managed to achieve with the alcohol. He had the extreme physicality of an apex predator, his body tempered by years of fighting, the thick muscles corded with sinew and veins. His Power was a heavy, sulfurous force that pressed her into the mattress.

She struggled to sit up. Suddenly he was bending over her. He eased one huge arm underneath her shoulders to help her upright. She scowled and glared at him. "Look, you can't stay, and that's all there is to it. I'm all right. I handled everything."

He snapped, "You have a knife wound between your ribs!"

"You should have a look at the other guys," she told him.

Her words hit a stone wall. "We're done discussing this," he said. He walked over to the other bed. "What do you want to take with you?"

She pressed a hand to her side. "Get back over here so I can smack you."

"Yeah, I'll get right on that."

"I mean it. Get your ass over here." There she was, back to what was fast becoming her favorite subject.

"I'm so motivated to do that since it's clearly in my best interest. I'm just going to assume you want all of this." He stuffed things back into the bags.

His back was turned to her. She stared at his ass again. Really, it was the sexiest ass she had ever seen. First she got a close-up of his front, and now she got treated to the back view. Tight, taut and clothed in black like it had been gift wrapped just for her.

She patted him on the butt and told him, "Nice buns, cowboy."

She started to pull his wallet out of the back pocket, and he grabbed her hand. Spoilsport. She sighed, opening her fingers, and he patted her as he let her go. "I'm taking the bags out to the car," he told her. "Be right back."

He walked out, and just like that she lost what little control she'd had over her life. She tobogganed right out of the fun bit of the drunk and plunged into the snowdrift labeled the sorry stage.

He came back and scooped her into his arms. He was such a mean barbarian, and he was being so careful with her, so gentle and nice. And she couldn't let herself rely on him. She couldn't let herself totally rely on anyone ever again.

⇒ THREE ⇐

Tiago tried to figure out how he could have wrecked his life so completely in just a day. One day. Twenty-four hours. Yesterday he had been merely irritated with cooling his heels in New York and doing unimportant stuff that could have been handled by someone—almost anyone—else.

Tonight in Chicago, he had lost all sense of irritation and had become downright desperate.

He paced in the parking lot of another motel, a Red Roof Inn, as he called Dragos, who answered on the first ring. Tiago said, "Got her."

The dragon let loose a long exhale. "Good."

"She was wounded. She's okay, but she needs to see a doctor soon." He explained what happened, or at least what he had found and what he had surmised, while his long stride ate up the distance of the parking lot.

Glowing streetlamps were surrounded with blurred yellow halos. A light rain had started to fall, miniscule silver meteors streaking through the illumination. Tendrils of fog rose from the sun-warmed asphalt. The tendrils twisted and curled around his steel-toed boots as though he stood in a Gorgon's nest of transparent snakes.

He stood several feet away from the building and scanned it and the surrounding area with a hypervigilant gaze. The motel building had a couple of floors, rows of identical doors stacked on top of each other. He had secured a ground-floor room that opened directly onto the parking lot, so they could leave in a hurry if they had to. It was late enough that the motel was quiet, and the cars that dotted the parking lot were cool to the touch. He pivoted at the curb to start another lap.

"What do you need?" Dragos asked.

"You should send a cleanup crew to the Motel 6 where she was hiding. Oh, and she said she left a stolen car in a Wal-Mart parking lot. She said she wiped her prints off the steering wheel and car door handle, but she admits she's been pretty rattled since the attack and hasn't been thinking very clearly. The car needs to be cleaned and returned to its owner."

"I'll get Tucker on it. Hold on."

He waited while Dragos relayed orders. Then Tiago said, "Dragos, you've got to help me get a handle on her before there's a murder-suicide here. She's bawling her eyes out. I'm here to tell you, there's nothing worse to be around than a forlorn faerie."

Dragos coughed. "O-kay. Hold on."

Tiago's sharp ears caught Pia in the background, saying, "You're all Neanderthals, what else did you expect? What, *me* talk to him? Oh no—" The phone must have exchanged hands. Pia sighed, "Hello, Tiago. I'm so glad you found her. What's going on?"

Another female. He nodded. Smart. Speaking in rapid sentences, he filled her in. "You've got to help me get her to stop crying," he demanded.

"You just told me she's drunk," Pia said. "Don't you think she'll stop as she sobers up?"

"That's not soon enough," he growled.

"Have you tried talking to her?" Pia asked.

He pulled the phone away from his ear to give it a quick glare. Was that sarcasm in her voice? He said, "Of course I have. I came all this way to help her, and she keeps insisting I go away. She didn't even want me to look at her wound. What the fuck is that about?"

There was a long pause on the other end of the line. Pia said, "You want me to deal with this in a five-minute conversation."

He told her in a grim voice, "Does it have to take that long? I'm just looking for a way to survive the night."

He glanced at the door to their motel room, which he had left cracked open a few inches. He could still hear her crying.

The worst of it was how quiet she tried to be, sneaking sobs into her pillow. She probably thought she was hiding it from him. *Argh.* He wanted to stab something in his ears.

"Alrighty," Pia said. "Gray and I have been discussing Niniane today since she's been on all our minds. Did you know she barely escaped with her life when Urien led the coup that slaughtered her family?"

Tiago stopped pacing. His hand tightened on the cell phone. "I knew Urien had killed her family and she had escaped, but I don't know the details."

"She was seventeen years old," Pia said. "Seventeen. Did you know she saw the bodies of her twin brothers, and she watched Urien's men as they gutted her mother?"

His stomach clenched. Her mother, gutted before her eyes. He wondered how old her brothers had been. How they had been killed. He had to clear the gravel out of his throat before he could reply. "No," he said. "I didn't."

"So, here's my five minute fix," Pia said, her voice soft. "Niniane is under a lot of stress. When she was just a child, a family member, maybe even someone she had cared about and trusted once, slaughtered everyone she loved. Now she's survived an assassination attempt from yet another family member, and somehow she's got to find the courage to go back into that palace where she lost everything in the world that mattered to her. So if you tried talking to her in the tone of voice you just used with me, Tiago, I suggest you come back to New York. Any one of the other sentinels would be glad to come take your place. *They* love her."

He sucked in a sharp breath. Way to stick a knife in when he wasn't looking. He stopped pacing and stood rigid. He listened to the roar of denial that had erupted inside when Pia mentioned him being replaced. Fuck if he was going to let that happen.

"Are you still there?"

"I'm here. Hold on," he growled. He fought his temper, won the struggle for self-control and kept his voice as soft and even as hers. "Nobody else is coming out. I've got her, and I will look after her."

"The right way," Pia said.

"The right way," he replied. He sent a grim smile into the halogen-lamp-lit night. "Pia, you're a bitch. Thank you."

In the background, Dragos said, "Hey."

"Ease off, big guy," Pia said, half muffled. "It was a compliment. At least I think it was." Her voice came back fully. "Anything else, Tiago?"

He turned to look at the motel door again. "No."

"Please call if there's anything we can do."

"You know I will." He hung up and pocketed the cell.

Moments later he eased into the room, and shut and locked the door. It was silent inside. Too silent. Was she holding her breath? He stretched his neck to ease tense muscles. Way to screw things up, Dr. Death.

His predator Wyr eyes adjusted quickly to the more intense darkness inside. The room had a king-sized bed, a bland beige decor echoed in motel rooms across the country and no smoking. He had requested that specifically. Niniane was curled under the covers of the bed, her small form scooted to the side closest to the wall, as near to the edge of the bed as she could be without falling off. It was almost like she was wishing she could get as far away from him as possible.

He shook his head and indulged in a little mental ass-kicking. Then he walked over to the bed. He removed his most obtrusive weapons, put them on the bedside table and made sure his Glock was close at hand. All the while he listened.

Yeah, shit. She was definitely holding her breath.

He sighed and eased onto the bed on top of the covers. She was lying on her good side, favoring her left with the knife wound.

She asked, "Did you call ho—New York?"

"Yeah. I talked briefly to Dragos and Pia."

Her head turned slightly toward him. "I like Pia. We didn't have very long to get to know each other, but I'm already going to miss her."

"She likes you too," he said. He carefully curled around her small, tense body and wrapped an arm around her. She started breathing again. It sounded choppy and uneven. He laid his head on his bent arm and hugged her back against him.

She whispered, "Don't be nice to me."

"Why not?" he asked, confused. Didn't Pia just tell him to be nicer? He tucked his nose in her hair. She had taken out those ridiculous pigtails, and her hair was downy soft and loose. She smelled like cigarettes, herbal shampoo and the unique feminine scent that was all hers, all Tricks. Niniane. Whatever. Niniane was a pretty name, he realized. It suited her.

"When you're nice, it makes it harder."

He thought of her tearful good-bye several days ago and the round of fierce hugs she had given everybody, himself included, before she left for the airport. He thought of the seventeen-year-old who had lost everything in the world that had mattered to her, and of the many obstacles in 1809 that one small, hunted Fae girl must have faced in getting safely from Adriyel to sanctuary in the Wyr demesne in New York.

He thought of the recent assassination attempt and how she still intended to go live with the Dark Fae, some of whom might still want to kill her, and all because it was far better to have a good person in power than to risk having another Urien take the throne.

He wanted to rip Urien to pieces all over again.

Her hand kept jerking. He raised his head. After a moment he realized she was plucking at the edges of the bedspread. He wrapped his hand with care around hers, stilling the nervous movement. Her fingers felt small, delicate and cold. She tried to pull away from his touch, but he wouldn't let go.

"How drunk are you now?" he asked.

"I don't know." She sniffed. "I can feel my feet again. My side hurts. Not very, I think."

She had to be exhausted. He hated that she was in pain. He wanted to offer her medication, but he wasn't sure what might be safe after she'd downed so much vodka. He told her, "Everything's going to be okay."

Her head moved slightly. "'Course it will."

He didn't know how she managed to make the perky statement sound so awful. He sighed. "You get some rest now."

She nodded. "Okay."

"We can talk more on the way to New York," he told her.

She lifted her head. "What?"

"I said I'm taking you back to New York." He kept his voice patient since she was obviously still inebriated. "And we can talk more on the way."

She sighed. "Tiago, I'm not going back."

"Of course you are," he said. "Your apartment in the Tower is secure, and we can set up a reliable security detail for you while the attack on you is investigated. Don't worry. I'll take care of everything."

He tried to think if there was something else he should say, but he wasn't Dr. Phil. He was Dr. Death, and he thought he had covered all the important bits. He held her a long time. Funny. He was doing it for her, but it felt pretty damn good to him too. She was curvy and soft, and no bigger than a minute. She fit perfectly in the curl of his body as he spooned with her.

Finally her stiff body went lax and her breathing deepened. She was asleep. He eased away from her, one careful move at a time. She never stirred when he stood.

He picked up the duffle he had set against one wall earlier. It held a toiletry kit and a couple changes of clothing in his size, along with a lightweight laptop in a protective case and extra weapons. He slipped into the bathroom and eased the door shut before he turned on the light.

He stripped and showered. After washing and rinsing, he braced his hands on the shower wall and leaned on them. He stood with his head down as hot water cascaded over his neck and shoulders. The wet heat felt good after his flight from New York, and it soaked into well-used muscles. Water dripped off his nose and chin. What a day.

He should do the smart thing. He should listen to what Pia had said, and call New York to have one of the other sentinels come take his place.

He should go with his troops to their next assignment.

He wasn't going to do the smart thing.

He was going to do the only thing he could. He was going to stay and make everything okay for Niniane. Because he had promised her that it would be okay. And because he didn't seem to be able to make any other choice.

He turned off the tap when the hot water started to run luke-warm. After toweling dry, he slipped on a clean pair of black fatigues and a black T-shirt. He switched off the light before he opened the door. He waited a moment for his night sight to return then slipped into the room, placing the duffle back against the wall.

He paused to check for her breathing, expecting the same deep, even rhythm of sleep.

Except there was no breathing, no sense of another living presence.

He flipped on the light.

The room was empty. She was gone. So were her shopping bags. So were the keys to the SUV.

So was his Glock.

Fury erupted. *"Goddamn you, Tricks!"*

Tiago couldn't have tortured her with any greater efficacy if he had tried.

Coming after her all the way to Chicago to make sure she was okay. Being all mean and barbaric and sexy.

She could handle that. She had lived with and been vastly entertained by it for two hundred years. All of Dragos's sentinels were mean and barbaric and sexy. Even that weird harpybitch Aryal, who she might have a teensy girl crush on. You know, in a totally hetero kind of way.

But then Tiago had turned nice. She hadn't known he had a nice speed. She had thought he had only two speeds, the killing speed and full stop.

The warlord sentinel, being nice to her. It burned her skin as if he had poured acid all over her.

He had come up behind her in the dark. He curled that powerful muscled body of his around her, enclosing her, and made her feel safe and warm and cared for. He caressed her hand like he cared. It made her wild to get away from him.

What was he thinking? Returning to New York was out of question. She couldn't go running back to the Wyr demesne just because things had gotten a little rough. That would be political suicide. She would look weak and unfit to rule, not just to the Dark Fae but to all the other demesnes as well.

He told her everything was going to be okay. Damn it.

How was everything going to be okay? For how long? For a few days or a few weeks, or for however long he might decide to help her out? Then what?

He would get on with his life, that's what, and leave her a solitary monarch on the Dark Fae throne. Meanwhile she had a hundred second cousins. No doubt some of them were lawabiding citizens, but she would bet a good number of them were every bit as ambitious as Geril or her uncle Urien had been.

Stupid Wyr. *Nothing* was okay.

She couldn't run away to New York. Now that she was no

longer drunk or in shock, she knew she couldn't run anywhere else either. All the news networks had been telling the same basic story by the end of the evening. Human police and Dark Fae authorities were collaborating on getting a major manhunt underway to find her.   .

She'd had her time-out and a chance to react, and now she had to go back to the Regent and meet up with the Dark Fae delegation. There wasn't any other realistic option. When she had chosen to go public with her real identity, she had started down a path of no return.

The delegation was a traditional triad that was comprised of three of the most powerful officials of the Dark Fae government. The first was Chancellor Aubrey Riordan, who belonged somewhere on a distant branch of the Lorelle labyrinthine family tree. Aubrey had been old when Niniane had been born and had retired from public office about fifteen years before her family had been massacred. In the late 1950s Urien had brought Aubrey back into government.

Aubrey's wife, Naida, had been absent from the group that had met Niniane when she arrived in Chicago. Niniane had heard that Naida was quite a bit younger than her husband. Niniane was interested in meeting the other woman. She looked forward to having conversations with someone that weren't quite so weighted with political considerations.

The second member of the delegation was Commander Arethusa Shiron, who was the current head of Dark Fae military forces. Arethusa was a cold-eyed, silent woman who intimated Niniane just by the force of her presence. The third was Justice Kellen Trevenan. Kellen was a rarity among the elder Dark Fae, for he was so old his hair had turned white.

All three members of the delegation, Aubrey, Arethusa and Kellen, were hardy survivors if nothing else. They had all lived through her father Rhian's reign. Her father had been a progressive ruler who had embraced change and developing Dark Fae relationships with not only the long-standing American Indian population but the fast-growing number of European settlers that spread across the continent after the American Revolution in the latter part of the eighteenth century.

Then the members of the delegation had weathered the coup that Urien had led against her father. Urien had been the leader of a conservative faction of Dark Fae that opposed Rhian's open door policies toward the onslaught of new European arrivals.

To the best of Niniane's knowledge, none of the three in the delegation had actually participated in the coup itself. They had witnessed Urien's rise to power and the throne. They had not only lived through his segregationist rule, which had isolated Dark Fae society from the rest of the world, but they came to hold positions where they wielded considerable power. Now they were witness to yet another shift in the monarchy.

While she didn't want to believe they could be involved in what had happened, the fact was, any of them could have been responsible for the attempt on her life, either by acting on their own or in collusion with another. Or they might have had nothing to do with it, and her cousin Geril and his accomplices had acted independently. Or the attack could have been instigated by someone else entirely.

It had been hard enough to face the delegation the first time when she had arrived in Chicago. The thought of facing them now made her gut clench and her palms sweat. The Dark Fae were known for subterfuge and silent political allegiances, and she had been gone for so long, she was a virtual stranger to it all. What she knew of her heritage read like a short encyclopedia entry colored with adolescent emotions and memories. It was an antiquated snapshot, two hundred years out of date, of a culture and a government that was thousands of years old and Byzantine in its convolutions.

A traitorous part of her longed to run back to the only safe haven she had known for centuries, and it wouldn't stop whining. See, even *she* thought running back to New York was weak.

She supposed she had been happy there, or at least she had been happy enough. She'd had an adopted family of sorts. They had kept the threat level contained so that she had come to know a measure of contentment, if not peace. Living her life as she had in the confinement of bodyguards and under the constant expectation of attack, she hadn't ever really felt free; but many people lived their lives under the constant threat of war, and they were far more constricted by poverty and a lack of opportunity than what she had enjoyed. If she hadn't appreciated the constrictions on her life, still she had known how blessed she had been to have the resources, both in friends and finances, to more than adequately meet her needs and to indulge in a serious shoe addiction.

But no matter how much she might want to go back to New York and hide in the safety of her former life, she couldn't bring that kind of political tension down on the Wyr, not after they had opened their hearts so generously to her for so long. Dragos had enough on his plate as it was. He was adjusting to having a new, pregnant mate while at the same time contending with the fallout from his trespass into the Elven demesne, along with the potential political repercussions from Urien's death.

She knew what she had to do. She had to suck it up and go back to the Regent and get on with her sucky life, for however long it lasted. Why was she driving in circles? She couldn't believe she was being such a flake about this. She hadn't realized she was so messed up. Her breath shook and her vision blurred. She scrubbed at her eyes.

She came to a halt at a four-way stop sign. She hadn't felt up to facing the challenge of the strange fast-paced highway that cut past their second motel, so she had turned instead into a residential area. Modest houses with well-kept shrubbery dotted tree-lined streets that were ribboned with pale strips of sidewalk. Most of the houses were dark and quiet.

She adored neighborhoods like this. They were so exotic. Whole families lived in these houses. The parents went to work, and the children climbed into yellow buses and went to school. They shared suppers together as loads of laundry wrinkled in clothes dryers. (Imagine washing your own laundry. What fun!)

Sometimes at Christmas she would slip into neighborhoods just like this one. She would walk along the streets and peer into windows at family and holiday gatherings, and marvel at the shiny gold, crimson and green decorated trees covered with tinsel and twinkling colored lights, while she wondered what it must be like to experience the beauty of such an ordinary, unattainable life.

The light rain from earlier in the evening had grown heavier. She looked over the readings on the dashboard of the SUV as she searched for the windshield wiper switch. Wow, this was a really nice SUV. A hybrid. She only understood half of what the dashboard told her. The clock read 3:32 A.M.

By now Tiago was hot on her trail and breathing fire. She could practically feel him coming up behind her. The tiny hairs at the back of her neck rose. The air felt charged, full of static.

Hey, maybe she should stop to get some breakfast. If she was already in a restaurant, he couldn't yell at her so much, could he? Besides, it would be rude if she showed up at the Regent before dawn with a furious Wyr sentinel in tow. She would wake people up and cause a ruckus.

She accelerated when it was her turn and looked for a driveway that she could use to turn the SUV around. She remembered seeing an IHOP restaurant about a half a mile back. Gorging on pancakes with strawberries and whipped cream might make her feel better and solve all her problems. Okay, so that seemed like it was a long shot, but she was willing to give it a try.

A violent wind rose from one block to the next. It whipped through the surrounding trees. Lightning speared the air. White light burned a jagged path across her retinas as it struck a tree. The accompanying thunderclap was like the explosion of a roadside bomb. The concussion assaulted her eardrums and shook the body of the vehicle. She startled so badly she almost lost control of the SUV.

Then not twenty yards in front of her a gigantic bird of prey with a thirty-foot wingspan plummeted down. For one split second he was caught full in the headlights of the SUV, enormous wings splayed high in the air and razorlike sword-long talons outstretched. He was shaped like a golden eagle, but his color was a dark sooty black.

Lightning flashed in those great fierce eyes. Thunder roared as he changed in midair and landed as a massive hawk-faced man in black fatigues and combat boots. He strode toward her, rage carving his body into a hard-edged weapon.

She shrieked and slammed on the brakes. She hit them too hard and the vehicle went into a skid. Tiago leaped forward. His hands slammed like twin sledgehammers into the edge of the hood.

He stopped the SUV dead.

She sat frozen as she stared at him, her mouth open. The fancy hybrid engine bawled a complaint and stalled.

Tiago came around to the driver's side and yanked the door open. He gripped the edge of the roof with both hands and glared at her. He was already soaked. She watched with eyes gone huge and round as a drop of water slid down one lean, hard cheek where a muscle twitched.

The knife wound had hurt too much for her to put on the seat belt. Wincing, she swiveled with care to face him. The rain pelted her bare legs and arms.

Maybe it was time to get cute. Her lower lip stuck out and her forehead wrinkled. In a small uncertain voice, she said, "Sowwy?"

If anything, that seemed to make him angrier. Worse, he looked offended. He snarled, "Don't pull that manipulative sex kitten shit on me."

She shrank back, her eyes crinkled in worry. "But what if I am a manipulative sex kitten shit?"

His grip on the car roof accentuated his heavy arm and chest muscles. He was breathing hard. His lightning-filled gaze fell, and he stilled.

She looked down. When she escaped from the motel room, she had figured stealth and speed were more important than getting dressed, so she was still in the camo shorty-shorts and midriff T-shirt. The rain had quickly soaked her front as well. Her nipples had puckered in the chill wet and were quite visible underneath her thin sports bra and shirt.

She looked up again into his dangerous face and said, "That's not my fault. I'm just sayin'."

He shoved his head and shoulders into the vehicle as he captured her by the back of the neck. His open mouth drove down onto hers. He was digging deep inside her mouth with his tongue before she fully knew what happened.

She made a sound, a whimper of surprise that he swallowed and gave back to her in a throaty growl that raised goose bumps along her bare arms and legs. The force of his kiss pushed her head back against his hand as he gripped the nape of her neck. She was trapped between his hand and his mouth. Her hands fluttered. She clutched at the front of his soaked T-shirt.

His kiss was brutal, ravenous, but his grip on her was gentle. He slid an arm around her waist and eased her forward until she perched on the side of the seat. He held her in place, an arm locked at her waist and a hand at her nape, as he nudged between her legs and slid the massive bulk of his long torso flush against hers. All the while he speared into the depths of her mouth and ate at plump lips that had gone soft in amazement.

The taste and texture of him was a shocking assault to her senses, the cold rain slippery on hot, aggressive lips. His jeans felt rough against the tender skin on the inside of her thighs,

and a hard swollen length pressed against her pelvis. She felt
his body move as he sucked in air. He was huge everywhere, his
body over twice her size.

She couldn't have stopped him if she'd tried.

She didn't want to try. She relaxed in his hold, trusting her
body to the solid support he offered. She tilted up her head to
him, eyes closed to the rain, and she kissed him back with all
the starved passion she had stored up inside.

Tiago felt the tension in her body melt away as her ripe,
wicked little mouth and eager tongue worked under the onslaught
of his. The surrender of her body was so damn erotic he almost
came in his fatigues.

Fucking hell. He fell into a tailspin.

What the hell was he doing?

She's been hurt. *Careful*, no frenzy allowed. She suckled at
his tongue as he thrust in her, and her slender white legs wrapped
around his waist. Okay, maybe a little frenzy. He groaned
and rubbed the hard length of his erection against the sweet wel-
coming arc of her pelvis. He wanted to palm those beautiful
breasts of hers and tongue that gold ring at her navel. He wanted
to spread her out and feast on her with the intensity of a starving man.

Delicate fingers dug into his short wet hair. He felt the tiny
prick of fingernails in his scalp like kitten claws. He wanted
them raking down his naked back. He wanted her to draw blood
as she screamed and climaxed in his arms. Her breath came in
jagged spurts. She was burning up, but violent shivers began to
shake through her small frame.

Sanity bulldozed its way into his thick skull. He dragged his
mouth away from hers with a harsh gasp, tilting his head up to
the rain as he tucked her face into his neck. "Goddammit," he
hissed. "I'm sorry."

"Of course you are," she muttered. "Not one single thing has
gone right for me today. Why should this be any different?"

He glared down at the top of her head. What the hell did she
mean by that?

She pushed her nose into the hollow where his neck met his
shoulder as her trembling increased. Too many things were
happening in her body. The knife wound felt like it was on fire.
She was so hot yet freezing at the same time. Weakness invaded
her limbs, and the sharp, empty ache between her thighs had

crazy thoughts running through her head, like how easy it would be to unzip his fatigues and take that swollen, hard cock in her hand. Like how much she wanted to explore the strange sensual terrain of his flesh and pump him until he spilled all over her. Her breath hitched.

Headlights swept over them as a car approached. He scooped her out of the driver's seat, carried her around and deposited her in the passenger's seat. Then he strode back, climbed in the driver's side and started the SUV so that he could park it by the side of the road. The engine was already warm, so he turned the heater on full blast before he turned to her again.

She was a bedraggled mess. The manipulative sex kitten had turned into a half-drowned rat. Her black hair glittered wet and sleek against the graceful curve of her skull, and those gorgeous erect nipples of hers, God help him, were dark raised pebbles underneath that porno T-shirt. She was shaking visibly. Grinding his teeth, he leaned past her to reach for one of the shopping bags she had thrown onto the passenger's seat floor. Not caring what he grabbed, he pulled out an item of clothing and began to stroke her wet bare arms and legs with it.

She muttered, "I had this whole thing going a lot differently in my head."

"I hardly dare to ask," he said. His white teeth bit at the air.

"For one thing, I was going to retain control of the car," she said. Her teeth chattered. She pushed his hand away. "There you go, being nice again. Stop it."

"What, you prefer abuse?" he growled. "That can be arranged. Just keep pushing at me, faerie."

"Pushing you." She snorted a laugh. "Don't tempt me. You haven't even seen me get started."

He cocked a sleek, sardonic eyebrow at her. "I'm actually afraid you might be right about that."

She grabbed the sweatpants from his hand and began to dry herself off. The material was thick and absorbent. She would have shrugged and slipped them on except she thought the twist of movement needed to pull them over her hips would hurt too much. Instead, she dug one of the T-shirts out of the bag.

Tiago's hands came over hers.

"I know you're hurting," he said, dropping his bad-tempered attitude for the moment. He had a powerful battlefield voice, deep and rich and penetrating, but now it was throttled down to just a dark murmur that was so gentle it shook her soul. "Let me help you."

He was right; she was hurting, and she was still trembling like a leaf. She bit her lips and nodded. He eased the shirt on, guiding the arm on her injured side. She managed to say, "Thank you."

"Where were you going, anyway?" he asked.

"I want pancakes with strawberries and whipped cream." She sniffed as she spread the sweatpants over her lap for the warmth.

"You left to get breakfast." The flatness of his voice and the cynical expression on his harsh features said he didn't believe her.

She rolled her eyes. She told him, "I left to get away from you."

"You must still be drunk if you thought you could give me the slip," he snapped. "You didn't have a chance in hell."

Well, no. She opened her eyes very wide. "I got your car and your gun when you weren't looking, didn't I?"

He clearly didn't like what he heard, if his scowl was any indication. His glare could peel paint. What the hell was the matter with her? She was needling a pissed-off thunderbird, for God's sake.

She groped for some sanity and told him, "Look, running back to New York is not an option. I don't have the energy to keep arguing with you about it. Will you just buy me some breakfast at IHOP and then take me back to the Regent?"

His attention shifted away from her as she spoke. His gaze narrowed on the car that had just passed them. The car's brake lights came on, shining bright red in the rainy night.

"What did you do with the Glock?" he asked. His face, voice, body remained calm.

Her stomach gave a sickened lurch. She dug into a shopping bag and put the gun into his outstretched hand. The car that had captured Tiago's attention reversed with a sharp squeal of tires.

Tiago was already exiting the SUV. He moved so fast he was a blur. He said to her telepathically, *Lock the doors and get down on the floor. NOW, Tricks.*

"Dr. Death" wasn't just a nickname she had made up on the spot. It was what the other Wyr sentinels called Tiago behind his back. He was a killing machine quick to anger and fueled by immense Power.

She had years of experience working with the Wyr sentinels whenever the threat level warranted she should have a detail of bodyguards. She knew when to fight, when to run away and when to get out of the way.

She wasn't a very old faerie and she wasn't all that Powerful. The low-level Power she did have was barely enough to cross over to an Other land or to achieve telepathy, which anyone, Elder Race or human, could do if they had a spark of magic. She also had a delicate sprinkle of charisma that gave her an edge sometimes in negotiations and knotty social gatherings, but it was worth squat in a combat situation. She had a small, light build, and now she was wounded. Her self-defense abilities were all artifice and had very little to do with natural aptitude.

She owed everything she knew to years of determined, patient training by the sentinels. Sure, she could kick ass, but she generally preferred for someone's back to be turned when she did so. Using poison on her stilettos was just another way to level a very uneven playing field. This was not a time for her to fight. This was a time for her to do as she was told and keep out of the way.

She locked the doors and pulled herself into a compact package on the passenger's seat floor, arms over her head. Her knife wound gave a throb so vicious it seemed to shoot to her spine. She could feel a gush of warmth against her chilled skin as it started bleeding again. It was the least of her worries at the moment.

She hated this part, hated it when someone she cared about put his life on the line for her. No matter how many times she went through it, it never got easier.

"Be okay," she whispered to Tiago. "Be safe."

That was when the shooting started.

═ FOUR ═

The sound of gunshots passed quickly. What she heard next was incomprehensible and just as frightening. There was a sudden explosion of glass shattering, a shout of rage and then a high scream of pain.

After what seemed like forever but was just a few moments, Niniane couldn't take it any longer. She broke a cardinal rule and disobeyed her bodyguard. She shifted and eased up on one knee until she could peer out the rain-smeared window.

The SUV and the other car's headlights, along with the streetlamps, caused the surrounding area to be unevenly lit and filled with deep shadows. Still, Tiago's aggressive black-clad form was unmistakable as he slammed one boot down on the head of a supine figure. The figure convulsed then lay still.

She covered her mouth, swallowing hard. There was another figure slumped at the steering wheel. The driver's window was starred with bullet holes.

Her gaze darted around. The Dark Fae tradition of working in triads extended to more than just legitimate groupings of governmental officials. If this was a Dark Fae triad, where was the third?

She pressed a hand to the wound at her side, and grimaced and panted as she began the painful process of wriggling back into the driver's seat of the SUV. Maybe she couldn't do much to help, but she could be ready to drive them from the scene if needed.

A dark figure lunged from the blackness of nearby shrubbery. The breath left her in a hiss. It was a shorter, slighter figure than Tiago and moved with killing speed as it threw something at him.

But Tiago was well aware of the threat and already acting. He dove to one side. He shot the other figure as he fell to the ground. The attacking Fae lurched and dropped. Tiago rolled. With a single leap that spanned at least twenty feet he was on the fallen Fae, who must have already been dead, because Tiago straightened almost immediately. He stared down at his fallen opponent for what seemed a long time. Then he spun to glare around at the scene. His raptor's eyes flashed eerily in the car's headlights as he turned toward her.

"That's it," he said. He knew full well that she could hear him with her sensitive Fae ears. "Don't give me any lip this time. We're going back to New York where I know I can keep you safe."

She stared at his angry face as he stalked toward the SUV. Her finger went out and hovered over the lock button on the doors. She pulled her hand away and left the doors locked.

Tiago reached the driver's side and pulled at the handle. He slammed his fist into the car. "What the hell are you doing now?"

"You aren't taking me anywhere," she told him.

"You are a crazy person. Open the goddamn door."

She looked into his fierce gaze and shook her head. She knew he wouldn't break the window, or do anything that might risk hurting her. She touched the glass where his fist was planted. She was filled with a yearning to let him take her home, to make the nightmare stop, but she knew he couldn't. Then she put the SUV into gear and pulled away.

Tiago watched her drive away, his clenched fists planted on his hips. As she looked at him in the rearview mirror, blinding-hot lightning struck the pavement near his feet, and the scene flashed black and white.

He roared, *"GodDAMMIT, Tricks!"*

She drove with intense concentration, mindful of the speed limit and the furious thunderbird that shadowed her overhead. She was also quite lost. After a few minutes she gave up trying to figure out the route on her own and punched the destination into the GPS system on the dashboard.

It was a terrible journey and it felt like it took forever. She almost pulled over a couple of times to let Tiago take the wheel. Her chills came back and raked at her body from the inside, and her skin hurt. Then her heart started working too hard, as if she were running, and her gaze started to blur. She kept a death grip on the steering wheel, afraid to loosen her hold for even a moment.

The Regent hotel was located in Chicago's Gold Coast district on the near north side, a historic neighborhood that had arisen after the Great Chicago Fire. Located just a few blocks from the famous Magnificent Mile shopping district on Michigan Avenue, the Regent was a luxury boutique hotel with mahogany-paneled walls, antiques, artwork, fireplaces and an old-world charm that was much favored by the Elder Races.

At long last she pulled onto the short one-way street where the Regent was located, and she could see the hotel's well-lit portico ahead. There was also a mob of people milling about, huddling under umbrellas and awnings as they talked and drank coffee.

Camera crews and television vans. Of course.

And there was Tiago, wearing his mad assassin's face as he leaned against a crosswalk post and watched the oncoming traffic on the one-way street with those dark killer's eyes. He was quite the satanic figure, massive and motionless and clad in black, and wholly focused on her. She tried not to let the sight of him affect her as she looked away, but her hyperawareness of his presence added to her clumsiness. He looked so savage. No, sexy. No, savage. Oh, for Pete's sake.

She carefully pulled the SUV over to the curb and parked illegally in front of a fire hydrant. "Big, tough, scary Wyr," she whispered. "I'm not afraid of you."

Tiago's chin lowered to his chest as he looked at her. The downward angle of his eyebrows became more pronounced. The overhead streetlamp slashed black shadows across his hatchet-carved features.

The skin at the back of her neck tingled. She whispered, "You can't hear me whisper from all the way over there, can you?"

He tilted his head in silent acknowledgment. Adrenaline pulsed. Her bones were wiser and more sensible than her foolish brain. They reminded her that his mad face was the last thing many creatures saw before they died.

Phooey. The keys clacked as her shaking fingers turned off the ignition. The spurt of adrenaline was a weak one that fled as her muscles seemed to turn to goo. She slumped in her seat. It hurt to breathe.

A light tap sounded at the window. She forced herself to look up. Tiago stood at the driver's window again. His mad-assassin face had morphed into sharp concern. He put his flattened hand on the window. It looked as big as a dinner plate. "Faerie," he said. "Niniane. Please open the door now."

Her arm felt like it weighed fifty pounds as she pushed the lock button. He yanked the door open and leaned over her, his brow creased in a frown. He put a hand to her forehead and took in a quick breath.

"They all want Niniane Lorelle," she said to him. Her voice sounded tinny and weird, and echoed in her own ears. "But who am I kidding? That girl died a long time ago. Tricks is just going to have to fake it."

His expression gentled in a way she would never have believed if she hadn't seen it for herself. The satanic killer morphed into a handsome worried man. "Niniane didn't die," he said. He stroked her hair. "She just went into hiding for a very long time. She's a brave, beautiful woman who needs medical attention now."

"I know, it's infected," she said. She watched as a man from the crowd noticed them and began to walk toward them. A few others joined him, then more. An internal quaking rattled her limbs, and her breathing grew choppy. She gripped Tiago's thick, strong wrist, and her gaze clung to his. "Please don't leave me until I get better. I can't do this alone and sick. You're the only one I know I can trust."

Death came back into his face as he glared at the oncoming crowd. "You couldn't get me to leave if you tried," he said. "And you might recall, faerie—you've tried. Just relax. I'll take care of everything."

She nodded. He pressed a quick kiss to her forehead and pulled out of the SUV. He took the Glock from his waistband and pointed it at the crowd. People cried out and jerked to a halt. In his deep battlefield-carrying voice, Tiago said, "Her highness has survived two assassination attempts in less than thirty-six hours. Do not make the mistake of thinking I won't shoot you, because I will. Back the fuck up."

The crowd stumbled back, staring at him. Niniane stared at him too. He was pure aggression, from that powerful muscled body to his hatchet-hewn face, black hair shining wet from the rain and those hard, glittering eyes. The last of her strength ebbed away as she relaxed. He really would take care of everything.

"Thank you," she whispered.

A flicker of his eyes, a small, brief quirk at the corner of his lips. He told the crowd, "Everybody—move across the street. Now."

She must have closed her eyes for a minute, because suddenly there were uniformed police all around. She startled violently as her overtaxed body tried to pulse another alarm, but something must have happened when she wasn't looking. The police had recognized Tiago and were helping, not confronting him. They cleared the path to the hotel.

Tiago leaned into the SUV one more time to ease his arms under her shoulders and knees. She tucked her face into his neck as he cradled her against his broad chest. Cameras started to flash, sparking in the wet night like fireflies. Tiago's Power enveloped her, a warm masculine blanket of inexhaustible energy. She concentrated on his scent, on his massive strength, which kept the rest of the chaotic, dangerous world at bay. Thank you, thank you.

Uniformed staff held the doors as he strode into the Regent. He headed toward the reception desk, intensely aware of the small shivering female in his arms. She felt so vulnerable. Rage swept over him again as he recalled the footage of when she was knifed.

A distinguished, well-dressed human male with salt-and-pepper hair approached Tiago before he was halfway to the desk. The male was flanked by hotel security. Tiago bared his teeth at them when they were still several feet away. "Stop there."

The men froze and regarded him with wide-eyed wariness. The human in the suit said, "Sir, whatever we can do—please know the full resources of the hotel are at her highness's disposal."

"We need a suite on a secured floor," Tiago ordered. "It should be at least two floors away from the Dark Fae delegation.

And her highness needs medical attention. Get a doctor. Make it happen now."

The suit nodded and spoke in an urgent low voice into a handheld. He said, "If you'll follow me, sir." He gestured and they strode to the elevators. Security fell into step behind them. The suit looked at Niniane, then back to Tiago, worry in his eyes. Her knife wound had bled through the dressing and the T-shirt. A patch of red showed clearly against the light material. She had not bothered to slip on the flip-flops. Her delicate pale legs and feet seemed very bare. Tiago raged that her wounded nakedness was so visible to the public.

He and the suit stepped onto the elevator. Tiago snapped at the security guards, "Take the stairs."

They jerked to a halt. As the doors shut, they turned to sprint away.

He looked at the suit and said, "Do you know who I am?"

"Yes, sir. You're the Wyr sentinel Tiago Black Eagle," said the human. "Lord Cuelebre called personally and informed us of your involvement. It is my understanding Lord Cuelebre has also been in contact with Chicago PD. I'm the hotel manager, Scott Hughes."

Tiago nodded. The seven Wyr sentinels had a legal authority that had several things in common with that of a federal U.S. Marshal, although there were several discrete differences as well that mainly had to do with the chain of command. When Tiago was in the States, among other things he had the authority to apprehend fugitives from Wyr justice, enlist help from willing civilians, and protect Wyr judiciaries, dignitaries and witnesses. He assumed control of the current situation from a long-standing precedent. Niniane had been a public member of Wyr society for many years, and she had often been under the sentinels' protection.

It helped to have some of his road smoothed. Now was not the time to fuck around with an argument over jurisdiction and weapons privileges.

"Don't misunderstand me," Tiago said. "It was her choice to come back to the hotel, not mine. I am on a hair trigger, and I will kill anyone who moves too quickly or tries to get too close. Clear the floor of the suite and put guards on the elevators and stairway exits. In fact, if you haven't already done so, clear the hotel. You might have heard what I said outside—there have been two assassination attempts on her in less than thirty-six hours. I'm prepared to shoot and ask questions later. *Do not* let the Dark Fae delegation come onto that floor for any reason, not until we have some kind of independent authority and arbitration on-site."

"Some of the hotel staff and guards are undercover police," said Hughes. "They were put in place once it was decided her highness was staying here before crossing over to the Dark Fae land for her coronation. Lord Cuelebre has advised us that the Elder tribunal is sending one of its Councillors, who will be here shortly."

"I would have expected nothing less," said Tiago. The tribunal would not be sending either the Dark Fae or the Wyr representative, but a representative from one of the other five demesnes in order to maintain an impartial stance in arbitrating any conflicts that might arise. Tiago dismissed the subject and thought for a moment. Safety, shelter, food, clothing. "Is there a suite with a kitchen next to the one we're going to occupy?"

"Yes, all the suites on that floor are business class. They're equipped with small kitchens."

"Put a chef and an assistant in a neighboring suite. They'll be on call twenty-four/seven. Better put a hotel housekeeper in there too. Put one of those undercover cops in there. The staff stays sequestered for now. They eat whatever they cook, plus you need to make sure they can test for poisons in any grocery delivery. Also, she needs clothing. See that she gets some of her things from the penthouse. Make sure they are swept for poisons and thoroughly cleaned before they're delivered."

The hotel manager was looking more somber by the moment. "All right."

Tiago stared hard at the manager. "I'm holding you responsible. You don't want to piss me off. Understand?"

Hughes swallowed hard but kept a calm demeanor and nodded. "I understand."

Tiago ducked his chin and said gently in Niniane's ear, "Almost there now, faerie. Hang on."

She nodded, a wisp of her silky black hair tickling his chin, and whispered, "You need c-clothes too."

"Don't worry about me. I'll get my stuff in a bit," he told her. Soon as he got her settled, he would have Tucker bring his duffle back from the motel room.

She raised her voice. "Scott?"

Scott? Tiago looked up fast, eyes narrowed. The hotel manager's face had gone from sober worry to pure adoration. "Yes, your highness?"

"Thank you so much for everything. I don't know what I would d-do without your help." It was clear she was gritting her teeth to keep them from chattering too much, as shivers continued to rack her body.

"It's my privilege, your highness, whatever I can do. This has been a terrible ordeal. We've all been so worried about you."

Tiago turned to face forward toward the elevator doors, his expression turning wry. Of course. Niniane had already met the manager and staff, and had already worked her particular brand of magic on them. It seemed she made conquests wherever she went, except, apparently, with anyone intent on murdering her.

"Please thank all the hotel staff for me as well. As s-soon as I'm well enough, I want to thank everybody personally."

"I'll be sure to do so," promised the manager with a fervent smile.

Tiago sighed as he thought of Niniane coming within proximity of so many strangers. Yeah, he'd be sure to talk her out of that one.

The elevator stopped and the doors opened. Tiago gave the corridors a good hard look before stepping out. Then he and the manager moved at a rapid pace until Tiago stopped at a suite in the middle of a hall with a clear view of each end of the corridor. He nodded to the manager. The two security agents jogged through the stairway exit as Hughes opened the door with a key card.

"Are you two undercover cops?" Tiago asked. They looked at each other, at Hughes and finally at Niniane, who rested with such trust in Tiago's arms. The older one of the pair nodded. Tiago told the pair, "Guard the door. Knock when the doctor arrives."

They both nodded. Hughes held the door for Tiago as he strode down the short hall to the living room. He booted the coffee table aside and eased his precious package onto the sofa. He knelt on one knee and got his first look at Niniane in good light for a while. Her pale skin was sallow. Those normally lustrous overlarge Fae eyes were dull and circled with dark purple shadows. Her lips were shaking.

His jaw clenched. He knew her injury was not life-threatening. He was long familiar with the horrific casualties of war. For him her knife wound wouldn't even warrant an email back to New York. He knew she was going to be all right. None of that helped alleviate how he felt as he stared at her helpless suffering.

He snapped out an order. "Blanket."

Even as he reached out, Hughes was thrusting something soft, heavy and warm into his hand. He shook out the blanket and tucked it with care around Niniane. He rested one hand on her quaking shoulder as he studied her with a frown. He said, "Why are your chills worse all of a sudden?"

"Your body heat was h-helping," she gritted.

He paused, then with infinite care he picked her up again, sat on the sofa and settled her on his lap with the blanket tucked around her. She lay against him, head on his shoulder, a limp weight except for the shivering that clawed through her slender body. He placed the Glock on the sofa arm as Hughes approached from the kitchen with a chilled bottle of water.

"Here," said the manager, offering it to Tiago. "It's still sealed."

Tiago nodded in approval, propped the bottle against his leg and twisted the cap off while he cuddled Niniane in his other arm. He took a sip of the water, rolled it over his tongue, and decided it was safe enough to drink. He offered the bottle to Niniane.

She stared up at him. "Don't you ever do that again," she said. What her thready voice lacked in strength, she made up for in anger. "Don't risk yourself by tasting for poison. It's hard enough to live with you putting yourself on the line doing body-guard detail for me."

He cocked an eyebrow at her and tilted the bottle so that she was forced to drink or let the water dribble down her chin. She gargled and swallowed. He said, "That's not your call to make, your snippiness."

"Tiago," she said. She sounded like her patience was severely tried. "Who is going to be Queen? Me, not you. You are not in charge here. You can't be. Get over it or go home."

"Like that's going to happen," he told her, tilting the water bottle at her again. She was forced to drink more while storm clouds gathered in those amazing eyes. "You asked for my help, and you got it. Deal with it and shut up."

She pushed her chin up and turned her mouth away from the bottle, and he let her. She huffed, "Your bedside manner is sociopathic."

"Trying to care about that," he said. He cocked his head and widened his eyes. "Huh. I guess I'm not managing it."

Sarcastic son of a bitch. "Thanks for everything you've done tonight. I really appreciate it. I've changed my mind about you staying. You're fired."

"I came to Chicago whether you wanted me to or not, so I'm not caring about that so much either," he told her. He held the bottle up, and she flinched, slapping a protective hand over her mouth. "Come on, your recalcitrance, finish the bottle. On top of your wound being infected, you drank far too much vodka. You need the hydration."

"Which I don't get," she muttered. Since she was thirsty anyway, she reached for the water bottle, and he let her take it. "As much alcohol as I ingested, my whole body should be a sterile environment."

"Life isn't logical."

Between his body warmth and the blanket her chills had eased, and she was looking sulky and mutinous. The bottom lip of that luscious little X-rated mouth was sticking out. The clench in his gut started to ease until he felt almost cheerful.

He could see Hughes's expression out of the corner of his eye. The manager's usual dignified expression had given way to openmouthed fascination. Tiago scowled at him. Then he heard a sound. He had eased Niniane onto the sofa, grabbed the Glock and was striding down the hall before either Niniane or Hughes could react.

Someone knocked at the door as he approached.

"What," he said without opening it.

"The hotel physician is here."

He stood to the side and leaned over to peer through the peephole. The hotel security/undercover cops were standing back from the door, in sight of the peephole. Between them stood a slight, intelligent-looking male who carried a bag. Even through the door Tiago could pick up a whisper of magic about the man. The doctor was a witch.

Hughes had come to the door as well. Tiago pointed to the door. "Verify this guy," he said.

The manager took a look through the peephole. "That's Dr.

Weylan, the one I called. The hotel has had him on retainer for several years now."

Tiago opened the door, gestured the doctor in and shut and locked the door behind him. Then he pinned the doctor to the wall with one hand around his throat and introduced him to the Glock.

"Here are the rules," he said. "No second chances. I've been on battlefields for far longer than you've been alive. I have performed triage and I am very familiar with medical procedures, including magical ones. You do not want me to misunderstand anything you do. You do a single thing that seems off to me in the slightest way, and you're dead. And I won't lose a single moment's sleep over that decision. Got it?"

Paling, the doctor nodded. Hughes stared at Tiago, and from the living room Niniane exclaimed, "Tiago!"

He raised his voice as he snapped, "Let's revisit, your argumentativeness. There've been *two assassination attempts* in less than thirty-six hours. You won't let me take you back to New York, so it's shotgun justice until we have a safe base of operations established." He said more quietly to the doctor, "You got that?"

"Actually, I do," said the smaller man. Tiago eased his hold on the human male's throat. Steady, sharp eyes met his. The doctor gave him a tight smile. "You've made your point. Let me do what I came to do and treat my patient now."

Tiago took a deep breath and stepped back. He had lived a long life by trusting his gut. His gut told him that Hughes was for real, and that through the years the human doctor would have proven himself to the five-star hotel and its customers many times over.

Tiago's gut also knew that anybody could be gotten to, through bribery or coercion, through family or lovers held hostage or through religious or political beliefs. That was why he followed so closely behind the doctor as the human entered the living room, knelt beside the sofa and introduced himself to Niniane as he opened his bag.

Like Tiago had said to Niniane, life wasn't logical. It was often filled with uncertainties. At that moment he knew just one thing for sure.

That little manipulative sex kitten was not going to die tonight.

The fate of anybody else remained an open question.

. . .

Niniane huddled under the blanket and looked at her surroundings with a dull gaze. The hotel living room seemed unobjectionable enough. There were chairs, the sofa, tables, a flat-screen television, all the obligatory elements, but her exhausted mind seemed unable to absorb any details.

She had a weird kind of infection, she decided. Someone had tried to stuff an extra dimension in her head, and it didn't fit. Too-loud noises came and went. Her vision flickered around the edges.

Her knife wound hurt. The light was too bright and her eyes hurt. Her skin hurt, breathing hurt—hell, even her hair hurt. She felt like she barely had enough energy to lie on the sofa and live.

But whenever Tiago was near she seemed to have plenty of energy for arguing with him. It must be God's way of telling her how wrong he was.

She opened her eyes as three men entered the room. Hughes showed that he was a man of discretion, as he caught her eye and gestured that he would go to the kitchenette. She nodded in thanks to him. A slender human male knelt on the floor beside her, opened a medical bag and smiled at her. Tiago hovered just behind him, his dark face grim, and his murderous obsidian eyes tracked the human male's slightest movement.

She turned her attention back to the man kneeling beside her. His intelligent face was creased with kindness. "I'm Dr. Weylan," he told her. "It's quite an honor to meet your highness, but I'm sure we both could have wished it was under better circumstances. I hear you've been having a challenging couple of days."

"You can say that again," she said. Exhaustion kept her voice faint. Then she glanced pointedly at Tiago and rolled her eyes at the physician as she added, "And somebody tried to kill me too."

The doctor's eyebrows shot up and he laughed, while over his shoulder Tiago glared daggers at her. "Okay," Dr. Weylan said. "I'll explain everything I'm going to do before I do it. The first thing I want to do is to put my hands on you and give you a magical scan. I want to put one hand on your forehead, and the other one close to where you've been injured. Have you had one of these scans before?"

She nodded.

"Good, then you know it might tingle a bit but it won't hurt. It's just going to give me information while you tell me all about what happened to you. All right?"

"All right," she said.

He laid his hand lightly against her forehead, and after asking her, he placed his other hand against her side near the knife wound. The look in his hazel eyes grew intent. "Go on now, tell me what happened," he encouraged.

She sighed. "If you saw that stupid viral video, you know pretty well what happened. My cousin said he wanted to take me out to dinner. Then he and my two other attendants attacked me, and I got knifed. I cleaned the wound as best I could, but it's awfully deep. It must have gotten infected."

The doctor nodded. The room fell silent as he concentrated. After a moment, he pulled his hands away and smiled at her. "I'm glad to say you're quite a lucky lady, your highness. The wound is deep, and if the entry had been at a slightly different angle, your lung would have been punctured."

She looked at Tiago. His dark gaze met hers. If anything, he looked deadlier and grimmer than ever, although his hand was quite gentle as he reached out to tug at a lock of her hair.

The doctor went on, "And you're right, of course. An infection has set in. It will be simple enough to cleanse once we've gotten rid of some cloth fibers that are trapped in the puncture. You're suffering from shock and blood loss, but otherwise, you're quite healthy. I would like to set up an IV drip to help replenish your fluid levels—"

Tiago stirred. "No IVs," he said. "No injections. Not without having all your medical supplies tested first."

The doctor had frozen while Tiago spoke. Weylan continued, without having ever looked away from her gaze, "But barring that, I will strongly urge you to force liquids. Everything you need I can do in the privacy and safety of this suite. I can put a local anesthetic charm near your wound, and I have an extraction spell that will flush the wound and expel the fibers within ten minutes or so. It will feel strange, but it's much less painful or invasive than physically probing into the wound itself. After that, I can either cleanse the infection with a spell or prescribe a course of antibiotics for you to take."

"Which is better?" she asked. No matter how hard she tried to keep her eyes open, they drifted shut.

"It's six-of-one, half-a-dozen of the other," he told her. "The cleansing spell is quick and efficient, but it takes a system by storm. You would feel pretty weak and exhausted for a couple of days afterward. The antibiotics take more time, but they don't leave one feeling quite so mowed down."

She forced her eyes open again and looked at Tiago. "Maybe the antibiotics," she said. "So I can get back on my feet faster."

"No," Tiago said. He bent over her and took her hand, lacing her fingers with his. His hand was huge and enveloped hers. "You will have all the time you need to convalesce, and the world will wait for you. I'm here. I'm not going anywhere. You are perfectly safe."

She gave him a blank stare. *Perfectly safe.* She had no idea what that meant.

She closed her eyes. "Do whatever is best then," she said in a listless voice.

There was a pause. The doctor pulled down the blanket, pulled up the loose outer shirt and folded back the camo T-shirt. His touch was gentle and efficient. She could tell the moment the local anesthetic charm was laid on her stomach. She sighed with relief as at least some of the pain eased.

She kept her eyes closed and listened without interest as the men talked.

"She's going to lose more fluids when I use the extraction spell. I don't like her level of dehydration. What can I do to convince you that the bags of saline solution I have are safe?" the doctor asked Tiago.

The Wyr warrior said, "Do you have more than one IV needle?"

"Yes."

"Use one on yourself. After five minutes, you can transfer the rest of the bag to her."

"Fine, done." Weylan raised his voice. "Scott?"

The manager hurried into the room. "Yes?"

"Would you please get some towels from the bathroom?"

"Certainly." After bringing in an armful of towels, the manager disappeared again.

She flinched as a warm hand came down on her forehead and smoothed back her hair. Tiago's hands were much larger than the doctor's, rougher and more calloused. She rested her fingers on his muscle-corded forearm. He thrummed with so much latent Wyr Power he felt like a current of electricity wrapped in a tree trunk.

She opened her eyes briefly to see that he had knelt by her head. He was bending over her while he watched with a sharp raptor's gaze as the doctor removed the sodden dressing and wiped the puncture wound clean. The doctor had to work with care as he had attached his right hand to a bag of saline, which he had hung from a picture hook on the wall.

Tiago continued to stroke his fingers through her hair. It felt so good she might have nuzzled his hand just a little bit. He murmured to her, "You're no fun when the stuffing's been knocked out of you, your listlessness."

Did that require an answer? She sighed.

"You're like a rubber ball with no bounce," he said. He cradled her cheek in one large palm. "A worm that's lost its wiggle."

A *worm*? "Oh, please, the hyperbole." She put a hand to her forehead. "It's too flowery."

Somebody snorted nearby. The doctor said, "It's been five minutes."

Tiago told him, "You can use the IV on her. That bag only."

"I understand."

The doctor inserted the needle into her left hand, which was closest to the wall, taped it into place and hooked her to the IV. Then he tucked rolled towels along her side and cast the extraction spell. She made a sound and clenched her right fist.

It was instantly swallowed in Tiago's larger grip. "You all right, faerie?" he asked, his voice sharp.

"Yes, I'm fine," she said. She opened her eyes and gave him an unhappy look. "It just itches deep inside where things aren't supposed to itch."

He frowned and asked the doctor, "Can you numb her any more?"

The doctor was busy blotting the bright trickle of blood and fluid that had begun to spill from the puncture wound. He shook his head. "Not without resorting to medication. And I'm not injecting myself or anybody else without good reason." He looked up at her. "This is as bad as it gets. I promise. It'll be over with in just a few minutes."

"All right," she said in a flat voice. She shifted her legs in an effort to get more comfortable.

Tiago began to stroke her hair again. She stilled, and everything inside her focused on the warm comfort he offered. He met her gaze and said, "Guess what you get for being such a good girl at the doctor's?"

She was still flush with fever, and she hated the itchy-crawly feeling deep in her wound. She didn't want to smile at him. She didn't. One corner of her mouth lifted. She asked, "What?"

He crinkled at her. "How about some pancakes with strawberries and whipped cream?"

Her eyes brightened. "You promise?"

"Of course I do."

Her smile deepened. A dimple appeared in one cheek. "Well, now that you've promised I guess I'm getting pancakes whether I want them or not."

Even as she said it, she knew it was true. A certain knowledge settled deep into her bones. She may not know Tiago very well in some ways, but after decades of living with and interacting with Wyr sentinels, in other ways she knew him intimately. Once he set his mind on something, nothing would stop him. Once he gave his promise, he would never give up, never stop, until he had achieved whatever it was he said he would do. It might be infuriating at times, but it was something she could rely on, wholly and completely.

"Oh, come on, faerie. You're just being cranky." His white teeth flashed in that hard, rugged face. "You know you still want them."

A miserable, lonely and unsettled part of her eased into something resembling peace. She turned her cheek into his hand.

A look came into his dark eyes, a new expression she couldn't decipher. He stroked her lips with his thumb and stared at her like he had never seen her before.

Another knock sounded at the door. Hughes said, "I'll see what they want."

Without looking away from her, Tiago ordered, "Don't open the door. Don't let anybody in."

"No, sir."

Reality was trying to intrude. She didn't want it to. She wrapped the fingers of her free hand around his thick wrist as her forehead crinkled. Holding her gaze, he whispered, the barest thread of a sound, "*Shh.*"

Hughes returned. "The Dark Fae delegation is demanding to see her highness. They're denying your right to protect her and threatening war with the Wyr."

⇒ FIVE ⇐

She tensed. Tiago tapped her nose with a forefinger. "Wrong response," he whispered to her. "Remember, the world waits for you. Okay?"

She took a deep breath and made herself relax. "Okay."

Tiago turned, his demeanor calm and unhurried. "Hughes, what an asinine thing to tell a hotel manager. They can throw as much of a fit as they like, as long as it doesn't get them past the stairwell doors. Understand?"

The manager swallowed and nodded. "The floor's been searched and evacuated. There are two guards at each stairwell door, and the elevators have been locked down for now."

"Good. That's how things stay" He turned back to her. "How is it going?"

She said, "The itching has stopped."

"Excellent, and the wound is no longer draining," Dr. Weylan told her. "That means the extraction has run its course. I'm going to close the puncture with just a few stitches and bandage you up. Once I cast a quick cleansing spell, you can get some real rest."

She nodded, and the doctor was finished in no time. She put out a hand to stop him when he would have cast the cleansing spell. Tiago scowled, but she ignored him as she asked the doctor, "I'm already feeling shaky. I would like to get cleaned up before you cast that spell."

He smiled at her. "Good idea."

She had barely made a move to sit up when Tiago was there to slide his arms under her shoulders and knees and lift her upright. He hooked the IV bag onto a finger and carried her, still wrapped in a blanket, through the nearest bedroom and into its bathroom.

He set her on her feet with care. She turned and reached for the IV bag. He held it out of reach. "Stop it," he said. "I'll help you."

Feverish color touched her cheekbones. She frowned at him. "I don't think so. This is the end of the line for you, cowboy." He opened his mouth to argue, and she told him, "There are some things a girl likes to do on her own."

Amusement danced in his dark eyes. "There's nothing you could do that I haven't seen an army of uglier, hairier people do thousands of times before."

"That may be," she said with dignity, "but you haven't seen *me* do any of it before. Please don't argue with me on this one, Tiago. I'm tired and I hurt all over, and I want to go to bed."

His mouth tightened, but he nodded. He checked the back of the bathroom door and hung the saline bag on the hook he found. "Don't lock the door," he told her. "I'll be right on the other side."

Who knew that the Wyr warlord's real animal form was a mother hen? She rolled her eyes and sighed. "Fine. Get out."

He shut the door.

She debated the possible merits of another shower while she used the toilet, but she simply didn't have the energy to figure out how she might work that with the IV needle in the back of one hand. Instead she washed her face at the sink and brushed her teeth with the complimentary supplies.

There was so much to do, so much to plan for and an entire political minefield to maneuver, and the simple act of getting clean was almost too much for her. How long would Tiago stay to help? He had promised he would stay until she wasn't sick any longer, but what did that mean? Would he leave after she slept and he had seen her into safe hands? That was the reasonable thing to expect.

She was shaking again and feeling irrational as she opened the bathroom door. Tiago was leaning against the wall just outside, arms crossed as he waited for her. He straightened when the door opened. She asked, "Can you help me get this bloody T-shirt off?"

He took one look at her distressed face, and his expression softened. "Of course I will." He put the toilet seat down and guided her to sit. Then he knelt in front of her and stroked her hair as he looked with concern into her eyes. "Is it the T-shirt that's got you upset?"

Her gaze fell away from his. She shook her head and her lips trembled.

"Then what is it?" He bent his head and tried to catch her eye. She wouldn't let him. "Talk to me."

She had to say it to somebody, at least just once. "I wanted a cousin who liked me," she whispered. Her face crumpled.

The breath left his lungs as if she had sucker punched him. He gathered her close. She put her head on his shoulder and cried as he rocked her. He was so big he filled the bathroom. It felt so right to lean on him, to breathe in his scent and let him stroke her hair and rub her back and murmur to her. It almost made her believe in good things. She was too tired to fight it. She rested against him and let her cold, tired bones soak in his strength and warmth.

"It's never going to happen again," he told her. "I swear it. I wish to God I had been there to prevent it from happening the first time. It sucks that I wasn't. But I'm telling you now, faerie—it's never going to happen again."

She rested her cheek in the hollow above his sturdy collarbone. The thick muscles of his chest were tight, and she could feel the ridges of his bunched biceps as he wrapped his arms around her. He spoke with all the force of a vow as he cupped the back of her head, and she hid her face in his neck. She gave up thinking *that's impossible* and instead gave herself over to his keeping.

Tiago sensed a presence. He turned his head to glare daggers at the doctor, who had come to check on them. The human male raised his hand with a sympathetic wince and backed out of sight. Tiago turned his attention back to the small bundle of misery he held with such tense protectiveness.

He put his cheek to her hair. The scent of cigarette smoke had faded, leaving the soft, silky black hair smelling of herbal shampoo, rain and woman. He pressed a kiss to the delicate contour of her temple.

What was it about her that got him so messed up? He had

never paid that much attention to her other than to cock an amused eyebrow at something she had said or done, or to shake his head whenever he saw yet another person fall victim to that indefinable, effervescent charm of hers.

Her wounded vulnerability—it was a scourge that raked underneath his skin, scoring him deep inside in places he hadn't even known existed. His hand fisted in the hair at the back of her head.

The vengeful warlord in him longed to destroy Geril, except the Dark Fae male was already dead. Tiago wanted to cause somebody major structural damage, but there was no one to fight. The lack bewildered him. He had all this fury and nowhere to vent it. Heaven help any fool who might try another assassination attempt. Tiago would come down on them with all the force of the frustrated cataclysm he had pent up inside.

She was too exhausted to cry for long, as the fever continued to rack her with shivers. Tiago sat back on his heels when he felt her tremble. He took a knife from the leg pocket of his fatigues and cut the T-shirt off her body. Underneath, the little camo shirt with spaghetti straps was also the worse for wear, the area under her breasts spotted with blood. He cut that away too, leaving her in the sports bra and those ludicrous shorts.

Then he carried her into the shadowed bedroom, tucked her into the large bed and hung the IV bag on the handle of the bedside lamp. He sat on the edge of the bed and stroked the hair off her forehead as she lay shivering under the covers, those large dark gray eyes glittering jewel-like under half-closed eyelids.

He called for the doctor, who came at once into the room to cast the cleansing spell. For several moments her body was filled with a strange tingling energy. It faded soon enough and left a bone-deep lethargy in its wake. It would take her body a little while to catch up to the fact that there was no more infection to fight off. The doctor left a couple of bottles of water on the bedside table and promised that he would check on her after she awakened. When he stepped out of the room, he left the bedroom door open a few inches, which threw a band of light across the foot of the bed.

Tiago stretched out on the covers beside her, the ever-present Glock near at hand on the table alongside the bottled water. "I'll stay until you're asleep," he said, turning on his side so that he faced her.

For a panicked moment her overtired brain thought he meant he would actually leave when she was asleep, but it was too soon for him to go. She wasn't ready to survive on her own yet. Then sanity caught up with her as he folded her hand in his. She nodded and let her eyes drift shut.

Tiago asked quietly, "Why are you doing this? Why did you insist on coming here earlier when I said I was taking you back to New York? It's admirable you're working to keep someone like Urien from taking the Dark Fae throne, but you've made it clear that you don't really want to be Queen."

She was silent for a long moment until he thought she had already fallen asleep. Then she said, "I don't know if I can put it into words in the right way. I appreciate what you said outside, that Niniane didn't die, she just went into hiding, and in a way you're right. But in a way, I'm right too. Urien killed that teenage girl just as surely as he killed her family. Going back and claiming the throne is the only way I can get justice for her, and for her parents and brothers."

He took a breath and squeezed her fingers tight. "Justice," he murmured. He could understand that. "It's been a long time coming, hasn't it?"

She whispered, "I remember what happened like it was yesterday. That night hasn't ended for me. I just learned to live around it." She turned her head and looked into his dark eyes. "I have to put them all to rest. I have to bring to justice any of the Dark Fae who worked with my uncle, and help those he victimized like he victimized me. I don't even want to do it, but I have to go back. I have to find peace or die trying."

His Power mantled and covered her, a swift, invisible storm of protective Wyr male energy. He cupped her chin, a quick hard hold, his hawkish face turning blade sharp. "I don't want to hear another word like that. You will wipe that from your mind and your vocabulary right now."

His personality was too forceful, too much. It beat against her hypersensitive skin. She murmured, "Tiago." That was all, just his name. She closed her eyes.

After a moment the angry force of his Power eased and became soothing. Hard fingers stroked her cheek, and his mouth covered hers in a brief warm caress. "Poor tired faerie. Sleep now," he whispered. "Don't worry about a thing. Just sleep."

She had no other choice. She fell off a cliff into darkness.

• • •

As soon as Niniane had been settled in bed with some degree of comfort, Tiago shifted into high gear. He yanked out his cell phone and punched in a call.

Rune picked up on the first ring. "What do you need?"

"We got a shitload of trouble postmarked for our address," Tiago told him. "If it hasn't hit the fan yet, it will soon."

"You guys safe?"

"Yeah." He told the other sentinel their room number. "We're good."

"How's our favorite princess?"

"She's okay," Tiago told him. "She's stressed out, of course, and exhausted. The wound was infected, so the doc had to give her a cleansing spell. She just fell asleep."

"So about this shitload of trouble."

"There was another attack."

"You happened to mention that precious fact when you threatened to shoot a gaggle of reporters, camera crews and paparazzi outside the Regent. I'm here to tell you, son, you are one motherfucking public relations nightmare." Rune did not sound concerned. He cracked gum. "You look cute on TV though."

Tiago paced the living room. "Would you trust your life to anyone in Chicago? Really. Trust."

A short pause grew invisible talons and fangs. "Spill it," said Rune. The other sentinel's former amiability had vaporized into the flat, cold tones of the Wyr warrior that had fought his way to become Cuelebre's First.

"There was a triad involved in the attack," said Tiago. "They were dressed to look like they were Dark Fae, but they weren't. Rune, they were Wyr."

Niniane stayed in a deep, dreamless sleep until bodily needs forced her awake. She struggled to get out of bed and knocked a bottle of water off the bedside table. Suddenly Tiago was there. He carried her into the bathroom, and this time he insisted on staying. She felt so weak and leaden she didn't have the energy to argue with him or to be embarrassed. Instead, she leaned against him, eyes closed, as he helped to pull her underwear down and ease her onto the toilet. When she had finished and they had washed their hands, he scooped her up again and carried her back to bed.

"I want this damn thing off," she mumbled as he tucked the covers around her.

"What damn thing?" he asked. He smoothed the hair off her forehead.

She twitched the hand with the IV. "If I have to pee, I'm not dehydrated enough to need this anymore."

He squeezed her fingers. "I'll talk to the doctor."

A few minutes later the doctor came into the bedroom. He eased the IV needle out of her skin and covered the puncture with a small section of cotton pad folded under a Band-Aid. She muttered thanks, curled up on her unwounded side and fell back asleep.

The rest of the day flew by for Tiago. He was on the phone more often than not. Fifteen minutes after he had dropped his bombshell, Rune called back. It was too late to send a cleanup crew to the scene of the second attack. The police had already been called, and the crime scene was being processed. Rune and Aryal were headed to Chicago to investigate the Wyr involvement in the assassination attempt.

In the meantime Tiago triangulated with the gargoyle sentinel Grym, who was head of security back in New York, and the Chicago police commissioner, until they came up with a list of senior level police officers they could all agree upon for a task force specifically set up for Niniane's protection.

Once the list was solidified, Tiago began to work with the leader of the CPD task force. Lieutenant Cameron Rogers, a twenty-year veteran of the Chicago police, arrived at the Regent within the hour. She was a tall, sandy-haired, freckled woman in her early forties with the strong, bright energy of a self-confident athlete, and she combined sturdy efficiency with a sense of humor. Once the hotel floor was locked down with more than just two undercover cops posing as hotel guards, Tiago turned his attention to other things.

Tiago refused to leave Niniane's bedroom door unguarded. After Tucker delivered his duffle bag and Cameron brought it up to him, he dragged the kitchen table over so that he could set up the laptop and work.

The next item on his list was to look over the personnel files of the staff Hughes chose to cook and houseclean. He rejected a few, sent the rest to Grym to screen, and by the afternoon they had settled on four staff that would, along with Dr. Weylan, occupy the two neighboring suites. Weylan volunteered to magically screen all the delivered food supplies for poison. The CPD task force dealt with the details of settling in the hotel staff and developing a secure food delivery system.

Tiago ran into a snag when the Dark Fae delegation, located on the penthouse floor, refused to "legitimize his interference" and send any of Niniane's possessions down. Rogers was the one to knock on the suite door and inform him.

She said, "Incomprehensible bastards. Why would they refuse to send her some pajamas, for God's sake?"

Tiago stared at the long-limbed lieutenant without really seeing her. "They're maintaining a precedent for when the representative of the Elder tribunal arrives," he said. "They're going to claim I am holding her here illegally. If they cooperate, it will weaken their argument. They're going to try to get rid of me."

Stupid Fae. He would blow up the hotel before that happened. Preferably with the delegation still in it.

"Whatever they're doing, the result is kind of cruel. It leaves her without anything but complimentary hotel crap," said Rogers. The policewoman folded her arms as she stood hipshot. "I'll go out and get her some stuff. Just give me her clothes size."

He gave her a blank stare. "I have no idea," he muttered. "Hold on." He slipped through the silent bedroom to dig the ruined T-shirts out of the bathroom trash then moved back to the suite door. He told the lieutenant, "She's an extra small."

"Christ, she's just a teeny-tiny thing," the other woman swore. "Who could knife somebody like that?"

"Kinda like kicking a puppy," he agreed. He dug a money clip out of his pocket and handed a wad of bills to her.

Her sandy eyebrows twitched as she did a quick count of the cash. "You do realize you just gave me five thousand dollars, right?"

"What?" he said with a scowl. "Is that not enough?"

"No, I'd say that's quite sufficient." She grinned and turned to go.

"Wait," he said. When the policewoman paused and looked an inquiry at him, he rubbed the back of his neck and glared at the carpet as he tried to navigate in his head the foreign concepts involved in female frippery. "She likes pretty clothes.

And lipstick, she likes lipstick and dangly earrings and things like that, with all the colors matching. And chocolate—could you buy her a box of chocolates? Maybe some of the stuff could be gift wrapped."

Rogers's gaze softened. Tiago's face darkened as the police-woman gave him a kind smile that crinkled the corners of her eyes. She asked, "Anything else?"

He scowled as he thought. What was all the stuff that Dragos's mate got when she was convalescing? Well, aside from the diamond ring and shit. "Froufrou magazines," he muttered. "You know, the girly stuff."

"Are you sure you wouldn't like to go shopping for her yourself?"

His gaze jerked up to meet Rogers's, and he shook his head. Unless it involved the word *semiautomatic* somewhere, he wouldn't have the first clue. "I'm not leaving her," he said. "You'll have to do it. I'm sure what you pick out will be fine. I just want you to make sure it's nice."

"I will," she promised. "The hotel's surrounded by the best shops and department stores in Chicago. I'll stay close and be back soon."

"You do that," he said.

When Niniane fell asleep the second time, she tumbled back into the deep, dreamless rest of profound exhaustion.

Then she turned her head. What was that noise? She looked around. She was standing in one of the many hallways of the Dark Fae palace, its spare elegant familiarity turned strange in the dark, blue-shadowed night. A full moon shone through tall windows and threw glints of silver on dark, heavy furniture.

A single set of unhurried footsteps echoed through the silent halls, a quiet yet defined click of booted heels on hard polished floors. It was a small, ordinary, utterly grotesque sound. Death walked through her home and left no one alive. Dread and adrenaline pulsed through her, shaking her limbs and drying out her mouth. The owner of those footsteps was hunting for her.

She had to run. She had to escape from the charnel house that had once been her home, but she couldn't remember the way out. She ran down the hall, silent in bare feet, frantic to find an escape from the building. She slipped in a pool of warm, sticky blood and fell to her hands and knees. It was her twin brothers' blood. She looked up. Their small, lifeless five-year-old bodies had been flung into a corner like abandoned dolls.

There were so many windows. She could see the familiar silver-edged roll of landscape outside, but she didn't dare break the glass, because it would make noise and draw the attention of the monstrous thing that hunted her in the shadows. She couldn't find a door. She knew this place. Why couldn't she remember where the doors were?

The footsteps came closer. A chill Power ghosted through the rooms, curling around furniture, slipping under doors, tightening in the air like the coils of a boa constrictor wrapped around its prey. She blundered into a closet and fought through clothing to get to the back. She sank into a shivering ball in the suffocating dark as a scream built up in the back of her throat, but she couldn't make a sound. She would be slaughtered if she made so much as a whimper. She clapped both hands over her mouth. Her rattled breathing sounded in her own ears as loud as a shout. The footsteps drew closer, and she drowned in her own panic.

She plunged awake, both hands clapped over her mouth. She was shaking all over and drenched in a cold sweat that had nothing to do with her injury. For a few pulse-pounding moments the shadowed hotel bedroom was as grotesque and terrifying as the dreamscape she had just exited. Then reality re-formed and settled into place.

She forced her rigid body to relax, muscle by muscle, and lay with a hand over her eyes as her heart rate slowed and her breathing quieted. It had been a long time since she had dreamed of suffocating in her own panic as her uncle Urien hunted her. The nightmare had once been a nightly occurrence. She supposed she shouldn't be surprised at its return, but she sure as hell didn't welcome it.

Finally thirst spurred her to movement. She fumbled for a bottle of water, broke the seal and drank most of the contents before coming up for air. She sank back onto the pillows, cradling the water bottle as she yawned so hard her jaw popped.

If the doctor hadn't already warned her, she would have been alarmed at how lethargy weighed down her body. The wound still hurt but not with the same kind of inflamed throbbing it had when it had been infected. At least her skin no longer felt like someone had scored it with tiny razor blades. It felt like the fever was gone.

The bedroom was dark and cool. A band of light from the partially closed door shone across the foot of the bed. The television was playing in the other room. It sounded like a news channel. She yawned again and finished her water. She felt hollowed out, and still tired and shaky, but she didn't think she could sleep any longer.

She clicked on the bedside light, and a moment later Tiago appeared. His long, powerful body filled up the doorway, his lean hawkish features alert. He had changed at some point into a black T-shirt, jeans and boots. The cotton of his shirt strained across the wide muscles of his chest and arms. He wore a shoulder holster and gun. His Power filled the room as he glanced around, and then he looked at her.

She glowered as she remembered how he had helped her to the bathroom. He had shown no sign of unease or self-consciousness but instead had helped her with calm practicality. Still, she pulled the sheet up and tucked it under her arms. She was an earthy person. She wasn't used to being embarrassed by her body. Why was this any different? All she knew was he was so damn big and overwhelming, and she had an extreme awareness of her own vulnerability around him.

He strode over to her and sat on the edge of the bed, and she fought to keep from cringing from him. A couple of lines appeared between the dark slash of his brows. "How're you feeling?" he asked.

She ducked her head. "Tired and hungry. A little disoriented."

"Your wound?"

"It hurts, but nothing like it did before. How long did I sleep?"

"Almost twenty-four hours," he told her.

Her head came up. "You're kidding."

"You got up that once to complain about the IV and go to the bathroom, but other than that, you slept a day away. No wonder you're hungry. I don't think you've had anything to eat for over two days except for vodka and Cheetos." His frown deepened. "What's wrong?"

"Nothing," she said.

Those sharp dark eyes dissected her defensive, hunched figure. "I don't believe you. What's wrong?"

"Don't start poking at me until I've at least had a cup of coffee and a hot shower," she said on a spurt of irritation.

For a moment she thought he was going to keep digging at her, but then he smiled a little. "Fair enough. Do you think you can shower by yourself, or are you too shaky?"

"I'll manage," she growled as she clutched the sheet tighter to her chest.

"Okay," he said in a mild enough tone. "I'll make fresh coffee and order some food. Call if you need anything."

"I won't," she said. "Need anything, that is."

"Right." He contemplated her for another moment, as if she was a piece of museum art he didn't comprehend. Then he stood and walked out. He left the bedroom door ajar again.

She wobbled to her feet and steadied herself with one hand against the wall until she was sure she wouldn't pass out. When she felt steady enough she went to shut the bedroom door. She took a complimentary hotel bathrobe into the bathroom, shut and locked the door and showered. The doctor had covered her wound with a waterproof dressing. Her side gave a twinge if she didn't remember to move carefully, but otherwise it gave her little trouble.

Afterward she considered herself in the mirror as she brushed her teeth. The dramatic purple circles under her eyes had faded to dark smudges. After a cursory examination she ignored her depressed face. There wasn't anything she could do about her appearance anyway. She finger-combed her damp glistening hair, shrugged on the bathrobe and walked into the living room.

She hadn't been able to retain many details when they had arrived, so she took a moment to appreciate the understated decor before curling up at one end of the sofa. With a simple color scheme of blues and tans, the suite was plain but well-appointed with sturdy comfortable furniture that had good lines, along with dark wood tables and lamps that provided indirect lighting.

They were in a business suite suitable for someone staying for several days or weeks. It was complete with a small kitchen, or so she surmised from what Scott had said earlier and from what she could see from where she sat. The suite seemed very small compared to the $30,000-a-night rooftop penthouse where she had been staying with the Dark Fae delegation. That six-bedroom penthouse took up the entire top floor of the hotel and came complete with its own kitchen and staff, rooftop garden patio, indoor pool, library, an original Tiffany stained-glass window and a grand piano in the crystal-chandelier-lit foyer. It was very grand and luxurious, but she liked this one's coziness and functionality.

The living room had a disarranged appearance. A table with a laptop and chair was near the bedroom door. Shopping bags were piled against one wall. Weapon parts were laid out neatly on the coffee table. It looked like she had interrupted Tiago at cleaning his guns.

Headline News was playing on the television. The logo at the bottom of the flat-screen said it was 5:00 A.M. "Five o'clock," she muttered. "No wonder my body is still whimpering. I'm allergic to early mornings, but I couldn't stay in bed any longer."

Tiago approached with two steaming coffee mugs. "What a crabby little monkey you are," he said as he handed her a mug. "Are you always this way when you wake up?"

"I am when I wake up at 5:00 A.M.," she told him. She buried her nose in her mug and inhaled the rich aroma, using her coffee as a way to avoid looking at him as he settled on the sofa beside her. "Have you slept at all?"

"No, I've been too busy," he said.

She looked at him sidelong as she sipped the hot coffee. Busy with what? He was sitting so close she could smell his clean masculine scent and feel the warmth of his muscled denim-clad thigh. He seemed well rested enough, even relaxed, whereas she had to fight to keep from fidgeting.

She felt miserable, tied up in knots inside. She was affectionate by nature, a touchy-feely kind of chick who loved hugs and cuddling. She wanted to scoot closer and curl against his side, to soak up the comfort of his warmth and strength again, to lay her head on his shoulder and let him keep the world at bay.

She swallowed hard. Last night all her guards had dropped with a shattering crash. She had said things to him in the dark and had cried in his arms. Apparently he was fine with what happened, but now she didn't know how to act. A craven part of her wanted to keep leaning on him, even though she knew it couldn't last.

She bit her lips to keep them from trembling. They needed to talk. She needed to know when he would be leaving. She had to know how long she could rely on him and to brace herself for what came afterward. She opened her mouth to speak.

He beat her to it. He set his mug on the table between the gun parts and stood up. He told her, "Breakfast is going to be here in just a few minutes, but in the meantime, I have some things for you."

She was caught with her mouth hanging open. "What?"

He gathered up the shopping bags by the wall and brought them over to her. She glanced at them, for the first time registering the department store labels. Nordstrom and Neiman Marcus.

He gave her a patient smile as he handed her a bag. "I said I have some things for you. The Dark Fae delegation isn't being very cooperative." He nodded to her. "Go ahead, have a look. If you don't like any of it, it can always go back."

Feeling like she was moving in slow motion, she set her coffee mug on the end table and pulled out the contents. When she had emptied it, he handed her another bag, until she had gone through everything. There were clothes and lingerie in cool jeweled tones that would complement her pale skin and black hair. There were also cosmetics in exactly the right shades, and scented toiletries, a pair of soft slippers and another pair of simple flat-heeled shoes. There were even some new-release paperbacks and magazines. A couple of the packages were gift wrapped.

She stared at him, big-eyed, the gift-wrapped packages in a pile on her lap. "You didn't pick all this out," she said. She didn't say it as a question. He couldn't have. She knew he would never leave her asleep, alone and defenseless. That would go against every protective Wyr instinct he had.

"Of course not," he told her. "If it doesn't blow up, cut up, or shoot something, I wouldn't know what to pick. I sent someone. We used your things in the SUV and the T-shirts as size guidelines. I like this. The color suits you." He fingered the soft material of a sapphire blue tunic top then cocked an eyebrow at her as he nodded to the packages in her lap. "Aren't you going to open those?"

She looked down at the three packages she held in her hands, feeling as if he had sideswiped her. She took one and picked the taped ends apart. She pulled out a box of Neiman Marcus chocolates. She set it down, picked up another package and opened it. It was a small perfume bottle of Joy. The third box contained dangly earrings. Each earring had a moon of silver and several stars in different shades of blue that dangled at varying lengths.

Her mouth worked as she stared down at the presents in her lap. Long, hard brown fingers came under her chin and tilted her face up. Tiago's expression had turned quizzical, searching. "If you don't like anything, faerie, it can go back," he repeated.

"I love it, I love all of it," she said unsteadily. She moved away from his touch on the pretext of opening the box of chocolates. She took a bite out of one. It was too rich for her over-empty stomach, and she put the rest of it back in its place.

His quizzical look deepened. "Then what's wrong?"

She held on to the candy box with both hands. "We should talk about when you're going to leave."

Silence. Her senses were so attuned to his presence she felt when the relaxation left him and his body grew tense.

"I'm not leaving," he said in a calm voice.

Her knuckles whitened. "Well, we both know you have to, at some point."

"I know nothing of the sort," he said. He picked up his coffee and drank it. His Power flared and filled the room, turning smoky and menacing as it wrapped around her.

She tried again. "Tiago, I need to make a plan in my head so I know w-what to expect and when."

"I am not leaving," he said again. While he never raised his voice, his hawklike face turned into a blade. "Deal with it."

"That isn't helping—" she said.

He stood and stalked out of the room. She stared after him, disoriented. Then she heard someone start to knock on the suite door. Tiago opened it.

It was the hotel manager, Hughes. "I just wanted to let you know, the representative from the Elder tribunal has arrived and has taken over one of the floors between her highness and the Dark Fae delegation." He wrung his hands.

Tiago's gaze narrowed on the nervous movement of Hughes's hands. "Which Councillor did the tribunal send?" he demanded.

Hughes said, "The one from San Francisco. The next floor up has been taken over by Vampyres."

$=$ SIX $=$

"Is it true the Vampyre Councillor is a sorceress?" the hotel manager asked.

Tiago rubbed his face as he briefly considered lying, but he was more interested in getting back to the interrupted conversation with Niniane. "Yeah, it's true," he said.

The manager's expression was a combination of dismay and fascination. If Tiago was a sympathetic type of person, he might have felt sorry for Hughes, whose entire fancy ass hotel had been overrun by Elder politics in just a matter of days.

He scowled. Why was Niniane so interested in getting rid of him? And why was he just as determined to stay?

He started to close the door in Hughes's face, but just then the door to the neighboring suite opened. A uniformed woman pushed a laden room service cart into the hall and angled it toward him. Only the thought of how little sustenance Niniane had taken in over the last few days kept him from slamming the door, throwing the chain and going back into the living room to pick a fight with her. He sighed and held the door open wide.

The living room was empty of both Niniane and shopping bags, and her bedroom door was closed. He moved the laptop as Hughes asked for permission to set out their breakfast. The hotel manager helped the woman arrange the table. The humans glanced often at Tiago, the closed bedroom door and the disassembled weaponry on the coffee table.

Tiago rubbed the back of his neck and resisted the urge to pace. The humans were fussing over the frickin' table setting like it was some kind of religious ritual. They settled a white cloth into place and arranged a small vase of fresh-cut flowers just so, not precisely in the middle of the table but a little to one side. What was the big deal? All they had to do was throw down two plates, knives and forks and the food. Plus they were taking far too long. They were probably hoping to see her bloody mindedness. He gritted his teeth.

The bedroom door opened. Niniane walked out. She was dressed in a pale peach lounge suit with a top that buttoned down the front, loose flared capri pants and the new slippers that had been selected for their sleek look and comfortable fit. The color brought richness to her delicate pale skin and emphasized the depth and hue of her dark gray eyes, while the cut of the suit flattered her small hourglass figure.

Inclined to feel brutal, Tiago studied her with a critical eye. Actually, she looked ridiculous. Her nose tilted up at the end. Her face was too angular, her eyes too big, her mouth too full. She had freckles, and the tips of her long ears were pointed. How did all of those things combine to make her so mouthwateringly beautiful? What was that elusive quality she exuded until it seemed to dance in the air? It was like the twinkle of sunlight on water, impossible to capture or define; it was just Niniane.

Both Hughes and the woman lit up when Niniane appeared. They gave her awkward but deeply felt bows.

That was when Tiago witnessed firsthand the effect she had on people. He watched Niniane light up in response to the humans' presence. She walked over to them, her hands outstretched. She greeted them like they were long-lost friends. She beamed at the fresh flowers and asked after Hughes's children (who knew? Tiago sure as hell hadn't, nor did he care). She learned that the other woman's name was Esperanza, an avid gardener and lover of flowers. Hughes held out her chair, and Niniane thanked him as she sat.

Every ounce of Niniane's attitude was sincere. She was a bodyguard's worse nightmare, a recognizable famous woman with charm who genuinely loved people, and they adored her in return.

Tiago's hands fisted. He didn't love people. If people weren't such a goddamn pain in the ass, he wouldn't be at war all the time. He wanted to smash Hughes's face for holding out her chair before he could think to do it. He wanted to knock these humans' heads together and toss them out of the suite, preferably out the window. He wanted to rile Niniane up and watch her sputter, then pin that little sex kitten down, cover her with his body and show her who was boss. Breathing hard, he turned away.

Silence fell. Then Niniane said, "Tiago? Are you going to come eat your breakfast?"

His neck muscles tightened. She sounded like she was wary of him.

Yeah, there was a reason for that.

He forced his body to relax and to turn around in slow, controlled movements. Niniane looked at him with wide eyes, and the humans smelled nervous. No matter how polite he might try to act, some subliminal part of them would always recognize that he was a predator. So he didn't bother. They withdrew almost imperceptibly as he strolled to the table and sat.

"Thank you," he said to them, his voice curt, dismissive. Hughes sent the woman Esperanza to tidy the kitchen and make fresh coffee, while he collected their coffee mugs from the living room area and joined her.

"I don't know what the hell's the matter with you," Niniane muttered as she glared down at the gleaming metal cover on her plate. "As far as I know, it might be a congenital defect and not your fault. But whatever it is, cowboy, you've got to dial it down or—"

His hands shot out. He planted one on the table and the other at the back of her head as he lunged forward and drove his mouth down onto hers. He felt the shock of it bolt through her body. Her soft, pretty mouth fell open under his onslaught as he pushed his tongue deep inside her, and there was nothing sweet or romantic about it. It was a marauding capture that fed a hunger that had been gnawing at him from the inside and making him bat-shit crazy.

Her hands flew up and touched his face. Her mouth moved, either to protest or to kiss him back. Or both. Breathing heavily, he pulled back.

She blinked devastated, dazed eyes at him. She whispered, "You're a menace."

"And you're tap-dancing on my last nerve," he growled. He removed the metal cover from her meal and slammed it down on the table. "Shut up and eat your breakfast, faerie."

He released the back of her neck and settled back in his seat to uncap a porterhouse steak and a mountain of scrambled eggs.

Tap-dancing on *his* last nerve? Well, he was driving a Sherman tank over hers. Trembling in reaction, Niniane looked down at her plate. She put her elbows on the table and covered her mouth as she stared at her meal. Of course. He had fulfilled his promise. Fragrant fluffy pancakes were topped with fresh strawberries and melting whipped cream. There was a side plate with a scrambled egg and two crispy slices of bacon.

For a heart-pounding moment she didn't know if she wanted to eat her meal or grind it into his face, but then a surge of hunger consumed her. Unable to think about anything else, her mind shut down. She dove into her breakfast and didn't come up for air until both plates were clean. At some point Esperanza brought them fresh coffee and iced water with lemon slices, then she left with Hughes.

If Niniane could have come up with any excuse for them to stay, she would have. She sat back and cradled her mug in both hands. She stared into the fragrant hot liquid to avoid looking directly at the lunatic Wyr that lounged at the table beside her.

She could see him out of the corner of her eye. He folded his arms and balanced his chair on its back two legs. He was topheavy as most of the warrior Wyr were, with massive muscles in his chest and arms from heavy sword work and wielding other weaponry. His stretched-out legs went on forever. She kept her feet tucked under her own chair to avoid coming into contact with him in any way.

She pretended to sip her coffee as the tiny hairs along her arms rose. He was staring at her, a moody, brooding look from under level black brows, while his Power pressed down in the room with the sulfurous weight of an impending thunderstorm.

"Of all the shit I've got to think about and deal with right now," she remarked in a cool voice. "You should not even make the list."

"So you think you can 'deal' with me," he said. The insolent, silken tone of his voice stroked down her spine even as it raised the danger level in the room. "You can try."

She raised her head and met his gaze. She watched her own hand move out, grasp the stem of her iced water and toss the contents into his face.

Water cascaded down his face and neck. His chair came down on all four legs. His eyes filled with lightning. She pushed to her feet and backed away from the table as he came to his feet in a leisurely movement.

A sharp rap sounded at the door. His head snapped around, and he glared as the rap sounded again. She took that moment to escape toward the bedroom. His soft growl followed her. "Goddammit, Tricks. Go ahead, try to run. See what good that does you."

She scowled. Try to run? Hell, no. She stormed out of the bedroom and into the kitchen. She flipped the kitchen faucet on and started pulling all the mugs and glasses out of the cabinets. She filled each one with water and lined them up on the kitchen counter.

She'd had it. And she had not just merely had it—she had really most sincerely had it.

Just a week ago, before she had even left New York, she had ambushed Tiago so she could smack him in the back of the head and yell at him for cursing at her. They had lived for her entire stay in New York—two hundred years, to be exact—as near strangers. Then all of it sudden it was "Goddammit, Tricks" or "Tricks, goddammit" with him. When her temper had finally erupted, he had had the gall to laugh in her face and call her *cute*.

Ordering her around. Acting like a world-class bastard. He was rude. He was crude (well, okay, maybe she didn't have so much of a problem with that). He hardly paid attention to a thing she said. One word from her, and he went ahead and did whatever the hell he liked anyway. He scared normal sane people and manhandled her without permission, and maybe his particular brand of crude, dominating sexuality was exactly the kind of thing that made her knees melt and her foolish heart go pitty-pat but that didn't give him any *right*—

In the meantime, Tiago stalked to the suite door and yanked it open, his anger fueled by the fact that he hadn't been paying attention and hadn't heard someone approach the suite door until they had knocked. That damn faerie was messing with his head and screwing up all kinds of finely honed instincts.

Cameron Rogers stood with her hand raised to knock again. He barked, "What."

The lieutenant's hand lowered as she stared at him. Her cinnamon-sprinkled features became suffused with sudden strain. "Ah," she said with a cough. "Looking a little damp there, sentinel."

"Fuck you," he snapped. He swiped at his dripping face with the back of his hand. "What do you want?"

The policewoman's mouth twitched but she quickly sobered. "Councillor Severan will speak with her highness at her earliest convenience. One of her attendants has been insisting on delivering that message in person."

He mentally dismissed the attendant. Tiago and Cameron had already agreed; nobody was allowed on the floor that wasn't on their preapproved list. "Tell Severan her highness is indisposed. We'll get back to her when we're ready."

Rogers lifted a sandy eyebrow. "Are you sure you don't want to tell the Councillor that yourself?"

"I've got my hands full at the moment," he muttered. He slammed the door shut and glared at it as he heard Rogers laugh.

Niniane listened as Tiago spoke with whoever had knocked on the door. Soon enough his arrogant, oversized silhouette filled the kitchen doorway.

She turned off the faucet, picked up the nearest full glass and threw the water on him.

He stood absolutely still, a giant statute of carved muscle and bone. Something dangerous throbbed in the air between them. Her heart pounded. "You did not just do that," he said in a conversational tone. "Nobody is that suicidal."

"You can't do anything to me. You swore you would protect me, and I'm injured." She picked up the next full glass and threw the water on him. "What is my name, asshole?"

He tilted his head and put his hands on his hips as he regarded her. His obsidian gaze glittered with a strange light.

"My name," she said between her teeth. The next one was a mug. She threw the water on him. "You know what it is. I've reminded you often enough. Funny enough, it is not 'Tricks, goddammit.' And if you ever shorten it to Ninny, *I WILL BITE YOUR NOSE OFF!*"

His broad, powerful shoulders jerked, and the clear sharp lines of his stern mouth spasmed. "Back in New York you told me I was supposed to say something else. What was it again? Oh yeah. Goddamn, ma'am."

"Don't you dare laugh at me!" she shouted. She grabbed hold of the next mug with both hands.

Suddenly he was behind her, his sodden chest pressed against her back. His hands encircled her wrists. He said in a strangled voice, "Lady, back away from the kitchen sink."

She clung to the mug with all her strength as he tried, gently, to pry her fingers away. Water sloshed over the rim, splashing their hands and drenching the countertop. "It's the last one," she panted. "I've got to throw it."

He buried his wet face in her hair and exploded. She tried to twist her wrists out of his grasp, quite without hope of getting free, as he roared with laughter. He managed to say after a moment, "I don't think you have a single sane synapse firing in your brain."

"I don't think you're any judge of sanity," she snapped. Disgusted, she dropped the mug onto the counter. They had jostled all the water out of it. "And in case you're thinking of patting me on the head and calling me 'cute' again, I'll have you know all of my weapons are still poisoned."

He let go of her wrists and turned her around, pressing her back against the counter. His drenched T-shirt soaked wet patches into her lounge suit, the muscles of his hard torso flexing with sinuous strength. The sparkle in his eyes turned smoky as her curvy body wriggled against his. "Oh, I don't want to pat you on the head, faerie," he said low in his throat in a deep purring growl that vibrated through her body. He bent closer until his lips brushed hers. "I want to fuck your mouth."

Said mouth dropped open, and the breath left her body. She couldn't believe what she just heard. "You–you what?"

The world swung as he picked her up and carried her in long, swift strides to the bedroom. He set her on the bed. She suddenly found herself lying down, as he planted a knee on the mattress by her hip and pinned her wrists over her head with one hand.

She looked up his body, from those strong legs that went on forever to the tight angle of his hips, the lean, long torso and the cut of his muscled arms. He bent his head until his mouth just brushed the sensitive skin of her open lips, and he spoke the words right into her body. "I said I want to fuck your mouth, first with my tongue"—he licked her lower lip—"and then with my finger, and then with my cock. Maybe that will shut you up."

"You can't talk to me that way," she whimpered. He was outrageous, completely uncivilized. She had to find the switch in her head that would turn off her traitorous arousal. She twisted her wrists against the long fingers that held her with such ease.

"Why not?" Sharp white teeth nipped at her upper lip. "Don't you like it?"

Like it? Like was far too insipid a word for how she reacted to what he did or what he said. His raw sensuality was whipping up a hurricane in her body. Confused and a little scared, she shifted restlessly, and his black glittering gaze swept over her.

"You said you were sorry. Right after you kissed me," she said. She hadn't meant for it to sound so breathless or accusing.

"Hell, yes, I was sorry, but not because I kissed you. There I was, eating you alive while you were exhausted, wounded and burning up with fever. I had no idea I could be such a low-down, self-serving bastard," he said. He brought his other hand up under her soft loose shirt, and he gently cupped her ribs where her knife wound was. "How are you feeling, faerie? Does it hurt?"

The concern in his face was genuine. She took a deep breath, released it in a shuddering sigh, and melted just that little bit further. "Yeah. But it's not too bad if I'm careful."

"We'll be careful," he murmured. "No more fever?"

She shook her head.

"Well-fed and rested?"

She nodded, mesmerized by the dark Power that blanketed her and by the intent focus in his hawkish face.

"Then kiss me," he whispered. He spread his hand on her torso and caressed down the curve of her hip.

He was a master of lightning. His request sent a bolt of it shooting down her body. It pooled between her legs, causing her to throb with hungry need. She moved her lips lightly against his in a sexy pout. "Why would I kiss such a low-down, self-serving bastard?"

He gave her a slow smoldering grin, a white rakish slash across the dark brown of his skin. "Because you like me," he said in a low voice. "And because you know in your bones it would be good."

No, she knew in her bones it would be wicked-bad, quite

possibly the worst thing she could do to herself. She already wanted too much to lean on him, to rely on him. Kissing him, getting more emotionally involved with him than she already was, would be nothing short of self-destructive. She felt like a gambling addict galloping into a casino with a week's pay in her pocket.

But there he was, untamed and uncensored, crouched over her like a lion waiting to pounce. Her breathing roughened.

Oh, what the hell, she thought. It's not like I'm known for my common sense.

She tilted her head, and with a light, delicate touch she caressed the line of his sensual, tough mouth with hers.

Whatever she had expected, it wasn't this. Strangely enough, her reaching up to touch him of her own volition seemed to calm down the unpredictable violent storm that had seethed through his energy since before they had breakfast. The kiss turned into a sweet, gentle exploration of him while he held himself poised over her, rock-steady, and he submitted to her touch.

She murmured something wordless as her own hurricane calmed, her heart sped up, and pleasure spun out in a slow, expanding liquid spiral. He teased her lips open and eased inside, an expert invasion she discovered she relished. When he let go of her wrists, she ran her hands up his arms to grip his shoulders as he pressed into her mouth more deeply. The hand stroking her hip shifted to cup her between her legs and pressed against that sweet, hungry ache.

She stiffened, and he lifted his head to whisper, "Shh, easy now. You're injured and we're not doing anything. Just relax."

She met his gaze. They were dark cauldrons of sexual heat. He ground the hard heel of his hand against her as he bent his head back down. He took her mouth again, this time hard and rough, while he rubbed her clitoris through the soft folds of her clothes. She sobbed out something incoherent as she ran shaking hands down the contoured landscape of his taut body. Feeling as if something inside of her had broken loose, she cupped both hands over the long length of his own arousal, which pressed against the zipper of his jeans. He hissed against her mouth and pushed his hips at her, moving against her touch.

"Goddamn," he whispered unsteadily, running his lips down the side of her neck. "You feel like heated silk."

She gasped out a laugh and gave him a gentle squeeze. He

hissed again and licked her collarbone while he worked her, and her pleasure spiraled higher. He bent down to bite at her nipple through her shirt.

He was a puzzle box constructed of aggression and thorns. She didn't want to want him, but oh gods, his hands and his mouth felt so good. She wanted his tongue, his finger, his cock in her mouth. She wanted his body covering hers as he pushed inside of her and drove the rest of the world away.

She shook her head as some part of her rebelled against the pleasure he sought to give her. She was her own puzzle box of contradictory feelings. He touched a place so deep inside, she couldn't bear to have him there. Her breathing roughened as anxiety tightened her muscles. She pressed a hand to her ribs as her wound gave a warning twinge, and she took hold of his wrist with the other. "Stop," she gasped. "Please."

He froze and searched her damp, bewildered gaze. "Did I hurt you?"

She bit her lip and shook her head. She turned her face away, covering her eyes with one forearm. "I–I can't do this."

She waited for some explosion of temper or aggression, but he held still, kneeling over her. Moments trickled by as his breathing deepened and steadied, and then he shifted onto his side beside her. He covered the hand she had pressed against her ribs and settled a heavy muscled thigh across her hips, pinning her in place.

"You were with me," he said. "What happened?"

She shrugged. "Reality intruded, I guess. I'm sorry."

"Niniane," he said in a calm voice. He fell silent, studying her face.

Hearing him call her by her real name tugged again at that spot deep inside of her, that place that was more private and vulnerable than even the place where his hand still rested.

"Would you please give me some privacy?" she asked, forming the words with some difficulty. "I need a few moments alone."

For a moment she thought he was going to refuse and push at her boundaries again, but something about her trembling mouth and unsteady voice must have made him pull back. He gave her a small smile and pressed a kiss to her forehead. "I'll go make more coffee," he said. "Then we'll talk. All right?"

She nodded and turned her face away as he pulled off the bed and walked out of the room. He left the bedroom door cracked and strode into the small kitchen to go through the mindless motions of starting a new pot of coffee. The suite was beginning to feel too confining to him. Maybe if she was up for it, he could sneak them out of the hotel and they could go for a drive along Lake Michigan while they talked. He could use a blast of cold, sharp air in his face.

He braced his hands on the countertop and shook his head. Back in the bedroom he had almost said to her, "Niniane, we're going to become lovers, so we've got time. That's all the reality you need to know."

Somehow he had managed to stop himself from saying it, because in that moment there had been something breakable in her expression and some instinct had held him back, for her sake.

Not for his sake. He knew in his bones what he had almost said to her was the truth. She prevaricated and tried to push him away, but he would have her in the end.

He would have her. He wouldn't stop or rest until he did.

The edge of the countertop cracked under his hands. He frowned, and for the first time he acknowledged that he wasn't acting as rationally, or nearly as calmly, as was normal for him.

Not rational. Not calm.

Obsessed with her. Unable to let go.

She was a long-lost goddamn faerie princess like something straight out of a hybrid Disney/horror flick. She would soon be Queen of the Dark Fae, an Elder Race well known for its relentlessly Byzantine politics. She was a constant pain in his ass.

She couldn't fight worth a damn without cheating (well, okay, maybe he didn't have so much of a problem with that). All her pretty designer clothes were named strange things. What was a shrug or a gladiator stiletto or a Vera Wang? What the fuck was wrong with calling clothes what they really were, like dresses or shirts or pants or shoes, anyway?

And he was old, very old and not just middle-aged old, and set in his ways. He was self-contained, well-used to the autonomy of command, comfortable in the violent roaming of his life, satisfied with army life, a predator, a warlord that liked pounding the shit out of things, and a Wyr sentinel.

This fixation he had developed for her was beyond insane. It was incomprehensible, a recipe for a perfect storm disaster.

He rubbed his face hard with both hands. First things first.

Rune and Aryal would be here within the next twenty-four hours. While they investigated the rogue Wyr in yesterday's attack, they could help with bodyguard detail. Their presence would dilute this impossible, intense one-on-one craziness he had going on with Niniane. Then things would calm down.

From the direction of the bedroom came a thump and a muffled cry. He lifted his head and called out sharply, "What happened, did you fall?"

There was no reply. His stride turned into a lunge. He slammed the bedroom door open with a flattened hand, his sharp gaze darting around.

The room was empty, as was the adjoining bathroom. The silence in the suite roared in his ears. The bedside lamp was on the floor. There was a strange wild scent in the room, a sense of an immense expenditure of Power, a wild upsurge in energy that was already fading.

The bottom of his stomach dropped away. Unbelievably, she was gone again, but this time it was not of her own choosing.

"Oh shit," he whispered. "Niniane."

⇒ SEVEN ⇐

`

She had lain on the bed staring at the ceiling for long moments after Tiago left the room. Without the vitality of his presence stimulating and supporting her, the lethargy from the cleansing spell stole through her body again. At first she wasn't sure if she could get her shaky limbs to support her.

Finally she managed to find the strength to push herself to an upright position. She thought about trying to change into more public attire, but that sounded like more than she could handle, let alone trying to deal with Elder politics. She should send messages out to everyone that she needed at least another day to recuperate.

Like Tiago said, let the world wait for you. *Pleh.* She wondered how he would like it if she applied that to him. But no, she already knew how he would like it—Mr. Bulldozer would push through every objection she might make, so she supposed they were going to have that talk he wanted to have. Then maybe she could lie down and watch old movies on the TCM channel. She could eat the box of chocolates he had given her in between naps and pretend for a little while that the outside world didn't exist.

When she thought she could stand without falling down, she pushed to her feet with a pained grunt.

That was when the cyclone entered the room.

From one step to the next she was standing in the middle of

a maelstrom of energy. She threw a hand over her eyes, staring through her fingers, as a man formed in front of her. Long raven-black hair whipped around an elegant, spare, pale inhuman face. Narrowed crystalline diamond eyes showed through the strands. The rest of his body solidified. He was as tall as Tiago, but he had a lean, graceful frame that matched his face. He wore a linen tunic and trousers that, while simple, seemed foreign. When he saw her, one corner of his mouth lifted in a triumphant smile.

It was a smile that looked all too much like it might say *gotcha*.

She backed up sharply, bumped into the bedside table and knocked over a lamp. She sucked in a breath to scream. The male grabbed her, moving so *fast*. He clapped a hand over her mouth while wrapping the other around her waist. He held her in a steely grip. She squealed and clawed at the back of his hand.

The howling windstorm rose again, and this time the world fell away as the cyclone swallowed her whole.

Terror rampaged through her mind. The only thing solid or stable was the creature that held her prisoner against a hard, lean-muscled body. Then the world began to reappear around her: walls, ceiling, furniture, and a floor beneath her feet.

She didn't wait to look around or get oriented. As soon as those steely arms loosened and she had enough freedom of movement, she pushed away from him, pivoted and punched her kidnapper in the face as hard as she could.

She threw the punch right-handed, from her dominant side, which also was her uninjured side. She got lucky. She felt the male's nose crunch as his head snapped back.

Those strange diamond eyes flared. She panted and staggered back a couple of steps, hand pressed again to her wounded side. Champagne-colored liquid trickled from one fine-etched nostril. The crooked break in his nose straightened back into place as she watched.

"You're Gumby Man," she said in awe, and with not a little resentment. Did all his other body parts straighten into place like that when he got injured? How could you fight and win against a creature that wouldn't stay broke when you broke him?

He didn't bother to reply. He wiped his face with the back of one hand as he regarded her with a lazy malevolence.

"I should have warned you to take care," a woman said from behind her. "The Dark Fae heir apparent is small and cute, but like a Tasmanian devil, she can be vicious when cornered."

Niniane knew that voice. It was one of the most beautiful voices in the world, and also one of the deadliest. Eyes widening, she turned to face Carling Severan, Councillor of the Elder tribunal, sorceress and Vampyre Queen.

The speaker was as beautiful as her voice, with a heartbreaking, life-threatening loveliness. Clad in a classic black Chanel suit and about average height for a modern woman, Carling Severan was slender with an exquisite bone structure. She had a patrician Nefertiti-like neck, long almond-shaped dark eyes, shining black hair that fell in a heavy curtain to her waist, high cheekbones, smooth luminous skin the color of honey and a treacherously sensual mouth. She had been ancient when Rome was born, but she still bore the face and figure of a thirty-year-old woman.

The Vampyre Queen was one of the oldest recorded surviving Nightkind, if not the oldest. Even at rest her Power filled the room, until Carling did something either to rein it in or camouflage it somehow, so that it receded like a tide flowing away from shore and she resembled a simple ordinary, beautiful human woman.

She was a poisonous king cobra that masqueraded as an innocent, bright green garden snake.

That was so not right.

"Councillor," Niniane whispered, through numb lips.

The illusion of innocuousness vaporized as the Vampyre walked over to her with a swift, fluid, inhuman grace that was as terrifying as everything else was about her. Carling stopped just in front of Niniane, dropped a slender hand onto her shoulder and looked at the male creature. "That will be all for now, Khalil."

The male creature's nostrils flared. He said, "I have paid in full one of the three favors I owe you."

Niniane could still hear the wildness of the cyclone in his deep voice. She shivered, and the unbreakable hold on her shoulder tightened. The Councillor said, "You have indeed. Until the next time, Djinn."

A howling wind rose and died. Niniane looked down again and cupped her eyes to protect them from the whipping ends of her hair. That was when she noticed a bright yellow band of sunlight from a nearby window that slanted across both of her legs and also those of the Vampyre's. Niniane stared. Carling wore no shoes, and her slender, beautiful honey-colored feet were limned in light. Such contact with direct sunlight would have reduced a lesser Vampyre to ash within seconds. Niniane's shivering increased. Even for a creature that many regarded as unnatural, Carling was unnatural.

The Councillor said, "This is where you may ask whether I am a good witch or a bad witch."

Niniane looked up, into that gorgeous, ancient smiling gaze. She said as steadily as she could, "I'm not sure I would want to hear your reply."

Carling said, "It is a wise little heir. I heard you had been injured. I can smell the blood from your wound, and a Demonkind prince is not the most beneficent of taxis. Sit."

Carling's hand on Niniane's shoulder compelled her toward an armchair and supported her as her shaky legs threatened to give out. Grateful to ease into the support of the chair, she sank down, although she was far from relaxing.

Carling flowed into a nearby armchair. By the simple act of sitting she turned it into a throne. Niniane watched her sidelong, envious of the other woman's imperial grace even as she kept her wary dial turned on high, the needle squarely pointed to emergency red. She had interacted in a cordial fashion with the Councillor several times over the years but always in a public, formal setting. Although not Wyr, Carling was every inch a predator, and Niniane would do well to remember it.

Strictly speaking, Carling was no longer Queen of the Nightkind. In an unprecedented move, she had formally abdicated when she became Councillor of the Elder tribunal. Carling had taken advantage of a legal loophole that had existed when the U.S. Elder tribunal had been created in the 1790s, which had barred any Elder ruler from holding office but had neglected to forbid such a position from former rulers. At Carling's abdication, her progeny Julian Regillus had become Nightkind King. While the legal loophole had since been closed, it was long accepted that Regillus acted upon his progenitor's orders and that Carling remained the de facto ruler of the Nightkind while also holding the power of her seat on the Elder tribunal.

Niniane became aware that they were not alone in the room when Carling gestured and an attendant, a blonde, pale, pretty woman with downcast eyes, left silently. Niniane looked around. She noted the similarities this hotel suite shared with the one she and Tiago occupied. She also noted the changes that had been made in furniture and decor, such as the exquisite damask silk draped over the coffee table and the antique inlaid-mahogany chest that had been set against one wall. The television console and hotel paintings had been removed, making the room feel larger, more spacious and alien.

She kept her breathing unhurried and her hands folded together in her lap as she absorbed the silent message written in the space all around her, that she was now within Vampyre territory.

She said, "Having a Demonkind prince indebted to one must be quite a rarity. It seems an extravagant use of a Powerful favor to use him just to transport me up a single flight of hotel stairs."

"Your Wyr was being obstructive and disrespectful," said Carling. The Vampyre's expression turned into an exquisite ice sculpture. "He needed to be taught a lesson."

Niniane's hands tightened on each other as she fought an upsurge in anger. Her Wyr. It was almost as if Carling had called Tiago "her pet." A part of her noted Carling's subtle, inexplicable smile. Curious. She wondered what that smile meant, even as she said with a careful lack of emphasis, "I would like to believe that no one intends disrespect, Councillor."

Niniane paused to let the multiple meanings of her statement settle into the silence of the room. The Vampyre sat across from her, exhibiting a patience that was as inhuman as the rest of her. Carling's inexplicable smile widened as she said, "I am sure Dragos will miss having you as one of his diplomatic resources, although it must be said—you are not Dark Fae Queen yet."

What did Carling mean by that? It was clearly a warning of some kind. Niniane couldn't tell if the warning was a friendly one or not. Her tension increased. If she didn't understand, then it was best to ignore it for the moment, at least in conversation. She said in apparent agreement, "There have already been a number of challenges, and I'm sure there are more to come. I am grateful that the warlord sentinel Tiago came to my aid when he did. You may not yet have heard that he was in time to stop another assassination attempt."

Carling's graceful eyelids lowered. For a moment the Vampyre maintained a perfect stillness, an incomparably beautiful woman set against a backdrop of ancient silk and mahogany. The tableau was so vivid and anachronistic that Niniane felt a ripple of disorientation, as if she stared upon a painting crafted by one of the European Old Masters or as if time itself had opened up to give her a glimpse into the distant past. Then the hotel air-conditioning came on. The cold air curled against her bare ankles like an invisible snake and dispelled the illusion.

Carling asked, "Another assassination attempt. When was this?"

Niniane could tell nothing from the Councillor's face. For all she knew, Carling had already heard of the second attempt and merely wanted her to tell the story. She shifted in an attempt to become more comfortable, her wound and fatigued muscles aching, the return of stress making her head pound. "It happened early yesterday morning when I was returning to the hotel. It was another triad. None of them survived for questioning. I didn't recognize them, although that doesn't mean anything. I wasn't close enough to get a good look."

"Curious, when the Dark Fae need you so badly," said Carling.

"What do you mean?" she asked.

The Vampyre lifted an elegant shoulder. "Ultimately the Dark Fae did not fare well under Urien's rule. Elder historians will eventually concur on that point, although his isolationist policy did allow him a great deal of control over trade and business agreements. I'm sure his personal fortune has become quite extensive."

"I'll bet it has," Niniane said between her teeth.

Carling continued, "But Urien closed off Dark Fae society at a critical juncture in this country's development. With the Dark Fae talent for metallurgy, they could have become a much more powerful and prosperous demesne than they are. I believe certain intelligent people among the Dark Fae will have realized this by now."

Old fury surged at Carling's words. Niniane pressed her lips together to keep it contained. She had raged at just such a fact many a time throughout the Industrial Revolution. "Despite the political rhetoric he spouted, Urien never did act in the Dark Fae's best interests," she growled. "He only acted in his own."

"Indeed," Carling said. "Urien was a metallurgist of some significant talent himself, and a Powerful sorcerer. I suspect you will find that while his fortune increased, the rest of Dark Fae society has grown stagnant economically and politically. As a people their numbers are too small for them to have thrived under such a separation from general trade and interaction with other societies, which is why they need you so badly. As heir, you will satisfy traditionalists like Justice Trevenan. You also have important ties with all the other Elder demesnes, which will appeal to the progressive-minded like Chancellor Riordan, and you have an unprecedented popularity with the general American population. You are a unique gift to the Dark Fae."

She snorted, and it caused her side to twinge. "All of that sounds good in theory, Carling, but I have to tell you, right now I'm not feeling the love."

The blonde Vampyre attendant entered the room again, carrying a tray. She set a wineglass filled with some kind of dark liquid on the table near Niniane's chair and set a sealed bottle of chilled water beside it. Carefully skirting the line of sunshine on the carpet, the attendant set another wineglass near Carling's chair, bowed her head to her mistress and backed out of the room.

Niniane's brows contracted. She lifted her glass to sniff gingerly at the contents. Power was steeped into the rich, dark red liquid, which emitted a gentle radiance against her hand. Herbs floated on the surface. She smelled cinnamon and cloves.

"It is a 1962 Rothschild," Carling murmured as she sipped from her own glass. "Yours is bastardized with a healing potion that will ease your discomfort, should you care to drink it."

Niniane kept her gaze downcast. She tried to think past the pounding in her head. She would not put Carling past anything in pursuit of her goals, including poison, but why would Carling bother to poison her? Carling and Urien had hated each other, which had only served to strengthen the Vampyre's alliance with Dragos and the Wyr. Niniane couldn't see Carling backing any other potential Dark Fae contender for the throne, especially anyone who might have been a supporter of Urien's when he had been alive.

On a personal note, Niniane and Carling had always been cordial. And the Vampyre was here in an official capacity as a representative of the Elder tribunal. Niniane needed allies, and Carling, if she were so inclined, was in an excellent position to make a friend and ally of the next Dark Fae Queen.

Also, the Power imbued in the concoction was a warm, gentle

glow against the palms of her hands. It felt good to her, in the way chicken soup smelled good when she was sick. She raised the wineglass and took a cautious sip. Her eyebrows went up. "Well, I didn't expect that," she said. "It's delicious."

Carling drank wine and watched her from under lowered lids. Niniane came to a sudden decision. She threw back her head and drank the healing potion down to the last drop.

A Powerful glow filled her body. She felt like she was an empty vessel being filled to the brim with rich golden light.

"Whoa-kay," she muttered. Her head lolled against her chair. She had to struggle to remember to lock her fingers around the stem of her wineglass and not just let it fall to the carpeted floor. A moment later she felt her fingers fall open and she lost hold of her glass. She tried to peer at the floor through the golden light that filled her head.

Then the diffuse Power concentrated on the wound at her side. As it ebbed from the rest of her body, she could feel the area around her wound grow brighter and hotter, until it shone in her mind like an internal star.

The star began to burn, as if someone laid a hot clothes iron along the puncture wound. It hurt. It hurt so much. *Ow ow ow.* She gasped and wrapped her arms around her middle. She could feel the torn flesh knitting itself together. You're not supposed to feel something like that. It was a thousand times worse than the internal itching caused by the cleansing spell.

She gasped, "A little warning would have been nice."

"You surprised me. I didn't expect you to just toss the potion back." Carling's beautiful voice penetrated her misery. "I'm told deep breathing helps."

Was that amusement in Carling's voice? Damn Vampyre. Niniane threw a glare in Carling's general direction as she tried the deep breathing. She couldn't tell how much it helped with the actual pain, but it focused her attention. She ended up panting through the pain.

After what felt like forever, the hot star dimmed until it died out. The pain and disorientation slid out of her body as if they had never existed.

She straightened with caution and pressed light fingers against the bandage. No pain. She took a deep breath, expanding her torso. Not even a twinge. Overcome with curiosity, she lifted the bottom of her shirt and peeled away the edges of the bandage to peer underneath. The only blood left was what had soaked into the cotton pad over the wound—or rather, over where the wound had been. All that remained was a small silvery scar, along with two stitches.

"Get out of town," she said. She poked the scar. "It's completely healed. I've never heard of a healing potion that strong."

"I am not surprised," Carling replied, "as I don't often stir myself to make them."

Niniane looked at her. "Okay, I totally buy that. Thank you so much, and I really mean it, but I'm mad at you too because that hurt a lot."

The Vampyre lifted an eyebrow. Still sounding amused, she said, "I expect you'll find a way to get over it."

She grinned. "Yeah, I expect I will too."

Niniane took another deep, pain-free breath. The potion had more than just knitted the puncture wound together. It had healed her bruises and contusions. She felt like she had before the attack, infused with a sense of vitality and wellness. Carling's healing potion was as far removed from Dr. Weylan's healing spells as the space shuttle was from a 1972 Toyota Celica. While there might be nothing wrong with a well-maintained Celica, it sure as hell couldn't defy gravity and fly.

She looked down at the bandage she had already half removed. She yanked it off the rest of the way, grimacing as her skin protested.

Carling's blonde attendant stood by her chair. Niniane managed to control her startled urge to shrink away. She watched as the pretty, young-looking Vampyre retrieved the glass she had dropped and placed it on her tray. The Vampyre held the tray out to her, head inclined, as she murmured, "If her highness wishes, I would be happy to dispose of the bandages."

She looked down at what she held. The cotton pad was blood-soaked. As well as she seemed to be getting along with Carling, giving a sample of her blood over to the Vampyre attendant of one of the most Powerful sorceresses in the world didn't seem like the best of ideas. She cleared her throat with a delicate cough and said, "Er."

"Of course Rhoswen will burn the bandages properly in the fireplace," Carling said, as she finished her wine.

She didn't bother to dissemble or apologize for her caution. "Thank you," she said. She dropped the bandage on the tray.

Rhoswen turned to take Carling's glass and place it on the tray, her expression the blank smoothness of the perfect servant. Both Niniane and Carling watched as Rhoswen placed the bandages in the fireplace and lit them with a taper. They watched in silence as the small flame flared and died.

Freed from pain and lethargy, Niniane's thoughts arrowed back to Tiago. He had to be worried about her, unless he had some way to track the direction of the Djinn's transport. She didn't have any idea about Tiago's capabilities as a tracker, other than Dragos always swore Tiago was the best at what he did. It was possible Tiago already knew she was safe with Carling (and she was, wasn't she?).

Maybe Tiago was relieved to be rid of her. And why wouldn't he be? He had made it clear from the moment he arrived that he considered the whole trip to be a pain in the ass. She bit her lip as she fought the urge to squirm.

Whether he was relieved or not, she knew the obsessive nature of a Wyr sentinel. She had been taken on his watch. He wouldn't rest until he got her back, which meant—

She sucked in a breath as certainty settled into place. He didn't know where she was.

"I'm sure Tiago has learned his lesson," she said to Carling. With an effort she kept her voice steady and devoid of all urgency. "Now I would like to let him know that I'm with you and that I'm all right."

A shadow of ugliness crossed Carling's lovely features. The Vampyre said in a smooth voice, "Why don't I just send one of my attendants with a message?"

Niniane looked at her. "Because we both know he might be too distracted to listen to anything your attendant might say. Then you could continue to take your revenge on him for blowing off your earlier message."

"Distracted," said Carling, dark eyes glittering. "I like that."

Whatever else might be communicated, one overall particular message was coming in loud and clear. You ignored the Vampyre Queen very much at your own peril. Carling wasn't going to budge on this unless she was pushed.

Niniane sighed and said, point-blank, "Give it up, Carling. You and I have a terrific chance right now to develop a good alliance. It's been a long time since you've had a good alliance with the Dark Fae. But it isn't going to happen if you insist on tormenting Tiago with my disappearance—or if you insist on tormenting him for any other reason."

"How interesting. You would put a potential Nightkind–Dark Fae alliance in jeopardy over one bad-mannered, bad-tempered Wyr."

Niniane tapped a finger on the arm of her chair. It wasn't wise to lose your temper with the Vampyre Queen either. After a moment, she kept her voice measured as she said, "I will remind you that Tiago followed me to Chicago after I went missing, and he saved my life. This is after the Wyr provided me with shelter and protection from my uncle Urien for almost two hundred years. Don't force me to choose between you, because you won't win."

Carling gave her a faint smile and conceded the point. "Fair enough."

Something crashed nearby. This time Niniane couldn't control her jump. She heard a sharp shout down the hall, a growl, and another booming crash. It sounded like a door had been slammed off its hinges. The Vampyre turned her head toward the hall. Carling remarked, "Apparently choosing a method of communication with your Wyr has become a moot point."

TIAGO! Oh gods, no. He couldn't attack the Vampyres or, with the mood Carling was in, she might very well have him killed.

Niniane bolted out of her chair and ran to the suite door. Somehow Carling was right beside her, long graceful fingers curling around the door handle. It seemed to take the Vampyre forever to open the door. As soon as she could, Niniane slipped through the opening and darted into the hall.

She took a mental snapshot of the scene in one horrified glance.

A heavy fire door lay on its side against a wall thirty feet away. Tiago's massive figure filled an open doorway that led to a stairwell. Three male Vampyres stood in a semicircle in front of him, each one a beautiful, lethal weapon. The blonde Vampyre Rhoswen had positioned herself between Tiago and her mistress. Several humans stood in open doorways, and some of them had guns. All of the guns were pointed at Tiago.

And Tiago—he was something out of a nightmare. He had weapons: a sword strapped to his back, guns in holsters. He had partially shapeshifted, a clear indicator of a Wyr caught in some kind of extreme emotion such as fear or rage. The bones of his face were alien, shifted into wrongness. His chest, arms and legs were wider and rippled with muscles where muscles weren't supposed to be. Talons tipped his powerful hands.

When Niniane appeared in the hall, Tiago's dark, savage face turned to her.

His eyes.

Their normal obsidian color and sardonic expression were gone. They blazed with white fire.

Niniane whispered, "Call off your people if you want them to live."

"My people will do their job," Carling said.

The Vampyre sorceress had lost her habitual amused detachment. Instead she stared at Tiago with a combination of anger and fascination. She also shimmered with vitality, her skin, eyes and hair more lustrous than ever.

After one quick, incredulous glance, Niniane dismissed the enigma that was Carling. She turned back to the tableau. Tension trembled in the air like the shiver of an avalanche before it crashed down a mountain range. She held a hand out and tried to smile at the monster down the hall as she walked toward him.

"It's okay now, Tiago," she said. She tried for gentle and soothing. Instead she got scared and shaky. Crap. She forced a false sense of conviction into her voice. "Listen to me. Everything's okay."

The monster's blazing gaze fixed on her. Tiago started toward her, and the avalanche came down.

The dark-haired Vampyre nearest Tiago moved to attack so fast he was a blur. If Niniane had been human, she might have missed it.

Tiago's enormous fist pistoned. He punched the Vampyre, whose body shot through the air and slammed through a wall. Tiago kept moving forward.

The other two Vampyres attacked. Tiago grabbed one. He spun on his heel and threw the Vampyre into the stairwell. With a wicked slash of fangs and talons, the third Vampyre leaped on him. Crimson blood spurted from wounds that appeared on Tiago's face and neck.

A blinding white-hot sear of flame flashed out of Tiago's eyes. Every light in the hall exploded as the lightning bolt struck the third Vampyre in the chest. The Vampyre flew back fifteen feet and slid along the ground to lie motionless. Thunder exploded in a rolling boom. It sounded like a rocket launcher had been fired in the hall. All the while, Tiago continued to plow toward her, an unstoppable juggernaut.

The humans armed with guns chambered rounds. They were far too slow for this kind of fight. Niniane would have called them cannon fodder except they were in addition to the Vampyres who were already occupying Tiago's attention. So many stood against Tiago, including Rhoswen, who hung back and stood in readiness to protect her mistress. Then there was the immovable object, Carling, the king cobra of the nest, who watched the conflict and waited in the background with all of her considerable venom at full strength.

Tiago against Carling. If those two came head-to-head, if they actually fought each other, neither would stop until one was dead. Between the two of them they could raze Chicago to the ground.

No.

For the second time in one day, terror mowed down her reasoning skills.

She didn't think. She didn't calculate risk or odds. She acted.

She flung herself forward and shrieked, *"STOP!"*

Niniane may not have much in the way of size or strength, but as a Dark Fae, she was slippery-fast. She was much faster than any of the humans. She was certainly faster than Rhoswen, who flung out a hand to stop her but acted far too late.

At her scream, Tiago spun from the fallen Vampyre. She leaped for him with her arms outstretched, blindly trusting him to catch her. She caught a blurred glimpse of that monstrous savage face and the white blaze in eyes, which were overcome with astonishment. He snatched her out of the air and whirled to place his body between hers and the others. One tremendous hand covered the back of her head as he jammed her face into his chest.

She grabbed fistfuls of his shirt, still wet from her earlier outburst of temper. The ferocious engine in his chest hammered against her cheek. His heavily muscled arms wrapped tight around her. He shoved her against the wall and covered the top of her head with his.

He sacrificed his ability to fight in order to protect her.

She had time to think, no, this wasn't what I meant. This is a unilateral disarmament.

They'll kill him.

She opened her mouth to scream.

Then in one of the most beautiful voices in the world, and one of the deadliest, the king cobra spoke a quiet foreign word filled with Power.

Everything stopped.

⇒ EIGHT ⇒

A nearby broken light fixture emitted a fitful buzzing. Other than that, the hall was filled with total silence.

For a moment it seemed the whole world had gone still. Niniane pressed her face against the warmth of Tiago's broad chest. She concentrated on the powerful rhythm of his heartbeat. She felt his ribs expand as he drew in a breath.

Then he released her. He pulled his sword and one of his guns. She pulled his second gun from its holster as he turned away. He let her take it. He ordered her telepathically, *Stay behind me.*

And let him get shot to pieces right in front of her?

Oh phooey! she snapped. She hopped out from behind to stand at his side. It earned her an infuriated growl.

Carling stood not five feet in front of them.

Drywall dust floated in the air. It lent a hazy dreamlike quality to the strange scene. Rhoswen stood unmoving in the center of the hall. The Vampyre who had first attacked Tiago was frozen in the process of crawling back through the hole where he had slammed through the wall. Another Vampyre lay sprawled on the floor, his chest singed black. The third male Vampyre had not reappeared from the stairwell. Eight humans dotted the hallway, each one held stationary by Carling's Power.

Five guns were still trained where Tiago had stood just moments before. He nudged her gently with the back of one hand and moved sideways with her until they stood several paces to the left.

Carling mirrored their shift down the hall in a loose-limbed prowl, her hands relaxed at her sides, an elegant and barbaric woman in bare feet and Chanel suit. She regarded Tiago with her head cocked, her lovely dark almond-shaped eyes bright with interest. Her earlier anger and its accompanying disfigurement of cruelty appeared to have vanished as if it had never existed. And, Niniane noted with a surge of baffled irritation, Carling looked even more radiant than ever.

"You would have sacrificed yourself for her," Carling said. "Interesting."

Niniane rolled her eyes. Carling was too strange. She gave up trying to figure out what made the old Vampyre tick. Instead she turned her worried attention to Tiago.

The slashes on his face were already healing. He was no longer the monstrous Wyr caught in midshift. His bones had settled into a more familiar shape, and the terrifying hot white blaze that had taken over his eyes had darkened again. But lightning still flickered at the back of his black gaze, the muscles in his arms were cut with rigidity and his Power felt razor-sharp, held in readiness for battle.

He exhibited a roaring disinterest in conversing with Carling. He said in Niniane's head, *I want you to move toward the stairwell. Do it now while she has her people in stasis.*

She took in a slow, deep breath and cast a leery glance down at the huge weapon she had pulled from his shoulder holster. It was a large-bore .50 Magnum Desert Eagle. It probably fit the width of Tiago's hand quite comfortably. In her much smaller grip it looked and felt like the hand cannon it really was. She had fired large-bore handguns before. They always knocked her on her ass unless she braced herself back against something. She found the gun's safety and clicked it on.

She said to Carling, "You created this mess. What are you going to do to fix it?"

"What, indeed." Carling lifted an eyebrow, turned her head to the side and said, "Rhoswen, make sure the guns do not fire."

The blonde Vampyre flowed into smooth motion as if she had never been frozen in time. She moved from human to human down the hall, taking their guns, ejecting clips and placing them on the floor.

Niniane never took her attention fully away from Tiago. She was already braced when he lowered his head and gave her a goaded look. He bared his teeth at her in a classic sign of Wyr aggression. She put her hand on his forearm. She could feel the current of tension jumping through his body like a live wire.

He was incredible. His outside appearance was scary enough. Inside, his Power was barely held in check by the uncertain leash of his temper. She had heard that he called the lightning when he lost his temper. She had not realized he *contained* the lightning. She felt like she had been given the merest glimpse into the vast unseen landscape that lay cloaked inside him.

Raw emotion flickered in his dangerous face, and her heart melted.

I know, I'm sorry it's hard, she whispered gently in his head. She stroked the hot skin of his forearm with a light touch, then she slipped his gun back into its holster underneath his arm. *I didn't do what I was told again. But Tiago, I am supposed to become a monarch. I can't take orders and I can't just run.*

If she had not been touching him, she might have missed the slight ragged edge to his indrawn breath. Her heart melted further.

Carling spoke another foreign word. Her Power pulsed in the unnatural stillness. Down the hall, humans jerked in surprise and cursed to find themselves disarmed. The Vampyre Tiago had thrown into the stairwell raced back into the hall and slowed to a stop, his gaze locked on his mistress. The lightning-struck Vampyre twitched and groaned as his rapid healing resumed.

A feral growl sounded behind Niniane. It came from the Vampyre climbing through the hole in the wall. His glowing red eyes focused on Tiago, his long fangs distended. Tiago swept Niniane behind him with one hand as he shifted to meet the threat.

Carling said in warning, "Cowan, stop."

The Vampyre launched with a hiss at Tiago. Tiago flowed into a defensive posture, sword held en garde.

Carling blurred. She caught hold of the Vampyre by the back of his neck. Her beautiful face was winter-cold, dark eyes twin shards of ice. In a move so fast Niniane couldn't track it, Carling tore the Vampyre's head from his body. The Vampyre's body fell to the floor. Carling looked down into the face she held between her hands. The Vampyre's mouth worked, as if he would say something, to plead for his life or to scream. Then his head and body crumbled into dust. Carling brushed her fingers together. She murmured, "He was always such an impetuous child."

Niniane stared at the small pile of dust on the floor that used to be a thinking, reasoning creature. She stuffed her fingers against her mouth. Tiago shifted, holstered his own gun, put a heavy arm tight around her shoulders and hauled her against his side. She leaned against him, rested her head on his chest and closed her eyes. She wanted to crawl into that hidden country inside of him.

A noise from the stairwell made her jump. She made a muffled noise against Tiago's shirt and his hold tightened on her.

The Dark Fae Commander Arethusa stood in the stairwell doorway, along with Hughes and a couple of the hotel security staff. They stared at the wreckage in the hallway, at Niniane and Tiago, and at Carling.

Niniane cleared her throat. She forced herself to say in a calm voice, "Everything is fine now. Scott, the bill for repairs on this should go to the Elder tribunal." If the tribunal had an issue with that, they could take it up with Carling. Elder politics tended to be hard on architecture and the general population. Niniane looked at Carling and silently challenged her to deny it. Carling curled a nostril, but as her Vampyres had been the ones to initiate an actual attack, she kept silent.

Hughes nodded and backed into the stairwell. His expression was a study in horrified dismay.

Niniane's gaze met the Dark Fae Commander's hard stare. Arethusa had the tall, lean build that was typical of most Dark Fae, but instead of giving her a willowy look, her leanness was coiled with long muscles that gave her a pantherlike grace. Her black hair was pulled into a tight queue at the base of her neck, and her large gray eyes and angular face were cold with censure as she regarded Tiago's arm around Niniane's shoulders.

The Commander said, "You meddle where you do not belong, sentinel. Release the Dark Fae heir now or face the consequences."

Niniane's temper spilled over. She straightened and stepped away from Tiago, her hands in fists. "That will be enough, Commander," she snapped. Arethusa's gaze swept up to her face. "Please inform Chancellor Aubrey and Justice Kellen that I will meet with the Dark Fae, along with Councillor Severan, in the penthouse in two hours."

"Your highness—" began Arethusa, her gaze turning flinty.

Niniane said between her teeth, "I am not having a good week, Commander. It is not a good idea to try my patience right now because at the moment I don't have any. That will be all."

The Dark Fae Commander's mouth tightened as her gaze flicked back to Tiago then to Carling, who lifted one slender eyebrow. After a moment Arethusa gave a curt nod and stepped back from the doorway.

Niniane concentrated on getting her breathing under control. She focused on a mote of drywall dust dancing in the air. She growled, "Now I am going to take a shower. I am going to put on some real clothes, and I am going to calm down. Does anybody on this floor have a freaking problem with that?"

No one replied. Okay, fine. She took that as a no. She nodded to herself and headed for the stairwell.

The leashed lightning that was Tiago shadowed her. She had just stepped into the doorway, when Tiago said, "Just one thing."

The rich, strong sound of his voice shocked her. She realized he had not spoken aloud since he had appeared. She swiveled.

He stood in the doorway facing Carling. His broad shoulders filled the space. Niniane could just see the outline of his profile. The planes and angles of his face were serrated. He hadn't sheathed his sword. The tiny hairs at the back of her neck rose as he pointed the tip of the sword at Carling in naked threat. Every one of Carling's people took a step toward him.

"If you do anything that puts her in danger again, I will burn down your world," he said. The lightning was in his voice.

Carling's eyes lit up. She smiled at him and said softly, "You might try."

Tiago's savage aggression. Carling's sinuous deadliness. It was just too scary.

Niniane shouted at both of them, "Oh, for crying out loud!"

She left them to their standoff and stomped down the stairs.

Death prowled behind her. She couldn't hear him but she knew he was there. She wouldn't turn around again. She wasn't going to give him the satisfaction of showing him how freaked out she really was.

She reached the next floor down. That stairwell door was

guarded by two uniformed police who stood aside as she approached. She smacked the door open with the flat of her hands and stormed down the hall. Last night she had been too sick to notice the number of the suite they had occupied, but it was easy enough to find. It was the only door with another pair of guards, a male and a sandy-haired lanky woman, standing at attention. Their bright smiles at her appearance vanished, and they paled as they looked at what followed in her wake.

She paused in front of the suite door and glared at it because she didn't have a keycard. The sandy-haired woman opened the door for her. Not trusting herself to speak, Niniane gave the woman a curt nod before she stomped inside.

Then she reached the suite's living room and came to a stop. Someone had come in to clean while she had been kidnapped. The breakfast dishes had been removed. The table gleamed with polish and a fresh bouquet of flowers. The coffee table was bare of gun parts, Tiago's canvass duffle set against one wall. She could see the corner of her bed in the other room. It had been neatly made. The second bedroom door was closed. The heavy living room curtains had been drawn to reveal a bright, sunny Chicago day outside. A cerulean sky was dotted with fluffy white clouds.

She pressed her fists against her temples as she struggled with a sense of disorientation. It looked so normal out there in the sunshine, outside of this hotel filled with crazy people. She turned as Tiago entered the room and finally sheathed his sword. He unstrapped the scabbard and laid it on the table. Then he removed one of the shoulder holsters and put that on the table too.

The cataclysm that had consumed his expression had vanished as if it had never existed. His face had become a smooth blank.

Had he calmed down already? How did he do that? She hadn't calmed down, not in the slightest.

Then he looked at her.

No. He wasn't calm at all. The cataclysm still raged inside him.

Her breathing grew ragged and her mouth shook. Something breakable uncurled inside her, causing her to open up her arms to him. For the space of a single heartbeat she pleaded with him in silence. Please don't reject this. Don't turn away from me.

Tiago took the short distance toward her in a lunge. He snatched her up. She wrapped her arms around his neck and clung tight as he held her in a grip that threatened to cut off her air supply. His dark head lowered, and he buried his face in the crook of her neck.

She cupped his head with a hand, stroked his short hair and murmured to him. She hardly paid attention to what she said. The words didn't matter. "I know. I'm sorry. I was scared too. I was so scared. Thank you for coming after me. Thank you so much for finding me."

He sank to the floor and sat on his heels, bringing her down with him until she straddled his lap. He rocked her, savoring with desperate focus all the sensual evidence of her, the weight of her body and shape of her graceful, delicate bones, her arms holding on to him as tightly as he held on to her, the touch of those small, gentle fingers.

When Niniane had disappeared, he had gone to a place he had never been to before.

He had panicked.

He reassembled his guns in seconds. He informed Cameron so she could mobilize police and call in a forensic witch to analyze the Power in the bedroom before it could fully dissipate. He called New York. Then he strapped on his guns and his sword and came to a complete standstill, because he did not have a clue how to track Niniane through the maelstrom of energy that had taken her.

She had vanished into thin air. She was just gone. The horror of it, the wrongness, had opened up a black hole inside of him that sucked away everything else—any sense of decency or perspective or moral compass—it all vanished until what had been left behind was a howling beast that would savage anyone or anything that got in its way.

Desperation drove him up to Carling's floor, which had turned out to be a stroke of sheer dumb fucking luck. He hadn't been capable or clever. He went to ask Carling to help him track Niniane down. He had been prepared to do something he had never done before. He had been ready to beg. Then he caught a whiff of Niniane's delicate fragrance in a place where it should not have been, and the beast consumed him.

If Niniane became endangered again, he might do more than just burn down Carling's world. He was a destroyer by nature. As the Wyr warlord, he could channel that violence in controlled, targeted ways that achieved a great deal of good.

The beast inside him was an entirely different matter. Unleashed, it might engage in wholesale slaughter.

And the beast wouldn't care.

"It's okay," he whispered. Even he didn't know who he was trying to reassure, himself or her. His lips moved against her fragile skin. "It's okay now."

She nodded, her cheek pressed against his. His heartbeat pounded against her breastbone. He was more than twice her size. He was as big as a moose, and as he was wrapped around her, he felt exactly like the right size. He felt like home.

I'm in so much trouble.

She froze. Wait. *Did I just say that out loud?*

"What do you mean?" Tiago said. He ran his big hands up and down her back. "What kind of trouble are you in? What happened?"

"What happened isn't my fault," she sniffled. "I'm just sayin'."

He raised his head and frowned at her. The raw, bruised look had not quite left his eyes. She had never seen him look like that before. She put her forefinger to the deep line between his brows and tried to smooth it away. He pressed his lips to her palm. The exchange did nothing to sway his attention from other things. He said, "How did you disappear, and why do you feel and smell like Carling's Power?"

"Actually," she muttered, "it's not so much what she did to me, as it is what she did to you. She has a Djinn who is indebted to her. He owes her three favors, or he did—he's now down to two. She had him transport me from the bedroom up to her suite. She said it was to teach you a lesson."

He growled, a deep rumble that vibrated through her frame. "What did that crazy bitch do to you?"

"Shh, remember everything's all right now," she murmured. She cupped his face in both hands and searched his eyes. They were obsidian without any telltale flickering of white. She stroked his lean cheeks. He was such a proud man, and he was so handsome when he wasn't looking like he might tear down skyscrapers or dismantle nations with his bare hands. "She healed me, and we talked for a bit. That's all."

His eyes narrowed. "Healed you," he said.

She opened her eyes wide. "Completely, Tiago. It's the most

amazing thing. See for yourself." She pulled back so that she could lift the top of her lounge suit and show him the silvery scar. "It hurt like a son of a bitch too. I could feel it knitting together inside."

Tiago touched the small scar. The brush of his blunt calloused fingers was featherlight. "It doesn't hurt anymore?"

"Not a bit. I feel like I did before the attack." She fingered the tiny stitches. They looked like baby spiders against her pale skin. *Ew*, actually.

He frowned. "Those need to come out."

She was opening her mouth to tell him she could take them out later when he picked her up and deposited her in an armchair as effortlessly as one might move a house cat. He opened his duffle bag, took out a toiletry kit and pulled out a small set of clippers. Then he knelt in front of her. She squirmed.

He smiled at her, a real smile and not his usual sardonic grimace, the kind that crinkled the edges of his eyes and revealed the handsome set of his features. "You sit still, faerie," he ordered as he pushed up her top. She kept her knees pressed together and angled to the right as she tried to do as he said.

He bent close to make sure of the snip. His gigantic hands that were so gifted in killing were remarkably gentle as they brushed over her skin. She stared at his broad shoulders and dark bent head, and dug her fingers into the arms of the chair, her stomach clenched against a stir of arousal.

His smile deepened. He could sense it, she knew. He could scent the changes in her pheromones. Blood heated her cheeks. She felt exposed and trapped in the armchair with his large powerful body pressed against her legs, but she didn't want to push him away. He snipped the stitch and told her, "Here comes the tug."

She nodded and he pulled the stitch out. He soothed the area, quite unnecessarily she thought, by massaging it with the ball of his thumb. Then he bent close again to remove the second stitch.

She waited for him to move, to straighten away from her, but he did nothing. Instead he tilted his head and stared at her scar. Something unfamiliar moved over his normally aggressive expression. It was a quiet reflectiveness that opened a window to that landscape hidden inside him and revealed—pain.

Her forehead crinkled. He was angry, irritable, rude,

protective and sarcastic, comforting in danger and calm under
fire and unrepentantly, aggressively antisocial. He was simply
an unconquerable spirit. It hurt her to think of him in pain or
distressed. She put her hand over his as it spanned her rib cage.

What he did then shocked her to her toes, as he bent close
and pressed his lips to the scar. A quaking started deep inside.
It spread out and collapsed her like a house of cards as he
straightened and sat back on his heels. She threw her arms
around his neck and fell against him, shaking and clinging to
him as if he were the only stable thing in the world.

And she was afraid. She was very much afraid that it might
be true.

"What is it?" he asked. That rough rich voice of his was
throttled down to a quiet murmur. He hugged her tight and
rocked her. "I thought things were better now."

She had to clear her throat before she could speak. "You
listen to me," she said. She pulled back, grabbed him by the
shoulders and tried to shake him. It was like trying to shake a
Mack truck: quite patently impossible. "Please don't argue with
me, threaten, posture or deflect. Just *listen* to me, Tiago."

He frowned. "I'm listening."

"Carling hates you. I don't understand it or know why. She
didn't say. Maybe you know?" She paused, and he shrugged,
his expression blank. "Okay, we'll put the why aside for now.
But she does. She hates you. I could see it when I talked to her.
I think she would love to find an excuse to kill you."

His eyebrows rose. "She might try," he said.

She wanted to smack him, but the problem was she didn't
think Tiago saw his attitude as posturing. "Yes," she said with
emphasis. "She might if she thought she could get away with it,
but I'm sure she doesn't want to make an enemy of Dragos."

He laughed. "Yeah, I'm quite sure of that."

She stuck her stiffened finger under his nose. "Don't laugh,"
she ordered. "This is not a laughing matter."

His face straightened, but the smile remained a lazy ghost in
his eyes. "Yes, your bossiness," he said. He grabbed her finger
before she could jerk it back and kissed the tip of it. "No arguing, threatening, posturing, deflecting or laughing."

"You're not taking me seriously." Her eyes burned and a
leaden rock settled in her chest. She looked down.

His big hands settled on her shoulders. "Hey," he said. The laughter had vanished from his quiet voice. "Look at me."

She refused. He bent his head to try to catch her gaze. She ducked her head further.

He sighed and rested his cheek on top of her head since it was the only thing she would let him reach. "Faerie, I'm sorry. I am taking you seriously, I swear it."

She pulled back and met his gaze, which had sobered. The skin across her cheekbones felt too tight. She said through stiff lips, "Carling really scared me, Tiago. Not for my sake, but for yours. She's Powerful, and she's dangerous, and for whatever reason, she would kill you if she could. I think there were only two things that held her back from trying earlier. One of them was Dragos. The other is she wants to build an alliance with me. Those feel like pretty flimsy protections to me."

He stroked her cheek with the ball of his thumb. He thought of the stark fear in her face and the suicidal leap she had made toward him that had almost made his heart stop. The impulse to rage at her for taking such an insane risk stormed through him, but she still looked so pale and had been through so much. He throttled back the storm.

"I understand," he said. "Forewarned is forearmed. I'll be careful, I promise."

Those huge gray eyes of hers searched his face. "Don't take unnecessary chances," she said. "Don't threaten her."

He could drown in those gorgeous eyes. Maybe he already had. Maybe this was what death was like, this beautiful torturous emotion. He tilted her back until he had her draped over his arm. He caressed the lovely, fragile white flower-stalk of her neck.

"I will do whatever I have to do to keep you safe," he said. He bent to press his lips to the pulse that fluttered at the base of her neck. He would lie, cheat, steal, murder. Break vows, drop friendships, abandon responsibilities. Start wars or end them. "Whatever I have to."

She knotted her small fists in his shirt. He loved it when she did that. He wondered if she realized how possessive the gesture was. Somehow he thought not. "Damn it, Tiago," she whispered. "You will not take unnecessary risks."

"You forget, my love," he said in a gentle voice. He had been a god of war, quick to wrath and violence. Gentleness was an exoticism that bloomed only in her presence. "I don't take orders either."

My love. He couldn't really mean that. Could he? It was just a term of endearment . . .

Then Tiago caressed her neck with his mouth, and Niniane lost herself in shocked voluptuousness.

She instinctively flexed as she searched for some stable point of reference. Her feet were on the floor, but he had her bent backward so far, he supported her full weight on one arm that he propped on the seat of the armchair behind her. He nuzzled at her neck then took a small piece of the tender skin between his teeth and sucked at it. The resulting pleasure was so piercing it pulsed down the length of her torso and centered in the soft vulnerable flesh between her legs. He was a master of the lightning that whipped down her body, that jumped along her nerves like a live wire, that awakened sensual urges she had not felt in far too long and stirred emotions she had never felt before.

She clutched at his wide shoulders and stared sightlessly at the ceiling as he suckled with such tender care at that one spot. This couldn't be happening. They didn't have time, and that was her fault. *She* had set the agenda for what happened next when she called for a meeting with Carling and the Dark Fae delegation in two hours' time.

Which had happened a while ago. Which meant the meeting was two hours from now minus something. And she should never try to do calculations or time estimates when the sexiest man she had ever known was licking up the line of her jaw to nibble at her ear, because she had never been that strong in calculus and he destroyed her utterly. Utterly.

Somehow her hands found their way to the back of his head, her fingers stroking through his hair, following blindly the whorls that were shaven in the short, silken black length. She gasped and arched against him as his teeth nipped with such care at her sensitive earlobe.

He had come for her. He had promised everything was going to be okay, and he had come for her, and he had looked so crazy-sexy. No, monstrous. No, sexy. Oh damn.

"Big trouble," she whimpered. I'm in big, big trouble now.

"Shh," he whispered. "Everything is all right. You're safe, we're not doing anything. You're not in any trouble."

"Tiago," she whispered. Her lips and her thighs shook. She tried to gasp for air.

He rose over her, an immense dark man that eclipsed the daylight. "God, you're so gorgeous," he breathed against her trembling mouth. "I could eat you up. I want to eat you all over. I want to eat you all day. But I know we've got to make that meeting."

What meeting?

Her mouth clung to him and her legs wanted to. They wanted to wrap around his waist and bring him into alignment with the aching empty cradle between her hips. She dug her fingernails into the back of his strong corded neck, and he arched against her with a shaken laugh that sent his moist, hot breath blasting along her lips.

He jerked his mouth away and gasped, "Reschedule it."

She blinked and looked at him with a dazed, unfocused gaze. "What?"

"Reschedule the damn meeting for tomorrow," he growled. He glanced down her little curvaceous body. He was rock hard and agonized with wanting her. "For next week," he amended.

Memory struck. The meeting! It was supposed to be in two hours minus a significant something now, and she still hadn't showered or put on street clothes, and she sure as hell hadn't calmed down. A sound broke out of her, a cross between a groan and a sob.

He put his hand between her legs and pressed the heel of his palm against the part of her that throbbed with an empty aching pain. "I can make it better," he whispered.

Her body pulsed at the dark promise in his voice. He could make it so much better. He could make it delicious, but in the process he would demolish what was left of her mind, and she needed her thinking clear and sharp if she had any hope of holding her own against Carling and the Dark Fae.

She clutched at his thick wrist and gasped, "No, Tiago. Not like this."

He groaned and went rigid as he bowed over her body, his eyes shut tight. She looked up at the harsh dark lines of his face and wanted to bite her tongue, wanted to take it back, wanted to claw at him and demand he give her everything he had. She teetered at the brink of losing control.

He opened his eyes and looked at her. Violence and sensuality teemed in that obsidian gaze, so that for a moment she thought he was the one who had lost control, and the part of her that had already plunged over the brink was fiercely glad.

Then he pressed his lips to her forehead with extreme gentleness. "No," he said, his voice hoarse. "Not like this."

Before she could protest her own edict, he rocked back on his heels and stood, and he drew her up along with him. At first her legs were too shaky to support her. She put her arms around his long, lean waist and leaned against him. They stood quietly together as he stroked the hair off her damp forehead, and for a moment she felt a crazed kind of desperate need to hang on to any part of him that she could before he slipped away and was lost to her for good.

Okay, now she was starting to scare herself. It was past time she got her careening harebrained self back on track.

She bit her lips and forced some iron into her spine. Then she stepped back, looked in the general direction of his face and gave him a sort of idiotic nod as if that meant anything. She turned away and—

His hand clamped down on her wrist. He yanked her back to him. The breath *woofed* out of her as she came up hard against his muscled torso. He grabbed her by the hair at the back of her head. Her mouth fell open. Before she could utter some version of the *what the hell?* that was ricocheting through her stuttering mind, he turned her face up and drove his mouth down onto hers.

There was nothing civilized about his kiss. He was rough, rampantly dominant, as he dug his hardened tongue into the soft crevices of her mouth, in and in and in, and it was such an invasive raw imitation of the sex act that desire roared through her like a runaway eight-thousand-pound freight train engine. Her inner muscles clamped down in involuntary need, and a high, thin whine broke out of her. She heard the desperate animal sound as if someone else had made it; it was that much beyond her control.

Tiago lifted his head. He was breathing hard as if he had just been sprinting, or as if he had just hurtled through the air in manic flight.

"Like that," he said. The burning words came from the back of his throat and singed her nerve endings. "It's going to be like that."

• • •

So how did one recover from Tiago's particular style of demolition and scrape together enough poise to meet with the senior officials of one of the oldest governments on Earth?

Along with Carling. Oh no, we mustn't forget Carling.

Niniane sat on the bed and stared at the bedroom clock for several heartbeats. And in a half an hour, no less. Yes, apparently she and Tiago had squandered away that much time.

Well. Whatever else happened, she would meet her fate clean.

She dug through the shopping bags and grabbed items of underwear and outer clothing. There was certainly no point in agonizing over what to wear. It wasn't like she had much from which to choose. She had two pairs of jeans, a polo shirt, a scooped neck tee, and a cashmere sweater. It was all Burberry Brit casual wear from Nordstrom and very nice, for what it was, but of course it wasn't suitable. All of her suitable clothes were being held hostage by the people she was going to meet. That might not rank high on anybody's list of affairs of state, but it ranked pretty high on the list of things she resented.

She went into the bathroom, closed the door and started the shower. When the water had warmed, she stripped off the peach lounge suit and stepped into the tub. She stretched and turned under the steaming cascade. It felt incredible to move freely and without pain. She could almost be grateful, except for that whole scaring-her-to-death thing when Carling—along with all of her people—had confronted Tiago.

Niniane knew herself pretty well. She read *Elle* and *People* magazines, not the *New York Times* or the *Wall Street Journal*. She had half a dozen lipsticks in her purse, all of them varying shades of pink. She loved pretty clothes, chocolate truffles and a good Pinot Noir. Her genetic makeup, not her designer makeup, was the only thing that qualified her to be a potential head of anybody's state. If the Dark Fae had a civil servant exam for the monarchy position, there was no way she could qualify even if they graded on a curve. She was not by any stretch of anybody's imagination a weighty faerie, but she was an efficient one. It had taken her two minutes or less for her mind to gallop back to the object of her obsession.

It's going to be like that, he had said. With such simple

words and a single kiss, he shredded her sense of mission and all of the convictions she had held about herself like they were so much party-colored tissue paper.

She squirted a dollop of lilac-scented shampoo into one palm. As she worked it through her fine black hair, she let herself wonder what it would be like to walk into the upcoming meeting and announce she would not take the Dark Fae throne. She could do it too. She could drop everything to be with this man. The frenzied passion he roused in her was that overpowering.

What would be the result?

Someone else would become Dark Fae King or Queen. Hell, as far as she knew, it would be someone far more qualified than she was. But it wouldn't be someone closer to the throne. There was no one closer. That throne had cast a shadow over her all of her life. Whoever became monarch would always know she was out in the world, the real heir with the unshakeable claim. It would undermine everything he tried to do. At the first test of his ability or crisis in government, it could shake him to his foundation.

The smartest thing for a capable ruler would be to solidify his power and rid himself of the threat, but then she already knew that. Walking away would not stop the attempts on her life. But would it gain her anything else?

She sagged against tiled wall. No.

It's going to be like that. With as many words Tiago signaled his intention to take her as his lover. She could follow him back to New York. She could work to make as much as she could out of the time they could have together—but sooner or later Tiago would go back to leading Dragos's troops and living his nomadic warring lifestyle.

She could follow him, if he would let her, but she cringed to think it, silly woman that she was, with her fashion magazines and makeup and pink lipsticks and high-heeled shoes and purses. Sooner or later he would grow to resent her, or worse, he would become impatient, contemptuous and bored. Even if she abandoned her heritage and left everything behind, she could still hope to gain only a limited amount of time with him.

So she would stay her course, not because of her convictions since Tiago had destroyed those. She would stay her course because there wasn't anything else to do. Days ago she had embarked upon a solitary road that had no turning point. She would be a good-hearted monarch, if not the most qualified or talented. That had to count for something, didn't it?

It was time to take another step along that road. As she had said to Tiago, the innocent young Niniane of the past had been killed along with her family. She could never become that Niniane again, so she would just have to forge a different Niniane for the future.

She wiped her cheeks. What kind of time could she manage to get with Tiago? A couple of nights together, maybe at best a week? She would have to hoard every moment, to concentrate everything she had on remembering the slightest detail, because the memories were going to have to last her a very long while.

Faeries could live for thousands of years. If something didn't kill them first.

That's what it was going to be like.

Something had happened and Tiago didn't like it. He didn't like it one fucking bit.

She had gone to take a shower, smelling of an intoxicating blend of bewilderment and intense arousal. He liked putting that shattered look in those gorgeous gray eyes and being the one to lavish attention on all her sexy pieces. He didn't like for her to walk away with that shattered look only to emerge again with the pieces put back together in a new unknown, cooler pattern. Unknown patterns meant something had happened in her head that might shut him out.

He was coming to understand why the other sentinels had nicknamed her Tricks. It wasn't just because they had taught her all the dirty fighting tricks they knew. There was something about her that was just not bloody quantifiable. It was more than the effervescence that winked out of her like sunlight on water. It was an unpredictable feminine quality that could start off at say, point A but then jump to, hell, he didn't know, an entirely different alphabet instead of going through a logical thought process that led from B to C then D and so forth.

That meant he couldn't track from where she had been to where she was now.

He might have to break down and ask her what she was thinking.

He scowled.

While he was on the subject of things he didn't like, he also didn't like her disappearing from his sight. The last time that had happened, a freaking Djinn had made off with her. The memory caused him to break out in a cold sweat. It held him shackled to the outside of her door, straining to hear her slightest move, the rustle of her clothing, anything to reassure him that she was still safe and sound in the hotel suite.

He'd had a couple of bad moments when she had been in the shower. For a heart-stopping while she hadn't seemed to move, and all he could hear was the steady sound of the water running. He had almost broken through the door to check on her. Then there had been a muffled clatter like she had dropped a shampoo bottle or bar of soap. The tight band around his chest had loosened, and he had been able to take a breath again.

It was okay when she ran the hair dryer. He could hear that all the way from the bathroom in the second bedroom where he dashed to tear out of his clothes, shower, towel dry and dress in clean black fatigues in five minutes flat. He was clean-shaven in just under two and a half minutes more. By the time she had clicked off the hair dryer he was back in the living room again with his steel-toed boots laced, buckling on his weapons.

He glanced up as she stepped out of the bedroom. In an instant he was so hard for her it nearly doubled him over. She wore jeans that molded to every inch of her tight, round little ass, a pretty shirt with a scooped neck, and a thin sweater that molded the sides of her curvaceous breasts, looked butter-soft and begged to be stroked. She wore the tiny flat slip-on shoes she had worn earlier. Her black hair was clean and shiny, and she had put on makeup. Somehow she had made her high cheekbones stand out, and glossy pink color emphasized those soft, plush lips. She had used a dark smoky gray eyeliner to devastating effect. It made her eyes even more enormous and compelling. They seemed to gather and reflect all the light in the room.

They also held an expression of distant composure that drove him insane. He stared at her in baffled fury. He was as hard as a rock from wanting her, and everything he had done to bring her to the peak of sensual awareness and desire—it had vanished as if it had never been.

"Are you ready?" she asked. She came to a stop beside him, and those breathtaking luminous eyes of hers narrowed on him. "What is it?"

He glared at what he held in his hands. It was a leather custom-made knife sheath with a leg tie.

He said between his teeth, "You're so goddamn beautiful it's about all I can do not to throw you down on the floor and take you right here and now, and even I know that's not acceptable behavior."

Dead silence. He shot a glance at her from under lowered brows. That fine clear skin of hers had gone white, the expression in her eyes turned stricken. Then she flushed a deep betraying red and her stricken look turned into a scandalized sparkle. She clapped her hands over her mouth and giggled.

Giggled. What a foreign, feminine sound. And he loved it.

One corner of his mouth lifted in response, and his fury dissipated and blew away on an intangible wind. He threaded the knife sheath onto his belt and buckled it. When he bent to fasten the leg tie, her hands came over his.

"Let me do it," she said. Her voice was breathless.

He froze and then straightened slowly as he stared at her.

Her eyes dancing, her piquant face alive with mischievous sensuality, she put those sweet, delicate little hands on his thighs as she sank into a kneeling position in front of him. She tilted her head back and looked up at him.

Holy fuck. His abdominal muscles clenched and the blood in his veins transmuted to slow-moving lava.

She reached between his legs. Her slender wrist brushed against the heavy muscles of his inner thighs. He broke into a fine sweat, his thinking crumbled into a wasteland, and his rigid cock strained toward her plump, smiling lips.

She pulled the two lengths of leather around his thigh and tied them together. "We're supposed to be upstairs in five minutes," she whispered. "We have no time right now. But when we do—"

She leaned forward to put her arms around his hips. His hands fisted in the air above her head, and he broke into a fine trembling as she nuzzled the pulsing bulge at his crotch. She rubbed her cheek against his cloth-covered erection, and it was such a happy, sensual, affectionate thing for her to do, he almost fell to his knees in dumbfounded worship.

He gasped her name, an incoherent hymn.

"When we do have time," she said against him, her breath warming and moistening the cloth over his cock, "I want it to be just like this."

• • •

The penthouse suite was just three flights up from their floor, but one needed a key to access it by elevator. Rogers was still doing guard duty in the hall. The tall policewoman offered the penthouse key to Niniane as they stepped out of the suite. Niniane paused to have a brief exchange with the other woman that had Rogers's pleasant freckle-sprinkled face alight with pleasure.

He didn't pay attention to what the females said. He was too busy struggling to get his raging hormones under control, to actually let Niniane walk away from the hotel suite and not drag her back inside, throw her on the floor and do what he had threatened to do. Each step they took down the hall was an uncertain, hard-won triumph.

Then his brain started working again, really working, and he began to think about the attendees of the upcoming meeting.

Not one of those elegant elderly piranhas was going to welcome his presence, and wasn't that just too fucking bad. There wasn't a Power on Earth that could keep him from guarding Niniane's back.

One of the two guards at the stairwell already held the elevator open for them. They stepped inside. After Niniane inserted the key and pressed the button for the penthouse floor, he took her hand and threaded his fingers through hers. She gave him a startled smile that faded as quickly as it had bloomed. Her sparkling sensuality had vanished again, leaving her a pale, sober stranger.

The elevator purred to a stop. He reached out to punch the door-closed button, and she looked at him in surprise.

"This time you listen to me, faerie. Everything will be all right," he said to her small, tense face that was turned up to his so trustingly. "No one who will be in that room will hurt you. We go in as a united front, and we leave as united front. Got it?"

She nodded. "Got it. Thank you, Tiago."

"You're welcome." He smiled at her, let go of the button, and the doors opened.

He couldn't have been more wrong on all counts. They walked in to the penthouse, and their united front got slaughtered.

⇒ NINE ⇐

Niniane squeezed Tiago's power-corded hand and then released him as they stepped into the quiet, cool luxury of the penthouse.

Carling's attendant Rhoswen appeared in the foyer, blonde hair pulled back in a sleek chignon and face smooth, serene. In profile she resembled a perfect cameo. The Vampyre had been young when she had been turned, perhaps eighteen or twenty. What had been so compelling at that age to make her seek out vampyrism, and what had convinced the Vampyre that had made her? Young humans were much like any other species, Niniane had found. They were all sure they would live forever. Whereas when she had been eighteen, she had been sure she would not live out the year.

A weight settled on her chest as Rhoswen walked toward her across a polished parquet floor. The problem with forging ahead with the Niniane of the future, she realized, was that she still loved reading *Elle*, still loved every shade of those damn pink lipsticks in her purse every bit as much as her old persona, Tricks, had, and she felt woefully inadequate for the challenges she faced.

She had to come up with a better coping strategy and fast. Why was she struggling with the thought of meeting again with the Dark Fae delegation and Carling? Tiago towered behind her, a menacing black-clad figure that promised death to anyone who dared to threaten her.

Not that anybody would threaten her to her face. If the attacks weren't two separate incidents, if there was an actual mastermind behind both of them, that someone would wait until she was alone and vulnerable before trying again. And besides, when she had worked for Dragos she used to have meetings all the time with heads of state and senior government officials, from both the human domain and the Elder demesnes. She'd had no problem dealing with them, even when her life had been in danger from her uncle Urien.

She tilted her head and pursed her lips. Maybe that was it. She should just pretend she worked for someone else. She would work for the real Niniane, who read the *New York Times* and the *Wall Street Journal*; who also read works of literature with deathless prose and haunting, tear-jerking endings (*bleck*); and who managed her own portfolio of stock options. That chick was a well-dressed bitch in a strand of pearls you didn't want to cross.

The fake silly Niniane smiled. "Hi, Rhoswen," she said. "Are all of you except Cowan settling in all right downstairs?"

For a brief moment the Vampyre looked disconcerted. It was a good strategy to keep Vampyres off balance whenever possible. "Thank you, your highness," said Rhoswen. She had a lovely speaking voice, a low, pure contralto. "We are doing well. We regret any distress Cowan's actions may have caused earlier."

Niniane lifted one shoulder. "Well, he did lose his head over it."

"As he should have," said Rhoswen.

Just as Carling had stopped the scene earlier from escalating to further violence, she could have stopped Cowan with one Power-filled command, but no Vampyre master would tolerate anything but complete obedience from her children. The stance was a harsh but necessary one. A Vampyre who lost control in public was a menace to everyone.

Rhoswen's brief disconcertment had smoothed away as if it had never existed. The Vampyre said, "Chancellor Riordan, Justice Trevenan, Commander Shiron and Councillor Severan are all awaiting you in the library."

Ooh, that sounded like a game of Clue. Somebody was going to get bashed in the head with a lead pipe or a candlestick. Not that the real Niniane would notice something like that. The real Niniane already had a clue; she wouldn't play a game of Clue.

She said, "Lead on, Macduff."

Rhoswen inclined her head and turned to lead the way. "I was in theatre before my transformation," said the blonde, as her heels tapped on the hard wood floor. "Did you know, the real phrase is not 'Lead on, Macduff' but actually 'Lay on, Macduff, and damned be him that first cries, *Hold, enough!*'?"

Sometimes Vampyres got pedantic when they got older, which was a function of how their once human brains coped with their unnatural age. And the real Niniane would never stoop to squabbling with an attendant.

The fake silly Niniane told Rhoswen, "Yes, but I was not quoting the play. I was quoting the quote. Nobody says 'Lay on, Macduff' when they invite somebody to go ahead of them. That would sound stupid. Everybody says 'Lead on, Macduff.'"

She grinned over her shoulder at Tiago, who strolled behind them. He wore his harsh assassin's face, but his dark gaze contained a fugitive twinkle.

They came to the library's double doors, which had been propped open. The library was a spacious room with quality neutral-toned overstuffed furniture arranged around an Oriental rug, bookshelves stocked with a collection of hardcover classics and current *New York Times* bestselling paperbacks and a fireplace at one end.

The room's real claim to fame was the sumptuous original Tiffany stained-glass opalescent window that dominated one wall. The window depicted a sunlit pond in a forest populated with brilliant fantastic fish and birds that had never been seen on this side of Earth. Art scholars argued that Louis Comfort must have traveled to an Other land and seen the wildlife at some point in his life to have created such beautiful detailed representations, but the argument was not substantiated as the strange species were not documented in any of the Elder records about Other lands.

Niniane sighed as she thought of Scott Hughes's white, horror-stricken face from earlier when he had looked at the damaged floor downstairs. The Tiffany window sparkled with a strong anti-breakage spell, but such spells had a limited veracity. If a force greater than the strength of the spell hit the window, both window and spell would still shatter. At least a couple of the people in this room had that kind of Power. Poor Scott probably wouldn't be resting easily until the Dark Fae concluded their hotel stay.

Perhaps she should nudge that conclusion along. Urien had built a sprawling mansion on a gated, extensive tract of land that covered eighty acres in one of the most expensive urban areas in the country. The grounds encompassed the main crossover point for the Dark Fae's Other land. Originally she had been uneasy about going straight to the mansion from New York. She had wanted to take a more cautious route, to meet and talk with the Dark Fae delegation on more neutral ground, from which she might have some hope of escape if needed. The mansion on its gated property had seemed as if it could be too easily turned into a prison.

As it turned out, her impulse to caution had had some validity.

The four occupants in the room turned at her arrival. As one, their attention went to the silent menace that stalked behind her, and their faces grew cold and still. All, that is, except for the tall black-haired Dark Fae male with high cheekbones and crow's-feet at his eyes that deepened when he smiled at her. Aubrey Riordan, Chancellor of the Dark Fae government, strode toward her with his hands outstretched. She put her hands out as he reached her, and he brought them up to kiss them.

Aubrey said, "I cannot tell you how angry and distressed I was to hear of the attack made on you by Geril and his partners, or how relieved and glad I am that you are back to us safe and well."

Niniane searched the older Dark Fae male's face as he spoke. According to her truthsense, every word he spoke was sincere. But she, and even Dragos, had believed that Geril and the others had spoken the truth too. As Dragos's mate Pia in New York had argued just a week ago, there were ways to get around truthsense if someone had a talent with words and misdirection. That had been how Pia had survived a potentially deadly encounter with Urien when he had kidnapped her. But Aubrey's eyes were kind, and Niniane so badly wanted to believe him. She squeezed his fingers before she let him go.

Carling moved with silent ghostly grace to sink into an armchair. The Vampyre was still barefoot, but she had changed out of the black Chanel suit. She now wore a loose plain caftan of undyed Egyptian cotton. Somehow she made the simple garment look like haute couture. She had pinned up her long, shining dark hair with two slender stilettos. The knives and the caftan appeared to be the only things she wore. The Vampyre watched the scene with interest, but unless there was a gross violation of demesne law or someone's life was threatened, as Councillor from the Elder tribunal, she would do nothing to interfere.

Commander Arethusa stood ramrod-straight behind one couch. The powerfully built Dark Fae woman glared at Tiago. "The Wyr is not allowed here," Arethusa gritted. "He must leave. Now."

Without warning Niniane's temper leaped from the cool green side of her shit-o-meter into the red zone. Her fists clenched. It was actually a good thing she didn't have either a lead pipe or a candlestick.

"Hey, you know what, Arethusa?" she said. "I am going to be your sovereign. You can't speak to me like that. EVER. I don't care how valid you think your point is or how strongly you may feel about it. Let's pause there for a minute. While we're on the subject of what you can't do, you can't EVER treat me again like I am a pawn to be maneuvered. If any of you EVER again deny me any necessity, like, oh, say, my clothes or toiletries or a goddamn blanket, just to set yourself up for some kind of legal precedent, I don't care how many years of service you have given to the Dark Fae or what you think may be owed to you. I will have you strung up on the nearest tree, and you should count yourself lucky that that's all I will do, because I know my uncle would have gutted you for such an offense. You may be too old for me to teach you any real decency. But that does not mean I will allow you to treat me with anything but the utmost care and respect. Are we quite clear?"

Though her attention was focused on the Dark Fae Commander, she happened to catch a glimpse of Carling out of the corner of her eye. Was that a glimmer of approval in the old Vampyre's gaze?

Arethusa's expression underwent a change so rapid Niniane would have sworn her look of shocked contrition was sincere. "Your highness," said the Commander. "My most profound apologies. I did not mean any lack of respect to *you*—my comment was meant to be directed at *him*."

"It is my decision to have Tiago here," she said. "He volunteered to come to Chicago and to help and protect me. He hasn't hesitated to provide generously for my every need without being asked, without trying to maneuver for political gain and without asking for repayment. In fact, every item of clothing I have on right now is because of him. It is certainly not because of any of you. So what you say to him, you are saying to me."

It was clear the Dark Fae Commander didn't care to hear that, for her face tightened and she shot another glare at Tiago, but she remained silent. It was Justice Kellen who cleared his throat and spoke for the first time. The aged Dark Fae male was one of the finest legal minds of any Elder demesne, the elegant bones of his face covered in a fine tracery of wrinkles, his long white hair pulled back in a queue. Niniane remembered him from when she was a child, but then she remembered all of them, just as she remembered her uncle Urien's cool, clever charm that had, to the happy undiscriminating child she had been, seemed so affectionate.

"Our decision to refuse to cooperate with sentinel Black Eagle was not well done of us," Kellen said to her in his gentle, cultured voice. "And for that, your highness, I do most sincerely apologize. The only thing I will say in our defense is we did not conceive of the possibility that your needs would go unmet."

Okay, so that stopped her shit-o-meter from boiling over. Kellen had always been a superb diplomat, and his nonaggressive approach was famous for cooling hotter heads than hers. She bit her lip and after a moment managed to give him a curt nod.

The Justice said, "We also have had deep misgivings at the Wyrkind's participation in recent events. As Commander Shiron has indicated, we feel it is imperative to distance ourselves immediately from any further involvement with them."

If that didn't sound like an opening to a litany of complaints, she didn't know what did. Niniane sighed as she walked over to sit in an armchair opposite Carling. She gestured for the others to be seated as well, and they arranged themselves in a rough circle, with Kellen and Arethusa on a couch and Aubrey in the last chair.

Tiago moved silently to take a standing position behind her. As she glanced at him, she saw the massive muscles of his biceps and chest bulge as he crossed his arms. She remembered his favorite position leaning against the wall during conferences with Dragos and the other sentinels in Cuelebre Tower, and a wave of homesickness washed over her. She shoved it aside. She had no time to indulge in memories or maudlin feelings.

As far as the general public was concerned, Urien had died in a riding accident, but there were a few individuals throughout the Elder Races who had enough Power to scry for the truth. The governing bodies of the different demesnes knew very well that Dragos had really killed the Dark Fae King.

"If you are referring to how Urien was killed, he had just kidnapped and attacked Dragos's pregnant mate," she said pointblank. "He got what he deserved, and everybody in this room knows it. And that's without even discussing any of his older crimes, which include slaughtering my family and his King."

"Regardless of Urien's crimes and how anyone may feel about his death, the fact remains that the Lord of the Wyr killed the Dark Fae King," said Kellen. "And regicide is a very serious matter. But that event is not to which I refer, at least not on its own." The Justice's gaze shifted to Tiago. "We must wonder at the deep game the Wyr are playing, and why after sheltering you for so many years they would make an attempt on your life."

"What are you talking about?" she said. Even as she spoke the words, Tiago shifted with a sudden muttered curse.

Tiago's broad hand came down hard on her shoulder. He said, quiet and urgent, "Niniane, I need to talk to you for a moment."

She glanced at him with a puzzled, impatient frown. He wanted to talk to her now, of all times? She shook her head at him then said to Kellen and the others, "You've mixed something up badly. There've been two Dark Fae attempts, but there's been no Wyr attempt on my life. That's ridiculous."

Arethusa took a deep quick breath. Kellen and Aubrey gave her a keen, searching look. Carling regarded Tiago with her eyes narrowed and eyebrows raised, her strong, lovely mouth pursed.

Tiago's hand tightened on her to the point of bruising. He said in her head, *I need to talk to you right now.*

Aubrey spoke. "Your highness, please forgive me for contradicting you. The first attempt on your life was made by Dark Fae individuals, for which we cannot express enough our chagrin and outrage—"

NINIANE, Tiago thundered telepathically. She gave her head a quick shake, as if to dislodge his mental shout along with the other formless roar that had begun to fill her mind like white noise.

Despite the cacophony between her ears, she could hear Aubrey perfectly as he continued. "But preliminary police reports on the second attempt are quite unequivocal. It was made by three individuals who were disguised to look like a Dark Fae triad, but they were, in fact, Wyr."

Were, in fact.

The white noise took over her mind. She couldn't think, couldn't hear any more. Several people in the room were talking at once.

Were. In fact.

Wyr.

She turned to Tiago with a look of such utter incomprehension, his expression turned savage and he started swearing.

She did not even bother to ask him. His reaction was all she needed to know for sure. Aubrey spoke the truth. The Wyr had tried to kill her. A jagged landscape opened up inside her. It cut at her vital organs and made it difficult to breathe. Her longtime friends? The people she had hugged with such love when she said good-bye, who even now she missed so much, the people who were—

Her adopted family?

Well, didn't that sound a little too familiar.

Tiago knelt in front of her. His mental voice was sharp and urgent. *Goddammit, don't look at me like that. I was going to tell you but you were hurt. Then we ran out of time and I forgot, that's all, I just fucking forgot. Niniane—*

He reached for her hands. She cringed away from him. He froze and looked as if she had knifed him.

"Thank you for everything you have done on our behalf," said the future Queen of the Dark Fae in a still, cold voice. Her face was polite and as blank as a doll's. "We will see that you are fully compensated for all of your expenditures. You will leave us now."

For one pulsating moment she was sure he would refuse. Absolute anarchy flashed across his face, and she knew in that moment he was capable of doing anything at all. She huddled back in her seat, unblinking.

She did not know what checked him. Something changed in his expression, an awful pained sadness. Then a barrier slammed into place, like a granite slab covering an open wound in the earth. He stood quietly and left.

She talked with Carling and the Dark Fae delegation for another hour. The group laid plans. Since Dark Fae had been involved in one assassination attempt, Carling and her Vampyres would provide security for Niniane while both attacks were under investigation. Then assuming it could be established for a certainty that none of the senior officials in the room had been involved, Carling and her Vampyres would phase out on security and Arethusa and her forces would take over.

In the morning the party would leave the hotel. They would move into the mansion where Aubrey's wife, Naida, was preparing for their crossover journey. From there they would finalize preparations for crossing over to the Other land. Once they crossed, it would take several days of travel by horseback to reach the palace at Adriyel. Niniane's coronation would be held a few days later.

She agreed to everything they requested.

After the meeting, Niniane went to her room in the penthouse. There wasn't any reason not to. She had left the bedroom in a mess after showering and getting ready for dinner with her new cousin and his attendants. Geril had flirted with her on the flight out from New York, which she had not exactly welcomed. They had gone out to eat at a Greek restaurant, and he had persisted over *saganaki* and stuffed grape leaves until she was forced to politely but firmly shut him down.

A second cousin flirting with the heir to the throne. I mean, come on. She hadn't considered it exactly subtle, but she had slogged through the rest of the meal determined to keep an open mind and try to find something likeable about the man.

Yeah, well.

Her bedroom was the largest and most sumptuous of the six in the penthouse, and it was now immaculate. She lay down on the bed. When she closed her eyes, she saw Tiago's tight, angry face, the sadness in his eyes as he looked at her, the muscle jumping in his jaw.

They were in fact Wyr who had attacked her?

Now, just wait a minute.

Now that she was no longer dealing with the Dark Fae

delegation, the cacophony in her head had a chance to subside. The quiet opened up the way for all the memories she shared with the sentinels to come rushing back to the surface.

The hours upon hours they had spent drilling her on self-defense techniques, repeating each thing until she had mastered it. Despite her lack of aptitude, they wouldn't quit and they wouldn't let her quit when she got discouraged.

The outlandish rambling faerie-to-harpy heart-to-hearts she had shared with Aryal over the years.

The times when the gryphons had teased and flirted with her as they patiently put up with "babysitting duty," when they had been pulled from their regular responsibilities to act as her bodyguard.

The gargoyle Grym's quiet, undemanding companionship as he provided guard duty on her walks through neighborhoods during the holiday season, and the Christmas presents of hand-carved wooden puzzles he had created just for her.

Dragos's loyal support of her sometimes controversial choices on how to handle knotty PR issues, and his smiles of fierce satisfaction when she was proven right.

Tiago's protectiveness, the gentleness with which he handled her, the way he had removed the stitches from her side and then pressed his lips to the scar.

She pushed upright as a rock-solid certainty settled back into its rightful place. The people who had attacked her and Tiago might have been Wyr, but Dragos and his sentinels had nothing to do with it. Of course they hadn't.

Oh, Tiago.

She started to look around for her cell phone before she remembered it was still in her evening bag in the suite two floors down. Using the phone by the bed, she asked the hotel switchboard to dial the suite. She listened to it ring. Disappointment bowed her shoulders as no one picked up. When the voice-mail system clicked on, she said, "Tiago, it's me. I'm sorry I sent you away like that. It—the whole thing—just came as such a shock, that's all. Please call me back if you get this, okay?"

She hung up slowly. He might have already gone back to the suite to collect his things and leave. It certainly wouldn't have taken him long to get his things. He traveled light. She picked up the phone again and dialed the front desk. When a pleasant-voiced woman answered, she said, "Hello, this is Niniane Lorelle."

"Your highness! Good afternoon, what can I do for you?"

"I'm trying to get a hold of sentinel Black Eagle and he isn't picking up in the downstairs suite," she said. "Have you, by any chance, seen him recently?"

"Yes, he left about fifteen minutes ago," said the woman.

This time the disappointment was crushing. She covered her eyes. "I see."

"Would you like to leave him a message?"

Would he even come back to the hotel or was he already on his way back to New York? "Yes," she said, her voice leaden. "If you see him, please tell him I need to speak with him. It's very important."

After the woman promised to do so, Niniane hung up. And why wouldn't he return to New York? He had seen her to safety, just as he had promised. After everything he had done for her, she had pretty much kicked him in the teeth.

She couldn't think and didn't want to feel, so she curled up on the bed again and closed her eyes instead. She must have slept because the next thing she heard was a soft knock. Rhoswen's pure voice asked if Niniane would like a supper tray brought to her.

"No," she said.

She closed her eyes again. She heard quiet, grotesque footsteps echoing in the shadowed, silent palace halls. She stumbled in the pools of blood from her brothers' small bodies. Blood had a raw-meaty smell and a consistency that was impossible to mistake, a slippery stickiness that coated her hands and knees as she fell. She scrambled to her feet and ran from a chill Power that hunted for her. It tightened the air like an invisible boa constrictor as she hid in the dark and smothered in her own panic.

The bedroom was fully dark when she next awakened. Disoriented, she fumbled to turn on a light and dig for her wristwatch. She hadn't worn her watch to dinner because it hadn't gone with her pretty red halter dress.

9:30 P.M. *Gah.* Sleeping through the day was a stupid thing to do. Now she would be up all night. She sat up and stared at the floor, feeling thick and slow, like molasses moved in her veins or she was only half alive because a vital artery had been cut and she had been bleeding out while she slept.

She looked at the silent bedside phone, and her eyes filled with tears.

Oh no. No, she didn't. She swore under her breath and pushed off the bed, grabbed a bottle of water from the small fridge and left the bedroom. There had to be something in that damn library that she could lose herself in. If she could not find a book, then she could by god find something to drink. Or maybe both.

When she opened the door, two Vampyres stood in the shadowed hall, the male that Tiago had thrown into the stairwell and Rhoswen. With her sensitive Fae hearing, she could hear people moving quietly about in other rooms in the penthouse. It sounded for the most part like people were spending the evening in their rooms. She imagined a quiet night was a welcome respite to everyone after the drama of the last couple of days.

"Do you require anything?" Rhoswen asked. "Perhaps some sustenance?"

Niniane shook her head. "I'm going to the library."

The blonde Vampyre inclined her head. Niniane walked to the library, which was dimly lit by a small table lamp and the jeweled glow of moonlight shining through the stained-glass window.

At first she thought she was alone in the room. Then she saw the still, silent figure in the armchair. She paused and almost left again, because she wasn't sure she could handle more of Carling that day. But something about that entirely still figure drew her forward.

Carling still wore the Egyptian-cotton caftan from earlier. She had removed the stilettos from her hair. The slender knives lay on the side table by the armchair.

"Carling?" Niniane said.

The Vampyre showed no response. Niniane took a step toward Carling then another, watching the incredible perfection of that profile against the jeweled backdrop of sapphire, ruby, gold and emerald in the stained-glass window behind her. Carling's stillness was complete. Those long, dark eyes were fixed and blank, her lush lips slightly parted.

Ice slithered down Niniane's spine. All Vampyres could be eerie in their stillness, since they did not need to breathe.

Rhoswen and the male Vampyre had been unmoving when Niniane had walked out of her room, but still they had retained a quality of alertness. She could sense they were aware of her.

Carling seemed to be in a different condition altogether. She looked like she was a mannequin or like she was some kind of Stepford Vampyre waiting for someone to flip a switch and turn her on.

Stepford Vampyre. *Ew*, actually.

Niniane cleared her throat and said in a louder voice, "Carling?"

"Macbeth was on to something," said Carling.

Niniane almost leaped out of her skin then felt like a fool. Carling had spoken in a quiet, absentminded voice and had made no sudden moves. Get a grip already, doofus.

She asked, "What do you mean?"

"In his soliloquy. Tomorrow and tomorrow and tomorrow really does creep in its petty pace from day to day," said Carling. "What will the last syllable of recorded time be, and who will be the one to write it? No matter how long we live, we still wonder when our world will end and how."

Niniane's unease increased. Carling had appeared to respond to her name, but she still seemed absent, her expression unchanging. She referenced *Macbeth* as if she were responding to the conversation that had occurred between Niniane and Rhoswen in the hall, but that had happened hours ago. Something was wrong, perhaps badly so. Niniane's stomach clenched.

She said in a quiet neutral voice, "Would you like for me to get Rhoswen for you?"

Carling's dark gaze snapped up to Niniane's face, and in an instant the sense of wrongness was erased. "Gods, no," said the Vampyre with a weary amusement. "Her frantic devotion is so tiring."

Niniane regarded her. She had a feeling she shouldn't ask, but she couldn't help herself. "Are you all right?"

Carling smiled. "I am not doing too badly for an old, diseased woman. We Vampyres are the lepers of the Elder Races, you know, since we were human until we were infected, and of course all of the Elder Races are immune to the disease. I've always felt a somewhat irrational connection with the Wyr because of it. As the lepers and the beasts of the Elder society, neither of us are quite as acceptable as the rest of you."

Niniane quirked an eyebrow. "None of us are that accept-able, Carling."

The Vampyre chuckled. "Too true. Sit, little Niniane. We did not have a chance to finish our earlier conversation when your Wyr so rudely interrupted us."

He's not my Wyr.

A vicious surge of pain came out of nowhere. She took a deep breath and managed to keep the words from tumbling out of her mouth. Then the memory of Carling twisting the head off her own Vampyre and staring at its eyes as it crumbled to dust flashed through her mind, but Niniane stepped forward anyway to sit in the chair Carling indicated.

"I don't understand you," Carling said, as she tilted her head and regarded Niniane.

Niniane blinked. "*You* don't understand *me*?"

"Is that so difficult to believe? You don't maneuver for power around me, and yes, sometimes you are afraid, but underneath it all sometimes it seems that you . . . like me. Even though that isn't wise or safe. And you are sad at the same time. I find that puzzling."

Funny, how accurate Carling was at describing Niniane's reaction to her. Niniane gave the Vampyre a lopsided smile then looked at her hands. She couldn't possibly tell Carling that she thought the Vampyre was something precious and horrific, an enigmatic tragedy like the ruins of a historic battlefield.

She settled for a small truth. "I do like you, even if maybe I shouldn't. And sometimes I get sad when I think about all the friends or associates that you must have outlived. I don't just mean humans. Losing human companions is painful enough. I'm talk-ing about people who have our kind of life expectancy, I guess."

"You have already lost more than enough people in your own time," Carling said, her voice gentle.

Was that gentleness an illusion? Did Carling mimic human behavior, to manipulate or to be social, or were there tattered remnants of humanity still left inside that exquisite exterior? Niniane sighed. Whatever the ultimate truth was about Carling, Niniane would not be the one to discover it. "I wanted to ask you something, if you don't mind."

Carling gestured with a few fingers.

"Why do you hate Tiago?" The words dropped like stones thrown in a pond, causing a ripple of reaction that moved outward to an unseen shore. Carling never moved, but Niniane's chest grew tight. She forced herself to breathe evenly as the silence stretched taut between them. She said, "I just want to understand."

The tension splintered as Carling exhaled an angry laugh. "The reason is so old it hardly holds any meaning, and he doesn't even remember, which makes me even angrier. I met him once in Memphis."

"Memphis," Niniane said, taken aback.

Just as she was going to ask what Carling and Tiago were both doing in Tennessee of all places, Carling said, "Of course it wasn't called Memphis then. That came much later. Then it was called Ineb Hedj. It was the capital of the entire world, and at dawn the sun would shimmer on the Nile like a sheet of hammered silver overlaid on jade and lapis lazuli."

Niniane caught her breath. "You met him in Egypt."

"Yes, a very, very long time ago. Tiago was a god, and I was a commodity. I was young and still human, taken out of poverty and the river mud because of my looks. I was given to a god to entice him to stay with our people. I was entirely desperate, but he did not even look at me. He left and I was punished for it."

Niniane had gripped her hands together at the small, dry telling of the ancient story. She said, "That's horrible."

"It's ludicrous," said Carling. "I didn't want him. I was just a child with a pretty mouth, and he terrified me. I was glad he left."

Niniane forced her hands to relax. "What happened after that?"

Carling's lush lips pulled into a smile, as if she were the Mona Lisa of demons and had just swallowed a soul. "I clawed my way to a better life," the Vampyre said. "I learned poisons and warfare and sorcery, how to rule over others, how to destroy my enemies, and how to hold a grudge with all of my heart. Then I discovered the serpent's kiss that turned me into a god as well, and no one ever took a lash to me again."

Serpent's kiss. Niniane stared at her. "You're talking about the time when you became a Vampyre." Carling inclined her head, and Niniane saw in the gracious, imperial gesture how much Rhoswen imitated her mistress. Niniane asked, "And Tiago never realized what happened or who you were?"

"No." Carling's expression turned wry. "But when I look at him, I want to strangle him all the same."

"I'm so sorry," Niniane said.

"Child," Carling said. The Vampyre's dark gaze was quizzical, somewhat bored.

"I don't care if it did happen eons ago," Niniane told her on a flash of ferocity. "I don't care if there's a more sophisticated way to respond or if it doesn't matter to you anymore. I am sorry for what that girl went through. I'm sorry for what the girl *I* was went through. We may not be those girls anymore, but their ghosts live on somewhere inside us, if only in the memory of what happened, and someone ought to say it: those children deserved better."

Carling's gaze dropped. The graceful wings of her eyebrows pulled together. She said, "You are right, of course. They did."

Niniane had slept too long, and none of it had been refreshing. Her eyes felt dry and scratchy. She dug the heels of her hands into them and rubbed. "It happened so long ago, and Tiago didn't mean to do anything wrong. You do realize that, don't you?"

Again Carling gestured with a few fingers. She made poetry of the movement through a couple inches of space.

"Do you think you could try to set aside your grudge?" Niniane asked. "I'm asking that you do this as a favor to me, in the interests of building an alliance between us."

"You care about him." Carling spoke as if she savored the words, even as she stared at Niniane with intense curiosity.

There wasn't any point in denying it. She said, "Yes."

"Even after he withheld the truth from you about the second attack?"

She sighed. "Yes."

A shadow of a scowl crossed Carling's face. The youthful, impetuous expression was a startling incongruity amid such disciplined, mature perfection. The Vampyre said grumpily, "Oh fine. I won't do anything to him as long as he doesn't try to do anything to me."

Niniane sagged in her chair. "Thank you," she said. "That means a lot to me."

Carling gave her a hard look and said, "Perhaps it means too much to you. You should be careful where you step next, Niniane, and in whom you place your trust. You are in a fragile place right now."

Niniane's spine stiffened. "I am well aware of the place I am in."

The Vampyre's expression softened. "I know you don't want to believe that Dragos had anything to do with the assassination attempt. I could feel the struggle in you earlier."

She was startled by the context of the conversation. "You can . . . feel my emotions?"

"Yes, of course. As Vampyres grow older our senses become more acute. The eldest of us eventually lose our taste for blood and we feed on the emotions of those around us. I have not partaken of human blood for several centuries now."

Good grief, Carling was a succubus. Niniane said, "You sense what other people are feeling."

Carling shrugged. "I sense the feelings of those who are alive, at any rate. Other Vampyres are of no use to me when it comes to sustenance."

What an intrusive ability. Niniane's forehead wrinkled. Well, that explained how glossy the Vampyre had looked at various times today. Niniane wondered what the jagged landscape inside of her tasted like to a succubus. Could it taste as bitter to Carling as it did to her?

If she asked, would Carling tell her what Tiago felt about her? Would the Vampyre tell her if that sadness she thought she had seen in his eyes just before he left had been real or feigned? She clenched her fists and jaw so tight her teeth ached, in order to keep herself from asking the pathetic question.

It wasn't as if knowing could change what had happened or bring Tiago back.

Carling said into the small silence that had fallen, "After two hundred years' sanctuary with the Wyr, you may want to believe that you have forged an unbreakable bond with them. But remember, what was almost your entire lifetime is not so very long a time to those of us who have lived so much longer."

Niniane's mouth tightened. "I'm also well aware of my relative youth and inexperience, thank you."

"It is not my intention to point out your inexperience or to make you feel inadequate," said Carling. "And I don't have answers for the challenges you face. I merely wish to caution you and give you food for thought. Stronger and longer alliances have certainly been broken, and the Great Beast is older than all of us. He is old and wily. His first priority will always be the Wyr, and you are not Wyr."

Did Carling really mean to provide food for thought, or was she trying to sow distrust between Niniane and Dragos? Niniane shook her head. "Everything you said is technically correct. Old alliances can be broken, and of course Dragos's first priority is the Wyr. But I don't buy that as an argument for Dragos's possible involvement in the attack against me. It doesn't make any sense. Why would Wyr who were disguised as Dark Fae attack me, while another Wyr kills them to defend me?"

"I do not know." Carling pursed her lips.

Niniane said, "If for some unfathomable reason Dragos wanted me dead, it would have been much more simple and efficient for Tiago to have killed me himself."

"We do not have enough information," Carling said. "Perhaps there is a schism within the Wyr of which we are only now becoming aware. Perhaps the Great Beast is playing a much deeper game than any of us can understand right now. I have always liked and respected Dragos, but I never completely trust him."

Niniane took a careful breath. Could Dragos have played such a deep game that even Tiago did not know what it was? Dragos was certainly capable of it, but she would not believe that of him in this case, not unless she was faced with indisputable proof.

After a moment she forced herself to speak out loud again. "Thank you, Councillor. I'm glad we got this chance to chat, and I will think carefully on all that you have said."

"Be sure that you do," said Carling.

≡ TEN ≡

"I like your duck waddle across the parking lot," Tiago told Clarence "JoBe" Watson. "It made its own statement. Maybe it wasn't the one you wanted to make. But it was definitely its own statement."

Tiago had found Clarence hanging with three of his homies on South Damon Avenue. They were wearing gangsta bling, displaying their colors and jamming to 50 Cent. The brothers had taken one look at Tiago striding toward them in his black fatigues, barbed wire tats and visible weaponry. The gods only knew what they saw in his face. Flares of white lightning kept flashing in his eyes. He had hidden them behind sunglasses. The brothers had bolted like so many rabbits flushed by a wolf.

Tiago had increased his pace to a quick walk. He had caught Clarence three quarters of a block later, grabbed him by the back of the neck and slammed him into the side of a brick building.

Tiago said, "You might be wondering if you could have gotten away if you'd had your pants pulled up instead of hanging down around your thighs."

"What the fuck, man?" Clarence shouted.

Clarence was twenty-two years old, six-foot-one and one hundred and ninety pounds. Tiago took hold of his jeans by the waist. With a heave, he lifted Clarence two feet off the ground. In one quick jerk Tiago shook him the rest of the way into his pants.

"I don't think so," said Tiago. "But we can always try this again." He stepped back. "Go ahead. Run."

"I'm gonna take you out." With a flick of his wrist, Clarence opened his switch as he whirled around. "You crazy mo-fucker!"

Tiago took the knife from the child, pressed the flat of the blade against the nearby brick wall, and snapped it at the hilt. He said, "That was just another one in a long series of unwise choices, son."

"You whack-job sum-bitch from hell." The whites of Clarence's eyes showed.

Tiago spun the guy around. "Here's the good news, Clarence," he said. "It pains me to say this, it really does, but you get to live."

"Whatever it is I didn't do it!"

"Oh yes, you did. If you hadn't posted your little impromptu film footage, those of us in New York might not have found out about the shit going down in Chi-town in time for us to stop some more shit from happening. Now here's the bad news."

Tiago grabbed him by the back of the neck and the seat of his pants, and threw him into the wall. Clarence accelerated from a baritone, took the freeway past soprano and hung a sharp exit to arrive at a teakettle shriek.

"Life for you is going to get really fucking painful for a little while," Tiago told him. "You might get away with only a few broken bones. And you don't get to keep any of your toys." He dragged Clarence to his feet again and pinned him by the back of the neck to the wall as he fished through the pockets of the kid's jeans and jacket. He confiscated a nine-millimeter and continued his search. There had to be one. "I've been to your crib. I've taken out your PlayStation, your Xbox, your Wii, your laptop and two PCs, the 52-inch, the TiVo, the Blu-ray, the Pioneer and the home theater system. Oh, and your Flip, of course. Speaking of which, that's a mighty lot of toys for someone who has no job on record. You dealing or did you just steal the shit?"

Ah, there it was. He pulled out an iPhone, dropped it to the pavement and ground it under one booted heel, which prompted more teakettle whistling. He picked up Clarence and reacquainted him with the wall.

"Now I'd have to stop doing this if some witness chose to call 911," Tiago said. "What do you think, Clarence? You see any dots that connect from, oh, say the attack you watched and filmed the other night without doing any goddamn thing about it to your current state of discomfort?"

The teakettle whistle dissolved into a soggy snivel. Tiago reached down to pick the guy up again.

A strong, lean tanned hand came down to grip one of his wrists.

Rune said in his ear, "You got the chance to discipline him, T-bird. That's enough."

Tiago turned toward the gryphon. Rune had lion's eyes the color of sun shining through amber. Whatever Rune saw in Tiago's expression made those golden eyes turn careful. "Hey, buddy, it's time for a debriefing," Rune said. "You need to catch me up on what's happened since we last talked."

"I fucked up," Tiago said. "It was a stupid fucking mistake and it hurt her. Bad. I don't know how bad."

Rune gripped him by the shoulder hard, his keen gaze steady. "All right. Whatever it is, we'll fix it."

"I had to walk away," Tiago said. His voice had turned guttural, harsh. "Give her a little space. I don't know how much space to give her. Couple hours? The rest of the night? I was just"—he looked down at Clarence, who had crumbled in a heap at his feet—"I was killing something. Killing time I guess."

Rune looked down at the guy too. Clarence had stuffed his bleeding nose into the sleeve of his jacket. Rune said to him, "You know what a lucky little pissant you are that I came along when I did?"

"Yeah, I thick so," said the kid. He swiped at his streaming eyes.

"Wyr don't forgive easily," Rune said. "And we never forget. You need to become a model citizen now."

"Cross by heart," Clarence said into his sleeve. "I bean it. I thick I saw Jesus in the wall just now. I'b gonna start going to church with by bob again. Baybe I'll join the arby."

No matter how sumptuous and inviting her penthouse bedroom was, Niniane had no desire to go back to it after her conversation with Carling. She wandered with aimless restlessness throughout the penthouse's common areas.

She paused by the grand piano and opened the lid to finger the cool, smooth keys. It was a Steinway, the black surface polished to a high shine, and she suspected it was in perfect tune. She loved music, loved to sing and adored dancing, but her piano playing skills were desultory at best. Besides, the time had to be well past ten o'clock by now. That wasn't terribly late and the Vampyres would be wide awake, of course, but some of their human companions and the Dark Fae might be readying for bed. She eased the lid back down with a sigh.

She looked up at the Vampyre who had become her soundless shadow. It was the stairwell Vampyre again. He was beautiful as Vampyres tended to be, with cool dark looks and a slim frame that hid what she knew would be a tensile inhuman strength. Rhoswen had disappeared, perhaps to attend to her mistress.

She couldn't keep thinking of him as the Stairwell Vampyre any more than she should keep thinking of Carling as the Step-ford Vampyre. She asked, "What's your name?"

"Duncan," he said.

"It's nice to meet you, Duncan."

"Thank you, highness." He watched her with an attentive dark gaze and a calm neutral expression. "It is a pleasure to meet you as well."

"When you came back out of the stairwell this afternoon, I was glad that the first thing you did was look toward Carling and that you didn't go after Tiago again," she said. "But I'm curious. What made you do that?"

Duncan said, "We could all feel when she stopped us. At least the Vampyres could. I'm not sure about our humans. Their senses are so much less than ours. When she released us and I returned to the hall, it was important to find out what had changed, preferably as quickly as possible."

Niniane's eyebrows rose. No wonder Rhoswen had no sympathy for Cowan. He'd gotten two warnings to stop before he lost his head.

Duncan spoke with a slight pleasant accent. Normally she loved to talk to people and to find out about their lives—or spooky undead existence, as it were—and the impulse to ask him more questions drifted through the back of her mind. The impulse faded almost at once. She wasn't able to muster up a social mood.

She asked, "So what's a girl got to do to get a drink around here?"

"She has merely to state what she would like," said Duncan. He smiled at her. "It would be my pleasure to get her whatever she desires."

He had an attractive smile and a pleasing manner. Niniane knew better than to believe those were the only qualities that won him a place in Carling's entourage. "I'd like a bottle of red wine, please," she asked.

"Anything in particular? Merlot, Beaujolais, Syrah?"

She said, "Alcoholic will do just fine."

She went onto the slate-tiled patio where potted trees and plants were arranged attractively around a couple of wrought iron tables and chairs. She sat and looked out at the city lights while a warm breeze played with her hair. A few minutes later Duncan brought a tray out. He placed a glass of wine in front of her. He murmured, "I thought perhaps a Malbec."

"Thank you," she said.

He placed the bottle on the table, along with an assortment of cheese, crackers and fruit. Wishing him gone, she thanked him again, and he gave her another smile before he stepped away to take a position by the doors.

Her life felt like too much of a burden to pick up and examine at the moment. She sipped her wine and tried to exist in the now, but she couldn't turn off her thoughts.

You should be careful where you step, Niniane. You are in a fragile place right now.

Yeah, thanks for that reminder, Carling. Like I hadn't noticed.

Niniane downed the contents of her glass and rubbed at her forehead. On the plus side: Her identity had been easily verified so that it was no longer in question. Nobody could contest her right to the throne.

Wow, that was on the plus side? That was the *only* thing on the plus side?

On the negative side: Aside from her releationship with the Wyr (which was *not* in jeopardy), she had no strong alliances upon which she could rely with any degree of confidence, she had no real Power to speak of and she had a long estrangement from Dark Fae politics and society. She had no idea which of the delegation members she could trust.

And her relationship with the Wyr was a long-distance relationship. Her father's relationship with the Wyr had been in good standing as well. That hadn't saved him or his family.

She really was up shit creek without a paddle. If she was in a betting pool, she would give herself less than a year.

Then a thought occurred to her. Perhaps dear dead cousin Geril wouldn't have tried to kill her if she had been less obvious about how unwelcome his attentions had been. Perhaps that was why he had taken her out to dinner first then tried to kill her. Otherwise why bother to feed her? Had he really thought his distant connection to the throne would be enough to make a play for it on his own? That was hard to believe. Or had he been working with someone else and decided to play all angles of the game? If she had responded to his flirtation, he might have thought he had a shot at sharing the throne with her.

Anxiety gnawed at her. She wished she had a pack of cigarettes. She took the bottle, tilted a liberal amount of wine into her glass and tossed it back.

If she wanted to lose at that betting pool and live longer than a year, she had to make an alliance with someone who had power. Or Power. Working to build a good relationship with Carling was all well and good, but that would be a long-distance relationship too, and she had to do more than build a distant alliance with another demesne. She had to make an alliance with someone close at hand. What did she have to offer that she could hope would make someone's loyalty stick?

She looked at her plus side. Well crap.

She said out loud, "I'm going to have to marry."

The warm wind took her words and blew them away. Not that it changed anything. She was going to have to marry to solidify her position and survive. She was going to have to find someone who wanted the throne, who couldn't get it on his own and who had enough political clout or Power, or both, to help her hold on to it. She needed someone who had as much of a vested interest in keeping her alive as she did.

This time when she reached for the wine bottle she didn't bother with the glass.

A rush of immense wings sounded overhead, and for a wild, heart-leaping moment she was so full of *hope*. She jumped to her feet as she searched the sky. A pale film of clouds draped the dark blue night sky, and a gorgeous nightmare descended onto the patio.

The creature had the form of a tall female with a wingspan large and powerful enough to support her long, flowing muscular form. She was a study in pale and dark grays and black, her lower torso and strong legs covered with short, fine feathers. She had a wide rib cage and chest that supported long flight and fast speeds, high slight breasts and magnificent sooty wings that deepened to midnight toward the primary feathers. Her long hands and feet were tipped with razored lethal talons that could slice through metal or split open a person's skull with a single swipe, and the lines of her angular face were severe, upswept. In her human form, the Wyr sentinel Aryal had a strange, gaunt beauty. In her harpy form both strangeness and beauty were accentuated, her stormy eyes magnified, and her long black hair moved in the wind as if it had a life of its own.

Duncan blurred past Niniane with his Vampyre's lethal strength and speed. The harpy picked him up by the neck and slammed him onto the patio so hard the slate tiles underneath him cracked. She held the Vampyre pinned as she inspected him curiously with her piercing raptor's gaze.

"*Hmm*, pretty," said the harpy. She looked up at Niniane. "If you don't want him, can I have him?"

A confused tangle of emotion roared up inside, gladness mingled with a bitter disappointment. She said, "Aryal, don't hurt Duncan."

"I wasn't going to hurt him," said Aryal. "Not unless he asked for it." The Vampyre's eyes had started to glow red, and his fangs had distended as he strained against Aryal's powerful grip. The harpy tapped his temple with one curved talon. "That's even prettier. Dude, you ever taste harpy's blood? We're rarer than shit so I'm betting not. Want to go out for a drink sometime? If you put out, I might let you have a sip."

"Aryal!" Niniane exclaimed.

"What!" The gorgeous winged nightmare blinked at her. "You know how hard it is to get a date in New York."

The Vampyre looked so confused and aggressive, but at the mention of harpy's blood, a startled avarice crept into his bloodred gaze.

Niniane started to laugh. She couldn't help it. "Duncan is a very nice guy. Would you let him go, please?"

"But I'm not done sexually harassing him." Niniane dipped her chin and glowered at the harpy, who scowled back and grumbled, "Oh all right."

As soon as Aryal's grip around his throat loosened, Duncan

sprang to his feet and lunged to take a stance between Niniane and the harpy. It was a brave, stupid and totally useless gesture of protection.

Aryal blurred into a Wyr's shapeshift as she rose to her feet as well. In her more human form, she was a six-foot-tall powerful woman, armed and dressed in leather, with an angular face, lean muscles, tangled black hair and stormy gray eyes. She said to the Vampyre, "You wanna hug it out?" She feinted forward and Duncan jerked back a step. "Yeah, I didn't think so." She bounced once on the balls of her feet and gave Niniane a feral grin. "Hey, pip-squeak."

Aryal looked so happy to see her, the pleasure on her odd gaunt face so sincere and uncomplicated, for the moment Niniane's disappointment that Aryal wasn't Tiago took a backseat and she was simply glad to see her friend.

Niniane put a hand on the Vampyre's shoulder and pressed down, silently telling him to stay put as she told him, "You know, Duncan, I have seen this harpy drunk on her ass more than a few times. Once she even—"

"Don't say it," Aryal warned.

Niniane grinned. "She even let me put pink lipstick on her and her hair up in pigtails."

"Traitorous bitch!" Aryal said. "You carp-carp-carped. 'Lemme just see what you look like, Aryal. C'mon, Aryal, I won't tell anybody. Five minutes and you can wipe it right off.' And now what do you do? You tell every freaking body you can every chance you get."

The Vampyre relaxed only slightly at their banter. He asked, "How did she look?"

"You know how she looked just now when she smacked you down?" Niniane asked.

Duncan's eyes narrowed. "Yeah."

Niniane started to giggle. "She looked a lot scarier."

The harpy rolled her eyes. Still laughing, Niniane launched forward. Aryal grabbed her and hauled her in for a tight hug. "How are you doing, pip-squeak? I was awfully proud of how you kicked the shit out of those three Dark Fae assholes, but you gave us quite a scare when you disappeared like that."

She pressed her cheek against Aryal's leather vest and her laughter dissolved into a harsh sob. "I've had a *rotten day*."

"Whoa," said Aryal. She sounded alarmed. She patted

Niniane's back. "You know how tears freak me out. Who do I have to kill to make it better?"

"I don't KNOOOOOW."

Aryal said over her head to the Vampyre, "Go guard the inside of the patio door. Pretend you can't hear us."

"Count me deaf and gone," said Duncan.

Aryal's hug turned bone-bruising. Niniane tilted her head back. She gasped, "Let go already. I'm not going to cry anymore."

Wide, worried storm gray eyes looked down at her. "You sure?"

She nodded. Aryal released her and she sucked in a deep breath. She turned to walk back to the patio table and sit. The harpy threw herself into a nearby chair and sprawled, arms crossed and long legs stretched, her piercing gaze fixed on Niniane's face.

Niniane said, "What are you doing in Chicago?"

"Rune and I are here to investigate those fuckers who attacked you and Tiago," Aryal told her. "Tiago called us just after you got back to the hotel and saw the doctor. We blew in a bit ago. We were barred from coming up through the hotel to see you. Then we heard from a Chicago PD chick that you and Tiago had separated. Rune went to find Tiago. I took the alternative route to see you." The harpy tilted her head. "Now it's your turn. Why isn't Tiago still with you, and why are you having a rotten day?"

"Oh gods, where to start." Niniane put her elbows on the table and hid her face in her hands.

"Wait a minute, you were awfully spry just now when you jumped at me," Aryal said suddenly. "What happened to your knife wound?"

"Carling," Niniane said. Speaking between her hands, she told Aryal everything that had occurred since she and Tiago had returned to the hotel. Well, minus the blisteringly personal stuff. She hugged that to herself, to be examined in private later when she had the chance. "I went into shock when I found out that it had been Wyr and not Dark Fae in the attack. I've been dealing with old bad memories anyway, and to hear about it in the meeting—well, that wasn't a good way to find out."

"I bet," Aryal said. The harpy sat forward to put her elbows on the table as well. "Tiago should have told you."

Niniane sighed. "He tried to tell me he got busy and forgot. I just wasn't able to hear it at the time, so I sent him away. Now I can't get ahold of him to apologize."

"He's used to giving orders. He's not used to sharing." Aryal narrowed her eyes on the plate of cheese, crackers and fruit. She raised her eyebrows at Niniane who gestured for her to help herself. Aryal popped a piece of cheese into her mouth.

"It didn't make any sense," Niniane said. "Why would you attack me?"

"We wouldn't," Aryal said. "That's ridiculous. We love you."

There was the reality she knew. Niniane whispered, "Yeah."

The harpy patted her back. "And forgive me for being brutally practical in saying this, but setting aside personal feelings, it's to our advantage to have you safely on the throne. That would give the Wyr an alliance with the Dark Fae for the first time since your father was alive."

Niniane nodded. "Of course. It was one of the reasons why the Wyr attack came as such a shock."

"I'll tell you what's even more ridiculous," Aryal said. "Those Wyr attacked when Tiago was with you."

Niniane looked up quickly. "I hadn't gotten that far in my thinking," she said. "They wouldn't have if they had known who he was, because it was a death sentence for them."

"Exactly. Do you know any Wyr in his right mind who would go up against Dr. Death?" Aryal said. "And nobody but Dragos and the sentinels—well, and of course Pia—knew that Tiago had come out to look for you."

Niniane said, "So those Wyr were either working on their own, or they were working for someone else. Carling brought up the possibility that there might be a schism in the Wyr we didn't know about."

"Okay," said Aryal. The harpy hooked the heel of one boot on a rung of her chair. "Maybe there's a supersecret anti-faerie Wyr faction out there that we haven't heard of before. Maybe they don't want us in an alliance with the Dark Fae."

Niniane watched the harpy's face. Aryal was in charge of Wyr investigations. "It doesn't make sense that you would know nothing about a faction like that," Niniane said. "Factions tend to grumble, write manifestos, protest, maybe blow things up. They often claim responsibility for things too."

Aryal ate a grape.

"So what makes the most sense?" said Niniane. "Somebody wants me dead, and if they succeed in killing me, great. But if they fail, the next best thing is to drive a wedge between me and my strongest allies, because that would leave me vulnerable for when they try again. And they do want me dead, because if they just wanted to drive a wedge between me and the Wyr, there are lots of ways to try to achieve that that are much less potentially dangerous than an assassination attempt."

"Ding ding ding. Give the girl a gold star." Aryal grinned and popped another piece of cheese into her mouth.

Niniane told the harpy about Geril's flirtation on the flight to Chicago and at dinner out at the Greek restaurant.

"I was wondering what happened to you for those couple of hours before the alley attack," Aryal said.

"Again, there was no reason that I can think of for Geril to kill me if he was acting on his own," Niniane said. "We didn't know each other. There was no direct line of inheritance between us, and his connection to the throne was too diffuse for him to make a play for the crown himself. I may not be all that connected with the ins and outs of current Dark Fae politics, but I know that much."

"Right now, I have just one question," said Aryal. "Are we looking for one entity—one person, conspiracy, or faction trying to kill you—or two?"

Since before 1842, the Cook County morgue in Illinois had conducted an official inquiry on every questionable death in the county, which included the city of Chicago. Shortly before the Great Chicago Fire had occurred in 1871, the morgue opened its Office of Magickal Inquiry to investigate every questionable death relating to matters of Power or the Elder Races. In 1976 when Cook County established its Office of the Medical Examiner, the Office of Magickal Inquiry was placed under the Medical Examiner's purview. The outdated term "Magickal" was dropped and the office given the simpler name of Paranormal Affairs.

The intent behind the move had been to modernize this section of the morgue and rename it with a view to greater accuracy and political neutrality, but in this attempt the county officials failed miserably. Many of the Elder Races, including several humans with Power, were offended by the name. *Paranormal* was a term that indicated something was outside the realm of normal experience or scientific explanation. Opponents to the term argued that it was racism and bigotry of the highest order.

Or so Dr. Seremela Telemar informed Tiago and Rune in her History of the Morgue 101 as she led them to the Paranormal Affairs section. Telemar was a medusa of late middle age, as evidenced by the length of her head of snakes that dangled down to her shapely hips. Medusas guarded their young ferociously. Tiago had personally never seen one of their children, but he knew young adult medusas had slim, short snakes that covered their heads like curly undulating afros.

A medusa's head snakes were semi-independent sentient creatures that shared a symbiotic relationship with their host, which included an exchange of sensory input and thought impressions. A medusa never had her back turned if one of her snakes was looking at you. For the most part the head snakes remained as peaceful as their medusa, but if a medusa felt frightened or threatened, they had a venomous bite that could paralyze most creatures and might, if the snakes were induced to multiple bites, cause death. When Telemar reached old age, which for her species would be between four hundred and fifty and five hundred years, her snakes would reach her feet or perhaps trail a little on the ground. For now, she bound them back gently in a loose headcloth like they were dreads.

The medical examiner's skin was a pale, creamy green that was several shades lighter than her snakes, and it had a faint iridescent pattern that resembled snakeskin. Her blue-green eyes had vertical slits for pupils and a nictitating membrane that flicked into place as she looked over her shoulder at the sentinels who followed close on her heels.

"Like other morgues across the country, my department doesn't usually see anything near the kind of traffic that the main morgue does," she said. Several of her head snakes looked around her waist and over her shoulder at them, tasting the air curiously with their flickering tongues. "It is a significant event for us to get six bodies back-to-back. The main morgue conducts around fifty-two hundred autopsies annually, and usually I spend half my time working with them. We're lucky if we see two hundred."

"Lucky?" Rune quirked a sleek tawny eyebrow at her. The gryphon was working his male charm on the medusa. She was, like every other female Tiago had seen around Rune, falling for it hook, line and sinker.

"Well. Perhaps 'lucky' is not the right word, but you get what I mean." She widened her eyes and smiled at Rune as she tucked a few of her snakes behind one shoulder. She pushed through a pair of swing doors and Rune and Tiago followed. "As you no doubt are probably aware, most Elder deaths are not even reported to a medical examiner's office. Many of them happen in Other lands and/or they are processed and investigated by their own demesnes. The deaths that tend to come to me are human ones that involve a Power exchange or discharge of some kind. This has been a real kick in the pants in more than one way."

"I can imagine," Rune said. "Politically as well as medically."

"Quite," said the medusa.

When Rune and Tiago had arrived at the morgue, the medusa had given Tiago one startled look that took in the implied threat flowing like silver mercury through his massive physique, his dark glasses and the banked aggression stamped in the strong bones of his face. Then her nictitating membranes had snapped shut and she kept herself busy looking anywhere else but at him.

Tiago was down with that. The gryphon and the doctor's conversation was more blah-fucking-blah as far as he was concerned. The First stood in an easy stance, his thumbs hooked into the back pockets of his jeans as he chatted with Telemar.

Tiago let Rune run interference. It left Tiago's mind free to pick over the pieces of the puzzle they had to date, and to grapple with what raged inside of him. He had a precarious hold on the beast. It would not take much to send him over the edge again, and he could tell that Rune knew it. Rune kept his body language casual and relaxed, but somehow he managed to always stay between Tiago and other people.

At least Aryal had texted Rune to let him know that she was with Niniane, and that Niniane was okay. But Aryal was known for not being girl-savvy. What did *okay* mean to the harpy—not coughing up arterial blood? Hell, by that standard, Tiago had left her *okay*. He had known she would be physically safe under Carling's protection. Mentally and emotionally were two different matters.

The need to get back to Niniane gnawed at him. Every minute he spent away was agony. He kept having something like a PTS-fucking-D reaction every time he saw in his mind's eye how she had flinched from him and turned lifeless as a little doll, and that had happened goddamn hours ago.

It helped to have an agenda. He had stuff he had wanted to accomplish. He had corralled Cameron Rogers and they had gone to the nearest police station to look at the reports that had been filed on the two attacks. He hadn't gleaned much more than he already knew, but it always paid to be thorough. He had taken a gander at Clarence/JoBe's rap sheet, which was mostly full of petty shit involving break-ins and robberies. Tiago had memorized his address. After he had parted ways with Rogers, he had gone to check out Clarence's crib and then gone to find Clarence himself.

Checking out the morgue was the last thing on his list. He wanted to see the bodies for himself and get what information he could from them. Then Tiago was going to head back to the hotel, and nothing, not the freak-show Vampyres, not the snippy-ass Dark Fae delegation, not even Niniane herself, was going to keep him from having a word with her, or maybe even three or four.

The room they had stepped into was utilitarian, full of steel and industrial-painted concrete, with tall cabinets in one corner that had to contain magical tools, for the cabinets gleamed with Power. There were no windows, of course. Tiago had been in many a morgue before—he had even been in the original Cook County morgue once—and he automatically loathed the place. The autopsies on the bodies of the three Dark Fae males had been completed. They were stored in drawers awaiting release for cremation or burial. The three Wyr were still being processed. Their bodies were laid out on tables and half covered in sheets.

Tiago prowled around the tables, looking at the males, his lip curled. That one—yeah, he remembered that one. The Wyr had died of blunt-force trauma to the head. The trauma had been Tiago's boot heel coming down on him. One side of the Wyr's face was now concave, but there was enough left of the other side to get an idea of what he had looked like.

Rune was still ostensibly chatting up Dr. Medusa What's-her-name, but he said telepathically to Tiago, *You recognize any of these gentlemen, T-bird?*

Just from the attack, Tiago said. *You?*
Nope. They're all new to me.

One advantage to conducting an autopsy by magical means was that the examiner could use disinfecting spells instead of chemicals. The decision was a tricky one for the examiner to make, as it depended on the forces involved in a death, since spells could disrupt any lingering Power that might provide vital clues, or they could even have a toxic effect when certain kinds of differing Powers combined.

These jokers were not that complicated. Death-by-stupidity was the cause as far as Tiago was concerned. Who the fuck didn't know by now that Niniane had been sheltered and was supported by the Lord of the Wyr?

The most important thing about these autopsies was how any information might aid in the investigation of the attacks. Dr. Medusa What's-her-name had foresight. She knew the Wyr would have a keen interest in the proceedings and had kept the autopsy procedure clean of any scent contaminants. Tiago found a box of gloves on a corner cabinet and snapped on a pair. He caught movement out of the corner of his eye as the medusa took a sudden step forward. Even her head snakes looked alarmed. Rune put a restraining hand on the medical examiner's arm, smiling down into her anxious face.

"It's okay," Rune told her. "Tiago knows what he's doing. He won't mess with your results."

She nodded although she looked uncertain. They both fell silent and watched as Tiago examined the bodies. The visual inspection didn't tell him anything he did not already know. Inspecting them by scent was more complicated, as the bodies had accumulated layers of different scents. No matter how tightly a crime scene might be processed, a certain amount of scent contamination occurred. Aside from their individual scents, these bodies carried scents from the last places they had been, including the scene where they had died, along with residue from the plastics and rubber gloves that had been used in transporting, storing and examining them.

He could detect the faintest hint of cigarette smoke on all three. He checked the teeth and gums of each dead guy. None of them had smoked, which didn't surprise him. Wyr, with their greater sense of smell, tended not to. Did that offer a clue to where they might have been, or had some police officer fucked up and taken a smoke break at the scene of the attack? Frowning, Tiago moved from the Wyr themselves to their clothing and possessions, which were sitting bagged and tagged on a nearby table.

None of the guys had carried an ID. All they had carried were weapons and cash, and one of them had a half-empty packet of Chiclets. Still, their possessions helped to solidify scent impressions much better. Confident now, Tiago said, "They met at a bar. Someplace that serves draft beer, greasy food, and allows smoking, because none of these guys smoked."

"That's certainly consistent with the contents of their stomachs," said the medusa. She gave Tiago a look of surprised approval. "Two of them ate a meal of fish and chips, and the other one had a large cheeseburger with jalapenos. All three had consumed a certain amount of alcohol, maybe some form of Dutch courage as they were gearing themselves up to fight. I don't have a tox report back yet, but at a guess I don't think they would have imbibed enough to impair driving or motor skills. That takes some heavy drinking for Wyr, and there's no other evidence to support it."

Tiago looked at Rune. "There are other scents of Elder Races on their things, but no one scent stands out. I just keep getting hints. We need to have someone canvass the bars in the area that are frequented by the Elder Races."

Rune nodded. "Somebody served dinner and drinks to these fuckers. We might get lucky and get a positive ID on one or all of them, which would mean we could look for where they lived and check to see if any of them received any large amounts of money recently. They had some motive for the attack. Maybe they got paid to do it."

"We might also get a description of somebody they met," Tiago said.

The two sentinels exchanged hard-edged predatory smiles. They didn't have to ask what the other one was thinking. In that moment both Wyr were of one accord. It felt good to go on the hunt and not stay stuck in a position where they were forced to react to a situation beyond their control.

"Skeert of the both of you," muttered Dr. Telemar.

A cold voice spoke from the doorway. "Or maybe you're hoping to plant evidence that leads other investigators away from the Wyr," said Dark Fae Commander Arethusa. The tall female stepped into the room. "I should not be surprised to see you here contaminating the autopsy results on the three bodies."

The beast in Tiago lunged to the end of its chain and clawed at the air. Everything dropped away except the sight of the Commander's anger-filled face. Growling, Tiago started forward. Arethusa drew the two short swords she had strapped to her back.

A Mack truck slammed into Tiago. He crashed back into a wall. The truck turned into Rune, who pinned him with a muscled forearm across his neck. Dragos's First went nose-to-nose with him, his fierce golden lion's eyes blazing. "*No*, Tiago."

Tiago swore and tried to heave Rune off him. He was heavier than the other sentinel and stronger, but Rune was faster than shit and had the weight of his long, lean body distributed too well for Tiago to shake off. He said, "She's been asking for an ass-kicking for a while now." His voice had changed, turned more guttural.

"My give-a-shit button's broken. You're my boy, and I say no." Rune slapped him in a controlled flat-handed blow. It dislodged the sunglasses on Tiago's face. They fell to the floor with a clatter. "Snap out of it."

Dr. Telemar backed into a far corner. Arethusa stared at them, her face whitening.

Tiago snarled at Rune and heaved again. He gripped Rune's imprisoning arm with taloned hands and shoved as hard as he could, but he could get no leverage with which to break the other sentinel's hold.

Rune stared point-blank into Tiago's gaze, his handsome face hard and unflinching. The First said in a calm voice, "I know you're in there. You can hear me or you would have drawn blood by now. Think for a minute. Who needs us?"

Tiago sucked in a deep breath that shuddered through his frame as he fought to contain the beast. He turned his head to one side and growled, "Niniane."

"That's right." Rune lowered his voice to a barely audible murmur. "You better listen to me. You fuck things up now and you can't go back. They'll never let you get near her again. Got it?"

That snapped Tiago's head back into place like nothing else could have. He stopped straining against the other sentinel's hold and said, "Got it."

Rune's tawny eyebrows rose. He lessened the pressure he had been exerting against Tiago's clavicle. Tiago remained quiescent, as he maintained a hard grip on his beast. Rune nodded, let go and clapped him on the shoulder.

Rune turned to face the Dark Fae Commander. He said, "Okay, first, you've been harshing my good friend's chi. I'm not liking you so much right now."

"I'll add a second point to that," said Dr. Telemar, who stepped out of her corner. All her head snakes were looking at the Dark Fae Commander. "I'm not into inter-demesne politics, but you just maligned the integrity of my office and I'll not stand for it. There's not one damn thing out of place with my autopsy procedures, up to and including how the bodies of these Wyr are being processed."

Despite getting her ass chewed on two different fronts, the cold anger in the Commander's angular face dissipated. She straightened out of her defensive fighting crouch and looked thoughtful as she sheathed her swords. A couple of the medusa's head snakes turned to blink at Rune. He gave them a what-the-fuck shrug.

Arethusa looked from Rune to Tiago. She said, "I heard what you said."

Tiago might have gotten a grip on his beast's leash again, but he didn't trust himself to speak. The muscle in his jaw jumped. He bent to pick up his Ray-Bans and slid them back on his nose.

Rune was the one who replied. "To which bit are you referring, Commander?"

Arethusa looked at Tiago. He noticed she took care to remain on the other side of the room, but the scent of aggression had faded from her pheromones. She said to him, "Whatever else the Wyr could be involved in, it really does matter to you that the Dark Fae heir might need your help."

"You think?" Tiago said from between his teeth. Sometime he wanted to get just one good shot at the Commander's face. One of these days, Alice, he thought as he stared at her. Straight to the goddamn moon.

Rune said, "I have to ask you, Commander. What part of this"—he made an all-encompassing gesture that included the three dead Wyr, and Tiago and himself—"makes any kind of sense to you? Why would we send Tiago to find and protect Niniane and then send these bozos after her too? There are a lot easier and more straightforward ways to execute a couple of guys."

Arethusa sucked a tooth as she considered them. "When I came in, you were talking about trying to get a positive ID on these three so you could look for a money trail. That's what we did for Geril," she said. "We looked for a money trail. You know what we found? He had a new Bank of America account in which he had received a substantial deposit this week from an Illinois company owned by Cuelebre Enterprises."

Tiago's eyes narrowed. "Which company?" he asked.

"Tri-State Financial Services," Arethusa said.

Tiago looked at Rune, and they both started to smile.

Dr. Telemar spoke up. "I missed something. What is there to smile about in that?"

Tiago crossed his arms as he leaned back against one of the autopsy tables. He told Arethusa and the medusa, "Somebody made another mistake. Cuelebre Enterprises doesn't own a company named Tri-State Financial Services."

The Dark Fae Commander's eyes narrowed, her expression full of skepticism. "And you know this so conveniently how?"

Tiago said, "Cuelebre Enterprises owns six companies that are based in Illinois. Thanks to Urien's and Dragos's recent fight over Urien's attempt to secure a U.S. defense contract, those companies have come under a great deal of scrutiny at the head office in New York. Stocks have taken a dip, and Dragos is tired of fucking around with them. He's working on getting them stabilized so that he can sell them off. If you dig deeper into your information, I think what you're going to find is that you've got a dummy corporation on your hands."

Arethusa stepped forward. She gripped the edge of an autopsy table and leaned on her hands, her mouth pursed as she regarded the corpse in front of her without appearing to really see it. "Okay," she said after a few minutes. "I'll check it out. Now what do you mean, somebody made another mistake?"

"Whoever set Geril and his buddies on Niniane didn't know how much self-defense training the sentinels had given her," Tiago said.

"Which was a lot," Rune added. "She was not exactly an easy study. That's simple enough to verify. Just ask her. We had to keep going over and over some things. That training was what saved Niniane's life."

Tiago continued, "They also didn't know how much scrutiny Cuelebre Enterprises' Illinois companies have been under recently in New York, or they might have chosen a different, less easily verified way to frame the Wyr. They also didn't know that I had come to Chicago, or they would never have sent these guys after her. And that's not all. We've now got two attempts to frame the Wyr. What do you have when you have the same MO in two different crimes?"

This time Dr. Telemar stepped forward to join the circle around the autopsy table. She cradled a snake head in her hands and pet it, her eyes wide with fascination. She said, "You've either got a copycat or you've got the same perp."

Rune smiled at the medusa. He said, "It's possible we could have a copycat, but unlikely. A copycat would have to know some pretty obscure information that we're only just now piecing together, which would indicate some intimate knowledge of the perpetrator of the first attack. He would also have to have the means with which to act very fast in setting up the second attempt. The odds are we're looking at the same perp for both attempts."

Tiago buried his chin in the heel of one hand as he regarded the Dark Fae Commander from under his brows. Arethusa cocked her head at him and said, "What."

"Something else occurs to me," he said. "We're only talking now by accident. And if we hadn't talked, we wouldn't all know what we know."

Arethusa said, "Are you thinking someone has been counting on that lack of communication between the Dark Fae and the Wyr?"

Tiago nodded. "Maybe if we start sharing more on our investigations, we should keep it quiet. That might give our perp the opportunity to make another mistake."

The Dark Fae Commander's eyebrows shot up. "Well, nobody's going to see me chatting up you guys in public," said Arethusa. "Everybody knows I think you're all a bunch of rat bastards."

More blah-fucking-blah happened. Other people called it pleasantries. Polite chitchat. Tiago called it agonizing. The beast crouched inside him and waited, and its silence took over his mind.

He watched the slight rhythmic flutter of the pulse at the Dark Fae Commander's neck, and took note of the increasing flicker of the medusa's nictitating membrane. The medusa did not look at him directly again, but half a dozen of her head snakes peered at him from around her waist and shoulders. They tasted the air as they watched him with their tiny jeweled eyes glittering.

Tiago's sharp hearing caught a slight buzz, and his entire attention focused on tracking it. The tiny sound emitted from the front pocket of Rune's jeans. He watched as Rune dragged out his iPhone, checked the screen and frowned. Rune started to put the cell back in his pocket while he began uttering good-bye blah-fucking-blahs.

Tiago's breath stilled, and every muscle in his body tightened. He knew in his bones that the message Rune had received was about Niniane. And Rune didn't appear to be inclined to share.

Before the instinct had the chance to fully form in his mind, Tiago sprang forward and snatched the iPhone out of Rune's hands. The Dark Fae Commander grabbed one of her swords and the medusa made a high-pitched sound and leaped back two feet. All her head snakes whipped around to hiss at Tiago as Rune swore and spun to snatch at his phone. The other sentinel might be famous for his speed, but Tiago caught him by surprise and he was too late.

"Goddammit, Tiago!" Rune swore. His lion's eyes blazed. *"GIVE IT BACK!"*

Tiago drove the heel of his hand into Rune's chest and knocked him backward as he tilted the phone to read the screen.

It was a text from Aryal:

OUT 4 BEERS + SHOTS. PD CHICK > BIG RED'S = GD COP BAR. FARY NEEDS STRSS RLIEF BAD. GNNA TRY 2 GT HR LAID.

Tiago's beast snapped its leash.

≈ ELEVEN ≈

The thunderstorm rolled over Chicago in a matter of minutes. It blanketed the city with heavy, sulfurous black clouds, a deluge of lashing rain and flashes of jagged lightning that split the sky, followed by rolling sonic booms that rattled skyscrapers.

The predator hurtled through the storm. When his huge wings rose and hammered down, the sky roared in response and the earth shook.

He ignored his pursuer. In flight, he was the one who was faster, his powerful body streamlined for slicing through the air. He was also the creator of the storm. It fulminated around him while hurricane-force winds buffeted the one who fought to follow. The storm blew that one behind.

The predator was one of the world's best trackers. Locating his prey was child's play. She was too innocent. She had not known to hide from him. As he fell to earth, he changed to wear his human skin, but the beast that raged inside him was far older and much more dangerous than a human being. His clothing, absorbed when he took his Wyr form, settled into place again on his body.

He slammed open the doors of the Big Red bar and stalked inside.

The predator paused for a heartbeat as human sights, sounds and smells assaulted him. Laughter, music, liquor and food.

Perfume, perspiration and aftershave. He ignored the fragile humans. He noted the location of the real possible threats, the harpy and the Vampyre. They leaned against one end of the bar while they talked and watched a crowded dance floor, their alert, watchful, roaming gazes belying their bodies' casual posture.

Then he caught sight of her, his prey, on the packed dance floor and she was—

He gave his head a sharp, disbelieving shake. The beast inside him roared.

She was a small, exquisitely boned, deliciously curved, raven-haired beauty who shimmered with so much molten light as she danced, she looked like she was a creature made of sunlight and lightning. Enormous gray eyes glittered under sultry lids, and her soft, glistening lips were painted the intoxicating color of poppies. Her slender, curved white legs with those narrow delicate knees were naked, and her tiny feet arched in four-inch fuck-me silver high-heeled shoes. She was a teacup temptress, undulating in that silvery light slip of scandalous something that she wore—

Dress, it was a dress—

That depraved piece of skintight luminescence wasn't a dress. It was a heart attack waiting to happen. It was covered with so many tiny, sparkly silver dangling *sequins*, and it was so low in the neck and so high in the hem, it barely covered her nipples and her sweet little round ass. With every graceful flirtatious dance move she made, the neckline and the hem hovered on the edge of unveiling the treasures they were intended to guard.

And didn't every red-blooded male in the building know it. The room reeked of sexual interest. Hot interested males from all over the room watched as she danced, undressing her with their eyes. He growled low in his throat.

Mine.

The predator bared his teeth and promised them all murder as he advanced across the room.

Normally Niniane loved to go out. But tonight, no matter how she threw herself into the effort, she couldn't relax and enjoy the moment.

The whole thing started when Aubrey and Kellen stepped out on the patio to protest the harpy's presence. Heaven only knew where Arethusa had gone, or Niniane had no doubt the Commander would have joined them. Then Carling had strolled out to take a seat at the table, listening without comment to the argument.

Not that it was much of an argument for long. Niniane told them all, "I know that Dragos and his sentinels had nothing to do with the attack."

Deep lines bracketed Kellen's mouth. They scored his face from fine-molded nostrils to the sides of his mouth, evidencing his displeasure. He said, "Your highness, please."

"Try not to be more of an idiot than you can help," Aryal told him. The Justice glared at her, his expression full of offense. The harpy clicked her tongue at him, looking remarkably avian despite being in her human form.

Niniane swallowed a bubble of hysterical laughter. Carling met her gaze. "Never send a harpy on a mission of diplomacy," the Vampyre murmured. "Are you sure about this?"

"I have examined the facts, and yes, I am sure," she replied in a firm voice. She looked hard at Aubrey and Kellen to make sure they heard her.

Aryal turned to Carling in a sudden movement. "The Wyr have the right to investigate what happened," the harpy said. "If there are other Wyr involved, we are responsible for bringing them to justice."

The warm breeze ruffled the hem of Carling's caftan, the plain cotton rippling around her bare feet. Carling's perfect face remained impassive, her gaze on Niniane.

Niniane looked from Carling to Aryal then to the two Dark Fae males. Both Aubrey and Kellen frowned at her, their gazes intent.

You should be careful where you step, Niniane.

You're in a fragile place.

Her back muscles were rigid from the tension she would not let show in her face. She would not deny her friends, but if she was not careful, she could also alienate two Powerful government officials and much-needed Dark Fae allies.

A heavy fullness pressed at the back of her throat. It tasted a little like grief. She said to the two males, "The Wyr have been friends of the Dark Fae before. They are my good friends now. You must accept this."

A slow feral smile began to spread over Aryal's angular face.

Niniane turned to the harpy and continued, "The crimes have been committed against me, not the Wyr. There have been more than one, and they have occurred within the Dark Fae demesne. There is no doubt in my mind that those involved acted without the official sanction or knowledge of the Wyrkind. It must also be said—those Wyr were not the only offenders. Therefore, it is up to us to dispense justice, and you must accept this."

The harpy's smile froze in midformation. She searched Niniane's expression with a sharp unspoken question. The fullness entered Niniane's eyes and turned them damp, but her face remained composed. She watched as comprehension came to Aryal. The harpy bowed her head in silent acquiescence.

Niniane said, "We do recognize how important it is for the Wyr to be engaged in this process. They must demonstrate their good intentions to the Dark Fae during this time of transition."

"Uh," Aryal said, her voice subdued. "That makes sense."

Niniane dropped the more formal speech. "And I have had a difficult week. A visit from my good friends is a comfort to me. Please accept my invitation to join us until the coronation. I know Dragos will send a representative anyway, and I would be grateful for the companionship and the chance to say good-bye properly as I return home."

She looked at Aubrey then, and she couldn't keep the entreaty out of her eyes. There it all was, said as best as she could manage under the circumstances. It was an assumption of authority, an official declaration of alliance and a statement of loyalty, and a compromise and promise to change, all wrapped together into one package. And it would not be a bad thing at all to show everybody that she had Powerful friends as allies, even if they would not be staying with her for long.

Aubrey studied her then glanced at a sober-looking Aryal. Finally he assessed Carling's neutral expression. Come on, Niniane urged him. This is a good thing. Accept it and back me up.

Aubrey turned back to her. *Please forgive me for asking this, highness,* he said silently. *Are you willing to share the facts as you have examined them with us at a more private time? I do not mean to question your judgment, only to ask that you help allay my concern for your safety.*

She smiled at him, warmed by his care for her dignity in front of the others. She told him, *Of course I will.*

Aubrey took a deep breath. "We must not forget our own responsibility in all of this," he said aloud. "I am the one who made the appalling mistake of choosing Geril, who is, after all, the one who caused you the real injury. I cannot apologize enough for that." He offered her a small grave smile. "And how could you not want your friends at a time like this? It must be difficult to leave behind the home you have known since you were a child. I believe this will be a very good way for you to transition."

Niniane breathed out a sigh of relief that was shakier than she would have liked. She turned to the harpy. "So will you guys come—if Dragos approves, of course?"

Aryal touched her shoulder with a smile. "Be real, pipsqueak. How often has the Old Man said no to you? We wouldn't miss this for the world."

So. Not quite up shit creek, not quite without a paddle—yet.

It was agreed that the sentinels would work with Carling's entourage to provide security for Niniane as part of the short-term arrangement until the investigation into the attacks was concluded. "We will be visiting together anyway," Niniane said. "They have guarded me many times over the years and we know each other well."

Then Niniane nodded to Aubrey, Kellen and Carling as they each bid her goodnight and withdrew. At a gesture from her, Duncan withdrew to stand just inside the patio doors again where he went into a statuelike stillness. When they were all gone, or at least as gone as they were going to get, she sat back in her seat.

Niniane muttered, "So you'll be around for a couple of weeks now. At least that's bought me some time."

Aryal narrowed her eyes. "What are you talking about, bought you some time?"

She slumped forward with a groan. She laid her cheek on the table. "Time for the investigation on the attacks, time to find out who I can and can't trust. At least a little bit. At least for some things."

Aryal snorted. "That's easy."

Niniane smacked the harpy's knee. "I know I can trust *you*, goofball," she said. "I don't know what I was thinking to let myself get shaken even for a few minutes. I mean, any harpy that will let me gussy her up in pink lipstick and pigtails—"

Aryal smacked her in the back of the head. "Will you shut UP about that. God!"

She gave Aryal an evil grin then sobered. "I'm talking about the people I'm going to be living with for the rest of my life. I have to make Powerful friends fast in the Dark Fae 'hood, or the brutal fact of the matter is, I don't think I'm going to last very long."

Aryal laid her head on the table too, facing Niniane, her gaunt features turning serious. "You're going to be okay," Aryal promised. Her scowl promised other things as well, like she would rain hell down on anybody that tried to say otherwise. "You're going to live for a long damn time. We'll work it out."

Niniane tried to swallow past a dry throat. Her fingers were cold. She rubbed her hands together. "And since we're on the subject of finding people to trust, I've also got to find somebody to marry."

Aryal's head reared up. "What?"

"I've made a shopping list for a husband," she whispered. "He's got to be Powerful and influential, and someone who wants the throne but can't get it on his own because he's got to have a vested interest in keeping me alive."

The harpy's stormy eyes widened. "Oh, good God, *gak*."

Niniane felt her eyes flood with tears again. This time, no matter how she tried, they spilled over, and then there was no containing the harpy's panic.

Which was why Niniane was now dancing and trying to pretend she was having a good time.

Because Aryal talked to Duncan who talked to Cameron, who cooked up the idea of a trip out to Big Red's. Big Red's was a nearby bar owned by a retired cop and frequented by cops. It was a sturdy place rather than a fancy one, with solid wood furniture and a sizable dance floor and a small kitchen behind the bar that served a limited menu of food, primarily sandwiches and fries. The building was easily defended, and even better, Cameron knew the owner and vouched for his integrity. Niniane, who would have given almost anything to get out of the hotel from hell, jumped at the chance to escape for a few hours. She threw herself into the venture and put on makeup, an outfit, shoes, the whole works.

Besides, she adored music and loved to dance. She did, really. Get her under some stress, and she was bound to turn manic and do something like this anyway. Aryal knew. Niniane had closed down more than a few nightclubs in her time. She would close down Big Red's too. She would click into her groove any minute now, baby, and shake it out.

But clicking into her groove meant she first had to find it. Her body felt disjointed, graceless. She felt disconnected from the music blaring over the dance-floor speakers. It sounded like a great crash of meaningless noise. The human policewoman, Cameron, dressed casually in jeans, a tank top, and a light summer jacket that hid her gun from casual view, threaded through the other dancers. The floor was packed with a rowdy, good-natured crowd, so Cameron stayed close, while Aryal and Duncan kept watch from one side.

Niniane forced herself to smile, and it felt horrible and fake, a rubbery stretch of tired facial muscles. Nobody else seemed to notice. Cameron smiled back, her cinnamon-sprinkled features lit with pleasure at Niniane's apparent enjoyment. The whole thing was gruesome, really.

Today had been one long, strange day from hell. Where was Tiago now? Aryal said he had met up with Rune. Maybe now that Rune and Aryal were here, Tiago really would head back to New York. He had kept his promise to her. He had stayed until she was healed. She knew how important keeping a promise was to all the sentinels. Would he leave without saying good-bye or returning her calls? He was such a proud, aloof man, and she had rejected his support in front of Carling and the whole Dark Fae delegation, so he might very well be gone.

Yes, he had made a mistake when he forgot to tell her about the Wyr, but after everything he had done for her, he deserved better than what she had given him.

She kept remembering that flash of anarchy in Tiago's face when she had sent him away. She had hurt him, and oh God, she missed him so much it was like suffering an amputation, and she wanted to ask somebody how she had suddenly gotten transported into a Victorian novel.

A marriage of convenience? Really?

She coughed out an angry, hurting laugh. The dance music obliterated the sound.

Look at this progression. First she was afraid to have an affair with Tiago. Then she was afraid she would only get a little time with him. Then she was grateful she might get any time at all with him. Then she lost any hope when she sent him away. Now, when Aubrey and Kellen agreed they would tolerate the presence of her Wyr friends for a few weeks, she didn't even know if Tiago was still around. If he was, there was a good chance he was no longer interested. Even if he was still interested, she didn't know how she could stomach having an affair with him while she simultaneously looked for a husband.

And that was just what was happening in her personal life.

How had everything gotten so twisted? She almost felt nostalgic for the time when all she had to worry about was Urien trying to kill her. Urien had been Powerful and scary, so she lived under his enemy Dragos's protection in New York. End of story.

Maybe she had put things together wrong in her head. (But she didn't think so.) Maybe a marriage of convenience wasn't necessary. (Even though she was pretty sure it was.) Maybe things would look different in the morning after a good night's sleep. (And too many tequila shots.)

And why did this have to be a nonsmoking bar? Her teeth clenched as she looked around. Everybody knew how much stress cops lived with on a daily basis. Somebody in this damn joint had to have cigarettes. One way or another she was going to beg or steal a pack.

The air grew static. The tiny hairs along the back of her neck and arms rose.

She knew that feeling. She knew it.

The lights flickered and dimmed. A speaker near the doors emitted a feedback shriek then another did, and a lightbulb over the bar exploded in a shower of sparks.

Agonized hope leaped inside. She turned, looking for him. She was too small to see over the heads of most of the people surrounding her. Then the speakers on the dance floor screamed, and the music came to an abrupt halt.

People stopped dancing. She heard snatches of good-natured grumbling. ". . . storm outside . . . must have been a lightning strike close by . . ."

That was when she saw him. He was still dressed in his black fatigues and weaponry. He was taller than most of the humans and infinitely more hazardous. The strong bones of his face were hatchet-sharp, his beautifully cut mouth drawn taut, and he wore dark glasses that turned him into an unpredictable stranger. His face was turned toward her as he shouldered through the crowd. A path opened on the dance floor between them as the people there took one look at him and backed away.

Her body reacted first as she stared at him. She started to shake. Her breathing grew choppy. Her pulse ratcheted up its speed, turning her veins into an autobahn. Then her emotions caught up with the rest of her.

Elation that he hadn't left.

Astonishment, as the sheer force of his presence jettisoned her into a different reality. Everything around her became sharper, clearer, more vibrantly colored. Everything inside her reached a level of intensity that had her nearly coming out of her skin.

And there was uncertainty. There was very much uncertainty. Because he looked so cruel, so sadistic. No, sexy. No, sadistic. Oh shit.

He stopped in front of her, an immense wall of muscled male aggression. His dark sunglasses angled down toward her, and his harsh-edged assassin's face was the one that had promised to burn down the world of the most Powerful Nightkind leader on Earth.

Whatever you do, don't say sowwy.

She tried speaking his name. It came out a shaky mess. "Tiago?"

"What the hell are you wearing?" he barked.

The question slapped her in the face.

Excuse me?

She fell back a step as hurt spread through her middle like a bruise. She may not have been able to get fully engaged in the outing, but she had still put effort into her appearance because she wanted to look nice.

She pointed to the door and said between her teeth, "You need to go outside and come back in with a different attitude, mister."

He snarled, "What I am going to do is take you back to your room so you can put some *goddamn clothes on*."

An invisible gremlin must have been in the room, because it doused her temper with lighter fluid and struck a match. A wave of heat flashed over her skin. She stamped her foot and shouted, "I look pretty!"

Dr. Death bent his head down to go nose-to-nose with her. He bellowed, "You look half naked!"

She disconnected from her body as she transported to a place only he could make her go. She didn't have to put up with this shit. She cocked her head sideways and glared at her reflection in his sunglasses. That was when she heard herself say, "So what are you going to do about it, spank me?"

The insolent words echoed in the air.

He stared at her in incredulity. A sliver of sanity whimpered and tried to crawl back into her head.

"Sure," said Tiago. "That works."

The floor fell away, and her world turned over as he snatched her up by the waist and threw her over his shoulder. She *oophed* as her midsection connected with hard muscle-covered bone.

"Wait," she tried to say. She had no air in her lungs, so it came out something between a squeak and a wheeze. "I take it back. I want a do-over."

"Tough shit," he said. He wrapped one arm around the back of her legs and strode off the dance floor.

"Do you understand how popular I am?" she hissed. She bent at the waist and flailed around until she managed to latch on to his ear with her nails. She pinched hard. He growled and jerked his head sideways, trying to dislodge her hold. "You can't spank a faerie princess in public in America. Do you want to get shot on sight?"

"Don't worry, your tempestuousness," he snapped. "There won't be any witnesses."

He spotted a hall toward the back of the building and made for it. There had to be restrooms, an office, something.

Niniane brushed her hair out of her eyes. Blood pounded in her face. His long legs rose like tree trunks in front of her upside-down gaze. She braced herself with a forearm against the small of his back and tried to look around. Her head bobbed. Where were the others? She tried again. "Tiago, it just fell out of my mouth. I didn't mean it. I'm just sayin'!"

"Shut up." His voice sounded shredded. He said to someone nearby, "Guard the hall."

A familiar voice cursed. She looked in the direction from which it came, and finally caught sight of Aryal and Cameron. They were herding the crowd back onto the dance floor, while people stared at them with varying degrees of curiosity, laughter and alarm. By the bar, Duncan shouted for someone to start up the music again.

Niniane thought she saw something odd as Aryal looked back at them. The harpy's eyes were narrowed, her angular face white with strain. Niniane might have been mistaken. Dangling upside down, everything looked wrong. People moved in weird ways, their smiles all turned down, and liquid spilled from drinks falling up. It was like looking in a carnival hall of mirrors in a dream.

Tiago strode down the hallway. Office, to the right. It was a small, cluttered cubbyhole, piled with yellowed papers. Restrooms. He could hear someone moving around in one and the whine of a small motor as a hand dryer started. Niniane wriggled on his shoulder and almost slid off. He hitched her light little body back into place and kept going. There, toward the emergency back exit, was an open door.

He veered toward it and strode into a shadowed room filled with metal shelves and boxes. One corner of the storeroom had been turned into a break area, with a battered comfortable-looking couch, a sagging armchair and a scarred coffee table with a pile of old magazines. A folded afghan blanket lay on the back of the couch, and a unit against one wall held a clunky thirteen-inch TV with an antenna and a digital converter box. A microwave sat on a middle shelf.

He came to the middle of the floor and stopped. She waited a moment. Nothing happened. Tiago's massive body stood rigid.

She let go of his ear, and maybe her fingers accidentally brushed along the side of his neck.

"I look pretty," she whispered. She rested her cheek against his wide, muscled back.

He took a breath. She felt it shudder through his whole frame. He laid one hand against the back of her thigh and stroked her leg. The light rasp of calluses on his broad palm left a trail of goose bumps on her sensitive bare skin.

Then he bent forward. With exquisite gentleness he eased her onto her feet. He kept his hands at her narrow waist until she had her balance back. They looked at each other, her head tilted up, his bent down. She felt absurdly tiny whenever she was this close to him, and warmed in a way that had nothing to do with their physical bodies.

"I am so goddamn old," he said. His voice was so quiet she almost couldn't hear him. "And you are the most beautiful thing I have ever seen."

She rested her fingers on his forearms so that she could relish the heat of his skin as she looked up into his half-hidden stranger's face. The aggression had splintered and left him looking shaken and—vulnerable. He was such a self-contained fortress. In all the years of their acquaintance, she had never seen him look this way. She reached up to take his sunglasses off. His obsidian eyes glittered in the shadowed room.

"If you think I'm beautiful, why didn't you say so?" she asked. Her breath hiccuped. "Why are you so mad at me?"

Listen to her. She was going to be the queen who stamped her foot and cried because her feelings got hurt. Whole nations would tremble in fear.

He cradled her face with both hands. They were so big they encompassed the graceful curve of her head. He growled, "You drive me out of my mind. You make me so fucking crazy I can't think straight. Did you even notice? Every male out there, along with several of the women, were undressing you with their eyes—and they didn't have far to go. You can't go out in public like this. I mean, Niniane. What. The. Hell."

He was winding himself tight again by talking about it. His face and body clenched. She blinked as she stared up at him. Light dawned.

He was so jealous and possessive, he was burning up with it.

That could only mean one thing. He still wanted her.

She said, "So you like the dress."

He glared at her, the picture of startled offense. *"That's not a dress."*

Delight tasted like honey mead and turned her drunk. She started to smile. "Then what is it?"

"It's–it's—" His gaze ran compulsively down the length of her body and grew ravenous. He had to swallow to clear his throat. He said, his voice gone husky, "Young lady, that thing barely covering your body is cause for a street riot."

Her smile widened. She took one of his hands in both of hers. His hand was huge and filled with killing strength. Veins patterned the expansive back and ran down long calloused fingers. She ran his hand down the sequins that covered the dress. "It feels good, doesn't it?" she murmured.

He had taken countless lovers throughout his long life, and they had all been strong-limbed warrior women who could take a good pounding. They hadn't expected anything afterward except to walk away. Niniane was such an exotic creature to him, with her love of feminine fripperies and the lush delicacy of her body. With the shabby storeroom as a backdrop, she looked shocking and glamorous, like shadowed lightning, and the bright, tiny dangling things as they ran over his fingers felt cool and hard like shards of ice. Entranced, he fingered one and breathed, "Hell, yeah."

Her smile faded, and her huge gaze gathered the shadows from the room around her. "I'm sorry I sent you away like that," she said.

His hand turned and he squeezed her fingers. "I'm sorry too, faerie," he said. "I knew about your past. I should have been more careful, and I wasn't. There's no excuse. I was thoughtless and I fucked up."

She reached up and laid her fingers against the warm, carved edge of his lips. For someone who could look so brutal, his mouth had a severe elegance, stamped as it was with both temper and sensuality. "I thought you might have gone back to New York," she said. "I missed you so much already."

He opened his mouth and took her forefinger between his teeth. He nipped at her with such sensual enjoyment it sent pleasure rippling down her body. "I already told you once." His voice had darkened, turned gravelly. "I'm not leaving."

He said the lie with such conviction her truthsense tried to convince her to believe him. She closed her eyes and explored his face with her fingers, reading the strong, heavy frame of his bone structure like Braille. His lips moved feather-soft against her palm. She felt like someone was dropping stones, one by one, on her chest, in a slow-building pressure. It was getting hard to breathe. Soon the weight would become intolerable and crush her ribs.

In the main room somebody finally got the music back up. It roared back on with a suddenness that made her eyes pop open. She looked so surprised as she tottered on her four-inch heels that Tiago laughed and yanked her against his chest. The Black Eyed Peas came over the speakers and rocked it out. The walls of the building vibrated as lyrics careened headlong through the air.

Still laughing, he picked her up, turned and put her against a wall. He held her up at a height where they were face-to-face. He made it look effortless, with one arm under her hips to brace her. With his face alight and his black eyes sparkling, he had such a barbaric beauty it took her breath away.

Then his Power mantled over her, and she felt a need for him that was so terrible it drew her knees up and sank into her DNA, and she knew in that moment she would never be free of it, or him. He was carving himself into the deepest, most secret places inside of her, and she felt herself reforming in response. She was Galatea, made of stone, coming to life as he fashioned her.

He nudged his hips between her knees and took hold of one of her ankles to draw her leg around his waist. She wrapped her other leg around him and locked her ankles behind him. She ran her hands across his broad-muscled shoulders. My God, she had to take an anatomy class. Every single one of those muscles had its own name.

She wound her arms around his neck and watched as that sparkle of laughter in his eyes turned dark with a different kind of savagery. He widened his legs and pushed his pelvis against her. Her head fell back as she felt the thick arch of his cock through the fabric of their clothes. She rubbed herself against him, whimpering, and he hid his face in her neck as he swore under his breath. The massive weight of his body as he pressed her into the wall was exquisite, as excruciating as everything else was between them. He wouldn't fit easily, she knew. He was too big, and it had been too long since she had last taken a lover. They would have to work to get him in, and it would burn so good as her muscles stretched tight to accommodate him, and then—and then—

She ground harder against him, aching for the burn. Gasping, he bucked his hips in response. He ran his free hand under the short hem of her dress, searching for and finding the thong she wore. He muttered something unintelligible as he shredded it, his hot breath blasting her cheek. He reached farther, curving his arm under her ass as he probed her plump, slick labia with gentle shaking fingers. She reached between them as well, arching her back against the cold concrete wall as she dug to locate the zipper of his fatigues.

He bit her neck, her ear, in sharp, stinging nips. He gasped, "You deserve slow, but oh fuck, I don't think I have it in me."

They couldn't do slow. Time was too precious, each irrecoverable moment arrowing into the past. They couldn't waste a single one.

"Just do it," she groaned in his ear. The lyrics of the song echoed her, eerily. *Do it do it do it . . .* He slipped the tip of one finger inside her, and it sent every one of her nerve endings into frenzy. She bucked and lost her grip on his zipper.

Niniane, I need to talk to you.

The sharp mental voice guillotined through the sexual haze that clouded her mind. She shook her head, disoriented. Who the hell was in her head? She managed to articulate, *What, now?*

Right now.

The mental signature of the speaker finally came to her. It was Rune. He sounded harsher and more commanding than she could remember ever hearing him.

Honey, you're killing him, Rune said. *You have to stop this. Shut it down. You're the only one who can.*

═ TWELVE ═

You're killing him.

The words were melodramatic, ridiculous. They made no sense. If they had come from anybody else, she would have lost her temper at the interruption.

But the words came from Rune, and they sent dread flashing through her system. She put her head back against the concrete wall and sucked in air. Her gaze darted around the room as she looked for danger. She found none. For the first time she took note of where they were. They were in a back storeroom of the bar.

Tiago angled his head to kiss her, his features flushed dark with sensuality, knifelike with need.

She jerked her face to the side. Somehow she managed to yank out the words. "We have to stop."

He froze and looked stricken. He sank down to his knees, and she slid down the wall with him. The friction tore sequins off the back of her dress. They scattered on the floor around them, winking like fallen stars. He let her body weight settle on his lap, braced both forearms on the wall over her head and put his forehead against hers. He ground out, "Don't do this, faerie. Not this time."

Rune had better have one compelling goddamn reason for this, or she was going to skin him alive.

She whimpered, "I'm sorry."

He threw back his head and shouted in silence as he drove

his fists into the concrete wall on either side of her head. The concrete cracked, showering gray dust down on their carpet of stars. The breath left her as she stared at his agonized face. She was appalled at what she had done. She rocked forward and threw her arms around his neck. His head came back down. He laid his cheek against hers to nuzzle her even as he hissed at her, his face contorted. His fists were still planted in the scars he had made on the wall. She sat on his thighs, legs splayed wide and felt surrounded, eclipsed by his tremendous body.

"I'm so sorry," she whispered again in his ear. She stroked his hair. He shuddered and remained silent as he struggled for control.

She couldn't see Rune, but he had to be somewhere close by to reach her with telepathy, probably just down the hall. She growled at him, *I just did a cruel thing to the both of us, so you start talking, and it better be good.*

Rune said, *Niniane, nobody will be sorrier than me if I'm wrong. But I've just spent the last few hours in Tiago's company. He behaved like I've never seen him behave before. He lost control more than once, and lost it bad.*

She listened to Rune's rapid words, her body clenched as tight as Tiago's. She cupped the back of his head protectively with both hands. He was breathing deep and hard and slow, like a runner in the middle of a marathon, his skin damp.

Nobody could blame you if you're looking for an affair, Rune said. *If you wanted some kind of comfort, something to hold on to for a little while before you assume the throne, and normally I would cheer you on. But I think Tiago is starting to mate with you, and you know what happens to Wyr when they mate. I hope to hell he hasn't gone too far already.*

She stopped breathing. Tiago, mating? With me?

How gorgeous, miraculous. How impossible and horrific.

Oh gods how I want it, and him.

I can't, shouldn't.

Several days ago the shocks had started coming. It had started with her uncle's death. Over the years, the thought of Urien dying had gradually become something like a fantasy, a vengeful daydream of what might happen sometime in a nebulous future.

When Dragos killed Urien, it catapulted her into a different reality. Every time she thought the shocks might slow down or stop, another one came along and smacked her upside the head. She was beginning to feel buffeted, incredulous, like she had gone swimming at high tide and the waves had caught hold of her. They were tumbling her head over heels, and she only just realized she might be drowning.

She did know what happened to Wyr when they mate. Wyr mated for life. Living in Dragos's Court, she had watched it happen more than once. The mating came from a complex combination of choice, sex, instinct, actions and emotion. All had to occur at the right intensity and time. Nobody fully understood when the mating became irrevocable. More deep than falling in love, it was a dangerous, often violent time. It was a rare occurrence for those long-lived Wyr known as the immortals. It was even rarer when a Wyr mated with someone who was not Wyr. All too often those pairings could have tragic consequences.

Pia's mother had mated with a human. When he had died, she had managed to hold on to life long enough to see Pia raised, and then she had faded away. Niniane remembered another time, around 1835, when a Wyr had mated with a Vampyre. They had been together until the American Civil War when differing loyalties had torn them apart. The Wyr had starved to death when the Vampyre left him.

I love him, she confessed to Rune in a small voice. As she did so, she admitted it for the first time to herself. Her arms and legs clenched on Tiago, and she held on to him with all her strength. She started to shake. She felt like she was coming apart at the seams.

Tiago swore, wrapped his arms around her and held her in a tight, bruising hold. "Okay," he said, his voice hoarse. "Don't shake like that, damn it. It's okay. Just tell me what happened. What went wrong?"

I just wanted a little time.

Rune's harsh mental voice gentled. *If you love him, then let him go, honey. You can't live his life, and the Dark Fae will never let a Wyr share your throne.*

She nodded but couldn't trust herself to speak for a few moments.

Tiago's head moved under her hands, his face turning toward her. "Faerie?"

Let him go, honey.

She dug deep inside, grabbed hold of her spine and straightened it. She forced her arms and legs to unlock. "Let me up."

He pulled back and frowned at her. She looked pallid to his sharp gaze, the layered black ends of her hair disheveled. Moments before she had looked rosy, flushed with desire. Now she looked like she was grieving. Those lovely enormous eyes of hers were dilated and depthless. He said in a quiet voice, "I don't think I should do that."

She looked at him steadily. "Please let me stand up now, Tiago."

His face clenched. He picked her up as he stood then let her slide down his torso, deliberately letting her feel the hard bulge of his erection, until her feet touched the floor. He watched the graceful slim line of her throat as she swallowed hard. She tried to pull away, but he took her by the elbows and held her to him. Every time he let her go something bad happened. He wasn't making that mistake again in a hurry. "Now," he said. "Explain what's wrong."

She put her hands on his chest and spread her fingers. There was not a spare ounce of flesh on him. He was all muscle, tendon and bone, his body carved out of an unimaginably long life spent fighting. She looked at her hands because it was easier than looking at his tight, concerned face.

She realized something that she had been picking up subliminally for a while. Dance music still pounded through the walls, but she heard nothing underneath it, no footsteps, clinking glasses, shouts of laughter, or any other sounds that normally filled a crowded bar. Aryal and Rune must have promised compensation to the bar owner and cleared the building, which was a measure of their sharp concern. The other sentinels would take watch and wait, guarding them and keeping everyone else away, because if Tiago was mating with her, right now he could be a danger to anyone else but her.

She wanted to say so many things to him.

Starting with I love you. Don't say it.

"You said you're not leaving," she said.

He stood unmoving under her hands, as steady and adamant as bedrock. "I'm not."

I need you. Bite it back.

"But you will," she told his chest. "You have to. You won't be able to help it."

"I'll stay," said the thunderbird as lightning flared outside. "And no Power on Earth can change that."

The intolerable pressure was building back in her chest. It goaded her on. "Dragos will call you," she said, her voice brittle. "And you'll fly back to him like a hawk to his wrist. Or another conflict will start somewhere in the world, and you'll take off to go to war. That's what you do, Tiago. You always take off. That's who you are."

He looked at her, breathing heavily, and said nothing. Pain blinded her.

She had not meant to tell him, but that pressure shoved the words out of her. "I am going to have to marry." The words blazed like meteorites between them. "I need to start looking for a husband right away."

His eyes flashed completely white. He enunciated, "Like hell."

Her stomach roiled. She had known this was going to be hard. It was so much harder than she imagined. "He has to be." She had to stop for air because he hadn't moved an inch but his tremendous body clenched into a weapon and his Power turned violent and heavy, a pressing weight in the storeroom. He looked murderous. "He's got to be Powerful and have influence—"

He moved faster than thought. He picked her up, whirled and slammed her back against the wall. She froze in shock. He shouted at her, "Like hell!"

She hit him. She couldn't help herself. She punched him in the chest. "And he's got to want the throne but not be able to get it by himself—"

Fury rampaged over his face. He sounded like a mortally wounded animal as he roared at her. "Nobody else can have you because you're mine!"

Dignity, sophistication, civility, they were meaningless strings of syllables in this place of raw emotion. She shouted back, "I can't be yours, and somebody's got to hang around so they can keep me alive!"

"Shut the hell up," he said, his voice savage. His features had reformed. He was a monstrous, merciless freak of nature, and she wanted him so badly she thought it would tear her to pieces from the inside.

She kept hitting him, the wild blows falling blind. "Will you get out of here, you son of a bitch? Go back to your life!"

She slapped him. She did everything she could think of to cause offense and drive him away. He took everything she dished out without a single flinch. He shook her once, a short, controlled snap of the wrist that rattled her torso, and he jerked her to him, his white eyes scorching. Then the monster's mouth slammed down over hers, and he devoured her, heart and soul.

She couldn't give either one of them to him fast enough. He dug into her mouth, his teeth and tongue hard, punishing. She clawed at his shirt as she kissed him back. She couldn't get him close enough, couldn't get the kiss deep enough.

Then he sank one fist into the hair at the back of her head. He forced her to look up at him. "Now you listen to me," he growled. "It's my turn to talk. I will not leave you. If Dragos or anybody else has a problem with it, they can take it up with me."

"The Dark Fae will never accept you," she said between her teeth.

"I don't give a shit about what the Dark Fae accept or don't accept," he snapped. "There's only one person and one thing that could make me leave, and that's you. Look me in the eye, faerie. Tell me you don't want me, and you better make me believe it."

Tears welled up and spilled out the corners of her eyes. They streaked down her cheeks to soak into her hair. She looked devastated. She worked to form the words, her mouth trembling. Someone else might have taken pity on her, but he wasn't a creature that knew much about pity. He knew a hell of a lot about fighting, though, and survival. He was fighting for the both of them now, if she only knew it.

She whispered, "I d-don't want you."

"What a bad liar you are," the monster whispered back to her. "I can smell how much you want me. I felt your wetness and all I want to do is lick it up. Your desire is coated all over my fingers. It's got me so hard I can barely stand up straight. You're a twist in my gut I can't unknot. I look for you when you're not with me. After you sent me away all I could think about was how much time I should give you before I came back to you. I counted it by hours, by minutes."

She stared at him, pinned and transfixed by his white eyes and the re-formed structure of his face. "That's just sex."

"Is it?" He showed her his teeth. "How bad did you miss me when you thought I went back to New York?"

"N-not bad." When she had found out he had left the hotel, she had curled up on her bed, unable to move.

"You said you missed me so much. How much is so much?"

"Not much."

He cocked his head. There was something almost plaintive about his ferocity now, a puzzlement that sliced at her. "Why are you still lying?" he asked. "Why can't you admit the truth to me? Is it such a horrible thing, to want me? Do you wish you didn't? Is that why you're trying so hard to drive me away?"

He was a lord of war. He instinctively knew more about assault tactics than she ever would. He had to know how he dug away at the foundation of her walls. It was a two-pronged attack, as he came at her from the outside but also from within, for she was her own worst enemy. She crumbled and sobbed, "I want you so much it's making me crazy."

"Then take me," he said. His grip in her hair loosened. He knelt in front of her, shocking her anew, and wrapped his arms around her waist as he laid his head against her breast. "Because nothing else matters."

She cradled his head and bowed over him, wiping her damp cheeks with one hand. "We're so different from each other."

"We live a long time. It's good to not be bored."

"I like pink lipstick," she sniffled. "And pretty shoes."

"Much to my surprise, I find that I do too," said the monster. His big hands moved up and down the shapely hourglass of her back, and cupped the back of her slender knees. Not once did he let the talons tipping his long fingers graze her thin, tender skin.

"I tried to think how I could walk away from the throne and follow you," she whispered. "But it's too late. Now everyone knows I'm alive. There would always be someone coming after me."

"You need me, faerie. I'll protect you." He rubbed his face in that extravagant, silly, wonderful heart-attack dress, and tiny strings of sequined beads tickled his nose. He smiled to feel those little fingers of hers thread through his short hair. Some time very soon he would have those kitten claws digging into his back while he made her scream with pleasure. His voice deepened. "You know we're good together. Even the fighting is fun."

They were so good. She buried her face in his hair. She whispered, "Rune was right, the Dark Fae will never accept a Wyr as ruler."

Rune? Tiago turned his head slightly away from her as he thought. He had known when the First had arrived at the bar, had heard when Rune and Aryal evacuated everyone, and none of it had mattered. That Rune had talked to Niniane—yes, that made sense. That explained it. She had been with Tiago all the way. Then she had changed so suddenly, he still felt mental whiplash. She had tried to drive him away, not for her sake, but for his. He was pretty sure he had Rune to thank for that.

Tiago would make a point of thanking him in person later.

But first things first.

"That dog won't hunt," said Tiago. "Because I don't give a fuck about ruling or the Dark Fae throne. But you should know, they're still going to object."

Her breathing stilled as she tried to think. It was hard to do, with hope twisting her into a pretzel inside. Could they do it, could they pull this off? The thought of Tiago coming with her was such a game changer, she couldn't compute the consequences.

Tiago tilted back his head to look at her. His white eyes had darkened to black again, and the lines of his face had returned to normal. He said, "Stop trying to think ahead to fix this. There's nothing to fix."

"But Tiago—"

"But nothing," he said. "I don't know all the answers. Nobody does; nobody can. Take hold of this, Niniane. Take hold of me, and don't let go for anything. We just need to do this one thing. We'll have some hellish fights ahead of us, and that's okay. We can meet whatever the future brings us. You knew you were looking ahead at a tough road anyway."

She touched his lower lip, studying him, her face grave. "You like to fight."

His lips pulled into a slow smile. "And I'm good at it."

It felt hazardous to her, but then everything did. Maybe she and Tiago would face a short life, but she was facing that possibility on her own already. With Tiago acting as her guard and protector, they would have a fighting chance, and she would no longer be alone. "You would be giving up everything."

He gave her a small smile. "You would be giving me everything that matters." Then his smile vanished and his face turned hard. "But if you take me, there'll be no one else for you. I won't tolerate it, faerie."

She already knew that. He was far too dominant and posses-sive. She could have told him that he was everything she could have hoped for, and far more than she had ever dreamed she might actually have. She might have confessed that she was every bit as possessive and jealous as he was. She should have reminded him that all her weapons were still poisoned and she knew how to use a gun.

Instead her lower lip stuck out. She pouted at him. "I haven't even had you yet," she grumbled. "Here you are talking about forever and only, but how do I know you're any good? I don't think it's exactly fair for you to be stomping and snorting about the pos-sibility of anybody else yet—"

He glared at her in disbelief. "Who keeps stopping?"

Her mouth fell open. "I get to say no if it's not right, mister."

"Did I say you couldn't say no?" he demanded. "No, I did not, even when it damn near castrated me. But it's a little much if you say no, and then you start complaining about the results, Niniane."

She narrowed her eyes and sneered at him. "Can I help it if I get cranky when I'm not sexually satisfied?"

The brutal angles of his dark face tensed, and his obsidian gaze grew vivid. His Power sharpened and turned predatory. He ran his hands up the side of her body. He stood. "Poor little faerie," he murmured. "Are you sexually dissatisfied?"

"Maybe a bit," she muttered. She blinked up at him. Good gods, he was built like a brick shithouse. He went long and grew wide, and he was looking at her like she was his newest favorite snack. She was doing much worse than teasing a tiger. She started to babble. "You've got to admit we've had some pretty frustrating moments in the last few—"

"Didn't I tell you once to shut the hell up?" he said gently. He took her dress in both hands and tore it from neckline to hem.

Sequins exploded everywhere. They showered the room in sparkling silver lights. She gawked at the wrecked material that hung off her arms. Maybe she needed her head examined. Tigers were pussycats in comparison to this walking, talking holocaust of a male. Then her teeth clicked together as she found her voice. "How could you, you stupid man? I loved that dress!"

"So did I," he breathed. He stared at her, transfixed. He had already removed her thong, and she wore no bra. She was as exquisitely made as his imagination insisted she would be, with round pink-tipped breasts in full, ripe bloom, a narrow rib cage and an even tinier waist, and a flat stomach that flared to trim hips. There, between slender thighs, was a small shadow of black hair.

He knew how silken that private, luscious tuft of hair was. He had stroked it so briefly not long ago.

And, good Christ, she still had on those four-inch stiletto-heeled fuck-me silver shoes.

He met her gaze and said from the back of his throat, "I'll buy you a thousand pretty dresses, a mountain of pink lipsticks and a queen's ransom in jewels, and I will never let anyone hurt you again."

Her pixie features shivered. The anger faded away to be replaced with things that were much more breakable and precious to him: trust and hope. She let her head tilt to one side, and holding his gaze, she slipped the ruined dress from her shoulders and let it fall to the floor.

He stepped forward, and it felt so right to pick her up in his arms. Pivoting on one heel, he carried her to the couch. He went down on one knee and laid her slender, curved body down on the cushions, then divested himself of his weapons, laying guns and fighting knife within reach on the floor.

She slipped off her shoes and stroked up his muscled arm, watching him. When he was through, she whispered, "Now your shirt."

He took a deep breath. Then he reached back, grabbed his shirt and dragged it over his head and flung it on the floor. He held her gaze as he unbuckled his belt and unzipped his fatigues. She felt herself growing drenched as she watched him undress, revealing, bit by bit, the massive architecture of his body. He stood, and the heavy muscles of his chest and arms flexed as he toed off his boots. He kicked off his fatigues.

It was the most beautiful gift, to feel this extravagant full-ness of desire.

She gorged on the sight of his nude body. His strong, sleek legs went on forever, his flat abdomen rippling with an eight-pack. His erect penis jutted over heavy round testicles that had drawn up tight underneath, unmistakable evidence of his own desire. She reached out and stroked him. He was so big she couldn't close her hand around him. As she massaged his penis's thick, broad head with her thumb, he sucked in a hissing breath and the muscles in his powerful thighs quivered.

She had enjoyed sex for a long time and made no apologies to anyone for it. She had bounced and shimmied through the 1960s with too much glee to be embarrassed or self-conscious now about their surroundings. But something had happened to her along that journey. She had grown, not indifferent exactly, but detached, unmoved by pretty men and frothy flirtations. Even though she loved sex, she found she no longer wanted any. She had stuffed herself on a banquet of dessert and walked away from the table unnourished.

This was the sweetest hunger she had ever known, leavened by the tenderness softening his hawkish face and how much she loved him. She caressed him, her fingers trailing along the huge velvet length of him, watching as sensual pleasure flushed over him and the tight clench of his body loosened.

He came down over her, and it felt more right than anything he had ever experienced to pin her down with his weight. He braced himself on one forearm and caressed her cheek and the side of her neck as he stared down at her. He was coming to a place he had never been before, a new and necessary place he hadn't even known to miss. It had all started with those first steps he had taken toward her in New York.

She still wore that breakable, breathtaking expression. She whispered, "It's been quite a while for me."

He stroked down the delicate line of her throat to her breast. He drew around her nipple and watched the succulent little bud tighten. He managed to remember to suck some air into his lungs. She was beautifully built and so small, and he was a great, crude, hulking brute of a male. "I'm glad you smacked me over the head and slowed me down," he whispered. "You need time."

He shifted to one side, lying on his hip beside her, his heavy erection resting on the curve of one of her hip bones. She shivered as his long-fingered hand played down her torso, stroking, drawing circles, pinching gently at her nipple, tugging the slender gold curve of her navel ring before moving down to tease the plump, hypersensitive flesh between her legs. He found the fluted opening of her labia and stroked. Her breath started coming in light pants as the most intense pulse of need she had ever felt careened through her body and jettisoned caution out the window. She gripped his forearm. "I don't care. Come inside."

He looked at her with a quick frown. "*I* care," he murmured. "We're going to make you ready. Ease your leg up, faerie."

She obeyed, bending her leg and propping it against the back of the couch as her gaze clung to him. He bent down to stroke her mouth with his as he eased a finger inside.

They both hissed at the sensation. Her stomach muscles trembled, and she whined high at the back of her throat at the sharp stab of pleasure.

Tiago started to sweat as that needy sound broke against his lips. He swallowed it down with greed. She was so sumptuously juicy and tight, her inner muscles clung to his finger. His cock jerked. Keep it slow and easy, stud. This is the most important thing you will ever do in your life. When her hand came down on his cock and she petted him, he thought he might explode.

He clenched his teeth. "Stop it."

She froze, looking at him with uncertainty.

He managed to give her a tight smile. "Let me make this about you," he gritted.

"It's about us," she whispered. She took her hand away from his cock and laid it against his cheek, and she lifted her head to kiss him.

His eyes closed, and he blissed out, kissing that ravishing sex kitten mouth as he fucked her so tenderly with his finger. Her hips moved with the rhythm of his hand, her liquid silk drenching his hand. He found the stiff little bud of her clitoris with his thumb and rubbed it as he suddenly drove his tongue hard and rough into her, and she gave a surprised muffled squeal and climaxed.

Shaken, he growled low and husky in her mouth. He licked at her lips and eased a second finger inside her dainty, tight sheath, and she arched her torso in response, stretching her body as she rotated her hips. "You're going to kill me," he breathed. "And I'm going to die so goddamn happy."

She gave a sexy whisper of a giggle, the long heavy lids of her eyes shuttered. His keen predator's eyes picked up every detail about her in the shadowed room, how her pale skin flushed dusky with arousal, all the way from her cheeks to her breasts. Her glossy lips were parted. He watched as her small white teeth dug into her plump lower lip as he began to rub her clitoris again.

When those fabulous eyes of hers flared open and she met his gaze, he felt a profound shock of connection. He took a step closer to that necessary place.

"I want to come with you inside me," she whispered. "Please."

He muttered something, he didn't know what, and rose over her.

She opened wide to him as he settled between her legs, looking down his torso as he carefully positioned his penis at her entrance. He braced his weight on his forearms, pushed the wide, warm head in and held rigid, panting.

It burned just like she knew it would. He felt so much better than she had imagined, like velvet-wrapped steel, and he was being so freaking careful it was driving her insane. She braced her feet on the couch and drove her hips upward, impaling herself on him as she raked her nails down his back and growled, *"Come on."*

She totally unzipped him. His beast came roaring out as he slammed into her. He pulled almost all the way out, looking down at her in incredulity, and then he slammed back in, and it was such a tight, liquid slide back, and he felt such a sweet tiny trail of fire along the skin of his back where she had scored him with her nails, just as he had fantasized for what seemed like forever, and she let her head fall back and, good fucking hell, she bared her throat to him in submission—*how did she know to do that*—and he went hurtling headlong into a climax.

He shuddered, gushing into her, taking her along with him as he ground his hips against her pelvis. She clamped her thighs against his hips as her climax rippled through her, deeper and richer than the first one. He slid a hand under her ass to hold her tighter to him as he rocked in her, his face buried in the slender stalk of her neck.

She stroked the edge of his ear, kissing his temple. I love you. Was it all right to say it now?

His head came up. He looked severe, desperate. He shook all over. "I'm not done," he gasped. "I'm not—I need—"

Oh gods, she had heard of this, what a Wyr was like in a mating frenzy. She grabbed him by the chin and made him look at her. Her eyes blazed with their own fallen light. "I need everything you have and everything you are. Don't stop."

He growled, withdrew, and flipped her over so fast her head spun. He yanked her body into place so that she was kneeling on the floor, bent over the couch. Then he knocked her knees as wide apart as they would go and shoved into her from behind. She shrieked into the couch cushion at the invasion. At this angle he felt bigger than ever, and when he drove in, he went in deeper.

He froze, bent over her, his heavy thighs pressing against the back of hers, his chest pressing against her back. She could feel how his heart hammered in his chest. His voice shook. "Are you all right, faerie?"

She turned her head to nuzzle at him. "I couldn't be better. I'm small and noisy; I'm not breakable."

He slid one arm underneath hers to spread his hand at the base of her throat. His fingers spanned the width of her collarbone as he ran his lips along the line of her jaw. "You could have fooled me," he muttered. He couldn't hold still any longer and started to move again. "You are so mine, young lady."

She caught her breath at the gorgeous sensation. "Yes, I am, aren't I?"

He closed his eyes, and his face tightened as he picked up the pace. She was a fever in his blood. "Mine," he growled.

"Yours," she told him.

He covered and surrounded her. Soon he drove into her with long hard powerful thrusts. She flung out her hands to brace herself. "Mine," he whispered into her ear.

She whimpered, "Yes."

He gripped her by the chin and turned her to look at him. His eyes blazed white-hot as he slammed her into the couch. He bared his teeth at her.

There you are. Her lips formed the words but she had no breath. He was so deadly, so beautiful, so sexy, so everything.

"Mine," the monster hissed.

Oh my God, yes.

A look of wonder came over his face. The climax blasted up the base of his spine. It was like riding the lightning, channeling the storm. His Power roared over her as he convulsed and spent himself. She screamed as it catapulted her into a climax with him. She clenched on him with everything she had and shook so hard she thought she might shatter into pieces, and for a few moments she thought she knew what it must be like to be him, for she felt like she was flying.

He wrapped both arms tight around her and crushed her back against his chest.

Here was the necessary place. Now that he had reached it, he said, "Of course. Now I understand." For the first time in his very long existence, Tiago knew what it meant to come home.

≈ THIRTEEN ≈

After several moments, his tight clench eased, and he carefully shifted his weight off of her. She collapsed forward,
shaking. He rubbed her back. "I took you at your word, faerie," he
said, breathing hard. "Now you tell me you're all right."

All right? *All right* was an ice cream cone on a warm afternoon, a press conference in which nothing disastrous happened,
or hell, just a day that passed without her uncle succeeding in
killing her. She was far too complicated for just *all right*. She was
deliriously happy, outrageously scared and completely immobi-
lized.

"I'm fine," she said into the cushion. "But all my muscles
have turned to Jell-O. I could use some help."

He kissed her shoulder. "Of course. Just a sec."

She could hear a pleased smile in his voice, and it sounded
very male, which in turn made her smile.

He cleaned her with a cloth, his touch light and gentle. "That
better not be your shirt, you lunatic, because thanks to you I've
got nothing else to wear," she murmured. She yawned. So many
things seemed impossible. Walking. Getting from here to, well,
anywhere. Making a decision. Facing other people.

She grimaced at that thought. *Ew*, actually.

He told her, "I'm using the inside of your dress."

"Okay." When he finished, she managed to push off the

couch. She wasn't kidding about having muscles made of Jell-O. Everything trembled.

He handed her his shirt. She turned the wadded material over in her hands, as her exhausted mind tried to deal with locating the neck and armholes. By the time she had it figured out and had pulled the shirt over her head, Tiago already had his pants zipped and was buckling his belt. The indirect light shining from the hall limned the wide arc of his back and shoulders, and one high cheekbone and lean cheek. He armed himself again with the two guns and the knife in its thigh sheath. He looked completely comfortable with the arm holsters strapped across his bare chest. He rotated his shoulders to settle them into place.

She took a deep breath at the sight of him, even as she swayed. He angled his head at her and lifted an eyebrow in inquiry.

"I can't, oh God, I can't," she told him. "But I want to."

A white smile slashed across his features and lit up his face. He looked energized, alert. He strode over to her, tilted up her chin and gave her a quick kiss. "You look gorgeous and edible, and I want to too," he said.

She snorted as she looked down at herself. "I look like a train wreck."

He ran a finger down the side of her neck as he surveyed her. Her silken black hair was tangled, and he had kissed all the makeup off her face. Her bare lips looked bitten, swollen and blushed with dusky color, and her eyes were smudged with exhaustion even as they held a wry smile. His black T-shirt came down to her narrow knees and gaped at her neck and arms. Her fingers and toes were painted pink. She looked like a woman who had been thoroughly made love to, and his groin tightened as he thought of all of the places he had not yet explored on her delectable body.

"You're my train wreck," he told her. "And you're more beautiful than ever."

She glowed up at him. Then she looked toward the hall. Her glow faded, replaced with tension and shadows. She sighed. He could see her visibly picking up the burden of her journey. It was a self-contained, lonely expression. She had accepted him, but she hadn't yet assimilated his presence. He knew that would take time.

She bent to pick up her shoes and started for the doorway.

He put a hand on her arm. "What are you doing?"

She blinked at him, puzzled. "We're leaving, right?"

He nodded his head toward her shoes and raised his eyebrows.

She looked at them too. Oh no. Her thigh muscles were much too overused for her to feel like she could balance on anything higher than the ground and even that was in question. "I can't."

"You're not walking around barefoot. Not in a bar and certainly not in the parking lot. There's bound to be broken glass around." Taking care to keep the material of the T-shirt pinned against the back of her legs, he picked her up in his arms.

"Whatever." She made a point to sound irritable, even as she nestled close, rested her head on his shoulder and let her aching body go lax.

He paused. "Faerie."

She opened her eyes and discovered him frowning down at her. "What?"

"We walk out of here a partnership. Don't let anyone try to persuade you otherwise. I am not letting you go."

She gave him a hesitant nod.

He looked severe, like he wanted to say more. Instead he gave her a swift hard kiss. Then he strode out with her in his arms.

Just as she had suspected, the only people in the bar were Aryal and Rune. They had evacuated everybody else, including Duncan and Cameron. The place looked abandoned and had a forlorn air. Half-empty glasses, and bowls of peanuts and popcorn still littered the tables. Aryal stood behind the bar, a bottle of tequila in front of her along with a shot glass that she spun in circles. Rune stood throwing darts in quick sharp movements at a board across the room. As they appeared, Aryal reached behind her and switched the music off, and silence crashed down over them all.

Niniane met Aryal's gaze. The harpy looked grim. Was that censure in her face? Niniane shrank back against Tiago's chest and went a little numb. She couldn't recall ever seeing Aryal look at her that way before. Was what they had done so awful?

Tiago took her to a barstool near Aryal and eased her onto it. He kissed her temple. *Stay right here.*

She set her shoes on the bar and swiveled to face him. His

expression gave no clue about what he was thinking. She asked, *Why?*

I have something I need to do.

Then Tiago pivoted on one heel and launched at Rune, who had just thrown his last dart and was in the process of turning around. Tiago tackled the other sentinel. They slammed into a table, close to five hundred pounds of solid Wyr muscle, and the table collapsed. Rune heaved, trying to dislodge Tiago, but Tiago was heavier and had him pinned in a headlock. Tiago's teeth were bared, his face feral with rage.

Oh shit. Niniane made a sound and rocked forward. Aryal grabbed her by the shoulder and held her in place. She struggled to shift the hold that pinned her, but the harpy's long-fingered hand felt like steel. "Let me go!" she said.

"Don't be stupid," Aryal said. The harpy's voice was as hard as her hand. "You know better."

She did, actually. Getting between two fighting Wyr was suicidal unless you were much bigger and stronger than they were. Dragos was the only one she knew who could survive tearing two fighting sentinels apart. She subsided as she stared at the males who struggled in silence. Aryal let go of her and took a long pull from the tequila bottle.

Tiago might never have managed to get Rune pinned if he had telegraphed his intention. He tightened his arm around Rune's neck and forced the First's body to arch backward in a painful bow.

You and I have been friends for longer than most modern nations have existed, he whispered in the First's head. *Which is why I'm not going to snap your neck right now. But if you ever try to come between me and Niniane again, I WILL END YOU.*

Rune sucked air as he struggled to ease the pressure on his windpipe. *Goddammit, T-bird*, he said. *I love that faerie as much as any of us, but I couldn't watch and do nothing while she becomes your* Titanic.

You crossed a line, Tiago hissed. *I choose her, I want her, and I am taking her.*

I was trying to save your fucking life! Rune tried to wedge his fingers underneath Tiago's forearm.

You were trying to control me, Tiago growled. *It's your choice. We can either come out of this as friends or we can come out as enemies, but you will not try to control me again. Understand?*

Rune grunted, *Yes.*

Tiago let him go and sprang backward as Rune flipped to his feet with a snarl, his golden lion's eyes flashing, and whirled to face Tiago.

One of these days, Tiago said. *You're going to find your mate. And maybe she'll be Wyr but maybe she won't. Then you will understand just what you almost did to me.*

With a visible effort, Rune throttled back his aggressive instincts. When both males took a deep breath and straightened, a palpable sense of danger eased from the room. Niniane felt as if she had just run a marathon. She wiped her cheeks and turned back to the bar. She reached for Aryal's tequila bottle.

Aryal shoved the bottle toward her without looking at her.

That stung. It stung badly.

Niniane took a few sips of tequila, and the fiery liquor flamed her throat. She said to the harpy, "What, you can't look at me now?"

"I'm too angry to look at you right now," said Aryal. She held her hand out for the bottle.

Niniane shoved it at her. Bitterness scalded her, along with a touch of fear. Rune and Aryal were supposed to be two of her and Tiago's closest friends. How much worse would the rest of the world react?

She said in a quiet voice, "After everything we've been through and all the time we've spent together, I would have thought I had earned better."

"I didn't say it was fair," said Aryal. "I just said I was angry." The harpy tilted the bottle up to her mouth and took several swallows.

"Okay," Niniane said. She put her hands to her face and rubbed, then dug her fingers into her scalp, trying to massage some life back into her tired brain. "Why?"

Aryal slammed the bottle onto the bar and glared at it. "I'm angry you chose the Dark Fae and you didn't choose us. You didn't have to tell God and everybody else who you were. Chances are your real identity would have died with Urien, because he sure as hell hadn't spread the news around. You could have stayed in New York. You were happy with us."

"We discussed this before I ever left," Niniane said. She was so weary she could barely sit upright on the stool. "You know why I did it."

"Yeah, but I don't have to like it, do I?" Aryal said. "And

you're not Wyr, and I hate it when one of us mates with someone who isn't Wyr. Let alone Tiago, good God. He's more Wyr
than most of us. So you're not only leaving us, you're taking one
of our strongest with you. I hate it and there's nothing I can do
about it, and you know how I hate it when there's nothing I can
do about something. That's why I'm angry."

Niniane felt slapped. "So it's okay to like me as long as you
don't like me too much? I had no idea you were so bigoted."

"Goddamn it," the harpy said. "That's not what I meant."
Aryal's stormy gaze met hers. The harpy said in her head, *What
happens in twenty or thirty years if you decide you and Tiago
aren't working out? You'll be able to walk away, but he will
never let go of you.*

That's just it, Niniane said. *That is bigotry.*

Aryal made an angry chopping gesture with one hand. *I've
seen what can happen. You have too!*

*I'm not talking about what can happen to someone else in
some other situation*, Niniane said. *I'm talking about me. The
bottom line is, you don't trust me to love him or look after him.
You said it yourself. It's because I'm not Wyr. I would never be
good enough or right enough for him, would I?*

Aryal glared at the tequila bottle and said nothing.

Niniane's eyes glittered. When Tiago's arm came around her
shoulders, she turned and put her arms around his waist, resting
her cheek against his warm bare skin. She couldn't bear to look
at either Aryal or Rune at the moment.

She knew her old life had ended and was coming to terms with
that, but she never thought her old friendships might end as well.

Maybe she was selfish to take what he offered. Her life
wasn't going to be any picnic. Maybe she should have tried
harder to push him away. He had said he would go if she could
tell him she didn't want him and she could make him believe it.
She hadn't been strong enough.

She said to Aryal, *I need him more than you do.*

Niniane's cheek felt wet. Tiago put a protective hand to her
head and shielded her face from the other two. He bent to
press his lips to her forehead. Whatever she and Aryal had said
to each other had obviously been painful. He wanted to slam
his fist into the harpy's face.

He held on to the impulse by the skin of his teeth. He could just hear how that conversation would go. She would say, Tiago, you can't fight all my battles for me. But he honestly didn't know why the hell not.

He picked Niniane up and cradled her close. She held her shoes against her stomach and put her face in his neck. He turned to the door and paused. Without looking at either sentinel, he said, "Don't come with us if you can't accept us."

He waited a moment to see if Niniane would contradict him. She slipped her arm around his neck and remained silent. He squeezed her tight and strode out.

Predawn was lightening the sky in the east. It revealed a sodden, bedraggled neighborhood that had been buffeted by the storm that had blown through in the night. Fast-food wrappers and plastic drinks containers were strewn across the parking lot. From the outside with the lights turned off, Big Red's bar looked tired.

He heard the sounds of boot heels on gravel and turned. Rune and Aryal had stepped out of the building. They looked tired too but resolute. They walked toward him and Niniane. The gryphon's tawny head topped Aryal's tangled black hair by a couple of inches. Both sentinels moved their long, lean bodies with fluid athleticism. They scanned the surrounding scene with sharp eyes. They came to a stop, one on each side of him. Aryal reached out and touched Niniane's hand. After a hesitation, Niniane clasped the harpy's hand.

Rune had been right earlier. Wyr were not good at forgiveness, and they never forgot.

They were also hellishly bad at letting go.

Niniane's exhaustion swallowed her whole. A formless fog filled her mind. She was vaguely aware that Tiago climbed into the back of a vehicle while still holding her. Rune said something to him, to which he replied, and then Rune shut the door. Other car doors opened and shut. Moments later Aryal started the vehicle, and she drove them through quiet gray-lit Chicago streets.

Then Niniane must have fallen asleep, or fallen into a state very like it. She dreamed of movement and quiet noises, but she only came awake when Tiago leaned over to lay her on a bed.

She cracked open bleary eyes and looked around. They were in her penthouse room, back in the hotel from hell. She pushed into a sitting position, her exhaustion-smudged face filled with alarm.

His hatchet-hewn features softened as he bent over her. He said, "It's all right. You're fine, it's safe."

Had it been a long, vivid, incredibly beautiful dream? She blinked, looking around. She wore a voluminous black T-shirt. Tiago was armed and bare-chested, and dressed in black fatigue pants.

She was sore in the most private places of her body. She relaxed marginally. It had happened. It hadn't been a dream.

"Are you going somewhere?" she mumbled.

"No," he said. He kissed the sleepy soft pout of her mouth. "I'm just stepping into another room for a few minutes. I need to call New York and talk to Dragos."

"All right." Her eyelids felt like they weighed about ninety pounds each. They fell shut and she couldn't pry them open again. Her head listed to the side. "I'll wait here."

He laughed, a soft exhalation of air. "I'm going to leave the door open, so I can keep an eye on you. I still haven't calmed down from when the Djinn took you. Lie down, faerie. I'll be back in a few minutes."

He put a hand on her shoulder and urged her down. She resisted for all of thirty seconds. Then she lay down and turned onto her side to hug a pillow as he tucked the bedcovers around her. She felt the brush of his fingers through her hair. He turned off the bedside lamp and walked into the bathroom. After a moment she heard him speaking in a quiet voice.

That was the last thing she remembered before she ran through a shadowed palace soaked in her brothers' blood.

Tiago positioned himself in the bathroom so that he could see the top of Niniane's black tousled head. He leaned against the bathroom counter and hit speed dial #1 on the iPhone he had stolen from Rune. He didn't need to double-check the number. All the sentinels had Dragos as #1 on their cell phones.

"What now?" Dragos said as he answered the phone.

Tiago rotated his shoulders, working to loosen the muscles

that had tightened after the fight with Rune. He told the dragon, "I quit."

Silence on the other end of the connection.

"Niniane is my mate," Tiago said.

He waited and listened to more silence.

He snapped, "You can't tell me Rune didn't find a way to get in touch with you in the last couple of hours."

"I'm waiting to hear from you whether you're still an ally or not," said Dragos.

"Don't be stupid," Tiago said. "Of course we are."

"All right. Keep her safe and stay in touch." The phone clicked.

Tiago shook his head and laughed silently to himself. When all was said and done, Dragos was the most efficient predator of them all. And, after all, what else was there to say?

He splashed off at the bathroom sink, found and unwrapped a new toothbrush and brushed his teeth. He went to the side of the bed where he undressed and set his weapons within easy reach on the bedside table. He exulted in the exotic intimacy of joining her in bed as he slid nude between the covers.

That was when he discovered she had curled in a tight ball. He pushed up on one forearm to stare down at her. She was clammy, her breathing choppy, and she had both hands clamped over her mouth.

"Faerie," he said in a sharp voice. His Power mantled in the room, seeking an enemy. He couldn't sense any other Power or influence nearby. He gripped her shoulder. She made a strangled noise and exploded into a hellcat. She kicked and punched at him, her movements wild and uncontrolled. He threw one heavy thigh over her thrashing legs, and he gripped her wrists as gently as he could and pinned them on the pillows on either side of her head. *"Wake up, Niniane."*

She hurtled into awareness, her heart slamming in her chest. For a nightmarish moment she couldn't remember where she was or recognize the dark silhouette of the male pinning her down. A terrified, despairing noise broke out of her as she tried to buck off his weight. He shifted immediately, easing off of her but not letting go of her wrists. Then he said her name again, and it snapped her reality back into place.

She stopped struggling and said in a ragged voice, "I'm awake. Sorry."

Tiago leaned on one elbow beside her and braced a hand on her ribs. He sounded as ragged as she did. "Fuck sorry. Just tell me what happened."

How strange that he was here, warm and naked, one hip pressed insistently against hers. Greedy for the feel of his skin, she burrowed into his side and rubbed her toes along his calf. The crisp hairs on his leg tickled her bare foot. "I was having a nightmare about the night when Urien and his men killed my family. I used to have it all the time. Then it mostly went away. Now it's come back again."

He growled deep in his chest, the menacing sound vibrating against her cheek. He sounded frustrated. "I want to kill that son of a bitch all over again. And again and again."

"It was just a dream," she whispered.

"No, it isn't, faerie. It's a terrible memory of a crime committed against you and people you loved."

"Yes." The word came out on the barest thread of sound.

He propped a pillow against the headboard, settled back against it and pulled her into his arms. She settled against him with her head on his shoulder, one slender leg hitched over his hips, an arm draped over his chest. He radiated heat and strength, the forcefulness of his presence filling the room and scattering the last threads of the nightmare that clung to her like cobwebs.

He stroked the hair off her damp forehead. "Can you tell me about it?"

She lifted her slender shoulder in a halfhearted shrug. "I'd much rather it just went away."

He cupped her shoulder, fingering the delicate bones underneath his shirt. "Maybe it will if you talk about it."

So she did, her voice halting at first, as the words came hard. When she got to the part where she found the bodies of her twin brothers, tears streaked down her face. She described watching one of Urien's soldiers as he murdered her mother with one efficient sword thrust, and Tiago rolled her onto her back and covered her with his body. His cheek rested against hers, and he covered her forehead with one huge palm. It was as if he was trying to hide her from the trauma of what had already happened. She rubbed his back.

"I never found out the details of what happened to my father, other than he and Urien fought, and Urien killed him," she said.

"My father had had a great deal of Power. I used to think nothing could touch him. Urien went after him personally and sent his soldiers to take care of the rest of us."

Tiago kissed her cheek, her temple. "How did you get away?"

She laughed a little, hardly more than an exhalation of air. "I was misbehaving. I'd snuck out to meet a boy. He wasn't acceptable, and I wasn't supposed to be seeing him, and it was really just a typical stupid teenage prank. I spent most of the night with him trying to decide if I wanted to have sex or not. I decided not, and I slipped back into the palace, and that was when I heard something. It sounded like people running in the hall, only they sounded quiet and furtive. My brothers' rooms were next to mine, so I went to check on them, discovered their bodies and ran to find help. Then I saw soldiers kill my mother, and I felt Power flare from Urien and my father's battle, so I knew I had to run. I slipped out the way I had come in."

Her apartment had a private walled courtyard with fruit trees and a marble fountain. Several of the apple trees grew within a few feet of the wall. Some weeks previously, she had stolen a rope from the stables and fashioned a rope ladder so that she could indulge in her illicit romance. Leaving had been a simple matter of climbing a tree and throwing the ladder over the wall.

Tiago pressed a kiss to the corner of her mouth as he thought. Adriyel was the seat of the Dark Fae demesne, deep in the heart of one of the largest tracts of Other land in the continental United States. He had never been to Adriyel himself, but he had heard that the journey to the palace from any one of the passageways took several days by horseback. He had to clear his throat before he could speak again. "Chicago was founded some years after you crossed over. In the early 1830s, if I remember correctly."

She nodded, watching her fingers as she traced his strong, sturdy collarbone. "Most European settlers called the area Fort Dearborn, which was built in 1803, and the American Indians called it Chickagou."

"Getting from Fort Dearborn to New York would have been hard enough." My God, the more he thought of the journey she must have made, the more it made him shudder. "How did you get from Adriyel to Fort Dearborn?"

"I went to the stables and stole a graewing," she said. "I

wasn't used to riding one though, so it was a pretty wonky flight. I managed to get it close to the crossover passage before we crashed. It was injured so I was able to get away from it."

He swore under his breath. Graewings were a winged species that bred in Other lands. They looked like giant dragonflies. Like their miniature cousins that fed on mosquitoes, they were efficient predators, but they fed on creatures much larger than mosquitoes. They were dangerous mounts, for not only were they difficult to control, but their flight capabilities were much like helicopters. They could dart forward and backward, or rise and fall straight in the air. Accidents from riding a graewing tended to be fatal. If the fall didn't kill the rider, most likely the graewing would. The Dark Fae had an elite force of fifty troops who were graewing riders that were traditionally led by their monarch. Urien himself had been famous as a proficient rider.

A body shouldn't feel so many things at once, Tiago decided. He wasn't sure if someone could explode from so many powerful emotions, but from the way he was feeling it seemed possible. He unclenched his jaw so that he could talk. "Okay," he said. "It happened a long time ago. You survived. That's all that matters."

She kissed his warm bare shoulder. "I just realized something," she said. She sounded drowsy now. "I always dream about my brothers. I never dream about my mother or my father. I mean, in the dream, I just know they're dead. I wonder why."

"Aside from the emotional impact of finding your brothers' bodies, that was when you discovered how your life had changed," Tiago said. "You had to have been going into shock by the time you saw what happened to your mother."

"Maybe that's it. I also always dream about hearing Urien's footsteps as he hunts for me, when the only footsteps I really heard were soldiers running through the palace. Anyway, after I escaped, Urien built the mansion and walled the grounds around that passageway, and of course he built outposts at the other passageways too so that he could control the traffic to and from Adriyel. I know I'm prejudiced against him, but it always sounded a bit like putting up the Iron Curtain to me." She yawned. They had stayed up all night, and she had already been exhausted, and talking about the nightmare and the memories left her feeling wrung out.

Tiago said quietly, "Walking back into the palace is going to be difficult."

What else could she say to that but the truth? "Yes."

He ordered, "You must tell me whenever the memories bother you. And you must swear to me you'll never ride a graewing again. I don't even want you within fifty feet of one. Understand?"

"That seems a bit extreme," she muttered. "It wasn't that bad. They're just so fast, and while I'd seen them in flight lots of times before, I didn't know what I was doing. Anyway, I'm s'posed to. Tradition. Need flying lessons first though." Her eyelids drifted shut.

"I don't care about tradition. If you ever need to have a flying mount, you will ride me," he said. He could protect her that way, and if she ever got dislodged, he could catch her before she fell. He frowned. Maybe they could create a harness for him to wear that she could use as a saddle. With a seat belt. And she was going to have to wear a helmet. And a life jacket if they ever had to fly over water. Would a parachute be too much, just in case?

"Fine. Whatever." She groped along his face until she could tap his mouth with an admonishing finger. "Shush now."

"All right, faerie." He pressed his lips to that slender pink-tipped forefinger. "You sleep."

By the time he eased his weight off of her again, she had fallen fast asleep.

The Dark Fae mansion and its eighty-acre tract of land lay a half mile northwest of Chicago's downtown Loop area. The grounds were bordered by a tall stone wall topped with rolls of barbed wire. The area had changed so much over the last two hundred years. Niniane didn't recognize anything in the stylish surrounding neighborhood as their SUV approached two tall iron gates.

This time Rune drove and Aryal rode shotgun. All of Niniane's things had been packed in suitcases and rode in the back, along with Tiago's duffle bag. Rune and Aryal had already sent their things ahead. Rune had dressed up for the occasion: the jeans he wore didn't have holes in the knees. Aryal wore her usual outfit of fighting leathers and weapons. Tiago rode with

Niniane in the backseat. He was dressed in a clean black T-shirt and fatigues, and of course he was armed as well. His hawkish face was alert and relaxed, his dark gaze constantly moving over their immediate surroundings.

She flashed back to earlier. She had awakened with the awareness of his long, powerful body lying next to her, one of his hands resting on the narrow frame of her rib cage. Even before she had opened her eyes, she knew she faced a day filled with profound differences. She had stirred and turned to him, and discovered he was already watching her, his expression pensive and strange with rare tenderness.

He had not spoken. Instead he kissed her. Then he eased her out of his T-shirt and caressed her breasts. He had taken his time as he bent his head farther down to lick and nibble at her most sensitive areas, her throat, the inside of her elbows, tonguing her navel ring as he learned what pleased her. Then he suckled her, tugging and nipping with erotic care at her nipples as he scraped the edge of his fingernails lightly along her skin until desire for him rose to that keen sharp, sweet ache that made her feel crazed, outside of herself, but he would not enter her no matter how she begged.

"You are too sore," he said. "I would hurt you."

"I don't care," she gasped, as she twisted under his clever mouth and hands.

"I do." He moved down her body and eased her legs apart. He settled on his stomach and stroked her swollen tender flesh, first with his fingers then with his tongue, and the sight of his wide shoulders and dark head between her legs as he worked at his intimate task jettisoned her into climax. Then he looked up the length of her bare torso with a steady intent expression and said, "Again."

She was too tired to handle this intense feeling of ecstasy. Her hands trembled as she stroked his head. "I can't."

"You can," he said. He spread the folds of her labia open and put his mouth to her clitoris.

And she did, sharp starbursts of pleasure flaring again and again, until at the last she sobbed, overwrought and wrung out, and he crawled up her body quickly to pull her limp body into his arms. She said, *But I haven't—you haven't—*

Listen to her. She could not even control her telepathy.

"I have taken exactly what I wanted," he whispered in her

ear. "I will have every part of you, until I live with you underneath your skin."

If that was his goal, he had achieved it. She sat quietly with
her seat belt on, her legs crossed at the knees, her hands folded
together in her lap. After they had finally showered, around
noon, she had dressed for the day in a simple black Givenchy
dress, modest peep-toed pumps, and a pearl necklace and earrings. The makeup she wore was minimal, her hair blow-dried
and fluffed with her fingers. The soft, expensive material of her
outfit was gentle against the marks left on her skin by their
lovemaking.

She gazed at the world with a patience that stemmed from
utter physical exhaustion, while she was filled to the brim with
a private pool of remembered eroticism. She looked at him with
a deeper knowledge.

There, his short black hair gleamed in the sunlight. She
knew what it felt like as it slipped through her fingers. There,
his elegant mouth. She knew how wise those lips of his were
as they traveled along the peaks and valleys of her body. There,
the movement of his long, strong fingers. She knew just how
those fingers felt as they curled around her ankles, how they felt
moving inside of her, where the calluses were on his hands
and the way they rasped along her skin. There, his restless,
intelligent eyes. She knew the steady promise in them as he
took her and took her, until there was nothing left of her to be
had for he had taken it all. Yes, he lived with her now, underneath her skin.

Rune pulled the SUV up to the black iron gates. There was
a guard booth next to them. A young Dark Fae woman in a
plain black uniform approached the driver's side to greet Rune.
Her fascinated gaze darted once to Niniane in the backseat, but
other than that she comported herself with discretion. Niniane
smiled at her, and after a hesitation, the guard smiled back.
After confirming their identity, the guard moved back to the
booth.

Nobody spoke as the gates opened. Rune drove through and
braked just on the other side. Niniane turned to watch as the
gates shut behind them. She looked through the bars at the
bright Chicago street. It was populated with the usual band of
frenzied paparazzi and news reporters who worked to capture
the event as she left official U.S. territory.

She would not see the outside of those bars again until she was Queen.

Tiago put his hand over hers in her lap. His huge palm enclosed both of hers. He squeezed her hands until she looked at him.

He was staring at her with that steady, adamant bedrock gaze. *I will do this,* that gaze said. *I will not leave you. I will take you and make you so completely mine, you will never know your life alone again.* She relaxed and gave him a slight nod, and he rubbed the back of her hand with a thumb.

Rune accelerated the SUV up a wide paved drive that was bordered by manicured shrubbery, flowers and trees. Everything within sight was rigidly controlled, trimmed and shaped to within an inch of its life, Urien's very own Versailles. A sense of nearby land magic tingled against her senses, and she knew what she felt was the nearby crossover point to Adriyel.

I meant to ask if there was any news on the investigation, she asked Tiago.

You will not trouble yourself with that, Tiago said. *You have more than enough to deal with right now. We're handling it.*

She sighed. Despite their unprecedented intimacy, Tiago had never acted as her bodyguard before this week, and they had a lot to learn about each other. *Ordering me not to trouble myself isn't helping. I need to hear details.*

There was a pause. Then he said, *The investigation has moved forward a few steps. Rune and I went to the morgue and inspected the bodies of the three Wyr. We had a run-in with Arethusa that turned unexpectedly positive, although we're keeping that under wraps for now. Why don't I give you a complete update later when we have time to relax?*

She gave him a quick smile. *That would be good, thank you.*

The SUV went around a bend in the drive, and the Georgian-style mansion came into view. It was an imposing structure, but she had expected nothing else. It stood three stories tall, with a stone facade that was half covered in dark green ivy. The front of the mansion had a roofed portico where carriages, and now cars, could pull and people could enter and exit from the building protected from inclement weather. The rows of tall windows shone with a hard polished gleam in the afternoon sun. There might be poison, innuendo, betrayal and murder within those walls, but there would not be a wayward speck of dust.

Her heart pounded. She whispered, "Urien's dead."

All three of her Wyr companions reacted. Tiago gripped her hands harder. Aryal twisted around to look at her. Rune took a deep breath.

Tiago said, "Urien may be dead, but this is still his house, and we have not been allowed to go through it. Remember, you need to go carefully. Whenever possible let one of us into a room before you."

Aryal asked, "Are you wearing your stilettos?"

Niniane nodded. The harpy was not referring to fashionable shoes, but to Niniane's pair of small sheathed knives with the thin two-inch-long blades. She wore them now, underneath her dress and strapped to her thighs.

The mansion's front doors opened as the SUV approached. Rune brought the vehicle to a gentle stop as people poured out of the house. The Dark Fae delegation had all transferred back to the mansion earlier that morning, along with Carling and her entourage of Vampyres who needed to get settled into shelter before daybreak. Now Aubrey, Kellen and Arethusa, and assorted guards and the household staff lined up on the steps to greet her.

It mirrored a similar scene that had occurred as she had left the hotel, where she had thanked the hotel staff and the various Chicago PD officers for their hard work on her behalf. There would be similar groups everywhere she went now. She had better get used to it.

The group at the hotel had been a special one though. She made sure to target Scott Hughes, Dr. Weylan and Cameron. As an expression of her gratitude for everything they had done for her, she invited each one to her coronation. Both Scott and Dr. Weylan thanked her profusely but said they had family and other obligations and would not be able to take time away on such short notice. Cameron, however, was a different story. After one startled moment, the woman grinned and said, "Seriously?"

Niniane leaned close to the police woman and whispered, "We both know Mr. Incredible did not know to buy me Joy perfume, or how to color-coordinate makeup and earrings with those new outfits. And who was it that arranged that absolutely smashing trip to Big Red's?"

Tiago leaned in close from behind to whisper in her ear, "Mr. Incredible is listening to every word you say."

She twinkled sidelong at him, and he had given her a slow smile in return. Cameron laughed, her face creased with delight. "I would love to come. I just have to arrange time off from work."

Niniane clapped her hands. "Oh goody! But taking time off of work can be tricky. Remember, time works differently when you cross over to an Other land, and you won't know for sure how long you'll be gone."

"I wouldn't miss this for the world," said Cameron. "I have a pension coming to me. I'll quit if I have to."

Niniane laughed. "We'll cross over for Adriyel in two days, so be sure to come by then if you can make it. I'll arrange at the gate for them to let you in."

She smiled now as she remembered Cameron's unaffected exuberance. The casual, easy comfort with which Niniane had interacted with the human woman stood in sharp contrast to how she felt as she looked at this current group waiting for her on the mansion steps. Many wore pleasant smiles, while others wore more neutral expressions. She noticed a tall, elegant Dark Fae woman who stood by Aubrey. The woman was almost Aubrey's height and was dressed in conservative dark blue tunic and trousers, her black hair swept back in a simple knot. Her hand was tucked into the crook of Aubrey's arm. She had to be Naida, his wife, who had stayed at the house to arrange the details of their journey back to Adriyel.

These were Niniane's people, and as she looked at them, she felt nothing except a vague sense of anxiety for all the places she could see in their clothing where someone might hide a gun or a dagger.

Clearly bonding was going to take a while.

⟹ FOURTEEN ⟸

Rune opened the door for Niniane. He offered his hand, and she took it as she stepped out of the SUV. Tiago came around the back of the vehicle and stepped into place behind her, so close she could feel his body heat. His Power surrounded her so that she felt it as an invisible cloak, a warm, protective living presence that pressed against her bare skin. It startled her, and she gave him a quick questioning look. None of the other sentinels had ever covered her with their Power like that before.

He gave her another one of those smiles of his that was so faint, if she hadn't known his facial expressions so well, she wouldn't have noticed it.

Rune said in her head, *Aryal and I will get your things upstairs. It will give us a chance to check out the space. Then we have things to do while we're still in Chicago. We'll see you later.*

She gave him a grateful look. *Thanks.*

Rune gave her a slight wink. *Knock 'em dead, pip-squeak.*

She smiled at him then turned away, and Tiago moved when she did. He remained always at her back, a silent towering figure that carried with him the promise of certain death for anyone foolish enough to try to harm her. She knew without checking that he had assumed his hatchet-hewn assassin's look. She could see it in the way that people reacted to them, as she moved to greet individuals in the group.

She went first, smiling, to Aubrey and Naida. Aubrey inclined his head and bowed, and Naida did as well. "Your highness," Aubrey said. "Welcome. We're so pleased to have you arrive here, at one of your homes."

"Thank you," she said. "I appreciate everything you've done to smooth the way."

Aubrey indicated the woman at his side. "This is my wife, Naida."

Niniane looked up at the other Dark Fae woman, who was several inches taller than her, and her smile widened. "It's a pleasure to meet you, Naida."

"Thank you, your highness. It is a pleasure to meet you as well." Naida's returning smile was smooth and pleasant, then her dark gray eyes moved to Tiago standing at Niniane's back and Naida's expression chilled perceptibly.

Don't react. Naida's reaction was only going to be the first of many. Niniane said, "I hear you have been working hard to get ready for my arrival and our trip to Adriyel. Thank you for everything you've done."

"I am pleased to be of service. I've heard how much you used to love horseback riding. I think I've found a mare for you that you will enjoy."

Niniane laughed, feeling warmed for the first time since their arrival on the property. "How wonderful! I've not been riding in years."

"I'm sure it will come back to you in no time," said Naida.

"Rather like riding a bicycle," she said.

Naida's eyebrows elevated at a slight angle. "That, I wouldn't know."

She opened her mouth. She almost invited Naida for bicycle riding lessons, but there was some quality to the other woman's composed and sophisticated self-containment that made her hesitate. She said instead, "Bike riding is great fun." She turned to Aubrey, "Perhaps we can have that chat soon."

Aubrey smiled, the fan of crow's-feet deepening attractively at the corners of his eyes. "I am at your disposal. When would you like to talk?"

"Why don't we get together after I've greeted everybody?"

Naida murmured to Aubrey, "I will see to it that refreshments are served in the study."

Niniane hesitated again. Why did that seem off to her?

Naida was only helping to smooth the way by acting as de facto hostess, but this was not the other woman's house, nor was she a servant.

Or perhaps anything would feel odd at this point. How should one welcome a long-lost heir to the Dark Fae throne to one of her own homes after her murderous uncle had just been killed? It was not exactly a social occasion covered by Emily Post. Not that Naida would have read Emily Post any more than she would have ridden a bike. Niniane didn't have time to examine the situation further, so she shook off her reaction and turned to greet Kellen and Arethusa, who responded with such warmth, it put the smile back on Niniane's face.

After greeting Naida and the Dark Fae delegation, they withdrew into the house and she turned her attention to the staff who took care of the property. She started with the steward, Brennan, who was an elderly Dark Fae male with a nervous gaze and restless hands. After greeting him she worked through the house staff and the gardeners. Then she spoke briefly with the captain of the guard, Prydian, who was a close-mouthed man with a shielded gaze who answered her in monosyllables. She also spoke with those guards who were not on active duty watching the gate or other parts of the property.

She made a point to say something to each member of staff, to ask their names and to make a comment or two about their work or to ask after their personal lives. To a person, they reacted to her attention with astonishment and varying degrees of pleasure. She suspected her uncle Urien had not been big on wasting his charm on anyone he deemed Powerless or without political influence.

All the while she carried an intense awareness of Tiago taking watch at her back. He moved when she did, a smooth and silent shadow. Then something different happened. His Power tightened around her as palpably as if he had reached out to grasp her shoulder. She paused, and only years of practice helped her keep from frowning at Prydian, the guard captain with whom she had been chatting. Keeping her movement casual, she took a step back toward Tiago, and his Power lightened again and became almost caressing.

Interesting. She made a point of looking around, as if to admire the front gardens, and she used the opportunity to glance at Tiago. He looked bland and no doubt as discreet as he could, but she noticed that she had come close to stepping out of the "safe zone" area, which would have brought her too close to a potential assailant while at the same time a shade too far from her guard. Tiago had corrected her course without interrupting her telepathically or using a physical gesture. Not long afterward she felt his Power nudge her more to the right, and again when she shifted to comply, the warm sense of his presence lightened as it brushed against her skin.

He would be forming his own opinions of the people she met, cataloguing reactions with names and faces as he conducted a risk assessment. She would make sure to ask him later what he thought of Brennan's nervousness and Prydian's guardedness. She couldn't dismiss everybody just because they had worked for her uncle. They couldn't all be enemies. Most of them had probably never even spoken to Urien.

It was also true, however, that this was property of some import as it was the main gateway from the Dark Fae lands to Chicago. As such, everything here deserved special scrutiny, although not everything had to be acted upon immediately.

After a half an hour or so, she turned to the house and motioned Brennan to her side. "I'm ready to be shown to the study now," she said.

"Of course, your highness!" the steward said. He rubbed his hands together, perpetually washing them. "I will be delighted to show you whatever you like!"

It was impossible to believe him. Even her rudimentary truthsense snorted in disbelief. Brennan wasn't delighted about anything at the moment. It was clear he was overcome with anxiety. No doubt he was afraid he was about to lose his job. She tried not to let her repulsion for him show. She wanted to snap at him to stop what he was doing and to slap his hands apart. The poor man looked like Montgomery Burns from *The Simpsons*. She gestured for him to lead the way.

As they stepped into the cool, elegant interior of the house, Tiago said suddenly in her head, *Be honest. How angry would you be with me if I squashed this bug?*

She glanced over her shoulder in startled glee. *That thing he's doing with his hands is making me crazy. But he must be a very effective steward to have survived under Urien's rule, and we cannot kill everybody we don't like.*

What if I don't kill him? Tiago said, his mental voice

thoughtful. *I could mash him up a bit around the edges and make him a size smaller.*

She pinched her nose hard until her eyes stung and managed to turn her laugh into a cough. This was what had been missing during their quiet drive from the hotel, all the sentinels talking smack. Even though Rune and Aryal were traveling with them to Adriyel, everyone had been feeling the impending separation.

She got a blurred impression of the grand staircase, foyer and the halls as they followed Brennan toward the back of the house. Polished wood shone everywhere. Marble floors gleamed. Every time she took a step, she could see the soles of her shoes just before her feet touched the floor.

An outrageous fortune in rare Dark Fae artwork decorated the foyer and the downstairs halls. The paintings focused on nature scenes from Adriyel. One painting in particular made her catch her breath. It depicted the palace and the spectacular waterfall of the Adriyel River behind it, the scene so unexpectedly familiar, it brought tears to her eyes. The slender flowing pieces of sculpture were all metal. They graced the air by achieving impossible heights and tinkled with a delicate virtuoso of Power that was as refreshing to the mind as the physical shape of the sculpture was to the eyes. Thanks to Urien's tight control of Adriyel's crossover passageways, Dark Fae art was difficult to get and fetched high prices at Sotheby's and other auction houses.

She wondered what statement Urien had been making with the artwork. Everything about the property was controlled, precise, from the Georgian-style mansion to the manicured grounds. The display of Dark Fae art here, in his property in Chicago, seemed as deliberate in its planning as was the rest of the estate. He would have entertained allies and business associates here. Had he offered them glimpses of Adriyel as an enticement, or had he merely been displaying so much artwork as a statement of his own wealth and Power?

She sighed. She was being haunted by a dead man. She hated how much time Urien occupied in her thoughts when all she really wanted to do was to jump up and down on his grave and sing "Ding-dong, the witch is dead." She suspected he would overshadow her thoughts for a long time to come, as she second-guessed the decisions he made and chose which of his laws she would reverse.

The thing was, and she hated to admit this to herself, Urien had been a very intelligent man. She wanted to despise everything he had done, but she wasn't sure she would be able to. The Dark Fae artwork decorating the front of the house was quite lovely. Now Niniane was no longer sure about many of her opinions. Maybe she needed to employ a count-to-ten policy whenever she encountered something she knew was Urien's creation. She needed to assess things on their own merit, not just reject them out of hand because her uncle had something to do with them.

Whatever Urien's taste in art had been, what Carling had said was still true. To most people, politically and financially the Dark Fae looked like they were in a strong position with regards to the other demesnes. However, those individuals, like Carling, who had an educated sense of the Dark Fae's real unmet potential, knew better.

They reached an open paneled doorway, and Brennan stood to one side of it and bowed to her. She thanked him and, without thinking, started to walk into the room first. Tiago's Power clenched on her even as he grabbed her by the arm. Brennan stared at Tiago, openmouthed.

Niniane rolled her eyes at the steward's reaction. She stepped back to let Tiago go in first as she said in his head, *Sorry.*

Don't sweat it, faerie, he said. *But just so you know, if the bug expires from shock, I'm not giving him mouth-to-mouth.*

She bit her lips to keep from laughing as he strode into the room, pivoted then invited her in with an outstretched hand. She walked in and stopped dead a few feet inside the door.

The study was very masculine, with heavy dark leather furniture that looked comfortable rather than stylish, a scatter of bookshelves, a large mahogany desk in one corner and a fireplace. Large windows overlooked the back gardens where the land dipped downward toward a small sunlit lake. A massive seascape painting by the English artist Turner hung over a wide fieldstone fireplace. Urien's personality seemed stamped in the room, more so than anything she had seen to date. She could see him sitting at his desk and looking out over that fucking immaculate landscape, all the while knowing he was master of all he surveyed. If she were Wyr, she would bet the damn place smelled like him.

Everything clenched. Gut, fists, face. Count to ten.

Tiago was beside her in three long, swift strides, his face sharp with concern. He put a bracing hand to her back. *Faerie?*

She raised a hand in a just-a-minute gesture as she struggled to unclench. It was just furniture. They were just books.

It was then she noticed that Aubrey was already in the room. He had risen to his feet at her entrance. Naida was also in the room. A tea service with three cups and plates, along with a tray of delicate pastries were arranged on a table in front of the couch. Aubrey watched her with a concern that seemed almost as sharp as Tiago's, while Naida looked at them both with a dawning speculation.

I am all right, she said to Tiago. She squeezed his arm. He nodded, still frowning, and rubbed her shoulders. *The place smells like him, doesn't it?*

There is a single predominant Dark Fae male scent here, he said. *It is very likely Urien's.*

All she could smell was beeswax and lemon polish. She decided that was a good thing. She smiled at him on a surge of tenderness. Really, he was the most scary-looking bastard she knew, and she knew a lot of scary-looking bastards. He was one of the most alpha males in the world. Once he had been a god. He was used to commanding troops of Wyr fighters, experienced in tactical maneuvers and making autonomous decisions. He had given up all of it. Today he had sublimated who he was just to walk in her shadow. She tried to imagine him living that way, year in and year out, as he suppressed everything he was just to be with her.

Oh God, Rune was right, this wasn't going to work.

She looked from Tiago to Aubrey then to Naida's shuttered expression.

Too many things were already happening in the room, and nobody had yet said a word. Panic threatened to take her over. She tried to stomp on it. She was too tired, overstimulated, stressed by just being on Urien's home turf and surrounded by all the evidence of him, and in the last thirty-six hours she had taken a whirlwind sightseeing tour of all the major stopping points on the emotional map.

She would much rather have gone on a sightseeing tour of Europe. How convenient, her bags were already packed. Maybe running away would solve all her problems. Okay, so that seemed like a long shot, but she could be willing to give it a try.

Tiago turned her toward him and gripped her shoulders. His Power had never left her once since they had arrived, and now it enfolded her, an inexhaustible wellspring of strength and warmth. He said in a calm, quiet voice, "Take your time."

She nodded and looking up, met his gaze.

Steady. Adamant. Bedrock.

She flashed back in memory to the last private conversation she'd had with Dragos. They had been in his office. The French doors and blinds had been open to a scorching morning sun. The room had been filled with hot yellow sunshine and sharp gusts of air.

They sat as they had so many times over the last two hundred years. The black-haired dragon had lounged back in his chair, his eyes more golden than the sun, booted heels propped on his desk. She perched on the desk beside his feet, cross-legged with her shoes kicked off.

"They may give you the throne, but you will have to take the power," Dragos said.

"That sounds a lot easier said than done," she muttered as she scratched at the tip of one ear. "Any advice?"

Dragos shrugged. "Assume you will make enemies. Work to make allies. Don't expect to make friends. Friends are a gift that happens over time. You have a lot of good things going for you. You're diplomatic, you're smart and you think fast, you see consequences and nuances, and you know how to cheat. But you have one great flaw when it comes to taking the throne."

She scowled. The gods only knew what would come out of Dragos's mouth next. She couldn't shapeshift, her swordplay was laughable, she had no fangs or claws with which to defend herself. It could be anything. "What is that?"

The dragon said, "You want to be liked."

Whatever else he had done or failed to do, Urien had never made that mistake.

She lifted up her chin, grateful more than she could say for the silent supportive oasis Tiago had given her. He gave her that subtle smile again, squeezed her shoulders and stepped back.

She should have a new personal slogan. WWDD—What Would Dragos Do? She turned back to Aubrey and Naida. Naida, who had apparently decided to join them uninvited for their private chat.

She said to Naida, "Thank you for requesting the refreshments for us. Please shut the doors on your way out."

Okay, she wasn't so sure Dragos would have said "please" and "thank you." He had only just started experimenting with trying out those three new words on his inner circle. But the message was still sent and received. Naida bowed her head and walked out. Tiago watched the Dark Fae woman leave, his expression impassive.

Niniane expelled a pent-up breath. She walked to an armchair and sat. Her legs felt rubbery again. Tiago moved in silence to take a position behind her chair.

Aubrey said, "Naida means well."

Niniane looked up. The Dark Fae male was watching her, his face troubled. She made a gesture of negation, waving away what had happened. She said, "Would you both please have a seat?"

Aubrey's gaze went to Tiago in quick surprise, but the Chancellor moved to sit at the end of the couch closest to her on her left. Tiago chose the armchair to her right.

Niniane tilted up one shoe to look at it. She said to the shoe in a flat voice, "I was in the palace when my family was killed. Tiago already knows. Taking this journey is bringing up a lot of old bad stuff, Aubrey. I get close to something of Urien's, like when I walked in this room, and I want to set it on fire."

Aubrey's brows pulled together. "I had no idea."

She said to her shoe, "Of course you didn't. How could you? You didn't even know I was alive until recently."

"Do you know how famous you are to the Dark Fae?" he said. That caused her to raise her gaze to his. The older male regarded her with a bittersweet expression. "You had simply vanished. There was no body, no evidence of your death. It was assumed you must be dead, but the question always remained, a rumor that you were alive and in hiding somewhere, and that one day you would return to rule. At first it was a comfortable whisper, one of those ghost tales told around a campfire, but over the last couple of decades the rumor grew to have quite a bite."

Her eyes narrowed. "What do you mean?"

Aubrey said, "Urien, and those who supported him, were reacting to many things when they overthrew your father. One of those things was the British losing the American War of Independence. I agreed with your father. When change comes, you must change to meet it. But his opponents claimed they were protecting the Dark Fae's status quo against being overrun by what they saw was a barbaric horde of heathens. They were really protecting the Dark Fae's Powerful elite, protecting themselves, but over time it came at the expense of the more ordinary of us, who might otherwise have thrived with all the advent of fresh opportunity that came along with those barbarian hordes."

Aubrey had never been ordinary in his long life, but she chose not to remark upon that. Instead she said, "Why, you sound almost democratic."

He laughed. "Perhaps I wouldn't go quite that far, unless it's possible to be a democratic-minded supporter of a benevolent, open-minded ruler?" He sobered as he continued, "At any rate, opportunities became rare, and they went to Urien's circle of friends and supporters, which grew fewer over time as our economy slowed. In the meantime, many of the ordinary ones suffered, and people began to speak of your legend with quite a dangerous sense of longing. It used to drive Urien into a rage. Of course now we know he knew the truth about you."

She gave him a grim look. "Indeed he did."

"I hated him," Aubrey said. He shook his head. "We're all adjusting to his death, I think, because it still feels dangerous to admit that. Your father had been a good friend of mine, and I, like so many others, had been half in love with your mother."

She smiled. "Really? I guess she might have been beautiful. I don't know, I don't remember that very well. What I remember is she was so funny and loving, and lively, and she made the room light up whenever she came into it."

"Yes," Aubrey said. "She was all of that. She would be so proud of you."

Niniane's eyebrows shot up. She was so shocked at his words, tears sprang to her eyes. "My goodness," she said. She laughed a little and wiped her nose. "Do you really think so?"

"I do," Aubrey said. "Not only did you survive against all the odds and turn into a beautiful woman, but you also learned skills and made connections, and you became someone she would have been thrilled to see take the throne."

"I don't know about that, but it means a lot to me that you said it."

She caught sight of Tiago out of the corner of her eye. He was smiling at her.

She said to him, "Thank you."

"For what?" said Tiago. He sprawled in his chair, his long legs stretched out and crossed at the ankles, his elbows rested on the chair's arms, his fingers steepled.

"You've been nothing but supportive today in all the right ways," she said.

"It's a complicated day," he said. "I'm trying to help." His words were neutral, but his Power stroked her cheek with a smoky tenderness.

"That means a lot to me," she said. She straightened her aching back and turned her attention to Aubrey, who had followed their exchange with close attention. She told Aubrey, "I have an agenda for this talk. First, I promised I would tell you why I know Dragos and the Wyr were not behind the second attack. Second, you need to know—Tiago is coming with me to Adriyel to stay."

The Chancellor's expression flared. "That's unacceptable."

"Is it now?" Tiago said. He tilted his head and regarded the Dark Fae male with a lazy predatory gaze. "Tough shit."

Tiago made an interesting discovery that day, as he guarded Niniane through two very different groups of people. She sure did an awful lot of talking. She spoke to every last person— yeah, there's no way that would always be possible—but somehow none of what she said ended up being blah-fucking-blah. She spoke to people with real warmth about matters that directly affected them, and they responded to her.

To him there was always something interesting to what she did, whether it was what she actually said, or how she wrinkled her nose and widened her eyes when she was feeling mischievous, or whenever she might get a particularly evil glint in her eyes. Sometimes he just watched her cute little ass as she walked, and he lost himself in remembrance of what had happened, in fantasy for the lovemaking to come.

He came to realize that all of her shoes were fuck-me shoes. Those little pretty froufrou strappy things she slipped on her feet could be categorized as weapons of mass destruction, because they obliterated the male mind. They elongated and defined those delicate, slender legs of hers. He would swear they caused her to walk in such a way that her hips swayed with a sexy little wriggle that had every male focusing on her like they were German pointers and she was the game they had just flushed out of the foliage.

She would be good on the throne, he decided with a sense of pride. She needed seasoning and confidence, and she had wavered once or twice at certain junctures, but all the raw materials were there, along with the not-inconsiderable added bonus that people fell in love with her wherever she went.

So he was content to stroll behind the little faerie and learn more about her. He catalogued potential threats, memorized faces, and noticed weaknesses in the layout of the property, such as the places where he would launch an attack or how he might break into the house. There wasn't a lot on that end; the place was well constructed and defended. But there were a few things he would change.

He also made a note of personalities and problems. He had been used to command for a very long time. Most people had tells, a twitch or nervous habit, or a manner of speaking, or a scent they gave off. Scents were interesting tags or identifiers, because they were an involuntary response to stimuli. It was an extremely rare entity that had no tells whatsoever. Often Carling or Dragos could manage it. Certainly the Elven High Lord could pull it off, but the Elven Lord's consort was more intriguing to Tiago, for she could pull it off with much more frequency than anybody else he had met.

Take the bug, for instance. He was pretty sure that nervous little man had a drug addiction of some sort. He had a scent that was too chemical but with no underlying layers to indicate he was taking something for an illness. Tiago was pretty laissez-faire about drug addictions—whatever a person chose to do was their own business—except when it came to people in positions of some importance or authority. An addiction meant impaired judgment and a weakness to exploit. Someone could be bribed or blackmailed, or hell, they might just fuck up. The bug smelled of fear. He was afraid he was going to get caught and removed from his position. He was right.

Another person of interest to Tiago was the guard captain, whose attitude toward Niniane held a veiled antagonism. Tiago had roused to urge her silently to step back toward him, while he assessed the man. Tiago continued to watch the captain without seeming to for several minutes after Niniane had moved away, watching the man's expressions and how he interacted with the people around him. If he were to make a guess, it looked like the captain had a problem with women in authority. It didn't appear that his veiled antagonism was directed at Niniane in particular. It was nothing personal—and the man was going to have to go, just as fast as Tiago could have a word with Arethusa to make it happen.

Naida, now. There was an interesting chick. Tiago was entertained by how a tea service and a tray of munchies could turn into some kind of subtle push for power or position. The kind of maneuvering for position he was used to tended to involve heavy artillery, a fight to get to high ground and his troops laying down covering fire. He watched and waited as his faerie assessed the situation, mulled it over and then sent the other woman away. Naida's posture and expression had been quite correct and compliant, but she couldn't hide her flare of scent aggression that filled the air as she walked out of the room. Naida couldn't be fired like the other two, but he thought he could learn a lot by keeping an eye on her.

The Chancellor was a different matter altogether. His face, scent and posture spoke of alarm, not aggression. Tiago took a plate, filled it and handed it to Niniane, who accepted it after a hesitation and a flare of surprise in her gorgeous eyes. He took another plate—there were three, he noticed, which was perfect, although not exactly what Naida had originally intended—and he piled that one higher then relaxed back in his chair and watched the Chancellor with cold killer's eyes. Tiago decided he enjoyed armchair warfare. It was so comfortable, and there were pastries.

Aubrey's face tightened as he suppressed some kind of strong emotion. It was a complicated scent Tiago couldn't yet decipher. The Chancellor turned to Niniane. "I apologize for my outburst, your highness," he said. "You said you had an agenda."

The guy was smooth, Tiago would grant him that. Maybe it was sincere and maybe it wasn't. Time would tell.

He could almost see his faerie give a mental oh-screw-it shrug. She slipped off her shoes, tucked her feet underneath her and selected one of the pastries Tiago had given her. The one she selected had chocolate in it, and the box of chocolates he had given her had already disappeared. He made a mental note.

Niniane took a bite of the pastry and set it on her plate, her face thoughtful. Tiago shifted his plate to cover the growing bulge in his crotch as he watched her lick powdered sugar off her fingers. Thinking and licking just became his two new favorite things to watch her do. What was going on behind that sweet pixie face of hers? Was she thinking through A and B to reach C or D, or was she jumping out of the logical alphabet again? He couldn't wait to see her when she was really conniving.

When she spoke next, it was to tell the Chancellor about her line of thinking about the Wyr, seasoned as it was by the intimacy of long familiarity, along with the conversation she'd had with Aryal. "So you see, it is nonsensical to believe the Wyr were behind the attack," she said.

"I see," Aubrey said. "Thank you for taking the time to explain it to me. When you explain everything that way, it does seem obvious that Dragos and the Wyr government were not involved, except in an accidental way as Tiago defended you."

Tiago enjoyed his snack while he watched and listened. Aubrey mentioned nothing of Arethusa's conversation with Tiago and Rune at the morgue. Arethusa must have decided to play her cards very close to her chest. Interesting. Apparently Arethusa didn't trust anybody at the moment. Given her familiarity with the other Dark Fae, what did that say about her, or them? Tiago let the puzzle pieces in his head connect, break apart and re-form into different scenarios.

"Now to move on to your second point," said Aubrey. The male looked at Tiago directly. "Please understand, this is not meant to be personal in any way. I have great admiration for everything you've accomplished. But no one will accept one of Dragos's sentinels, let alone his warlord, on permanent deployment in the Dark Fae demesne. It would be considered an act of aggression and cause for war. The Dark Fae are unsettled enough by Urien's death. While he had grown unpopular, he also ruled with a strong hand that gave many a sense of security they no longer have at the moment."

"That's why I quit," said Tiago. He popped another pastry into his mouth.

The other male sat forward, his gaze sharp. "Excuse me?"

"I said I quit," Tiago told him. "I am an independent agent. I no longer work for Dragos in any capacity."

Aubrey's astonished gaze shot to Niniane, who nodded. She said, "He's coming with me."

"I see," said Aubrey, but Tiago was sure he didn't yet. The man might be smart and well-placed in the Dark Fae government, but he was not as quick on the uptake on a few things like his wife was. His wife had taken one look at Tiago and Niniane and had gotten it. "Your highness, even if people believed that Tiago really has quit, they're not—"

"Aubrey," Niniane interrupted. Her voice, like her face, was calm, her eyes clear. "I'm not asking for permission or what people's opinion will be on this issue. Either Tiago is coming with me, or I'm not going. The last thing on my agenda for this talk is to see if we can come to an understanding with you on this. I want you to back me up. I want you to be my supporter. I want to talk to you, confide in you, and ask your opinions about things. I have to start developing relationships with someone, and to start trusting somewhere. Frankly, if we can't get you to accept this, I don't see any reason in crossing over. We might as well stay here and the Dark Fae can find some other person to try to put on the throne. You're some second or third cousin by marriage. Maybe that would be you."

"Please." Aubrey put up both hands, his face and scent flaring with deeper alarm. "Don't say another word like that. My family connection is distant, and in any case, *you* are the real heir."

"Then back me up," Niniane said. "If you support this, other people may grumble at first, and they may not like it, but eventually they will accept it. Tiago is my—"

"Chief of security," Tiago said.

She turned to him, surprised. "Is that what you are?"

Now that he had verbalized it, he tested it out in his head. There was no point in freaking out the faeries any further with talk of Wyr mating. What happened between him and Niniane was none of their business, and Niniane needed him to protect her, which was going to be a much more sophisticated and complex job than simply watching her back as her bodyguard. He said, "Yes."

She regarded him, her expression concerned. "That will be a difficult position to be in as a foreigner."

"I like a challenge," he told her. "And it's where I need to be, and it's where you need me to be." He added telepathically, *And I'll be hellacious good at it.*

Her gaze searched his. He gave her a nod.

She looked at Aubrey, who stared into the middle distance while he wore a deep frown. "If you truly believe that I am the real heir, then you also have to recognize that change is here to stay for the Dark Fae," she said. "I don't think any of you have fully accepted that yet. Some of Urien's old supporters are going to have a problem too, but there's no use in trying to resist it. This is Urien's legacy every bit as much as the laws he passed or the way he tried to cloister Adriyel from the outside world. Because of what he did, I had to escape and go somewhere else to survive."

Aubrey looked at her with pain in his eyes. "If I had known you were alive, I would never have stopped searching for you."

Her face softened. It was clear she believed him. There was so much sincerity in his voice, even Tiago almost believed him. She said in a gentle voice, "I appreciate you saying that more than you can know, but that's all water under the bridge now. The point I'm trying to make is, because of what happened, I became someone I wouldn't have otherwise become. I'm young for a faerie and I'm trendy, and the Dark Fae aren't used to that in a ruler. I like American pop culture, cheese pizza, reading romance novels, and shopping in Milan. Also, thanks to Dragos, I have independent relationships with every Elder demesne in the continental United States. Now I can compromise on a lot of things. I can take advice and bring change in carefully and gently, but I will not compromise on this. I trust Tiago with my life in a way I can't trust anyone else right now, not even you."

Aubrey rubbed his forehead and looked under his hand from her to Tiago. After a moment he said to Tiago, "I will withdraw my support at the first hint that you are really working for the Wyr."

"I would expect nothing else," Tiago said.

Aubrey pressed. "She is the last direct descendant of the Lorelle line, and the only thing left of her father. You must always act with Niniane's best interests at heart, and do everything in your power to keep her safe."

"That," Tiago told him with perfect honesty, "is not going to be a problem."

Aubrey said to Niniane, "Very well then. I will support you."

Niniane's face lit up. She slipped out of the armchair and

went to Aubrey to put her arms around his neck and hug him. Tiago tensed, hating her close contact to the other male but suffering through the moment, recognizing it as important to the other two, perhaps even necessary. Still, he watched Aubrey with jealous attention, noting the exact placement of the other male's hands and arms as Aubrey hugged Niniane back. He could only relax when the Dark Fae male and Niniane separated.

She turned to Tiago and searched his gaze. *I don't want to spring too much on him at once. Do you think I should tell him I intend to bring to trial the people who supported Urien on the night of the coup?*

Tiago studied the Chancellor's face thoughtfully. Change, tempered with patience. It was a good strategy. *Not yet. Remember your own advice and bring in change carefully. Prosecuting people for treason and murder can come after your coronation and we've had a chance to establish a secure power base. For now*—he smiled at her and said with deep satisfaction—*well done.*

═ FIFTEEN ═

Later that evening, Niniane climbed the staircase behind Naida, her movements slow with exhaustion. She had toured the gardens and the rest of the main areas of the house. She had made a cursory inspection of the accounts that maintained the property. Everything appeared to be in order. She and Aubrey had had a preliminary discussion of Dark Fae finances, which were not as robust as she would have liked, but after her talk with Carling she wasn't surprised.

He also gave her an overview on the status of her inheritance of Urien's personal fortune. The sum Urien had managed to amass was staggering. She reminded herself that her family's fortune would have been subsumed into his. She also met separately with Kellen and Arethusa to inform them that Tiago would be coming to Adriyel as her chief of security. Kellen had been outraged, Arethusa noncommittal.

Dinner had been rife with undercurrents and tensions. Carling had come to join the party at the table. The Vampyre had sipped red wine, listened to the conversation and said little. The meal itself had been exquisite, or at least the three bites Niniane managed to choke down had been. She made sure to step into the kitchens to praise the chef and her staff personally. The kitchen staff had been transported with surprise and delight.

Now Tiago climbed the staircase beside her, his powerful body moving with relaxed fluidity, his hands clasped behind his back and his expression impassive as it had been for most of the day. He looked like the aloof Wyr sentinel she had met in Cuelebre Tower. After consuming the huge plate of pastries, he had proceeded to eat a mountainous dinner. He appeared to be impervious to glares, dislike, snubs and innuendoes. She had felt quite an irrational desire to smack him several times over the head with her napkin.

Naida said over her shoulder, "Earlier your bags had been taken to the master suite, but Aubrey and I wondered if you might enjoy a more feminine touch in your rooms. There's a suite that has a lovely view of the back gardens. I hope you don't mind that I took the liberty of requesting that your things be moved back there?"

She sighed. She was too tired to tell if there were undercurrents in Naida's voice. No doubt Aubrey had thought to make the change after her reaction to Urien's study. She was just relieved she didn't have to step into Urien's bedroom. She'd had it up to her eyeballs with confronting all things Urien, his handwriting, his decor decisions, his approach to foreign policy and his outrageous expense accounts. Apparently he'd had a fondness for Elven wine and Vieux Cognac aged from the French Revolution, which everyone at dinner had been all too pleased to sample. It was probably the only thing they had agreed upon. If she had to look at his bed right now she might gak up all three bites of her dinner on what was no doubt a tasteful and very expensive carpet.

So she chose to be grateful and stuck to a simple reply. "That's great, thanks."

Naida looked back to smile at her. "Everyone has been clamoring for your attention today. I cannot imagine how tired you are."

"I'm pretty tired," Niniane admitted.

They walked down a second-floor hall. The hardwood floor was carpeted with a woolen wine-colored hallway runner and furnished with heavy dark antique tables and cabinets. Urien apparently had liked the English manor look to go with the Georgian-style architecture. Toward the end of the hall Naida opened a door then stood back to let Tiago enter first. He did so, turned and indicated that Niniane could step inside. She walked into a large bedroom that was a blur of green and cream.

A delicate floral pattern flecked with pink decorated the bed-spread and pillow shams.

She turned to Naida, who was studying Tiago with an inscru-table expression. Naida said to Tiago, "Your bag has been put in the room next door."

Tiago nodded, and remained silent. He stood relaxed, his hands on his hips, clearly not intending to go anywhere. His massive black-clad physique and visible weaponry were a bar-baric contrast to the room's light feminine decor.

Naida's sleek eyebrows rose a delicate fraction of an inch. She said to Niniane, "If no one has yet shown you, all the rooms are connected with an intercom system. You can request any-thing you want or need by contacting household staff through the unit on the bedside table. Is there anything else I can do for you?"

Niniane said, "No, thank you."

"I'll say goodnight then. Rest well." The Dark Fae woman stepped out, closing the door behind her.

Tiago said, "I think she likes me."

She burst out laughing and clapped her hands over her mouth.

He gave her that sexy, subtle not-quite smile of his. "Don't you? I'm pretty sure she's crushing on me right now."

Shh, remember how sensitive Dark Fae hearing is. She can still hear you! she said telepathically as she tried to stifle her giggles.

"I'm not at all concerned about that," Tiago said.

Her body couldn't stay upright any longer. She kicked off her shoes, staggered forward and pitched onto the bed face-first. She was so exhausted her muscles ached all over and she trembled on the edge of something, she didn't know what, as all the reactions that she had suppressed from the day threatened to come crashing down on her head at once.

She fisted her hands into the bedspread. She'd had that flash of conviction in Urien's study that Rune had been right, she and Tiago were making a monumental mistake, and it had been so strong and felt so real, it had frightened her so that she had stuffed it down and refused to look at it for the rest of the day. Now that the outside stresses had eased up, the memory of that conviction came roaring back.

She heard Tiago moving about the bedroom. He opened and closed the closet and bathroom doors. Then the bed dipped as he knelt beside her. His large hands ghosted over her. He found the back zipper in her dress and unzipped it. Cool air kissed her skin.

"I know I'm a high-maintenance girlfriend," she said into the bedspread.

"Fuck, yeah," he agreed. "The highest. You need a whole staff of full-time employees." He paused. "I just realized I'm not kidding."

"I panicked earlier in the study." He nudged her. She rolled to one side and he eased her arm out of the dress. Then she rolled to the other side, and he eased out that arm too.

"I got that." He tapped her at the base of her spine. "Lift up your hips."

She lifted and he pulled the dress down so that it slid off her legs. At least he didn't rip this one to shreds. Maybe he only ripped up dresses that had sequins on them. They knew so little about each other, but that still hadn't stopped them from plunging together. In retrospect the impetuousness of their actions made her shake. "I panicked about us," she said.

Silence. He laid a hand on her back. It felt huge, warm and heavy. "Why?"

She lifted her shoulder.

"That is not an adequate response, faerie," he growled. His Power lay in the room, a heavy brooding presence. "I require a series of words strung together that make coherent sentences."

"I looked at you and something happened in my head," she said. "All I could see was everything that you had left behind just to follow me throughout my day. I couldn't see how you could thrive doing that, and then what Rune said came back to me. Tiago, are you sure about this?"

He was silent a moment. Then he said, "Stay put."

"Okay." She snuffled into the bedspread as he walked away.

Tiago strode into the bathroom and inspected it. It was a large, luxurious bathroom, color-coordinated to complement the bedroom and dotted with the silver gleam of polished fixtures. He noted with approval that there were a lot of expensive-looking bottles of froufrou set out on the counter surfaces. She would like that. He uncapped one bottle on the tub and sniffed the contents. It smelled pink. He started a hot bath running and squirted some of the pink-smelling stuff under the gush of water. It foamed into bubbles. He swished his hand through the bubbles and water. The temperature felt fine to him, but his hand was so calloused he would have to be careful with her delicate skin.

He walked back into the bedroom and regarded his doubtful faerie's nearly nude backside as he stripped. That sweet little curvy body of hers embodied the definition of sexy with those two cute toothpick-sized knives strapped in sheaths to her slender thighs. The realization that those knives were poisoned and she knew how to use them made him hotter than hell. How could he ever think that big strapping women were his type? He promised himself a treat one day. He would watch her ride him while she wore those thigh sheaths and nothing else. He cocked his head. No wait. Maybe that pearl necklace too.

When he was nude, he unbuckled her thigh sheaths, unsnapped the back fastening of her bra and slipped her panties off. Then he scooped her up, took her into the bathroom and tipped her over the water. "Check that," he said.

She wiggled her fingers in the frothy mounds of froufrou-smelling stuff, dipped them into the water underneath and sighed. "It's perfect."

He deposited her in the tub and climbed in behind her so that she sat sandwiched between his legs. He leaned back in the tub with a grunt and pulled her to him. She moaned and collapsed against his chest. His engorged cock had been on urgent duty call from the moment he had slipped off her dress, and he had to shift a bit to find a comfortable spot. Then he wrapped his arms around her warm, wet naked body and contemplated the concept of perfection.

"We have agreed that you panicked in the study," he said.

Her head moved in a small nod.

"Do we also agree that you panicked over several things and not just about me?"

Another nod.

"Shall we consider the possibility that this was stress induced?"

"Yes," she muttered. "But Tiago—"

"No 'buts,'" he ordered. "And don't wriggle." She huffed but subsided, and he bit back a smile. It was a rare moment when she didn't have a comeback of some sort. She truly must be exhausted. He pressed a kiss to the top of her head. "Perhaps we should then conclude that what you panicked over may not necessarily be of any real concern."

"Tiago—"

"I'm hearing a 'but' attached to that," he said in warning. "It is implied, but it is still there." She growled in frustration even as she wrapped her arms around his to hug him back. "You must trust me to look out for myself. I had fun today."

"You had *fun*?" She tilted back her head to look at him in surprise.

He swooped in fast to kiss her pillowy mouth. "I did. Furthermore, I learned a lot. I learned things about you, and I learned things about the people around you. You might recall, I also figured out exactly what I need to be doing and how."

"Okay, I'll give you that."

He pulled her up higher so that she was lying on him, their legs entwined.

"You keep picking me up and carting me around," she muttered. "You know, when I'm not injured or drunk on my ass, I do have two perfectly functional feet."

"You are just so magnificently portable," he told her. She snorted out a laugh, her body relaxing against his, her head tucked under his chin. "I like carting you around." He loved how she felt in his arms. He asked, "So what is the moral of this story?"

She yawned. "Stop panicking?"

"Well, that too." He rubbed her back. "The moral of the story is you must learn to trust me. Don't try to do your job and worry about me too. It's too much and, more important, it's not necessary. You have an immense undertaking ahead of you. I need to be able to trust you too, that you're taking your best to your job. We both need you to succeed."

She kissed his neck. "We both need you to succeed too."

"I think that works out well," Tiago said. "Don't you?"

"Yes. Okay." The bubble bath was warm and lustrous, and Tiago's body made the most comforting bed imaginable. She slit her eyes open. His dark muscled chest looked intensely masculine against the mounds of bubbles that surrounded them. She looked at the massive bulge of his bicep as she traced the barbed wire tattoo with a finger. "What did you learn?"

"About you?" His deep, lazy voice reverberated in her ear.

"No, silly, about other people."

He shifted and kissed her forehead. He said telepathically, *From his scent and mannerisms, the bug is most likely an addict of some sort. Unless he can convince me he's ill and on some kind of medication that produces a chemical tinge to his scent, he has got to go. The guard captain has got to go too. My guess is he has a problem with females in authority, but it doesn't really matter. I don't like how he responds to you. I like most of the house staff. I don't have an opinion one way or another about the grounds staff as long as they follow security protocol, and I don't trust Naida as far as I could throw her.*

You could actually manage to toss her quite a distance, she murmured.

He conceded the point. *Okay, I trust her much less than as far as I could throw her. You get my point. I haven't made up my mind about Aubrey. Sorry, but I haven't. I think Arethusa is genuinely investigating the attacks, and she doesn't seem to trust anybody else. That makes me cautious. And I think Kellen is likely to be trouble, politically if in no other way. And there's one last thing.*

What is it? Her mental voice was flat, tired.

He could imagine how difficult hearing all this was for her. These were her people, and some of them were people she remembered from a happy childhood. Her instincts must be warring inside as she wondered who she should trust. His arms tightened. He said in as gentle a voice as he could manage, *Perhaps the attacks on you were engineered by someone other than the Dark Fae. But taking everything into consideration, including the timeline of events, I think it is most likely that the person behind the attacks is under this roof.*

She was silent as she considered his words. *What is your reasoning?*

She didn't just accept what he said, or react. Good girl.

I don't have evidence, he said. *And I could be wrong. But consider: who would have had the time to develop an alliance with Geril and entice him to commit a really bad fucking crime? Geril didn't just attempt murder. He attempted a political assassination. There had to be a damn-strong motive there, and I'm not sure that money alone would have done it.*

She stirred. *What do you mean?*

He explained about the conversation he and Rune had had with Arethusa in the morgue, and the payout Geril had received from the bogus Illinois company that was supposedly owned by Cuelebre Enterprises. *Remember, I'm just making suppositions,* he said. *But given how Urien controlled traffic to and from Adriyel, it seems less likely that an outside agent from another demesne could have had the time to persuade Geril to act. And why would another demesne do that?*

They wouldn't, she whispered. *They would have no reason to.*

Exactly, he said. *There's no motive. Look at it as a risk/ benefit analysis. You're already known to all the demesnes, and every last one of them is hoping to develop a good relationship with you. They may not like your connection to Dragos, but at worst they would watch and wait to see what kind of monarch you would make. Assassination could come at a later point if they feel you present an active danger to them. To try to assassinate you now wouldn't benefit any of them strongly enough to offset the risk of inciting war with the Dark Fae or of incurring Dragos's wrath.*

She was still, huddled against him, and silent.

Again, I have no proof, he said gently. *But what makes the most sense from what we know is that our perp was someone who crossed over from Adriyel to Chicago with Geril. Maybe it's someone with an allegiance to Uriel's old cronies; I am very interested in pursuing that line of investigation when we reach Adriyel. Our perp would have had time to work on him by promising a big enough reward. At the same time Geril would have perceived our perp as a big enough threat, so that killing you became more important than leaving you alive and trying to curry favor with you.*

She shook off suds from her fingers to rub at her forehead, which had begun to ache. *Geril was a weathervane on risk and benefit,* she said thoughtfully. *It seems the benefit of a romantic attachment with me would have outweighed the risk from his coconspirator.*

He might even have entertained giving up his partner, Tiago said. *Until it became clear you had no interest in him. At that point his original agreement with his partner became more imperative. And his partner had to be in Chicago, not back in Adriyel, because they had the means and opportunity to act quickly to set up the second attack. That's the best fitting profile we have right now. Everything points to it being someone in the Dark Fae delegation—or at least in their party.*

She had already known there was a strong likelihood that whoever had tried to have her killed was Dark Fae, but somehow it was so much worse to hear it all laid out in Tiago's cool, relentless logic.

She said aloud, "You sure know how to ruin a totally excellent bubble bath."

When the bathwater cooled, he picked her up and stepped out of the tub. Since he enjoyed carting her around so much, she decided to let him. He set her on her feet and handed her a towel. She scrubbed herself dry, her eyelids half shut. Then he swung her up into his arms again. She was asleep before he stepped out of the bathroom.

The next thing she knew she was warm all over, and her neck, cheek and ear were burning hot.

Irritable, she rubbed her neck and tried to burrow under her hard pillow, but she couldn't figure out how to get underneath it. Her pillow moved up and down, and her eyes opened. She was lying on Tiago who lay sprawled on his back, his head turned to one side. All of the feather pillows had ended up on the floor. She lifted her head to peer down the bed. All of the blankets had ended up on the floor too. They were both nude, and the sheet was their only covering. The window curtains had not been completely closed, and a brilliant yellow band of morning sunlight slashed across the bed. The heat from the strip of sunlight was what had awakened her.

She tilted her head as she studied Tiago. She had never seen him asleep before. This was only the second time she had shared a bed with him. Apparently he did not understand the concept of bed sharing that well. He owned every inch of the bed and made the queen-sized mattress seem as small as a twin.

He radiated heat. She could feel it when she held her hand an inch away from his sun-burnished skin. His face was turned away from the morning sun. The arc from his head down the long column of his neck to the heavy flare of his collarbones was strong and graceful. He had a large scar that sliced across the right side of his torso. It started at the base of his right ribs and slashed all the way to his back. His broad shoulders and deep chest, with those defined intercostal muscles that rippled down his rib cage, indicated the kind of leviathan strength that could catapult his huge Wyr form through the air fast enough to bring down a helicopter gunship.

She touched the scar. One of the persistent legends about Tiago that circulated the Tower was from a time in the late 1960s when he had troops pinned down by enemy gunfire from a gunship. His fighters were dying, so he changed into his Wyr form and slammed sidelong into the helicopter. He drove the helicopter toward the side of a cliff, and managed to pull up just before it exploded against the cliff face. He had sustained serious injuries, as one of the helicopter blades had sliced into him, and he had been forced to take a six-month hiatus. Remembering how he had leaped forward to stop her SUV dead in its skid, she could believe the story.

As she studied him, the extent of his handsomeness was revealed, with those proud high cheekbones, dark slashing eyebrows, lean cheeks, a bold forehead, nose and chin and that mobile expressive mouth. When he was awake, intelligence and aggression carved him into a natural biological weapon. He was such a battering ram of a male, his personality was the kind of force that could roll over a country and bring down a government. No wonder the Dark Fae reacted so strongly to the possibility of him moving into their lands and home.

He'd had fun yesterday. Fun. She thought of him sprawled in the armchair in the downstairs study, calmly demolishing pastry after pastry while Aubrey looked at him in shock. Or what about that god-awful dinner? A variety of people looked daggers at him and tried several times to deliver a direct verbal cut, while he plowed through alarming amounts of beautifully prepared food with evident enjoyment for the cuisine and a monumental indifference for anybody else's opinion. It wasn't that he didn't get that people had been trying to insult him. He just didn't care.

She pinched her nose hard and bit her lip to keep from laughing and waking him up. He needed so much less sleep than she did, and to the best of her knowledge he had not had a chance to rest since he had arrived in Chicago. She wanted to enjoy this rare treat of watching him while he slept.

She had to learn to trust him, he'd said. He was right. Yesterday he had gleaned a surprising amount of information just by observing people, and he had a clear, strong vision of what he needed to do. His ruthlessness, his aptitude for tactics and strategy, and his incisive logic and investigative skills were all natural fits for the position he had reached out and taken for himself.

She took a deep breath and sighed. For the first time in what seemed like forever, the tight, restricting band around her chest was gone. She felt lighter, full of hope and optimism.

Tiago's compilation of facts was persuasive. She believed as he did, that a killer lay in quiet wait in the house. But she now believed that the killer would be caught, and that she and Tiago had a fighting chance in this new life they had begun to carve out for themselves.

Belief, hope, optimism. Passion and laughter. A sense of safety. Look at the wealth of gifts he had given her. Just days ago she had been drunk, injured, frightened and alone.

Overcome with emotion, she pressed a kiss to his warm pectoral. She watched his face as he stirred, his beautiful mouth pulling into a sleepy smile. He put a hand to her cheek and fingered the pointed tip of her ear. She felt his penis stiffen against her hip, felt her own responding clench of hunger, and she indulged in a luxurious full-body stretch that moved her body along the length of his.

"Faerie, you sure do know how to make a man glad he's alive," he said. His morning voice was gravelly, deeper, and it rumbled against her cheek. He yawned.

"I notice that you are taking up the whole damn bed," she said. She kissed his nipple. It pebbled under her lips.

"It's comfortable so why not?"

"Tiago, it's my bed." She licked his nipple and nibbled at it and listened to his breath catch. It was the sexiest sound she had ever heard. Her hunger sharpened and became liquid as she felt his erection pulse.

His smile widened. He cupped her cheek with those long, clever fingers of his. "You're my faerie. Besides, I didn't hear you complaining in the night."

"I'm complaining now," she informed him. She nipped gently at the pebbled flesh. He sucked air.

"Is that what you're doing?" he said between his teeth. His legs shifted restlessly underneath her. "Take your time, tell me all about it. I'm a patient man for these kinds of complaints."

"I demand recompense." She slid farther down that long rippling torso, licking and kissing as she went.

He hissed, lifting his head to watch her with black glittering eyes. He cradled her head between his hands with tense care. "This is called recompense? I'm learning a whole new language here. Please, for pity's sake, have as much recompense as you want."

"I think I will." His erection lay along his washboard stomach, the head almost touching his navel. It was as beautiful as the rest of him, large, hot and velvet-skinned, his testicles voluptuous, tight globes underneath. She gripped his penis under the head, lifted it to her mouth and sucked him in.

His head slammed back against the mattress and he opened his mouth in a silent shout. The sight of his extreme pleasure was so erotic she moistened further, her hunger settling between her legs as a deep, insistent ache. She scratched lightly at the side of his ribs as she suckled him, and his torso arched off the bed.

His hands and heavy, powerful thigh muscles were shaking. She did this. She caused this man to shake. She purred, opened up her throat and took all of him in.

"Holy gods, Niniane!"

This peaceful sunlit bedroom was their oasis, their time to let go of outside stresses and dangers and relish the nurturance of their sensuality. When they left they would have to arm themselves with weapons and watch the world with wary eyes, but for now they had this moment and she would take everything she could from it before she let it go. Under the lavish generosity of so many gifts, she dared to think and say what she felt. She whispered in his head, *You're mine*.

He said between gritted teeth, "I couldn't be more yours. Take all of me, faerie. Don't leave one piece of me behind."

She held her hands out to him. He laced his fingers through hers. They held on to each other as she took him until the warm vitality of his climax flooded her mouth.

He wasn't done, of course. She had roused him to such an extent, he rose over her with his face desperate, stripped of all self-protection. He pinned her to the bed and drove into her. She turned her head at the gorgeousness of his entry, and the morning sun blinded her. The world around her was radiant, full of light. He stretched and filled her, and she clenched on him with all the strength she had. She caught the shadowed arc of his wide shoulders flexing over her. His head was flung back, eyes closed. People kill for this kind of beauty.

He took everything. It was unthinkable to keep one piece of her behind.

I love you. She heard the echo in the room and knew she had said it.

He framed her face and drove his mouth down on hers as he drove in her body. "So this is called love," he gasped. *"La petite mort."*

Drenched in gold, she lay transfixed by the surprise of him, the language of his body, the poetry of his mind.

La petite mort. The little death. More than a climax, a spiritual release.

Then they both took flight.

Late that afternoon, a hesitant knock sounded at the door. Niniane called out, "Yes?"

Vrayna, one of the household staff, said, "My apologies, your highness, I know you said you did not wish to be disturbed, but a Chicago policewoman is here to see you."

"Oh good, that's Cameron!" Niniane dropped the clothes she held to clap her hands. "Please show her up."

A few minutes later a second, firmer knock sounded on the door. She flung it open. Cameron stood in the hall, dressed casually in jeans, black shoes and a red summer tank top. Her sandy hair was pulled back in a plain clip, and her cinnamon-sprinkled face was lit with pleasure. Niniane threw her arms around the taller woman. Cameron laughed in surprise and hugged her back.

Then Cameron looked over Niniane's shoulder. "Okay," said the policewoman. "And you still intend to leave tomorrow?"

Niniane turned to look too.

The lovely bedroom was a rainbow-colored disaster. There were two armchairs arranged by a small table near open windows. The table held the remains of a meal on a food tray. Tiago occupied one of the chairs. He lounged with his long legs stretched out. He was dressed in jeans, a plain black T-shirt, boots, and just one visible weapon, a handgun in an arm holster. Jewelry boxes and toiletry bags were piled on one end of the bed. The other end was piled with dresses and other outfits. The closet spewed dozens of shoes on the floor. The second armchair was stacked with paperbacks, magazines, folder files and a laptop.

Tiago's lap was mounded with filmy garments in a variety of colors, pink, cream, royal blue, black, lacy red, and a few things that were patterned with flowers. He held in his hands a pair of pale pink high-heeled slip-on shoes with marabou trim. They looked absurdly tiny in his massive grip, the marabou feathers waving gently in a breeze that wafted in from the windows.

Cameron disguised her guffaw poorly as a cough. "Ah, looking a little frilly there, sentinel."

"Fuck you," Tiago said. His tone was amiable. He turned one shoe over and regarded it with a bemused expression. He blew on the marabou.

"Mr. Incredible has discovered he has opinions about women's fashion," Niniane said to Cameron, her eyes dancing.

"Has he, now?" Cameron shook her head. "I am speechless."

"I have very strong opinions about lingerie fashion," said Tiago. He looked at the pile of silken material in his lap. "All of this must come with us. I'll find room for it somewhere if I have to carry it in my own saddlebags." He held the bottom of the shoe up for Cameron's inspection. "She balances her entire body weight, which admittedly is not much, on these minuscule surfaces."

"It's a skill I never acquired," Cameron said. "Nor did I ever want to."

Niniane said, "I can run in those shoes too."

Tiago raised his head. His dark saturnine face turned intent. "I want to see. You have those pearls and knives somewhere."

"Not now," she told him, color darkening her cheeks. "We have company." She smiled at Cameron. "I hope you did not have to quit your job so that you could come."

"I did not," said Cameron. "I got a leave of absence. Given the circumstances with the time difference between here and the Other land, and the honor of the invitation, my superintendent was inclined to be lenient. I'm packed and ready to go." The policewoman raised her eyebrows. "You, clearly, are not."

"Oh *pfft*!" Niniane waved a hand. "We'll have pack animals, but most of this can't come with us anyway. I was trying to choose what I wanted to take, then Tiago got involved and he started asking questions and, well." Her tongue poked between her teeth as she turned in a circle. "We did make a bit of a mess."

Tiago was studying Cameron, his eyes narrowed in thought. He pointed the toe of one shoe at her. "I want to have a word with you."

"All right," said Cameron, who hooked her thumbs in the belt loops of her jeans. "What's up?"

"Have a seat in my office." He indicated the other armchair, then noticed it was full. "Faerie, do you mind if we shift some of this stuff?"

"No, go right ahead." Niniane rubbed the back of her neck, looking frustrated. "I still can't find that ivory inlaid box, and I know I brought it with me. Do you need me for this conversation?"

Tiago smiled at her. "No, I do not. Go find your box."

He helped Cameron clear off the second armchair as Niniane disappeared into the walk-in closet. Cameron took a seat, and he tapped the shoe against his lips as he regarded the policewoman. "I think I can make a pretty good guess at what you make in a year," he said. He named a figure. "Is that close?"

Cameron snorted. "Close enough. I've got twenty years on the force, but a police detective only makes so much."

"You may have heard that I am no longer one of Dragos's sentinels," Tiago said.

"Word's gotten around," said Cameron.

Tiago told her, "I am now Niniane's chief of security, and I'm starting from scratch. Come work for me for a year, and I'll triple your salary. If you want to leave at the end of the year, I'll help you relocate back to Chicago and find a new job."

Cameron stared. "You're asking me to come *live* in Adriyel for a year?"

Tiago shrugged. He switched to telepathy. *She likes you, and she's relaxed in your company. She giggles around you. You get the same pop culture references, and you understand that all this froufrou is important to her. Niniane and I have got to build relationships with Dark Fae, and we will. But right now, you're a trained detective, you're kind to her, and I think you like her too. And I trust you. As I look at you, it occurs to me everything you embody is a rather rare commodity.*

I do like her, Cameron replied. The human was frowning, not in negation, but in thought. *I like her a lot.*

Tiago paused. *Police work and bodyguard work are two different things, of course,* he said. *You would have a lot to learn, and you would have to learn it fast. I remember your employee profile said you have taken some martial arts training, but I doubt you've picked up a sword.*

Actually, I have done a bit of sword work, along with knife and crossbow work, said Cameron. *There's a course through the department for detectives like me who have a spark of Power and who might find themselves needing to cross over to an Other land in pursuit of a fugitive. It was just an introductory survey course. It wouldn't be enough, but it's a start. My God, I'm really thinking about doing this. Don't you have enough bodyguards already? Powerful ones? Rune and Aryal, and assorted Vampyres?*

Yes, but they all leave after Niniane's coronation in a week or so, Tiago said. *And I can't stay with her twenty-four/seven. I'll need to set up my own office when we get to Adriyel and lay the groundwork for developing my own intelligence network. And we have a killer in our group, someone who wants Niniane dead.*

Something fell in the closet, and Niniane swore. Tiago raised his voice. "You okay in there, faerie?"

"Yeeeeessss," Niniane said. She sounded aggravated. "The stupid box just found the top of my head."

He smiled a little. He said to Cameron, "Don't take your time. If you don't do this, I need to find someone who will."

"I'll do it," said Cameron.

≈ SIXTEEN ≈

Niniane was pleased to see Cameron, but she was all too aware that the other woman's arrival heralded change that she could no longer avoid. The sunlit intimacy she had shared with Tiago evaporated. She was glad they had managed to prolong their oasis for so much of the day but she still mourned its passing.

After he finished his talk with Cameron, Tiago stuck his head in the closet. "Faerie."

She sat cross-legged on the floor with the ivory inlaid box on her lap. She fingered the carved wood top. "Yes?"

"Are you all right if Cameron stays with you?" he asked. "I have things I should do. I want to check in with Rune and Aryal."

She nodded without looking up. "Of course."

He was silent. Then his boots came into her line of sight. He kneeled and slipped one hand under her chin to coax her face up for his inspection. He gave her a swift hard kiss. "Your endorsement of this idea is less than rousing," he said. His thumb stroked her bottom lip. "Are you sure?"

She cleared her throat. She told him in a stronger voice, "Yes, I'm sure." She met his dark searching gaze and gave him a small smile. "I just don't want our day together to end, but it's starting to happen in my head anyway. We both have a lot to do before tomorrow's crossover."

His expression was determined. "We will make time for ourselves. I'll not stand for anything else. I am a selfish man and do not intend to go deprived."

Her smile deepened, became more real. "I'll hold you to that."

He tilted his head and nodded to what she held in her lap. "What's in the box?"

She spread her hands over the top of the box. "Just some memories. I can tell you another time."

"All right." He braced his hands on his thighs and leaned forward. "One more for the road."

She put a hand to his cheek as she kissed him, savoring his clean masculine scent and the sensation of his warm, firm lips moving on hers. Then he stood and strode out. He took much of the day's light and warmth with him.

After a few minutes she stood, her arms wrapped around the box, and she walked back into the bedroom. Cameron was sorting through the pile of clothes on the bed, folding things into neat stacks. She had already sorted the lingerie. It sat on the end of the bed with the saucy marabou-trimmed shoes perched on top of the pile.

"You don't have to do that," Niniane said.

Cameron grinned. "Are you kidding? This is a blast. Your wardrobe is like going on a whirlwind shopping spree of the major couture houses."

"I know, I indulge too much." Niniane bit her lip. "Shopping is a stress response for me."

Cameron shrugged. "If you have the kind of budget that can support your habit, who cares?"

"I was listening to your conversation with Tiago," said Niniane. "I'm thrilled you're taking the job."

"Great," said Cameron. "I was just wondering if I should have run it by you before accepting. I'll need to email my notice to my supervisor and arrange with my brother to put my things in storage. But I can go out later to do that. Right now, what do you need?"

"You're already doing it."

Working together, they had most of the things sorted and put away in a short amount of time. Niniane kept what she was taking with her on the bed. She chose outfits suitable to wear when horseback riding and camping, jeans, T-shirts, sweaters, sneakers and boots. Toiletries were kept to what was strictly functional along with a few basic items of makeup. A rain-resistant jacket, scarf, all of the lingerie Tiago liked, the bundle that contained her knives, their various sheaths and the small vial of poison she used to coat the tips. Some jewelry, a few small mementos from her life in New York, a couple of paper-backs and the inlaid box. She would have more of her things shipped later and would expand her wardrobe in Adriyel with Dark Fae clothing, so she could afford to travel somewhat light on this trip.

Then she sat on the edge of the bed and opened the box. It contained a pair of 2-barrel .41 rimfire caliber Remington Double Derringer pistols with engraved silver handles, along with a couple of felt ammunition bags and cleaning materials.

"Holy crap, those are gorgeous," Cameron breathed, sitting beside her. "Are those 1866 Derringers?"

"Yep," said Niniane. She picked up one, checked to make sure it was unloaded then handed it to Cameron. "I bought them as soon as they came out. Derringers were so much easier for me to handle than the earlier bigger guns, and of course you can carry one in your dress or coat pocket or slip one in your boot."

Cameron inspected the small pistol with reverence. "You bought this when it was new. My God." She sighted down the short barrel. "Where are you going to store these when we cross over?"

"I'm not going to store them," Niniane said. "We're going to clean and load them, and I'm going to take them with us."

Cameron's sleek sandy eyebrows rose. "I don't understand. Technology doesn't work in Other lands."

"That's not quite true," Niniane said. She held her hand out for the pistol, and Cameron handed it to her. She showed the other woman how to clean and load it. "Dragos has done a lot of experimenting. Passive technologies like composting toilets or designs that utilize solar heat work just fine. In fact, we're tak-ing a Melitta coffee filter with us. Modern crossbow and com-pound bow designs work well too."

"Interesting." Cameron worked on cleaning the pistol she had been given. Her strong, long-fingered hands were confi-dent, capable.

"Magic is so strong in Other lands, Dragos thinks it acts as a sort of natural defense mechanism. He says it works like a body's immune system," Niniane said. "Once it recognizes something that acts on some sort of principle of combustion, the magic moves to block it. That's why guns misfire." Niniane loaded hers and handed a couple of bullets to Cameron, who took them with her eyebrows still raised.

"You're not inspiring my confidence with this little chat," Cameron said.

"Here's the thing," Niniane said. "Automatic weapons always seize or misfire as soon as they're taken over and used, but it can take the magic a little longer to recognize one of the primitive guns. You never know when they might explode, or misfire, so they're dangerous and nobody uses them, but they always fire at least once."

Cameron's face was hard, her hazel eyes clear and direct. "The gun might fire, but it might also kill you at the same time."

"Tiago and I were talking last night about a risk/benefit analysis." She sat with her loaded derringer in her lap. She met the other woman's troubled gaze. "The potential benefit might outweigh the risk."

"The situation would have to be extreme," Cameron said. "Someone would have to consider this a weapon of last resort."

Niniane nodded. She thought of slipping in her brother's blood. Then she imagined slipping in Tiago's blood.

She said, "And then nobody would see it coming."

She managed to persuade Cameron to keep the contents of the box to herself. As she told Cameron, if Tiago found out, he would go on a rampage and take them away from her. In all likelihood the guns would never be fired, and having them with her would give her a severe kind of comfort. Still the other woman remained resistant until Niniane finally snapped, "It's none of his business, Cameron! If I ever feel the need to fire one of these, Tiago won't be around to help me."

Cameron looked grim but at last fell silent.

Niniane had saddlebags and trunks brought up. She and Cameron packed the inlaid box, along with the rest of the things.

Soon after dawn the next day, the party that was crossing over to Adriyel gathered outside the stables. Dew still sprinkled the lawn, but the early morning air was fast losing its crisp coolness. The weather forecast stated Chicago was going to see a summer scorcher that day, with temperatures climbing into the mid-nineties.

Niniane watched the travel party from her upstairs window. It was a large, complex gathering.

The Nightkind had provided their own mounts, pack animals and supplies. Their eight humans were dressed in functional clothing much like what Niniane wore, jeans, boots, T-shirts and jackets. Three figures wore long-sleeved turtlenecks and gloves under robes and ground-length cloaks. They wore sunglasses and ski masks, with the hoods from their cloaks pulled over their heads. They wouldn't take chances with something as deadly as sunlight. Probably under all that protective clothing they wore 100+ full spectrum SPF sunscreen as well. Those three would be Rhoswen, Duncan and the third Vampyre whom Niniane had not yet met. One of them—guessing by the Vampyre's height and build, Niniane thought it was probably Rhoswen—held the halter of a black Arabian stallion. The stallion had a blanket on its back but no saddle. He snorted and tried to rear, but the slim robed figure held him firmly to the ground.

Each of the Dark Fae had their own group. They all wore some variety of Dark Fae travel dress, consisting of tunics, leggings, knee-high boots, and either thigh-length riding coats cut with a split to the small of the back or cloaks.

Arethusa waited with ten troops. She was dressed for travel as her troops were, in a plain brown battledress uniform consisting of a leather half-armor jacket, trousers and boots. The Commander was busy inspecting their mounts and the wagon train of supplies that the troops would be responsible for safeguarding.

Justice Kellen was striking, as he was the only white-haired figure of the party. He moved his tall, lean body with an energy and vigor that belied his white hair. It would be a fatal mistake to believe his age implied infirmity. He stood with his personal entourage of four attendants, his back turned toward the others as he appeared to converse with one of his men in a low voice.

Aubrey and Naida's group was not quite the smallest, but they shared just four attendants between the two of them. Naida wore a dark green embroidered riding outfit, her black hair pulled back from her beautiful face. Aubrey's tan and brown riding outfit complemented his wife's. He checked the stirrups and cinch straps on their horses. His long hair was tied back with a simple strip of leather.

Rune, Aryal and Cameron made their own small group within the much larger party. Rune's tawny head bent close to Cameron's. The human was laughing at something the gryphon had just said. Niniane smiled to see Rune working his usual charm. Aryal stood with her arms crossed. The harpy studied the rest of the travel party, her stormy raptor's gaze piercing, then she looked up and caught sight of Niniane at the window. Aryal sent a pointed sidelong glance to Rune and Cameron and rolled her eyes, and Niniane burst out laughing.

Then Carling came into view. Her body moved with the flowing sinuousness of a cheetah. A ripple of silence passed over the party as she appeared. The Vampyre's dark hair was not the raven black of the Dark Fae coloring. Instead hers sparked with auburn glints in the early morning sunshine. She had it pinned back with the two stilettos. She was barefoot and wore a plain black cotton caftan that was slit to midthigh at the sides. The garment flowed around her lithe honey-colored body as she moved. As Carling approached her group, she gathered speed and leaped onto the Arabian stallion's back. She gathered the reins from the Vampyre, and controlled the stallion easily with her hands and knees.

Tiago spoke from behind her. "Are you ready?"

"Yes," she said.

She turned away from the window. Tiago's massive figure filled the doorway. He was dressed in his usual black fatigues, two swords crossed at his back, hunting knife at his thigh. The shaved swirls at the back of his hair had grown out in the last couple of days. He had run hair clippers over his head that morning to eliminate the unevenness. The severe buzz cut emphasized the strong, elegant shape of his skull. He looked sharp and lethal as a blade.

He stood back from the doorway. When she stepped into the hall, he took one of her hands in his much larger, warm clasp. He shortened his stride to accommodate hers as they walked down the hall and descended the house's main staircase. The house staff had assembled in the foyer to witness her departure. They bowed when she reached the ground floor. She murmured good-byes to them as she and Tiago passed. They stepped out the front double doors into full morning sunlight.

As they walked around the house toward the stables, Tiago's Power mantled over her. She sighed with pleasure as a sense of his presence surrounded her. He felt fierce today and battle-ready.

He ordered in a low voice, "You will not at any time step out of sight of either myself, Rune, Aryal or Cameron. Is that clear?"

"Yes," she said.

She kept her reply neutral and patient, her expression calm. They had gone over all of this already. She felt quite sure she would be safe with the Vampyres and their attendants, but Tiago's protective Wyr instincts were roused by the size of their large travel party and the relative lack of progress made on the investigation.

He had been in a foul mood since he had rejoined her the previous evening. Rune and Aryal had conducted an energetic canvass of the bars in the greater Chicago area that catered to the Elder Races. They had discovered the bar where the three dead Wyr had met for dinner, and by talking with the bar staff and several of the patrons, they had gleaned a few names. Names led to addresses. The Wyr had lived and worked in Chicago and had frequented the bar, but they had pretty much kept to themselves. Examining their bank accounts revealed that each of them had received a $25,000 payment from Tri-State Financial Services, the same company supposedly owned by Cuelebre Enterprises that had made a payout to Geril, but there the trail ended.

No one had witnessed the three Wyr meet with anyone the night they had attacked. The sentinels searched their apartments but came up with nothing. Tri-State Financial Services had articles of incorporation filed with the Illinois Secretary of State, but the address listed on the bank transfers turned out to be a UPS Store.

That pesky company. It was a puzzle. Setting up a company with corporation papers took time, and that one factor threw everything else into question. None of the Dark Fae who had crossed over from Adriyel would have had the time to create Tri-State. At least Rune and Aryal had unearthed proof that it was the same person or partnership behind both assassination attempts. Rune had put a forensic accountant to research the origins of the company's money resources, but that kind of investigation would take time, and in the meantime the party was crossing over to Adriyel.

Niniane and Tiago rounded the corner of the house and came in sight of the group. Everyone turned as one to watch as she and Tiago approached. She smiled at them all. The party had a total of thirty-seven people, thirty-eight including her, and she could trust so few of them right now. It would be a huge step forward if she could just be sure of Arethusa, who commanded the troops.

Then she noticed Rune walking toward her. He led a horse she hadn't seen from the window, a sweet-faced Appaloosa mare with intelligent eyes. She had a shining black coat and signature white-spotted markings dappling her rump and face. The mare had the fine, graceful head and long slender legs that revealed an Arabian ancestry, and her bridle and saddle were polished black leather trimmed in silver.

Niniane lit up with pleasure. She said, "What a beauty."

She looked around for Naida to find both Naida and Aubrey smiling at her. Naida said, "Please accept her as our gift. I thought you might enjoy breeding her with one of our Dark Fae lines."

Rune added telepathically, *I've checked her and her tack over thoroughly. She's a sweet little mare. She's responsive and affectionate, she has a smooth, fast gait, and she's steady. She's nervous at my Wyr scent but not skittish. She'll adjust well to our presence and be a good mount for you.*

"This is so generous of you," Niniane said to Aubrey and Naida. She could not resist petting the mare's velvet-soft nose. The mare blew at her fingers and nuzzled her, and her heart melted. All thought of politics and maneuvering for position flew out of her head, and she lost herself in delight. "I love her," she said. She told the mare, "I love you." She looked at the Dark Fae couple. "Thank you so much."

Aubrey said, "It is our very great pleasure, your highness. I hope you get many years of enjoyment with her."

In that moment it was impossible for her not to believe in his sincerity. The sun was shining, the mare regarded her with great, dark liquid eyes, and everyone in the party was smiling at her pleasure at the gift. Perhaps one of them was the person who had tried to kill her. And yes, Tiago pushed hard for caution, and she would follow his orders. But that left thirty-six other people who may very well be friends.

She decided those odds were enough to make it a good day.

Tiago put his hands at her waist and lifted her into the saddle. Then he and Rune mounted their horses, great, sturdy draft crossbred horses that could carry the Wyrs' weight for days on end. Then nothing happened. Niniane looked around. Everyone was mounted but nobody moved.

She happened to glance at Arethusa who raised her eyebrows. Oh, right. They were waiting for her. Her cheeks warmed. She gave the Commander a sheepish grin and nodded. Arethusa inclined her head, smiling, and nudged her horse forward to lead the way on the path toward the point of crossover. Niniane and Tiago moved to follow Arethusa, and the rest of the party fell into place behind them.

The sense of land magic grew stronger as they neared the point of crossover. Niniane still didn't recognize anything, but landmarks changed over time, and the entire property had been landscaped and cultivated for many years since the last time she had seen it. She had also been stressed, moving fast, and not inclined to stop and memorize the scenery.

The path Arethusa followed went down an incline that turned into a shallow ravine with an old dry streambed, and then she recognized where she was. She tensed as she remembered staggering along the streambed. She had been dazed and in shock from the palace massacre, her escape and the subsequent graewing accident. It had not been dry then. The water had been icecold. She had slipped on the wet, slick rocks more than once, numb in spirit and body.

Tiago's leg bumped hers. He said, "Faerie."

"I'm all right," she said.

"I require proof of that," he said.

"I didn't say this wasn't difficult," she told him. She kept her voice cool, precise. "I just said I was all right."

She kept her back ramrod straight. She didn't look at him, because if she saw concern in his black gaze, she might start bawling in front of everybody, which would be mortifying. She might be a touchy-feely kind of chick, but she had too much pride for that.

He must have understood, because he pulled away to leave her to her own memories.

The party followed the streambed and the magic grew stronger. From one curve to the next the land changed, and so did the season. The wind gusted. It had turned sharp and cool.

She gazed at the altered landscape. For the first time in two hundred years she looked at the blazing, brilliant colors of Adriyel in the autumn.

It was so quiet.

Tiago kept his gelding in line with Niniane's high-stepping little mare as he studied the altered landscape. The party was bypassing the outpost that had been built to guard the crossover point. The outpost was just a squat three-story tower with a barracks attached at the base. Arethusa raised a hand to the guards who stood on lookout duty at the top of the tower. They gave a brisk salute in reply.

Even though they had left Chicago shortly after dawn, the sun was high in the sky in Adriyel, the day nearer to noon than not. The kitchen had worked through the night to supply the party with plenty of fresh-cooked foodstuffs, which were packed in nylon padded coolers in the supply train. They were going to have an easy first day out.

Once they had crossed over, the party spread out along the narrow dirt-packed road and fell into a natural formation of people who chose to ride together and talk. Tiago listened to the noise their party made. He could hear snatches of conversation wafting on the sharp autumnal breeze, along with the snort of horses and the earthen thud of hoofbeats, the jingle of harnesses and occasionally someone's sudden outburst of laughter. Avian wildlife darted and flew all over, singing and chirping alarm at their presence. There was the rustle of the wind in the trees.

Several of the troops kicked ahead to join Arethusa and guard the front of the train. A few rode to the sides, and the rest brought up the rear with the supply animals. The arrangement was a little loose and relaxed for him, but he was used to tight, silent defensive formations moving through war-torn areas.

The road followed a rolling landscape, its emerald carpet of wild grasses turning golden with the end of summer. The landscape was dotted with clumps of deciduous forest that had exploded with various shades of reds, yellows and burnt orange. Some late-changing trees were only just beginning to turn, the deeper green of summer lightening to lime and yellowing along the edges.

And it was so quiet.

He contemplated the roaring absence of constant traffic, the white noise of the city that he never could quite block out of his senses, the azure of a virgin sky that had never seen a condensation trail left by an airplane, and he smiled to himself. It was good to find something to smile about, good to take deep breaths of air that had never been tinged with exhaust fumes and other urban contaminants.

He looked behind him, caught Aryal's gaze and motioned to her. The harpy kicked her horse forward. Aryal said telepathically, *What's up?*

Hang with Niniane, would you? he said. *I want to do some recon.*

You got it.

He said out loud, "Faerie, I'm going to take a look around."

She had been silent for some time, her expression contemplative, closed-in, even sad, but she roused to give him a quick smile. "Fine, go."

He nodded to her and nudged his mount forward until he came abreast with Arethusa. "Scouting ahead," he said.

He had expected the Commander to get snarky, but Arethusa just frowned at him and said, "Of course."

He liked his horse. It was a no-nonsense worker and knew its job. He touched his heels to its side, and it broke into a canter. He rode away from the party at a fast, steady pace until he reached a copse far enough away he could be sure of some privacy. He stopped, tethered the horse, changed into his Wyr form and launched into the air.

The Dark Fae had grown used to Adriyel being protected. The faeries would have a conniption if they caught sight of a Wyr thunderbird soaring over their land, so he figured it was best if they didn't see him, at least for now. He had never asked for permission to fly before, and he intended to never ask for forgiveness, so he cloaked himself as he flew. The oldest and most Powerful of the Wyr, such as Dragos and his sentinels, had the ability to hide themselves from normal sight. They didn't spread that fact around to just anybody.

He flew several miles ahead of the party, and then he scouted to either side and took a look at their rear flank just to be safe. All was peaceful and well in the countryside. There were no sneaky faeries lying in wait. Niniane was safe. She might not be happy yet, but she would be one day. He swore he would make that happen. For now it was enough that she was safe and riding a pretty horse on a sunny cool afternoon with old friends surrounding her.

He dared to relax, just for a little while. The sharp wind blew. It lifted him high where the air was thin and sounded a mournful, endless song. The lustrous sun blazed with a greater clarity than he had seen in far too long, and the shimmering land magic rose to greet him as he soared, his great wings outspread.

And it was so blessed quiet.

⇒ SEVENTEEN ⇐

After his scouting venture, Tiago rejoined the party looking refreshed and invigorated. Niniane's spirits took an upward surge as she watched him approach. He was a superb horseman. His black-clad figure astride the huge dappled gray gelding was eye-catching as they moved across the land with power and grace. He was easily the largest male of the group. The Dark Fae males who reached his height had lean whipcord strength, but they appeared willowy and almost effeminate by comparison.

Tiago approached to check on her welfare, his dark gaze searching her features as she smiled at him. His Power enfolded her in a brief, vibrant, invisible caress. Then he took his leave again. He consulted with Arethusa, collected three soldiers and went ahead on the road.

Then the party reached a bend in a wide shallow river, where Arethusa called a halt for the day. The area had been used several times as a campsite, and the underbrush had already been cleared away. Tiago and his group of soldiers were gathering kindling and chopping wood, so setting up camp became an easy chore for the new arrivals. The temperature began a sharp drop as the sun moved low in the sky. There would be a hard frost that night. Soon several large campfires were set and blazing.

Many of the party had modern nylon domed tents, but Niniane's tent was a large, luxurious Dark Fae construction, warmed by woolen carpets and sectioned into two rooms by heavy, embroidered wall hangings. The outer sitting room had pillows, two cushioned wooden chairs, lamps and a campfire ring, where a small fire in a brazier chased away the damp and the chill. The second room contained her bed, a stool and a small travel desk, her saddlebags, another lamp that hung from a hook on a metal pole and the two trunks that contained her belongings. There was also, a Dark Fae female soldier informed her, a brass tub. If her highness would like, water could be heated for a hot bath.

Niniane almost groaned out loud when she heard. She and Cameron had hobbled into her tent to collapse in the chairs. They were among the worst off in the group. She didn't know if the Vampyre's human attendants also suffered. Cameron was a fit athlete but had never before ridden a horse for hours on end, and it had been many years since Niniane had.

"Is our pain that obvious?" Niniane asked. Cameron had sunk low in her chair and gave her a dour look.

"Yes, ma'am," said the female soldier. The other Dark Fae female's face remained impassive, but her gray eyes smiled in sympathy.

Niniane said, "I would be most grateful for a hot bath. Cam?"

"I don't have a firstborn," said Cameron. "But you can have mine if I ever do."

"We will heat water," said the soldier.

Soon she and two other soldiers brought in the brass hip tub and filled it with pails of steaming water. Niniane stripped without ceremony or self-consciousness and collapsed into the bath. As she soaked, Cameron brought her Aleve and hot spiced cider. Twenty minutes later she dried and dressed in fresh jeans and sweater. She was still sore, but at least she could move with more freedom. She left the other woman to soak and stepped out of the tent.

After the warmth of her tent, the air felt sharp and bracing. The camp had become well established. Her tent was in the most protected area, surrounded by others on all sides and well lit by campfires. The sun had dropped below the tree line. The rich evening light was beginning to fade. It had become diffuse enough that the Vampyres were able to shed their protective clothing.

Aryal sat on a log at the campfire in front of Niniane's tent, tending several rabbits she roasted on spits over the fire. A couple of nylon coolers were stacked near her long, lean legs. Rune stood near the harpy, his hands on his hips, as he watched the activity around the other fires. Tiago would be around somewhere, Niniane knew, but she couldn't see him at the moment, and his bag was nowhere in sight. Niniane frowned, crossed her arms and tapped her foot, thinking.

Rune caught sight of her. "Hey, pip-squeak. We've got supper here if you're feeling hungry. There's the fancy stuff in the coolers, and Aryal wanted fresh, hot meat."

"About fifteen more minutes and the rabbit will be done," Aryal said.

"Thanks. Where's Tiago?"

Rune said in her head, *He's been interacting with the troops, working to build a rapport. They seem to like him. I think he's trying to get Arethusa to loosen up. She said she would share whatever she found out on her end of the investigation, but then she went tight-mouthed on us. Maybe he can get her to talk.*

She nodded and frowned at the leaping flames of the campfire. All she wanted was to take a seat at the campfire, relax her aching body among friends and stay in the protected bubble that had been created for her, but she knew she needed to reach out to the Dark Fae as much as Tiago, if not more. She looked up at Rune, "I should tour the camp."

He nodded. "Okay. Let's go."

He fell into step behind her as she walked from campfire to campfire. She stopped to talk with the troops, learning each of their names, and she thanked them for setting up such a comfortable campsite. She left them smiling as she walked to Kellen's site.

The Dark Fae male was eating a simple supper of stew and pan bread. He set it aside to stand as she approached. She raised a hand. "I'm sorry. I just wanted to see how everyone was doing. Please, don't let me interrupt you."

"But your interruption is the highlight of my day," Kellen said. He smiled and gestured to the stool beside him. "I'm so glad you came. Please join me. I have such a taste for my man Huwyn's field stew. I ask him to make it every time we travel. May I offer you some?"

She sat on the stool he offered. She kept her expression bland. A traditional Dark Fae field stew was an autumn hunter's dish. It consisted of whatever wild game one could catch, cooked with dried berries, herbs and roots. Kellen's passion for the stew could very well stem from how safe he knew his meal was. She told him, "My supper is being prepared, but I would love to taste Huwyn's stew. I haven't had field stew in ages."

She felt rather than heard Rune move behind her. Kellen's smile widened. He gave her a knowing look. He offered her his bowl, from which he had already taken several bites. "I would be honored if you tried a bite of mine."

"Thank you," she said. She took his bowl and tasted the stew. It was a rich, hearty blend of sweet and savory. She took another big bite before she made herself stop, then she handed the bowl back to him. "That is delicious. Perhaps next time I can coax Huwyn to make a larger pot to share."

"I know he would be transported with delight," Kellen told her.

She talked with him for a few minutes about their day, letting the conversation develop a relaxed tone. Then she said, "I would like to run something by you, if I may."

"Of course," Kellen said, his intelligent gaze fixing on her expression.

She regarded the leaping flames of his campfire as she sought to find the right words. "I know how much tradition means to you, and how much it means to many of the Dark Fae," she said at last. "It is important to me to honor our traditions while also looking for ways to open up Dark Fae society to new opportunities. I think striking a balance may be tricky, and I'm hoping to talk with you from time to time about my ideas, if you're open to that."

"I would be delighted and honored to talk things over with you," he said at once. He gave her a smile that redesigned the tiny lines on his lean, spare face. "Sometimes I can be too hidebound. Your fresh ideas are just what the Dark Fae need right now."

"I hope so," she told him. "For example, while we were in Chicago, I looked around at that great big mansion and got to thinking. The property is fully staffed but for the most part it sits unused. I thought maybe it could be turned into a school. People could go to stay for six-week courses and learn about technology and take computer classes, that sort of thing. We have so many magnificent metallurgists. I wonder what they would make of computers and other electronic devices. We need to open up our borders and interact more with the outside world, and I thought that might be one way to stimulate innovation and economic growth."

Kellen's brows rose as she talked. As she fell silent, he said slowly, "I think that's an excellent and very generous idea. I also like the fact that the property is so protected. Chicago can be quite a shock to the system after one has lived in Adriyel for so long."

She smiled. "I'm so glad you agree."

They talked about the idea for a school for a while longer. It was easy to avoid difficult topics by focusing on a positive subject. When she rose, he stood also and reached out to touch her arm. "This was exciting," he said. "I'm glad you stopped by."

"I am too," she told him. "Let's talk again soon."

She wished him a good evening and walked toward Aubrey and Naida's camp, Rune a quiet shadow at her back. Inwardly she was in more turmoil than ever. She wanted to bond with Kellen. Admittedly they did not see eye-to-eye on some important things like Tiago coming to Adriyel, and her truthsense was not all that evolved, but she liked him. Under more normal circumstances she would have stayed longer and enjoyed his company. She wanted to look forward to relying on his legal wisdom and experience.

Naida and Aubrey were relaxed at their campfire, drinking mulled wine. Nylon food coolers lay open at their feet. Apparently they had no problem with eating what the kitchen staff had prepared for them. They both rose as she approached.

"Niniane," Aubrey said. He took her hands and kissed her cheek. "How nice of you to stop by. How are you doing on your first day out?"

She snorted. "After a hot bath and some medicine, I have achieved miserable."

Naida smiled at her. "I think you did remarkably well. You'll have your riding muscles back in no time. How was the mare?"

"She was perfect," Niniane told them. "A real joy to ride."

"Will you join us?" Aubrey asked.

She told them the same thing she had told Kellen. "I have supper waiting back at my campfire, but I would be delighted to join you for a few minutes."

She was pleased to note that Aubrey looked behind her to

Rune and made a special point to include him in the invitation. As far as Kellen was concerned, Rune had joined the metaphorical woodwork where all guards and servants existed. Rune sat, and the four of them talked about the day. Rune made an easy fireside companion. Niniane hid a smile behind one hand as she watched Naida grow brighter and almost flirtatious in the sentinel's presence. It was easier to enjoy Naida away from the pressure and tensions of the rest of the group.

Naida said to her, "That clothing you're wearing seems so wonderfully functional."

Niniane laughed. "You mean my jeans? Yes, they are. They can stand a lot of wear and tear, and they're quite comfortable." She hesitated then said, "I didn't bring much in the way of clothing with me, just some travel outfits and a few mementos. I've been noticing how elegant your clothes are, and I admire your sense of style. I hope you don't mind if I ask you for advice on clothiers. I am interested in developing a more traditional wardrobe."

Both Naida and Aubrey looked pleased. "I would be honored," Naida told her. "Perhaps we can spend an afternoon together so I can get an idea of the colors you like."

"I look forward to it." Niniane smiled and stood. "Please, don't get up. I've interrupted your evening enough."

But no matter what she said, they stood anyway. "I'm glad you came," Naida said, her voice warm. "Let's talk again soon."

Niniane nodded, gave them both a smile and turned away. As soon as her back was turned to the other Dark Fae, her smile dropped away, and she scowled. Rune fell into step beside her, moving with lazy grace, as she headed toward the Vampyre camp.

Rune said, "I notice our supper does not lie in this direction."

"I have one more stop I want to make," she growled.

"Perhaps you would enjoy your next visit with a sunnier attitude if it were accomplished after supper," he suggested.

"Oh shut up," she said.

"My case in point." He raised his eyebrows and looked bland when she glowered at him. "I'm just sayin'."

The evening still showed hints of the day's golden sunlight, but shadows were deepening across the clearing and glowing lanterns had begun to appear in strategic places as she and Rune approached the Nightkind encampment. Rhoswen, Duncan, the other male Vampyre and their human companions (attendants? servants? food supply?) were gathered around a communal campfire. The group looked relaxed. The humans had made short work of their portion of the supper supplied by the Chicago kitchen staff. Perhaps their air of relaxation was an illusion, but Niniane envied them their ease in each other's company.

She was amused to see that the humans were not prompt in rising to their feet at her appearance. They only did so after Rhoswen gave them a glare. She would miss modern Americans' casual ease of manner.

She said to Rhoswen, "I was hoping to have a word with Carling."

After a brief pause, the blond Vampyre said, "Certainly. The Councillor is down at the river. She invites you to join her."

"Thank you."

Niniane went in the direction Rhoswen indicated. She followed a short trail through bushes to arrive at the river's edge, while Rune kept pace at her back. As the evening sky darkened, the brightest stars began to shine. The river rippled silver in the fading light, and the fiery foliage colors on both banks turned muted. At first she looked along the near bank for Carling. It was only when Niniane saw pale material draped on a nearby bush that she thought to look out over the river. She found Carling's sleek dark head cutting through the water.

"Oh my God," she said. She shuddered. The water had to be so frigid it was bone numbing. Anybody who fell into it would run the risk of hypothermia in minutes if they were, well, alive. "You don't feel the cold?"

Rune looked amused as he parked himself by leaning against a nearby birch tree with his arms crossed. Carling's husky chuckle sounded over the water. The Vampyre swam against the current. Her lazy-looking breaststroke made it look effortless.

"I feel it," said Carling. She ducked her head under the water and came up to the surface again. "It just doesn't affect me like it does you."

"Is it the same as sunlight?"

"That is a different matter," said the Vampyre.

"How so?" Niniane had been dying to ask ever since she had seen Carling step into the sunshine at the hotel.

"I cloak myself with Power so that I can walk in sunlight. Otherwise I would have to cloak myself with clothing and sunscreen, like the other Vampyres do, or the sun would burn me to ash just as it would them. I can step through sunlight and can look upon it, but I can no longer feel it on my skin and survive."

"That must be exhausting."

"I would not want to travel for weeks in the daylight without respite, but this short trip is fine."

Carling swam toward the shore and walked out of the water. Niniane lost her breath. The Vampyre's sleek, wet, nude body glinted with the silver edge of the fading light. Her full breasts, slim waist and strong shapely legs were perfectly formed and sinuously graceful, but there any pretence to perfection ended, for she was tiger-striped from shoulder to thigh, her body covered with dozens of long white lash scars. Someone had beaten her badly when she had been human, beaten her so badly she must have been near death.

Niniane clenched her teeth and grew teary. Carling gave her a brief disinterested glance as she stepped to shore. Then the Vampyre's attention moved to Rune and paused for what could have passed for a heartbeat.

Niniane turned to Rune too.

He stared at Carling. His handsome face was carved into stark lines, the bones standing out. The lines of his body thrummed with tension, the muscles cut with rigidity. His golden lion's eyes blazed.

Carling turned from the sentinel. She plucked her clean caftan from the bush and shrugged it on, her movements languid and unhurried. Her expression remained bored, and her face and body gleamed with radiance.

"Perhaps we should talk in my tent," Carling said.

Niniane followed Carling back to the campsite. The Vampyre stepped inside her tent, which was a large, modern nylon affair with zipped-up windows. Niniane paused at the entrance. She said to Rune, "Please wait here. I know Tiago wanted me to stay with one of you at all times, but I'm only going to be on the other side of this canvas."

Rune nodded without speaking.

She hesitated. She didn't know what she was tempted to ask him, maybe just if he was all right, but his expression was tight, closed-in, and his body language warned her away. She sighed. Sometimes Wyr were inexplicable.

She stepped in the tent. Inside it was decorated with the damask silk hangings and the mahogany inlaid trunk from the hotel. There were no chairs, just a scattering of pillows on a rug. Carling poured two glasses of red wine. Her dark wet hair lay sleek against her head. She turned and offered a glass to Niniane, who took it. Then Carling sank down to sit cross-legged on a floor pillow. Niniane tried not to show her struggle as she eased her aching body down onto another pillow.

Carling sipped wine. "What do you need?"

"Some advice, if you can give it." Niniane rubbed her eyes. There was no point in beating around the bush. She asked the Vampyre, "Do you know if any of the Dark Fae in this group tried to kill me?"

"No," said Carling. "I do not."

Niniane struggled to verbalize her next question. It was surprisingly hard to ask. "How do they—feel to you?"

Carling shrugged. "They feel like people."

"I mean emotionally. Could you tell if one of them was feeling violent?"

Carling's eyebrows raised. "Certainly. I can also tell when they are feeling sad or angry, and when they feel dislike or joy. None of these emotions have anything to do with whether or not they have committed, or have conspired to commit murder."

Niniane ground her teeth and growled. "This is so frustrating. I just spent time with each one—well, except for Arethusa, who's been busy this evening. I enjoyed each one's company. They all acted like they liked me."

"No doubt they do like you, and why wouldn't they? You are an engaging person." Carling smiled. "But I have killed someone I liked before. I have killed someone and felt regret. I have also sensed violent emotions from you, but you have not erupted into violent action. Emotions are like colors, Niniane. Thoughts and actions provide structure and purpose to a person. It is only when you put them all together that they begin to form a real picture. The Dark Fae are a complex people, with many years of memory and motivation to influence their actions and ambitions."

"Okay," Niniane said. She swallowed wine. "I guess I was looking for a shortcut, and there isn't one."

"I'm sorry, no there isn't." Carling paused then said, "But now that we have a chance to talk, I would offer you a word of advice about something else."

"By all means." Niniane drank more wine. "Please do."

"I suggest you go carefully with Tiago. All of the Dark Fae are feeling threatened and aggressive about him, except perhaps for Aubrey, whose reaction has been surprisingly low-key."

Niniane asked, "How has Aubrey reacted?"

"I would say he's concerned, maybe even troubled, but I have not picked up feelings of aggression from him."

Did that mean Aubrey was taking Tiago's presence well, or did that mean he wasn't too threatened by Tiago's presence since he planned on killing her anyway? *Argh.* This kind of thing was going to drive her around the bend. She tossed back the last of her wine.

Carling continued. "I think there is only so far you can take your relationship with Tiago and hope to hold the throne in peace. No Dark Fae will ever tolerate a Wyr as ruler. In fact, I will take that statement further. No other Elder demesne will tolerate it. Power among the United States Elder Races is carefully balanced. The Wyr cannot be seen as taking more than their allotted share."

"Tiago and I have discussed that," Niniane said. "He has no interest in the throne."

"I am not talking about just Tiago," Carling said. "I am talking about any potential heir."

Niniane went still. Even her mind stopped working. She said past a sudden rasp in her throat, "You mean any children I might have?"

"Let me be blunt," Carling said. "You cannot take the throne, have children with Tiago and hope to avoid war, either civil war with the Dark Fae, or war with the other demesnes."

The restrictive band around her chest was back. She moved carefully to set her wineglass aside and forced herself to take slow deep breaths.

"I take it you have not considered these consequences." Carling's voice was gentle.

"I've been busy," Niniane said.

"You could consider a marriage of state," Carling said. "Have an heir and perhaps a spare, and maintain a private agreement with—"

"No," said Niniane. Everything in her reacted violently to the thought, and that was without taking into consideration how Tiago would react. He would never allow it. He would kill anyone she might try to marry. "That is not going to happen."

Carling was silent for a moment. Then she rose to her feet and went to collect the half-empty bottle of wine. She poured more for Niniane and then herself.

"Perhaps you can take your cues from history," Carling said. "Consider the English. Edward VIII abdicated because his government would never accept Wallis Simpson. To them, marriage meant she would ascend to the throne. Do you think the Dark Fae would accept a marriage between you and Tiago, and trust that he would not also share the throne?"

Niniane drank her wine and stared into space. "No," she said.

"Then there is Elizabeth I," Carling said. "I liked Elizabeth. She was a clever woman. She used the possibility of making a marriage by alliance as a diplomatic ploy, but of course she never followed through. If she had lovers, she was so discreet it could never be proven. And no matter how much her parliament pressured her to do so, she never named an heir, so she avoided making her throne vulnerable to a coup."

At that last, Niniane's gaze snapped to Carling's face. The Vampyre's expression was serene, Madonna-like. She grumbled, "Conversations with you never go as I expect."

She finished the bottle of wine with Carling then said goodnight and stepped outside. Rune fell into step beside her, and they walked back to her camp. Tiago sat with Cameron and Aryal at the campfire, eating supper. Niniane drank in the sight of Tiago. He sat with his elbows on his knees as he inspected the contents of an open cooler between his feet. He was not participating in Cameron and Aryal's conversation, but he was listening. He looked burnished. Vitality poured off him, yet he appeared more relaxed and at ease than she could ever remember him looking in New York. Adriyel seemed to suit him.

Then he looked up, caught sight of her, and his relaxation vaporized. He rose to his feet, and his face assumed a hatchet-edged aggression. He said in her head, *What's wrong?*

She looked at him, affectionate exasperation breaking through her tiredness. *How did you know?*

Your scent. In two quick strides he was in front of her. He cupped her elbows as he looked down at her in concern. *Tell me what's happened.*

Her eyes grew damp. She put a hand to his chest and stroked him. *I promise I will tell you all about it very soon, but I am not ready right now. I have to think about some things before I know how to talk about it.*

Okay, he said. "Why don't you sit and have supper? I heard you haven't eaten yet."

"I'm not hungry," she said. "I'm going to turn in."

His expression darkened. "Faerie."

She closed her eyes. *Don't push me right now, Tiago.*

He put his forehead to hers. *I can't make it better if you don't talk to me.*

Maybe you can't make this better. Sometimes things just hurt, she said. His hands tightened, and she opened her eyes to be jolted by his fierce stare. She steeled herself and said, *I will talk to you soon. Right now I am going to bed. I need to have some time to myself to think, so . . . I need to go to bed alone, please.*

His lips parted to reveal clenched teeth, and his Power pressed down on her. She knew it had to go against all of his instincts, but after a moment he eased back. His hold on her elbows loosened. *I will be in telepathic range,* he said. *You are to call me if you have the slightest need, do you hear?*

Telepathic range. That meant he would stay within ten or fifteen feet of her. She relaxed and nodded. *I love you.*

We will have that talk, Niniane, he said.

Soon, I promise.

He let her go and stepped back. The others had fallen silent, appearing to concentrate on their own thoughts as they ate. She nodded to them and stepped inside her tent. It was warm from the brazier where the fire had died down to glowing red coals.

She went straight to her bed, stripped down to her T-shirt and crawled shivering onto the pallet. There she curled into a ball as she waited for the bed to warm. Tiago would have had it warm in seconds. He would have warmed her heart too, in almost every way except for the one that was hurting now.

Nature seemed to compensate for those who were long-lived, and children were correspondingly rare and precious. Added to that, she had never dared to consider having children when her life had been under such constant threat. The possibility of having a child was always a part of some vague, undefined "sometime" in the future.

She had not considered that she might never be able to have children.

She ran through everything Carling had said again. Niniane could not fault the Vampyre's logic in the slightest.

The bed warmed but she remained curled in a tight ball. She fell asleep, huddled around that cold internal place.

A shout splintered the cool silence in her head. She bolted into a sitting position as someone shouted again. Heavy footsteps ran past outside.

She shrank back as Tiago tore past the wall hanging, his sword drawn. His face was savage in the shadowed tent. He said, "Get dressed."

Her heart hammered. "What's happened?"

"I don't know."

She leaped out of bed and slipped on jeans, boots and a sweater. Then she grabbed her stiletto sheaths and jammed them in the pocket of her jeans. As soon as she stood, he took her by the arm and marched outside with her. Cameron stood in front of the tent with a short sword drawn as well. The rest of the camp churned with chaos.

Tiago put an arm around Niniane's shoulders and clamped her to his side. She put her arms around his waist. Aryal pushed past several frightened attendants who were milling about. The harpy snapped at them, "Get the hell out of the way. Go back to your campsites and stay there until you're told to do otherwise."

They took one look at the harpy's expression and scattered.

Aryal strode toward Tiago, Cameron and Niniane, her raptor's eyes blistering with adrenaline and anger. The harpy looked ready, even eager, for a fight.

"What?" Tiago barked.

Aryal came to a halt in front of the other three.

She said, "Arethusa's dead."

≡ EIGHTEEN ≡

Tiago's skin was a thin layer containing an inferno of violence. It boiled in the air around him. Cameron gave him a
sidelong look and took two steps away. Aryal too kept her distance. Only Niniane moved closer. She leaned against him as if
his supercharged aura comforted her.

"What happened?" Niniane asked.

Aryal shook her head, her face grim. "At first glance, it
looks like she slipped on some wet rocks down by the riverside,
hit her head and fell into the water. One of her troops went looking for her and found her body fifty yards downstream."

Niniane's gaze flashed up to meet Tiago's. She asked him,
What do you think?

He shook his head slightly. *Arethusa moved like a panther.
There is no way in hell she slipped, hit her head and drowned
by accident. I don't believe it.*

What do you think we should we do?

He wanted to snatch Niniane up, take to the air and keep
flying until he knew he had her in a safe place. He wanted to
rampage through the camp and not stop until he found the mur-
derer. His hand clenched on his sword hilt until it shook. He
took a slow, careful breath. *Rune and Aryal should investigate*,
he said. *We need to know as soon as we can if they can clear
Arethusa's troops, so we know if we can rely on them.*

Her gaze searched his face. Then she nodded. Her expression

turned calm, and she gave him a squeeze around the waist and stepped away. In a voice pitched to carry some distance, she said to Aryal, "Please do whatever is necessary to verify the details surrounding the Commander's death."

"Right," Aryal said. She pivoted and stalked away.

Niniane looked up at Tiago again. His mouth tightened at the dark circles shadowing the delicate skin under her eyes. She hadn't rested well before he had awakened her because of whatever the hell was bothering her *that he didn't know about yet*, and of course now was not the damn time to ask her about it.

"Would you please follow me?" she asked.

"Of course," he said. Anywhere.

She paused. A hint of a smile crept into her tired eyes. She said in his head, *Would you please put away your sword first?*

He looked down at his hand, saw his white-knuckled grip and set his teeth. He growled, *I'd rather not.*

You are the real weapon, she said. *Believe me, nobody doubts it.*

"Fine," he snapped out loud. He reached over his head and slammed the sword into the scabbard strapped to his back. He surveyed the area. The campfire in front of Niniane's tent was quite public, but he wasn't about to take a chance with anything. He turned to Cameron. "Guard the tent."

"Of course," said the human, her face cop-calm and eyes alert.

Niniane turned and walked through the camp, her small, slender figure erect, and Tiago stalked behind her. He noted how everyone responded to them. They looked at him with varying shades of wariness and alarm, but when they looked at Niniane, their faces eased perceptibly and they calmed.

He didn't have to see her expression for himself. Niniane was damn good at public interactions.

She was also making straight for the Dark Fae soldiers' campsite. He said, *What are you doing?*

I'm doing what needs to be done, she said. *I am going to commiserate with and comfort my soldiers. They are not going to see me come to them too late after they have been cleared by Wyr investigators. They need to know I have faith in them. Arethusa picked them for this trip. I'm willing to take a chance on that, especially with you at my back.*

His protective instincts were in hyperdrive. Every last one

snarled at her plan to go among so many others, but he clamped down on his reaction and examined her reasoning. It was sound. Of course it was. *Fuck.* He let his tension out in an almost inaudible growl, and she glanced over her shoulder at him. She looked wry, apologetic and determined. He gave her a short nod, his mouth tight. She took a deep breath, turned away and went to talk with her troops.

They were huddled in a miserable tight clump around their campfire. They looked up as Niniane and Tiago approached. He had managed to get himself under better control and schooled his expression to impassivity by the time they grew close. He gave each of the ten soldiers a sharp, quick assessment. Their scents were stressed, and they looked shocked and grieving. A couple wiped surreptitiously at their faces as they all rose to their feet.

Niniane said, "Arethusa's death is an unimaginable loss, and others are doing what needs to be done. For now I came to share her memory with you, and to tell you how proud she was of each and every one of you."

She said other things, his faerie, and they were all the right and meaningful things one would say to people who were grieving, but she didn't really have to. If he knew how to do one thing well, it was how to read soldiers. With those first two sentences, those troops were hers, heart and soul.

Someone brought Niniane a stool, and they stayed with the group and talked about Arethusa until the sky lightened with the first pale streaks of dawn. Niniane made arrangements for the captain to take command until they reached Adriyel proper, where a more permanent arrangement would be made to appoint a new Dark Fae Commander. The captain's name was Durin, and he was a competent male with a respectful manner.

At last Niniane stood, and of course everyone else stood as well. She was just offering a last few words of encouragement to them when one of the troops sidled unobtrusively to stand behind Tiago. It was the slight, quiet male named Hefeydd, the one responsible for tending the draft horses that hauled the supply wagons.

Tiago was aware, of course. He was aware of everything that happened in the vicinity, aware of every thoughtless gesture, every hand that was raised, every sudden movement. He waited, balancing his weight on the balls of his feet.

A diffident voice spoke in his head. *Sir.*

Yes? he said. His mental voice was calm. He flexed the fingers of his sword hand.

Commander Arethusa gave me something that I was to give it to you if, well, if something were to happen— No, sir, please don't turn around! I th-thought you might not mind if I just slipped it into your hand?

Yeah, like that was going to happen, he almost snarled, but then he stopped himself. Hefeydd had been one of the ones with reddened eyes who lingered at the edge of the campfire's light. The soldier hadn't added verbally to Arethusa's impromptu wake, but Tiago had taken note of the grief in the Dark Fae male's gentle face.

Tiago sighed, put a hand at the small of his back and opened his fingers.

A flat leather-wrapped package slid gently against his palm. Even as his fingers closed around it, he sensed Hefeydd moving away.

Tiago tucked the package under his arm as Niniane turned to him at last. If she had looked tired before, now she looked utterly drained, her small face white with exhaustion. He throttled the impulse to scoop her into his arms and carry her away. They had to take such care when they were under others' scrutiny. He mustn't do anything that would make her look weak or less than capable in the eyes of her people.

She came over to him, and he had to content himself with putting a gentle supportive hand at her back. He shortened his stride to match hers as they picked their way through the shadowed encampment.

Back at Niniane's tent, Cameron still kept watch. Tiago's sharp gaze ran over the human woman's figure. Cameron looked tired but alert, her tall, slim figure held erect. He raised his eyebrows at her and she gave him a nod. She said to them, "I made coffee, if you want some."

Niniane shook her head, wordless. He held the tent flap for her as he said to Cameron, "I'll take a cup."

He followed Niniane, who came to a halt in the tent's sitting area. The brazier contained fresh coals, which warmed the area, and the lamps were lit. He dropped the leather package by one of the wooden chairs. Niniane turned to him. He pulled her into his arms and knew a fierce sense of relief as her small body nestled against his.

She buried her face in his chest. He stroked her silken black hair. "I am so proud of you," he told her.

"Don't be nice to me," she said, muffled against him. "Or I might bawl like a baby."

He cupped the back of her head with a protective hand. "You go ahead and cry if you need to," he whispered.

The tent flap rose and Cameron stepped in, carrying a metal cup full of steaming hot coffee. She hesitated when she saw them but then stepped forward to set the coffee by the nearest chair before turning to go.

Niniane lifted her head. "Do we know anything yet?"

Cameron said, "Sorry, not yet. The last I heard Rune and Aryal had finished examining the area and were canvassing the camp."

Niniane nodded and let her head rest against Tiago again. He stroked her silken black hair. He heard footsteps as someone approached. He took Niniane's shoulders to ease her away, so he could turn to face the tent flap unencumbered.

Just outside, captain Durin said in a quiet voice, "Excuse me, your highness?"

"Yes, Durin, come in," said Niniane.

Tiago noted with approval as Cameron shifted into a defensive position, mirroring his placement between Niniane and the tent opening. The tent flap lifted, and the Dark Fae male stepped just inside, his expression diffident.

"What is it, captain?" Niniane asked.

"With your approval, ma'am, I would like to set up shifts to guard your tent," the captain said.

Exhaustion made her slow to react. She looked at Tiago in tired surprise. He said in her head, *I approve. You reached out to them, and now they're claiming you for their own. This is a very good step forward.*

She nodded. She said to the captain, "It's an excellent idea. Work with Tiago to arrange the details. He is responsible for security, and you are to answer to him from now on."

"Yes, ma'am." Durin looked at him. "Sir?"

"Keep the shifts short and make sure rations are generous," Tiago told him. "Everybody's tired. I don't expect we'll be moving now until tomorrow morning. I'll come by later today to see if there's anything you need to discuss. That will be all for now, captain."

"Yes, sir." Durin bowed his head to Niniane and left.

"Speaking of tired," Tiago said. He looked at Cameron. "Get some bunk time while you can."

"Good idea, if you're sure you don't need me," said Cameron. She turned to go.

"No, wait!" Niniane said, her pixie face filled with alarm. She grabbed the other woman's arm. "Lie down in my bed."

Cameron's face softened. "Niniane, *you* need your bed."

"I don't need it any time soon," she said, her expression turning stubborn. "And I don't want you going off by yourself."

Cameron looked at him. He raised his eyebrows and said, "You heard her. Go to bed."

Cameron's face creased with exasperated amusement. "Remember, I've also heard you two when you argue. I never would have guessed you could present such a united front."

Niniane smiled at him, and for a moment all the shadows in her eyes had vanished. She said, "We're learning as we go."

"And we're doing a damn-fine job of it," he added.

"And on that note," Cameron said. She put an arm around Niniane's slender shoulders for a quick squeeze. Niniane gave her a quick fierce hug in return, and then Cameron retired to the other part of the tent and they were finally alone.

Tiago walked to the wooden chair where his steaming cup of coffee and the leather-wrapped package waited on the floor. He shrugged off his sword harness, placed the scabbard on the floor then sat and stretched his legs with a grunt. It was a good, sturdy chair of Dark Fae construction, with interlocking parts that could be disassembled for easier transportation. It bore his weight and size well. He approved.

"I have a lap that requires a faerie's presence," he remarked to the room in general.

Niniane's tired face lightened. She approached, and he gathered her up, wrapping his arms around her. She rested her head on his shoulder and let her body go lax with a sigh. He rested his cheek against her soft, fragrant hair.

I have been waiting quite patiently, he said. *For which you may compliment me any time you like, but now I want to know what upset you before you went to bed.*

He felt the relaxation leave her body. His mood, already not the best, darkened further. His arms tightened.

Silence stretched out. Then she said, "Can we agree that events have been moving at an extraordinary pace?"

He nodded thoughtfully.

"Have we not also agreed that we will trust each other to do our jobs?"

His eyes narrowed. Another nod.

She walked small fingers across his chest. "Shall we consider the possibility that our jobs might also entail assimilating all of these new events and decisions we have made?"

"Yes," he said between his teeth. "Faerie, you should know I am no longer enamored with this line of reasoning—"

"No arguments," she ordered. She tapped a finger against his lips. He sighed and pressed a kiss to the admonishing finger. "Perhaps we should then conclude that the troubles I went to bed with may not necessarily be of real concern at this point in time, especially with so many other urgent matters that require our attention."

"Nope," he said. "That was a good try but it doesn't fly. You promised you would talk to me about what upset you. I'm holding you to it."

Another silence, a tense one this time. Then she pushed upright to look into his eyes gravely. "I did promise, didn't I?" she said. "I'm sorry, Tiago. I talked with Carling, who pointed out some unpleasant facts about you and me and this new life we're trying to build with the Dark Fae."

"That crazy-assed bitch," he growled. "I swear to God I'm going to—"

She clapped a hand over his mouth before he could go further. She demanded, "Do you want to hear what I have to say or not?"

He took a deep breath, made himself calm down and kissed the palm of her hand. "My turn to apologize," he said. "I'm sorry, go on."

"There's not much more to tell," she said. "She just pointed out we can only hope for a certain amount of acceptance but no more. No one will believe that you don't intend to share the throne if we were to marry. And nobody, not the Dark Fae and certainly not any of the other demesnes, will accept half-Wyr children as potential heirs to the Dark Fae throne."

He grew grim as she talked. "What was the part that hurt you the most?"

Her gaze fell.

Everything clenched inside him. *Maybe you can't make this better*, she had said. *Sometimes things just hurt*. A ball of burning lava lodged in his chest. "It was the thought of never having children, wasn't it?"

She shook her head. "It started there, but you know, mostly I think I'm having a problem with the concepts of 'forever' and 'never.' I don't want to think in absolutes. I'm not dying to have children, but I also don't want to say I'll never have them, especially just to placate other people. And I am not thrilled with the thought of committing to the Dark Fae throne for the rest of my life, especially today of all days." She looked up, met his gaze, and the shock of the connection between them was deeper and more profound than ever. She whispered, "There's only one thing and one person right now I am wholly committed to, and that's you."

He made his lungs expand and discovered he could breathe again. He cupped her face in both hands and kissed her, savoring the texture of her soft open lips.

"Only one person," he whispered. *Only one thing*.

She put her cheek against his and nuzzled him. "Would you like children some day?"

"I don't know," he said. He ran his hands down her shapely back. "Maybe. I like children. I would like your children. I must confess, this is not a subject to which I have given much thought."

"Me neither," she sighed. She switched to telepathy. *You know, we might decide some day that I should abdicate. I would like to see how we feel about things after we've opened the Dark Fae borders and brought the rest of my family's murderers to justice. I don't think we need to stress too much over the long term when meeting our short-term goals is enough of a challenge.*

That is a good point, he said. *One step at a time. Now, about marriage.*

She kissed him. *What about it?*

Do you require this ritual for happiness? We can always marry in secret, if you like. He brushed a lock of her hair out of her beautiful eyes.

She stuck out her lower lip and grumbled, *I would like to point out I am actually much more Wyr than anybody has given me credit for thus far. I mean, hello, I moved in with you all when I was seventeen, remember. I know to a lot of you geriatrics that's not such a long time ago, but it's quite a significant length of time to me. Tiago, are we mated or not?*

We are indeed, he said.

She went nose-to-nose with him. *And will you have me and no other?*

I will. He touched her delicate skin. *And will you have me and no other?*

For the rest of my life. She smiled. "So I reckon that's that."

"I reckon it is." He smiled back.

"Here, drink your coffee before it gets any colder." She leaned sideways to pick up the cup on the floor by his chair and paused. She cocked her head. "What is this package?"

He leaned over and looked at it too. "It's the next thing on my to-do list after I talk with you."

"What's in it?"

"I don't know. It's a message from a dead woman." Niniane looked at him quickly, and he explained how he had acquired it.

"How could you not open it right away?" she exclaimed. She snatched the packet up and thrust it into his hands.

"It has quite a high priority rating," he said. "But making sure you were okay was the most important thing to me."

"I think that's one of the sweetest things you've ever said to me." She slid off his lap to kneel on the ground in front of him. She leaned against his legs and nodded to the package. "Hurry up, open it."

He turned it over in his hands, considering. It was roughly nine inches by six or seven, and more or less flat, wrapped in leather and bound with a thin length of cord that was firmly knotted. He pulled out a pocketknife and slit the strip. Then he folded back the leather cover. Inside was a manila envelope that had been folded in half. He opened the envelope and pulled out the contents.

The message from the dead woman came in the form of corporation papers, owned by a dead man.

The papers were for Tri-State Financial Services, complete with bank account and checkbook. The company supposedly had been incorporated by Cuelebre Enterprises, but the single shareholder listed was Urien Lorelle.

Son of a bitch.

· · ·

A little while later, Niniane lay curled in a pile of pillows on the floor near the brazier. Tiago had erupted out of the chair to prowl the confines of the tent when they had discovered the contents of the packet. After the stress of the broken night, her energy had already been at low ebb. He had far more stamina than she ever would. She couldn't keep up with him and didn't even try.

He had paused in his furious pacing to drape a soft woolen blanket over her curled form. Then he opened one of the nylon coolers that he had tucked into one corner of the tent the evening before. He piled a variety of foods onto a plate, which included quintessential American fare like fried chicken, potato salad, and cherry and apple turnovers. Then he slapped the laden plate on the floor in front of her and ordered her with a glare to eat, the warlord mother hen at his finest.

So she rested, watched him and nibbled.

Then Aryal's voice sounded just outside the tent. "So you two clowns are on guard duty now? Good for you. Move or I'll break your legs."

Niniane choked on a piece of potato, coughed and swallowed hard. She exclaimed, "Aryal!"

Tiago stopped pacing and turned to the front of the tent.

"What!" Aryal snapped back. The harpy sounded even more bad-tempered than usual. "They've been taking the same trip we have. You would think they would know by now they don't have to guard you from me or Rune."

Niniane let her head fall back on a pillow and covered her eyes with one hand. She said to Tiago, "Now is not the time for anyone to be working my last nerve."

"I feel you on that one," he said between his teeth. His upper lip curled in a snarl.

Then with exquisite politeness, a Dark Fae male said, "Your highness, forgive me for interrupting you at your rest. Wyr sentinels Aryal and Rune request an audience with you."

Close on the heels of that, Aryal's sarcastic mutter was clearly audible. "Ding-fucking-dong. Ooh, what a surprise. Someone's at the door."

Rune said, "This is why you have so few friends, dipshit."

Niniane clapped her other hand over her mouth. Don't laugh.

After a moment she managed to say, "Thank you for letting me know. . . ." She lifted her fingers from her eyes to squint at Tiago.

That one is Bruin, Tiago told her.

"Thank you, Bruin. Aryal and Rune may enter."

"Yes, your highness," said the soldier.

She muttered, "Although if they don't start pretending to have some manners I'm going to kick them out again."

Tiago put his hands on his hips. "You'll have to get in line, faerie."

She sat up as the sentinels stepped into the tent. Her exasperation faded as she got a good look at them. They were streaked with mud and dirt, and both looked tired. Aryal's gaze fell on her plate. The harpy's expression turned hopeful and she started forward. "There's food?"

Tiago smacked Aryal in the back of the head. It didn't look like a gentle blow. "Touch her plate and die."

"Ow!" Aryal glared at him and rubbed the back of her head.

"There's still plenty in the cooler," Niniane told them.

Rune had already gone to investigate. He bit half the meat off a chicken leg in one bite and chewed as he stretched his neck first one way then the other. "We've done all we can," he said around his mouthful. "Durin and one of Kellen's attendants have treated Arethusa's body with herbs and wrapped it, so it's ready to be transported to Adriyel for a proper burial."

Wyr tended to prefer cremation, so when Rune mentioned a "proper" burial, which was more of a Dark Fae concept, it was clear he was speaking to the two sets of ears on the other side of the tent walls. Tiago shook his head and strode outside. Niniane, Rune and Aryal fell silent. They listened as he told the two guards, "We have too many guards and not enough off-rotation. I'll send for the next pair when we need them. For now, go get some shut-eye."

"Yes, sir."

Tiago reappeared. He scooped up Niniane, blanket and all, and settled in a chair again with her in his lap. Rune carried the cooler to the second chair, and Aryal sprawled on the floor beside him. The two sentinels divided the cooler's contents between them.

Niniane rested her forehead in the crook of Tiago's neck and let her eyes drift half closed. Tiago told the other two, "Spill it."

Aryal licked sugar from a turnover off of her fingers.

"Inconclusive. We're Wyr on Dark Fae land. We can only request others' cooperation; we can't command it. We could only take things so far when we questioned people."

The growl started so low in Tiago's chest, Niniane was probably the only one who heard it. She put her flattened hand against his heavy pectoral, stroking, and he quieted.

Rune said, "Arethusa's body has a wound behind one ear, caused by a blow made with some kind of blunt object, but her death looks consistent with drowning. Theoretically she *could* have slipped, hit her head and drowned, but it's clear by how everyone is acting that nobody believes her death was an accident. The problem is, there's simply no proof. Whoever killed her knew just what to do. They watched and waited until most of the encampment was asleep or in their tents. They had to have waded in the water because there's no definitive scent in the immediate area."

"Don't misunderstand, there are plenty of scents and plenty of tracks," Aryal muttered. "We scoured every inch of the riverbank, and they're all over the goddamn place. And almost everybody has something wet or damp in their possession. The whole camp has been down to the river at some point, to either wash or haul water."

Rune opened the container of potato salad. He took the fork Niniane had left on her abandoned plate and began shoveling food into his mouth. He said, "I think the killer did the simplest thing possible and bashed her over the head with a rock, threw the murder weapon into the water and let the river take care of the rest. Maybe it was someone Arethusa trusted, or at least someone she discounted as a threat, or maybe it was someone capable of sneaking up behind her and catching her by surprise. It had to be one or the other. Arethusa wouldn't have turned her back to just anybody."

The thought of such quiet, calculating malice made Niniane shudder. Tiago cupped her cheek. His fingers curled around the back of her neck, underneath her hair, and he stroked her face with his thumb. He nodded to the manila envelope on the floor and told Aryal and Rune, "Look at what Arethusa left for me, in care of one of her men."

Aryal pulled out the checkbook and papers. The harpy held them up so she and Rune could both stare at them. Rune murmured, "That's motive right there, baby."

"Here's how I piece it together," Tiago said. "Someone works on Geril and gets him to try to kill Niniane. That someone also has access to Urien's mansion, finds this bogus company in his files and decides to use it. If Geril succeeds, he gets paid. If fallout from Niniane's death causes an investigation that uncovers the payment, the Wyr get blamed. Only Arethusa talked to us, so she didn't stop digging when she was supposed to, and she found this file. She kept quiet because she knew one of the Dark Fae had done it, but she wasn't sure who."

"She wouldn't have had the authority to dig through Aubrey's or Kellen's belongings, not without creating a big stink," Niniane said. "We would have heard if that had happened."

"And we didn't slink off in disgrace the way we were meant to," Rune said. He sat forward, his elbows on his knees. "So—what, you think maybe someone discovered this file had gone missing? I wonder where it was when Arethusa found it."

"Our someone wouldn't have wanted to keep something so incriminating," Tiago said. "The file was probably put back where it had been found in case it might be useful again, or better yet, it was hidden somewhere else, in a cubbyhole, or stuffed under towels in a linen closet. That was a big house. It had a lot of hiding places."

"Our someone likes to hedge bets," Rune said. "But he made another mistake by not destroying that file."

Aryal yawned. She had stretched out on the floor, her long legs crossed at the ankle. She said in a drowsy voice, "I could start bitch-slapping people. Sooner or later somebody would squawk."

Niniane was so tired. It had sunk deeper than her bones and become a cold ache that dragged at her spirits. It was exhaustion that made her eyes leak. It had to be.

She said, "I don't know why you're all being so circumspect. It's not like you to dance around something instead of just saying it."

Tiago's arms tightened. He held her with his whole body, but it was Rune who asked, "What do you mean, pip-squeak?"

"Anybody who had been in that mansion could have found that file," she said. "But the one who probably did was the one responsible for going through Urien's financial papers, as well as for overseeing all the other Dark Fae financial matters."

Aryal tilted her head to look at Niniane. The harpy wore a rare expression of sympathy.

Rune said, "You think the killer was Chancellor Aubrey."

"I don't want to think that," she said. Her voice sounded small, and as cold as the rest of her had become. "But suspecting him without proof would have been more than enough reason to keep Arethusa quiet." She tilted back her head to look up at Tiago. "What do you think?"

His hard-edged face was quietly savage as he looked at the pain in her face.

Aubrey had said to Niniane, *If I had known you were alive, I would never have stopped searching for you.* It had felt like the truth. What if the reasons behind the statement were much less benign than what Aubrey had inferred? Had he ever unequivocally refuted his distant connection to the throne?

Upon reflection, Tiago thought not. It disturbed him, especially considering how Aubrey was already centrally positioned in the Dark Fae government and secure in his allies and relationships. Now one of the major Dark Fae power brokers was dead, the checks-and-balance system built into their triad disrupted, and their army leaderless.

He kissed Niniane with lingering tenderness. Then he said, "I think we should get to Adriyel as fast as we can."

⇒ NINETEEN ⇐

Change of plans.

They could not take Aubrey into custody without proof, not with so many highly placed witnesses present, and they could not allow him to reconnect with his power base in Adriyel and possibly gain control of the army. The same applied to Kellen. Without proof, they could not conclusively clear Kellen of suspicion. For all they knew, Aubrey and Kellen might have struck up an alliance and were now working together.

Niniane had to leave, and quickly, but she also had to travel in the right way. If it were a simple matter of who reached Adriyel first, Tiago, Rune and Aryal could shift into their Wyr forms and carry her to Adriyel in a matter of hours, not days. But she could not be seen to take power through the Wyr.

She said to Tiago, "The troops need to go with us."

"Agreed," Tiago said. "Yesterday Arethusa told me the trip would take the group three days from this point forward. We had an easy day, so our horses are still fresh. If we travel light and push it, we can make Adriyel in a day, maybe a day and a half." He looked at Rune and Aryal. "You need to stay behind and monitor what everyone does when we leave."

Aryal stretched and sat up. "Should be interesting."

Cameron pushed through the hangings, shoes in one hand, scabbard in the other, her hair tousled and face creased. She said in a sleep-gravelly voice, "What about me?"

"You come up with us," Tiago said.

Cameron nodded. She looked unsurprised. She slanted a grin at Niniane and said, "My sore ass can't wait."

Niniane snorted. "Mine either."

Tiago passed a hand over Niniane's hair. "Do you need to sleep for an hour or two before we leave?"

She shook her head. "I rested and ate. I'll live."

"Right. Here's packing made easy for you. It'll be a food, water and weapons kind of trip." He stood and set her gently on her feet. "I'll go muster the troops and get our horses saddled. Plan to leave in half an hour. Less if I can manage it."

"Okay." She watched him leave then she looked at Cameron. "That gives you time to eat something."

Cameron looked around at the empty cooler and array of empty containers. Her eyebrows rose.

Niniane picked up her plate of food and handed it to the other woman. "I just nibbled around the edges. Mr. Incredible served me enough food to last a week. Finish that while I make us some coffee."

"You're the coolest princess I've ever met," Cameron said.

She filled a metal pot with water and set it on the brazier to boil. Then Rune and Aryal took their leave to wash and change into clean clothes and, as Rune said, prepare for mass consternation and misbehavior. They each gave Niniane a hard hug. "See you at the other end," said Rune.

"Be careful," she told him.

"You too, pip-squeak." He smiled and touched her nose.

When it was her turn to say good-bye, Aryal said, "Don't do anything I wouldn't do."

Niniane opened and closed her mouth. She said, "I have no idea how to respond to that."

"Yeah, well." Aryal's hug lifted her off her feet. Then the harpy followed Rune out.

The water in the pot boiled. She set about the comforting, familiar routine of making coffee while Cameron ate everything left on the plate. Niniane tried to drink her coffee but it was too hot. She had a sense of time flashing by too fast as it raced toward an inevitable, deadly foreign place, like a curtain of water that spilled over a waterfall to shatter on jagged rocks.

Her hands shook as she added cold water from a canteen to the steaming brew so she could drink the contents down.

Cameron did the same with her coffee. As the other woman drained her cup, Durin said from outside the tent, "Your highness."

"Come in, Durin," she said.

He lifted the flap and looked in at them both, his expression grave. "It is time to leave."

"All right." She stood, and Cameron grabbed her sword in its scabbard and shrugged into the shoulder harness.

Dawn had come and gone. In the full light of morning the area sparkled with melting frost. The area stirred with restlessness. Niniane could hear the jingle of horse harnesses and raised voices coming from the troops' area of the encampment. Durin stepped close so that Niniane was sandwiched between him and Cameron. He gestured to one side of her tent, opposite the direction of the troops. Cameron frowned, and Niniane looked at him in quick inquiry. "The troops are garnering a lot of attention from the others," Durin said rapidly in a low-toned voice. "We thought it would be faster and quieter to take you out this way. We must move quickly now."

She nodded and turned in the direction he indicated. Cameron put a hand to Niniane's back and turned with her, and Niniane felt the other woman's hand clench in a fist in the material of her sweater. Cameron threw her hard.

Wait, what?

Niniane stumbled forward, trying in vain to correct her balance as she bounced off the taut material of the tent wall. Then she reached the dipping point and fell forward. She tucked her shoulder as she had been taught, hit the ground and rolled. As she fell, she heard a ringing metallic noise that was the sound of swords clashing. Her mind still stuttering, she came up on her hands and knees. She spun around to look.

Cameron and Durin were fighting. Cameron shifted to block the Dark Fae male's sword thrust. Cameron's movements were athletic and confident, but Durin moved with such deadly, accomplished style and grace, it was clear the human woman was hopelessly outmatched. Cameron said to her, "Run."

She jumped to her feet, staring as she backed up.

An arm hooked around her neck, and she felt the cold, hard

edge of a knife at her jugular. The blade bit into her skin. The sting came a moment later, and she felt the wet trickle of blood.

"I might have known," Naida said in her ear. "Nothing's gone right since you crawled out of the woodwork."

Ah damn.

Durin surged forward, his sword flashing in a complicated series of movements, and Cameron's sword went flying. She spun and kicked, but he lunged forward, too close for her to land a proper blow. At the same time he reversed his hold on his sword and slammed the hilt into her jaw. Cameron dropped without a sound.

"Keep your hands where I can see them." The warmth of Naida's breath tickled her ear. "I have no intention of letting you poison me like you did Geril and his friends."

She held her hands up. Naida turned her around and marched her rapidly toward the edge of camp. Durin fell into place beside them. He kept his sword unsheathed as he looked around them with sharp eyes. She gritted, "I can't believe nobody is seeing this."

"They're all arguing and watching the soldiers prepare to leave," Naida said. Within moments they reached the edge of the clearing, and Naida forced her to move faster until they were running. Naida said to Durin, "What is taking so long?"

"Ryle can't get to the Chancellor," the captain said. "The Wyr bitch is watching him too closely."

Who was Ryle? Not one of the soldiers. One of Naida and Aubrey's attendants? Niniane's gaze slid sideways to Durin. The Dark Fae male's face was bleak.

I have killed someone I liked before, Carling had said. *I have killed someone and felt regret.*

"You did it," she said to him. "You killed Arethusa. She was your commanding officer. She trusted you, and you killed her. How could you?"

Durin's red-rimmed gaze flashed to her, then he looked away.

"He did it for the greater good," Naida said. They came to four tethered horses that were bridled but not saddled. Naida jerked Niniane to a halt. "Keep your hands up." She said to Durin, "Search her for weapons."

Durin sheathed his sword and ran his hands over Niniane. He

was as fast and expert in searching her as he was in doing every-thing else. She sighed as he took her stilettos from her pocket. He tucked the small sheathed knives inside his shirt. When she was disarmed Durin tied her hands behind her back with a strip of leather as she looked at Naida for the first time.

Naida's sophisticated, immaculate appearance was gone. Her sturdy travel clothes looked rumpled. She carried a leather pack slung on one shoulder. She looked exhausted, and her usu-ally sleek hair was tousled. Lines of stress marked her pale skin. Well, good. She ought to look like shit.

Niniane said between her teeth, "I'm a little surprised you're going to all this trouble. Why haven't you already killed me?"

"I wish you'd died on the first attempt, but things are no longer that simple. Actually I wish you'd never resurfaced," said Naida. Her indifferent gaze flicked over Niniane's figure, then she looked away. "You should have stayed in the past, along with the rest of your family. It's not enough to just kill you. We also need to survive so we can put my husband on the throne where he belongs."

The utter callousness in Naida's voice made Niniane's breath catch. Durin had tied her hands so tight she was rapidly losing feeling in her fingers. She twisted her wrists in an attempt to reach the knots, but she couldn't. But the binding was leather. Sooner or later, it would have to stretch. She worked her wrists back and forth.

Two of the horses had saddlebags slung on their backs. Why weren't they saddled? She was willing to bet there hadn't been time. Naida, Durin, Aubrey, Ryle and whoever else was work-ing with them were reacting to the moment. Did they really think they had a chance of getting away free and clear from any pursuers?

She said, "This is not going to go the way you think it will."

"Do you think not?" Naida shook her head. "We must improvise with the tools we find in front of us."

She watched as Naida knelt and put her pack on the ground. "Naida, listen to me," she said. "This has spun too far out of control. There are too many people involved. There are Carling and the other vampires, Kellen, Tiago and the sentinels, let alone the rest of the troops. They are never going to forgive or forget what Durin did to Arethusa."

She saw Durin flinch out of the corner of her eye. Was that a weakness she could exploit? Warmth slid along the skin of her hands, and she realized she had rubbed her wrists raw. Good thing she couldn't feel it very well. Maybe the blood soaking into the leather would help stretch it out. Okay, so that was a long shot, but she had no choice but to give it a try. She tucked her chin against her chest and kept twisting.

"The only two people we need to stop are you and your filthy animal," Naida said.

Filthy animal. She tucked her chin in further and gave serious thought to some head-butting action. Apparently they didn't want her dead right away. One really good crack, and she could break Naida's patrician nose.

Naida continued. "If we kill the both of you, there is no succession to protect. Aubrey is the only real choice for the throne. He has cared for the Dark Fae people and worked on our behalf for far longer than you and I have been alive. His wisdom and experience in governance is unparalleled. The Elder tribunal will come to see his ascension as inevitable. And the Wyr have no right to stay in Dark Fae land, especially since your animal has cut all official ties with the Wyr Lord. They will have to leave. I doubt the Wyrkind will be interested in an alliance with us after this, but I am not concerned about that. The Dark Fae have done well enough without a Wyr alliance for the last two hundred years. We will succeed, especially when we place the right Commander at the head of the Dark Fae army."

The right Commander. Gotcha.

"Greater good, my ass," she growled. "Durin murdered Arethusa so he could become Commander, and if Aubrey becomes Dark Fae King, you get to rule by his side, which is all that matters to you, you psychotic bitch."

Naida opened the pack. She said with edged calm, "You talk like the trash you have become. Speaking of tools, you know, exploring Urien's house gave me a fruitful education and some unexpected opportunities."

"If you're referring to Urien's fake company, we already know about it," Niniane said.

"That tool is no longer useful. I refer to more than just that." She reached into the pack and pulled out two sets of black chains with manacles. They radiated a kind of Power that raised Niniane's hackles.

"What the hell are those?" she whispered.

"Urien made them," Naida said. "He was such an expert metallurgist, and so gifted with Power. He was one of the most accomplished of us, and his notes on his research were meticulous."

"You've got to be joking," she said. "He was a treasonous mass-murdering, self-serving, Power-hungry bastard."

Naida sighed. "Oh, get over it." The Dark Fae woman regarded the manacles. Her gray eyes gleamed with admiration. "He designed these specifically to imprison Wyr. Apparently they worked so well they shackled the Great Beast himself. According to Urien's notes, even though the Beast freed himself, he was not able to break these bindings."

Oh shit. Niniane's breath hitched and she grew still. She had heard of those shackles. They had been used when Urien had had Dragos and Pia kidnapped and imprisoned in the Goblin stronghold. They had blocked Dragos's ability to shapeshift into his dragon form. Dragos had been able to gain his freedom only after finding the key to the shackles. Preoccupied with getting to Pia as fast as he could, he had lost the shackles and had been obsessed with trying to find them ever since.

A frigid gale-force wind howled through the trees, blasting into the clearing, and the bright sunlit autumn morning disintegrated as black clouds churned across the sky. Durin swore under his breath, and Naida looked up, her face blank with astonishment, as a massive bolt of lightning ripped the heavens. Thunder exploded.

Niniane didn't give herself time to think. She took a step forward, lifted a leg and slammed the heel of her boot into Naida's face as hard as she could.

Bone crunched. Blood spurted from Naida's nose as her head snapped back.

Durin lunged to grab her, but she knew she had no hope of getting away. She was only interested in inflicting as much damage as she could. Durin missed as she let herself fall back on the ground. Agony shot through her shoulders as she landed on her bound arms. She ignored it, rolled toward him and sent the most vicious kick she could muster to the side of his knee.

Durin hissed in pain and toppled sideways to the ground.

Holy cow. She actually managed to get in two good, solid hits in a row. The sentinels were going to be high-fiving each other at her funeral.

She rolled desperately, throwing all her strength into trying to get some distance between herself and the other two. Hey, miracles happened all the time. You never know, she might make it. She might—

An iron-hard grip clamped on to her ankle. Gasping hard for air, she flipped on her back again and tried to kick at whoever held her, but Durin pushed forward onto her legs, and though she screamed in rage and bucked and kicked as hard as she could, she could not dislodge him.

That was when the monster walked into the clearing. He moved with a speed that was shocking for one of his massive build. He carried a sword in each talon-tipped hand, and his teeth were too long and sharp. His eyes blazed white like twin stars, and oh gods, she loved him so much, and she knew why they had kept her alive for so long, because she was both bait and leverage, literally all they had to use against the onslaught of this nightmare.

Durin sank a fist into her hair and yanked her up until she was on her knees. He jerked her head back, and Naida moved up beside her to put the knife at her throat.

Naida said, "Stop."

The monster's blazing eyes fixed on Niniane. He stopped.

"Drop your weapons." Naida sounded ragged.

No no no.

His hands opened. The swords fell to the ground.

Vaguely she was aware of other people racing into the clearing, and something lethal and winged soaring over the trees. A harpy's enraged shriek sounded in the air overhead. Somewhere close, Rune swore and ordered people to stay back. None of them mattered. The world had narrowed to just her and Tiago, Durin and Naida, and the knife at her throat.

Durin bent, grabbed the shackles and threw them. They landed at the monster's feet. "Put those on," he said. "Run the chain behind your back."

The monster did not move.

Naida pressed the knife harder against the thin skin of her neck. Another sting, another small wound and warm trickle of blood. Naida said, "She is one slice away from death. Do it."

"No," she whispered. "Don't."

The monster held her gaze as he bent to pick up the shackles.

Durin and Naida meant to kill Tiago as soon as he put them

on. She would throw herself on the knife if she could. Maybe they had not gone too far on mating. Maybe he would have a chance to survive if she did. Maybe—she strained forward, but Durin's tight fist in her hair was rock-steady.

Tiago snapped one manacle into place on one thick wrist, ran the chain behind his back, and snapped the second manacle on his other wrist.

"My gods," Aubrey said from across the clearing. He sounded profoundly shaken. "My gods—Naida, *what have you done*?"

"As soon as we heard Urien had been killed, people started whispering," Naida said. "You were going to be King. Didn't you hear them? Everyone said there couldn't be anyone better, and there was no one left with closer ties to the throne. Then *she* appeared, and she had become nothing more than a plastic Americanized whore who had been in bed with the Wyr all these years—"

The monster growled, his face naked with hate.

Aubrey shouted, "She is your rightful Queen!"

"She is not Queen yet!" Naida shouted back. "Why can you not see—when she and her animal are put down, there will be nothing to stop people from supporting you again—"

Naida pressed the knife harder into Niniane's neck.

The monster bared his teeth and plunged forward.

Naida said to Durin, "Kill him."

Durin's grip in her hair loosened. She tried again to throw herself on the knife, but Naida shifted to take Durin's place, holding her jaw in a bruising grip and forcing her head back. Durin strode forward, and time fell its inevitable fall, both backward and forward, toward that jagged place where everything shattered into pieces forever, and she screamed out her heart as the Dark Fae male impaled Tiago on his sword—*oh god mother*—

And Niniane stared as Tiago thrust himself farther onto that murderous sword, all the way to the hilt, his powerful body the most real and dangerous weapon, as he snaked his head forward, and with one wicked-fast snap of his teeth he tore out Durin's throat.

Blood sprayed across Tiago's face. It poured in a river from the sword in his abdomen. Tiago spat out flesh as Durin's body collapsed to the ground. The twin blazing stars that were

Tiago's eyes fixed on her again. His face was slick and red. He went down on one knee.

"My gods, he's an abomination." Naida's breathing sounded in her ear, as harsh and ragged as her own.

She said between her teeth, "I told you this was not going to go the way you thought it would."

His head bowed. He sagged forward. Tiago.

Behind them, Cameron said in a hard, cold voice, "Drop the knife, Naida."

Cameron sounded so confident and her words seemed so misplaced, Naida actually twisted around with Niniane to look. Niniane tried to turn her head to keep her eyes on Tiago, but Naida's hand was clenched so tight on her jaw she couldn't move.

Cameron stood ten feet away. One side of her face had already blackened from Durin's blow. She had both of Niniane's derringers, the gun in one hand pointed to the ground. She held the other gun aimed at Naida's head.

"Do you think I would give up my only leverage now, especially for such a stupid and ignorant bluff as this?" Naida said. "Your weapons technology does not work here, human." She said to Niniane, "Get up. We will have to make for Adriyel, you and I, and then we will see what Urien's old supporters think of you—"

Naida started upright. Niniane didn't move. She didn't know if it was a smart thing to do or not. She simply could not leave Tiago.

Naida screamed in her ear, "Get up right now, or I will gut you in front of everyone!"

"Risk and benefit, huh," Cameron said with a grim smile. She pulled the trigger.

The gun exploded.

There was too much blood, of course.

The beast kept his face turned toward his mate as he fell to the ground. He kept his face turned toward her even though a haze came over his sight and blanked out the farthest reaches of the clearing so that he could no longer see her.

Someone with a tawny head bent over him. He almost lunged upward to tear out this one's throat too, but the tawny-haired one had a scent that was long familiar, and so the beast held back to watch and wait.

"Goddamn, T-bird, look at what you've done to yourself this time," said the familiar one. He took hold of the sword's hilt and pulled it out. The beast hissed at the liquid burning slide as the blade left his flesh. The tawny male tore off his shirt and pressed the wadded material against the beast's wound, and shouted, "ARYAL. Why isn't he starting to heal? Here, put pressure here."

Another familiar one knelt beside him, her eyes blazing with fear and fury, but it wasn't his mate. "Got it."

Then his mate was there, his beautiful, precious mate. His world had burst out of his chest when he had returned to the tent to find she had gone missing. Now she brought it back to him, and it was such a blessed relief to see and smell her—but she had bled from her wrists and neck—he snarled as he caught the fresh scent of her blood and struggled to rise up and slaughter the ones who had done this to her—

"Somebody cut me loose," his mate said. "Oh gods, Tiago, stay down."

He subsided and sighed as she bent close to press her cheek to his. "Only one person," he whispered to her. "Only one thing."

"I can't lose you," she said. Rune cut her hands free, and she wiped the blood off Tiago's face. She pressed her lips against his. She was trembling. "You have to fight for us. Fight as hard as you can, do you hear me? Hold on."

Always.

"He's talking to her but he hasn't come out of the partial shift, and he's still bleeding out," said Aryal between her teeth. "What the hell is wrong? We're going to lose him unless someone figures out what to do right now."

"It's the shackles," his mate said suddenly. "Urien made them to imprison Wyr—they suppress a Wyr's Power. These are the ones that held Dragos and we need the key—" She pushed to her feet and raced away, and his world grew dim again. "It isn't in her pack!"

His mate raced back. She fell to her knees beside his head. She was crying.

Rune surged to his feet. "Help him, Carling!"

That was when he saw the other woman who stood nearby.

She regarded the scene with an expression of mild curiosity, her gaze vague and unfocused. "That is not within my purview as Councillor of the Elder tribunal."

Rune grabbed Carling and shook her. She bowed backward under the pressure of his hands. He roared in her face. "What the hell's the matter with you? Snap out of it."

The Vampyre's gaze clicked into focus. She cocked her head and looked over the scene as if she had never seen it before. Her long almond-shaped eyes blazed with Power. She said to Rune, "If I do this, you will owe me. Not Dragos, not Tiago or Niniane. You. You will come to me in one week after we leave Adriyel, and you will do a favor of my choosing. Do you agree?"

"Yes," Rune hissed. "Just fucking do it."

Carling walked to Tiago. She bent over him with a Mona Lisa smile. "I'm told this might hurt a little."

He closed his eyes in resignation. Crazy-assed bitch.

═ TWENTY ═

Carling placed her hands on Tiago and spoke foreign words filled with Power. Niniane sagged in relief as she held his head.

There was a flurry of activity around Cameron and Naida's prone figures. Both women had fallen when the derringer exploded. Niniane couldn't think about that right now. She didn't care if Rune had to bargain for Carling's cooperation. She was only grateful that Carling was helping now and everything would be all right. It had to be.

Carling frowned, her gaze sharp. "The spell didn't take."

Niniane's head came up. Her gaze searched the strong, quiet features framed between her fingers. "Tiago?"

He remained silent.

"He's gone unconscious." Panic took her over. She switched to telepathy and screamed at him, *DON'T YOU DIE ON ME!*

He did not respond. She hit the jagged rocks and shattered.

The others were all speaking at once.

"What the hell use are you, anyway?" The vicious question came from Aryal and was directed at Carling.

Rune growled, "Cast it again. Make it happen now."

Carling ignored the two sentinels, her face intense with concentration. She spoke other foreign words that were so filled with Power, their vibration thrummed in Niniane's body. Then the Vampyre sat back on her heels. She wiped her face with the back of one hand. "I caught him in time. I have put him in stasis for now."

Niniane gritted, "What's wrong?"

"His injury requires a healing spell that must act along certain shapeshifting principles. His torn arteries and organs must knit together in order to stop the hemorrhaging. Normally the Wyr are particularly adept at healing injuries. It is part of their inherent ability to shapeshift. I think the Power in the shackles is blocking the spell." Carling's gaze met hers. "He stands at the threshold. If we do not find a way to remove those shackles, he will die."

Niniane didn't recognize her own voice. "You're not going to let that happen to him."

"I will hold him as long as I can." Carling regarded Tiago's still face as if he were a cipher she could not read. "But part of that is up to him. If his spirit chooses to let go and slip away, there is nothing I can do."

Tiago's face disappeared in a watery shimmer. She wiped her cheek on her shoulder. "He said he'd fight," she whispered. "He'll fight."

Rune and Aryal crouched, looking at each other. "Niniane checked Naida's pack," Rune said. "She didn't check Naida or Durin."

The two sentinels sprang away. Rune landed by Durin's body while Aryal launched at Naida's prone form.

You swore you would not leave me, Niniane said to Tiago. *You made me believe in you. You made me love you. Promises are all well and good, mister. Now it's time for you to make good on them. I can't—I can't take it if you don't.*

Aryal gave a sharp, triumphant hawk's cry. The harpy leaped to her feet, sprinted to Tiago and skidded on her knees as she landed beside him. Her long hands blurred as she unlocked the shackles. Then Rune rejoined them, and they all worked to ease the shackles out from underneath Tiago's body. "Take those away," Carling ordered.

Aryal's stormy gaze flashed up to meet Niniane's for the barest instant. Then Aryal whirled from them, the shackles gripped in one hand, and she was gone.

Carling said, "I have to remove him from stasis and then cast the healing spell. If you believe the gods take an interest in our lives, now would be a good time to pray."

Oh gods, please. Please. She threw the full force of her panic into the prayer. Then she pressed her lips to Tiago's forehead and said to him, *Tiago, you must stay with me.*

Carling spoke even more rapidly than before. The low-voiced Power-filled words made the world shiver, made Niniane's bones vibrate, made Tiago's body blaze with golden light. His back arched and he gasped as his face contorted in agony. Niniane wrapped her arms around him, cradling his head. He turned to bury his face against her breast as his talon-tipped hands dug into the ground.

She remembered the agony of her own healing. Her wound had been so much smaller than his. She suffered with him until gradually the tension eased from his body, and at last he rested against her, his face and body smoothing into their normal lines.

I've already told you more than once, faerie. I'm not leaving you. He spoke as if he had heard every word she'd said to him and was continuing the conversation. His mental voice was slurred, and his eyes refused to focus. *Some day you'll believe it.*

She sobbed out a laugh and held him closer. *I think some day just might be today, Tiago. I think it might be today.*

He slipped again into unconsciousness. Carling sounded confident when she said the danger had past, but Niniane could not relax until she had torn open his blood-soaked shirt and seen for herself the shiny scar from the sword wound. It was about three inches long and looked almost silver against the dark tanned skin of his muscled abdomen. She put her fingers to it. There would be another at his back where the blade had passed through his body.

A sober-looking Hefeydd and three other Dark Fae soldiers came with a stretcher improvised from blankets and two poles. Under her anxious supervision they eased Tiago onto it. She kept one hand on Tiago's shoulder as they carried him back to camp. Aryal and Rune kept a watchful pace alongside. The stretcher-bearers took Tiago to her tent without being asked. She directed them to lay him on her bed, and they did so gently.

"Please heat some water so I can bathe him," she said, her attention on Tiago.

"Yes, ma'am." Hefeydd lingered, and she looked up. The Dark

Fae male's brow was creased. He said, "If it pleases you, your highness, we want to help. May we do anything else for you?"

She tried to think. "He'll be hungry when he wakes up. He needs a lot of meat."

"With your permission, a few of us will go hunting."

She nodded. She frowned. "You were the one Arethusa gave the packet to."

Hefeydd bowed. "Yes, ma'am."

Her gaze narrowed on him. "Why were you so cautious about giving it to Tiago?" What had Hefeydd known but not said?

The soldier's eyes reddened. "None of us believed the Commander's death was an accident, and I did not think anyone had the ability to slip up behind her without her knowing. Her killer had to be someone she trusted and, therefore, was most likely someone I knew too."

She closed her eyes and nodded again, and he backed out of the space.

Rune had entered with them, carrying Tiago's swords. He set them on the ground beside the bed, then knelt alongside her and helped her cut away Tiago's bloody clothes. Without looking up from the task, she asked, "How's Cam?"

There was a pause. Then Rune turned to put his hands on her shoulders. He squeezed her gently as he said, "I'm sorry, sweetheart. She didn't make it."

It was too much to hear, on top of everything else. She rocked and keened quietly, and Rune hugged her tight. After a few minutes, she said, "Naida?"

"She's dead too," Rune told her. "The gun fired and exploded simultaneously."

"It's my fault. Those were my guns. I brought them with me."

"Stop it." Rune's voice was calm and firm. He stroked her hair as she leaned against him. "Naida had gone over the edge. Cameron saved your life. She did a brave, good thing and died like a warrior. Don't try to take that from her."

She bit her lips. After a moment she was able to nod. She said, *Thank you for getting Carling to act.*

I had to. It was T-bird. He pressed a kiss to her forehead.

She lifted her head to look at him. *Rune, be careful. Carling isn't quite sane.*

Yeah, I figure. He smiled, his gaze serene. "Don't worry,

pip-squeak. You know how the song goes. 'Every little thing is gonna be all right.'"

Trust Rune to quote Bob Marley. She would not have expected she would be able to smile back, but she did. She glanced back down to Tiago's stretched-out form, and her smile was replaced with rage. "We are done with diplomacy. I want you to scour the camp. I don't give a shit if it offends anybody or not. Use force if you have to. Durin and Naida mentioned someone named Ryle. Find him, and find out how much he knows. No one is exempt, not Aubrey, not Kellen. Nobody."

"Bitchin'," he said. His smile widened, and his amber lion's eyes flared with a predator's gleam. "Sounds like my kind of party."

"Niniane," Tiago said as he opened his eyes.

He was in her bed, in her tent. Someone had removed his clothing and bathed him. He broke into a sweat as he remembered the star of agony in his abdomen that had grown to fill his body with burning gold. He started to rise. Suddenly Niniane was there, kneeling beside him. She laid a hand to his cheek. "I'm here. No, please don't get up."

He looked at her hungrily. She was clean and dressed in a robe. The thin cuts at her neck were not covered, but her wrists were wrapped in bandages. Her face was drawn and pale, her lovely eyes haunted.

In his mind, he saw her bound and kneeling, her neck exposed and bleeding. One slice away from death.

His mouth opened as the breath left his lungs. He snatched at her and dragged her down. She grunted as he clenched his arms around her. He growled, "Every time I let you out of my sight, something bad happens."

She put her head on his shoulder, her small body flowing to align with his and accommodate his tense hold. He put a hand to the back of her head and turned his face into her fragrant hair. She whispered, "Everything's all right now."

She pressed her lips against the bare skin of his shoulder. She was safe and alive, and she was with him. He dragged her underneath the bedcovers and curled his body protectively around her. His mind raced. "The shackles."

She stirred. "Aryal has both sets of chains, and the key," she told him, muffled against his skin. "She swears she'll find a way to destroy them. She's saying 'my Precious' a lot and talking about dropping them into a volcano."

He took a deep breath and let it out. "Naida," he said. "Cam."

She swallowed hard and shook her head.

He rubbed his cheek in her soft hair as he listened to the sounds of the camp. People were talking and moving around quietly. Enough time had passed, then, for calm to return. "How long have I been out?"

"Almost thirty-six hours. You almost died," she whispered. "It was really close, really bad." He stroked her back, soothing her, and they held each other in silence for a while. Then she stirred. "There's food," she told him. "Venison stew and pan bread."

Hunger was a sharp, insistent ache, but his need for answers was sharper. He said, "Tell me everything, starting with when I left."

She did. Since she had learned things after the fact, she was able to add more to the story than what had just happened to her. Aryal and Rune had split off to keep an eye on Aubrey and Kellen, the most dangerous suspects. In the meantime, Durin received Tiago's order to get the troops ready to ride out. While Tiago collected food and water for the journey personally, and saddled his and Niniane's horses, Durin passed his orders on and went directly to find Naida.

"Everything Naida and Durin did from that point on was in escalating reaction," she told him. "Right up to the end, when Naida realized Aubrey would never agree with what she did or forgive her. Then she had nothing left to lose, and I think she just unraveled. Just imagine, a couple of weeks ago she believed Aubrey would be crowned and she would be Queen."

He growled, "Do you believe Aubrey?"

She tilted back her head and stroked his face. "Everybody believes Aubrey, Tiago. He has been beside himself. He has offered his resignation as Chancellor and asked to be taken into custody. And you know what? I finally learned where Duncan's talents lie."

He lifted his head to frown at her. "What?"

"Duncan, the Vampyre," she said. "It turns out in 1890 or so, he founded what has become one of San Francisco's premiere law firms. He's expert at questioning witnesses and suspects, and especially at cross-examination, although after everything that happened, people were more than happy to cooperate. Between his skill, and Aryal and Rune's truthsense, they're confident everybody else in the camp—including Aubrey—is innocent. One of Aubrey and Naida's attendants, a man named Ryle, was involved only peripherally. Naida had sent him to get Aubrey out of the camp quietly, but she hadn't told him why. Geril and Durin were her two accomplices. She must have done quite a number on them to play on their greed and ambition. She all but promised to get Durin appointed as Commander, right in front of me."

"So it's really over," he said.

She nodded. Her eyes filled with tears. "The sad thing is, Arethusa and Cameron didn't have to die. If we had achieved more trust and openness—if we had all just worked together better, they would still be alive—"

"Hush, you can't think that way," he said. "All we can do is work with the information we have at any given time."

The tears spilled over. "I know, but I liked Cam so much and she was so happy to come."

"I know," he whispered. He framed her face in his hands and kissed her damp eyelids, the tip of her nose, her mouth. "I wish I could take the pain away."

"I don't," she said. "She deserves to be mourned."

That may be so, but his faerie had suffered too much and he had had more than enough. If anybody so much as looked at her funny, he was going to come down hard on them with both size-fourteen steel-toed boots. Then he would consider seriously the merits of evisceration.

He kissed her again, gently, and she kissed him back. Then soothing became searching. She wound her arms around his neck, and he growled low in his throat and moved to cover her body. "Wait," she murmured. "Don't you want to eat first? You must be starving."

"It has quite a high priority rating," he muttered. He rested his weight on one elbow and ran his hand down the side of her body, looking for a way to open her robe. "It's next on my to-do list, but you're the first thing."

The most important, the most urgent thing.

There was a belt at her waist. It was tied. He untied it and pulled her robe open.

She was naked underneath, and he swallowed as he stared as

her gorgeous pink-tipped breasts, that narrow waist, the impudent little gold navel ring and the silken tuft of private hair at the sweet, graceful arch of her pelvis.

He put his forehead down between her breasts and swallowed hard. She was his life. It was as simple as that and he had almost lost her.

Niniane slipped her hands under his chin and gently urged his head up. Her face softened as she took in the harsh set of his face, his full glittering eyes. He shook his head. His throat had closed up, and anyway, he had no words.

"It's all right," she whispered. She stroked his face, his shoulders. She reached into the shadowed space between them, took hold of his erection and guided him between her legs. She pulled her knees up and cradled his long torso as he came inside her, came home.

Then the words came, and the force of his feelings shoved them out of his mouth.

"I need those chains back," he said. "I'm going to shackle you to me. We'll destroy the key. We're never going to be more than two feet apart again."

"Okay, we'll do that," she murmured. "I promise."

"Don't humor me," he snapped. He pushed all the way inside. Then he rocked his hips, moving slow and gentle as he remained buried to the hilt. He felt huge and hot and he stretched her wide, and he found just the right spot to hit. With every thrust he ground hard against her pelvis, as he dug in as deep as he possibly could.

"I'm not," she gasped. "I almost lost you too."

She flung back her head, her eyes closed. Her emotions were too naked, the pleasure too intense. She dug her nails into his flexing back.

He slid a muscled arm underneath her, his hand at the nape of her neck, and he clamped her to him so tight she could hardly breathe. "Look at me."

Her eyes opened and she looked. His hard-edged features were raw, but his eyes had cleared, and they were...

Steady. Adamant. Bedrock.

"You will never lose me, faerie," he said point-blank into her upturned face. "I love you too much."

Then he pushed his pelvis against her one last time in a slow, hard, voluptuous grind, and the explosion of pleasure was so intense it seared her soul as he destroyed her again. God, she adored him. He was such a walking, talking holocaust of a man.

They ate and slept, and made love again. Then laughter came back early the next morning, and they agreed it might be time to face the world again. They dressed and left the tent together, and while he clenched if she stepped too far away from him and she turned to look too often for the reassuring sight of his tall black-clad figure, they managed well enough.

While Tiago had been unconscious, she had written a letter of condolence to Cameron's family. Two troops had taken the letter along with Cameron's body back to Chicago. After healing Tiago, Carling disappeared into her tent and did not reemerge. When Niniane gave the word they were ready to break camp and resume travel, there were four, not three, wrapped and cloaked vampires who appeared the next morning. Niniane noticed that Rune glanced at Carling's cloaked figure often as she rode astride her black Arabian stallion, his eyes narrowed in a speculative look. But more often than not, his expression was closed and remote. She and the others respected his unspoken desire and left him alone.

Such, however, was not the case for Aubrey. With three bodies wrapped in herbs and carried in one wagon at the rear, it was a somber group, and Niniane set an easy pace. After they had ridden for most of the day, she caught Tiago's eye and gestured with her chin toward the Dark Fae male. Tiago turned to look. Aubrey rode by himself. His cloak was wrapped tightly around him, his chiseled features bleak and withdrawn.

Tiago set his jaw and lowered his brows in a scowl, but after a moment he nodded. Niniane nudged her sweet-natured little mare forward. As she came up on Aubrey from one side, Tiago came up on the other.

The Dark Fae male's head lifted. He looked from Niniane to Tiago and drew further in on himself. "Your highness," he murmured. His voice was toneless.

"You must know this won't do, Aubrey," Niniane said. "I refuse your resignation. I need you too much."

Aubrey stared sightlessly ahead. "After Geril and Naida, I no longer have the confidence that I can meet your need."

"The last time I heard, it was not a crime to think well of

people you know, especially those you care about," remarked Tiago to no one in particular as he surveyed the surrounding landscape.

Aubrey gave him a quick glance but said nothing. They rode in silence for a time.

Niniane sighed. "I don't know that I can afford to give you the choice. I know you need time to heal and mourn your wife, and I promise you will have that. But you must return to your position as Chancellor. If you won't do it for me, do it for the Dark Fae."

More silence. Then Aubrey said quietly, "I would do anything for you that I could—"

She interrupted him to stave off another rejection. "Good," she said strongly. "I need you to get together with Kellen right away. The two of you have to come up with a short list of people you would recommend for appointment as Dark Fae Commander. And I don't know how precisely you're going to do this, but I want you to research the history of Urien's finances since he took the crown."

A spark of curiosity enlivened Aubrey's dull gaze. "What do you need to know?"

She was too canny to let herself smile yet. She told him, "I want to know how much my family fortune was when Urien became King. It doesn't have to be exact if the records aren't precise. I'm just looking for a realistic estimate. You see, I was disturbed by the inequities in the numbers we reviewed. I think Urien benefited too much from isolating the Dark Fae all these years. I intend on taking only what was rightfully ours before my father died. Then I want to put the rest of Urien's fortune to work in developing opportunities for our people. You want to help me spend that money wisely, don't you?"

She glanced sidelong at him. Life had come back into Aubrey's expression in the form of startled interest and intellectual speculation. Riding relaxed in his saddle on Aubrey's other side, Tiago quirked an eyebrow at her.

Now it was time to smile. Maybe just a bit.

The road and the river meandered, moving apart and coming together again like quarreling lovers. On their third day the travelers started to come upon individual homes and villages.

Wide-eyed Dark Fae came to stare in wonder at the group. They were a handsome people and rich in creativity, but while their homes and properties were well kept and sparked with flashes of Power, their relative poverty was also painfully apparent.

Tiago had a quiet but intense conniption when Niniane dismounted to walk and talk among them. Thunder rumbled in the distance, which concerned certain individuals in the group very much. Niniane turned to glare at him. He fought a private battle and the thunder subsided.

Word spread, and people began to appear on the road. They brought fresh-baked bread and cheese, water and wine for the group, and they gave Niniane presents of flowers, hand-embroidered linen, quilts, gorgeously worked silver jewelry, and incense and spices. They began to follow until they trailed for a quarter of a mile behind the group. On their last night at camp, snatches of singing and laughter came from bright campfires that dotted the countryside.

"I have never seen anything like it," Kellen told Niniane over an excellent supper of hunter's stew.

She shook her head as she met Tiago's dark gaze over their own flickering yellow fire. "I don't know what to say."

"Then say nothing," Kellen told her with a smile. "Just rule well."

Then their last day of travel came. She recognized landmarks. There up ahead, she knew that twist in the road. Further up still, they passed underneath a bluff that one could scale and look out over the river that lay winking silver blue in the pale autumn sunlight. The road climbed in a low-grade incline for a time, and she knew exactly where they would crest the hill. Her heart began to pound. Her mouth dried and her hands shook.

"Faerie," murmured Tiago as he rode beside her.

"Just wait," she whispered. "Watch."

They reached the hill's crest and looked over a valley.

The land scrolled down, carpeted in green and gold. Clusters of pale buildings with spare, gracious lines showed through copses of trees dressed in brilliant fall foliage. The deep blue river bordered the valley. It came from an immense waterfall in the distance that was shrouded in a perpetual mist that sparkled in the bright chill afternoon.

The jewel in the scene was the palace by the river that gleamed pearl and pale gold. A double colonnade of immense sycamore trees lined the road that led up to the palace. The ancient trees towered several stories high, the curve of their white branches flowing upward in gracious outspreading fans. They were tipped with gold leaves that had not yet fallen, their trunks wreathed in lush skirts of scarlet-leaved vines.

Aryal nudged her horse up beside Niniane's. The harpy's eyes were wide with wonder. "So that's Adriyel. No wonder it's famous in poems and shit. We're finally reaching journey's end."

Niniane and Tiago looked at each other.

"No," he said. "Now we begin."

⇒ EPILOGUE ⇐

Early in the morning, one week later, Niniane sat at a table on her terrace and looked over her private walled garden. The day had dawned crystal cold and clear. She wore a fur robe, and braziers dotted the area around her. The garden was a jewel of a place, perhaps a third of an acre in size, with a luxurious carpet of thick well-tended grass, fruit trees, flowers and shrubs. She watched as the man worked in her garden. He had removed his shirt and rivulets of sweat glistened on his long, muscled torso.

Her coronation had occurred the day before. For his coronation, Urien had worn an outfit encrusted with jewels and gold. For hers, Niniane chose a simple, tailored gown made of deep midnight blue silk. She must have said the right things and given the right responses at the appropriate times. She couldn't remember. She had gone through the ceremony, her mind blurred with terror, trembling as the weight of her father's crown was placed on her head.

Afterward, she had held her first court. The throne was a ridiculously uncomfortable piece of furniture. She made a mental note to get a cushion. Tiago, dressed in severe, unrelieved black with two crossed swords at his back, had taken for the first time his position standing just behind her. Representatives from the American and Canadian governments and other Elder demesnes had presented her with gifts and statements of congratulations and promises of friendship. Well. Time would tell about that.

Then came the time for the Dark Fae nobles to pay homage to her. She noted both confirmed and potential allies, and she gave a cold smile to old enemies with friendly faces who bowed low before her. Tiago had put in a fruitful week of work already. He had five nobles targeted for arrest and prosecution for their involvement in the coup that killed her family. She affirmed Kellen as Chief Justice, and Aubrey as Chancellor, and appointed their strongest recommendation for Commander, whom Tiago also liked, a clever, accomplished and genial male named Fafnir Orin.

Afterward they held the coronation feast, and she danced first with Aubrey, next with Kellen, third with Fafnir, and down through the list of preapproved safe partners. She danced last with the one she loved the most. After the feast, they carried a mound of blankets out to her private garden and made love under a brilliant spray of stars, and it was good. It was very good.

Aubrey said from behind her, "Good morning, your majesty. Thank you for inviting me to breakfast."

She turned to give him a bright smile. "Good morning, Aubrey. I hope you don't mind a working breakfast."

"Not at all," he told her. "I enjoy an early start to my day, and we have a lot to accomplish."

The Chancellor joined her at the table. She poured him a cup of coffee. They looked at the man together as he worked his powerful body through a complex martial arts routine that stretched and toned muscles recently healed from serious injury.

"He will always be at war here," said Aubrey, his brow creased in concern.

In the midst of his work, the man glanced at her. He was aware of what had been said. He was aware of everything that happened around her. His Power mantled over her in a warm, invisible caress.

The Dark Fae Queen replied, "That makes him happy."

Turn the page for a special preview of
the next Novel of the Elder Races
by Thea Harrison

SERPENT'S KISS

Coming October 2011 from
Berkley Sensation!

"I am a bad woman, of course," said Carling Severan, the Vampyre sorceress, in an absent tone of voice. "It is a fact I made peace with many centuries ago. I calibrate everything I do, even the most generous-seeming gesture, in terms of how it may serve me."

Carling sat in her favorite armchair by a spacious window. The chair's butter-soft leather had long ago molded to the contours of her body. It cradled her like an old lover. Outside the window lay a lush, well-tended garden that was ornamented with the subtle hues of the night. Her gaze was trained on the scene, but like her face, the expression in her almond-shaped eyes was blank.

"Why would you say such a thing?" Rhoswen asked. There were tears in the younger Vampyre's voice as she knelt beside the armchair, her blonde head turned upward to Carling like a flower's to the sun. "You're the most wonderful person in the world."

"My sweet girl." Carling kissed Rhoswen's forehead since the younger woman seemed to need it. Although the distance in Carling's gaze lessened, it did not entirely disappear. "You know, those are painful and rather disturbing words. To believe that of someone such as I—you must acquire more discernment."

Her servant's tears spilled over and streaked down a young-seeming, cameo-perfect face. Rhoswen threw her arms around Carling with a sob.

Carling's sleek eyebrows rose. "What is this?" she asked, her tone weary. "What have I said to upset you so?"

Rhoswen shook her head and clung tighter.

Carling patted the younger woman's back as she thought. She said, "We were talking about the events that led up to the Dark Fae Queen's coronation. You persist in believing that I did a good thing when I healed Niniane and her lover, Tiago, when they were injured. While the results might have been beneficial, I was merely pointing out what a selfish creature at heart I really am."

"Two days ago," Rhoswen said into her lap. "We had that conversation two days ago, and then you faded again."

"Did I?" She stroked Rhoswen's pale hair. "Well, we knew the deterioration was accelerating."

No one fully understood why very old Vampyres went through a period of increasing mental deterioration before they disintegrated into outright madness and then death. Since it was rare for Vampyres to achieve such an extreme old age, the phenomenon was little known outside the upper echelon of the Nightkind community. Vampyres lived violent lives, and they tended to die from other causes first.

Perhaps it was the inevitable progression of the disease itself. Perhaps, Carling thought, in the end, our beginnings contain the seeds of our eventual downfall. The souls that began as human were never meant to live the near-immortal life that vampyrism gave them.

Rhoswen's tear-streaked face lifted. "But I don't believe you have to deteriorate! In Chicago, and later at the Dark Fae coronation, you were fully alert and functioning. You were present for every moment."

Carling regarded the younger woman with a wry expression. Extraordinary experiences did seem to help, as they jolted one into alertness for a time. The problem was it only helped temporarily. To someone who has witnessed the passage of millennia, after a while even the extraordinary experiences became ordinary.

Carling sighed and admitted, "I had a couple of episodes I did not share with you."

The grief that filled Rhoswen's expression was so epic it was positively Shakespearian. Carling's sense of wryness deepened as she looked upon the face of fanatic devotion and knew she had done nothing whatsoever to merit it.

She had squandered an almost unimaginably long life in the acquisition of Power. She had played chess with demons for human lives, counseled monarchs and warred with monsters. Throughout the unwinding scroll of centuries, she had ruled more than one country with unwavering ruthlessness in her slender iron fist. She knew spells that were so secret the knowledge of their existence had all but passed from this Earth, and she had seen things so wondrous that the sight of them had brought strong, proud men to their knees. She had conquered the darkness to walk in the full light of day, and she had lost and lost and lost so very many people and things that even grief failed to move her much anymore.

All of these fabulous experiences were now fading into the ornamented night.

There was simply nowhere else to take her life, no adventure so compelling she must fight above all else to survive and see it through, no mountaintop she had to scale. After everything she had done to survive, after fighting to live for so long and to rule, she had now become . . . disinterested.

And here was the final of all treasures, the last jewel in her casket of secrets that rested on top of all the others, winking its onyx light.

The Power she had worked so hard to accumulate was pulsing in rhythm with the accelerating deterioration of her mind. She saw it flare all around her in an exquisite transparent shimmer. It covered her in a shroud that sparkled like diamonds.

She had lost track of when it had begun. Time had become a riddle. Perhaps it had been a hundred years ago. Or perhaps it had been the entirety of her life, which held certain symmetry. That which she had fought so hard for, shed blood over and cried tears of rage over would be what consumed her in the end.

Who knew that dying could be so beautiful?

Another Power flare was building. She could sense its inevitability, like the oncoming crescendo in an immortal symphony or the next intimate pulse of her long-abandoned, almost-forgotten heartbeat. The expression in her eyes turned vague as she fixed on that ravishing internal flame.

Just before it engulfed her again, she noticed an oddity.

There was no sound in the house around them, no movement of other Vampyres, no spark of human emotion. There was nothing but Rhoswen's hitched breathing as the younger Vampyre knelt at Carling's feet, and the small contented sounds of a dog nearby as he scratched at his ear and then dug out a nesting place in his floor cushion. Carling had lived for a long time surrounded by the jackals eager to feed from scraps that fell from the tables of those in Power, but sometime over the last week, all her usual attendants and sycophants had fled.

Some creatures had a well-developed sense of self-preservation, unlike others.

She said to Rhoswen, "I suggest you work harder on acquiring that sense of discernment."

*E*very little thing is going to be all right.
    Recently Rune had quoted Bob Marley to Niniane Lorelle when she had been at a very low point in her life. Niniane was young for a faerie, a sweet woman and his very good friend. She just also happened to be the Dark Fae Queen now and the newest entry on America's list of the top ten most powerful people in the country. Rune had brought Bob up in conversation to comfort her after an assassination attempt had been made on her life, during which a friend of hers had been killed and Tiago, her mate, had nearly died as well.

And damn if that Marley song hadn't kept running through his head ever since. It was one of those brain viruses, like a TV commercial or a musical theme from a movie that got stuck on perpetual replay, and he couldn't find an off switch for the sound system that was wired into his brain.

Not that, in the normal course of things, he didn't like Bob's music. Rune just wanted him to shut up for a little freaking while so he could get some shut-eye.

Instead Rune kept waking up in the middle of the night, staring at his ceiling as his silk sheets sandpapered his oversensitive skin and mental snapshots of recent events shuttered against his mind's retina while Bob kept on playing.

Every little thing.

Snap—Rune's other good friend Tiago was sprawled on his back in a forested clearing, gutted and drenched in his own blood, while Niniane knelt at his head and held on to him in perfect terror.

Snap—Rune stared into the gorgeous, blank expression of Carling, one of the most Powerful Nightkind rulers in history, as he grabbed her by the shoulders, shook her hard and roared point-blank in her face.

Snap—he struck a bargain with Carling that saved Tiago's life but could very well end his.

Snap—Carling was walking naked out of the Adriyel River at twilight, drenched in silvery water that glistened in the dying day as if she wore a transparent gown of stars. The curves and hollows of her muscled body, the dark seal-wet hair that lay slick against her shapely skull, her high-cheeked Egyptian face—they were all so fucking perfect. And one of the most perfect things about her was also one of the most tragic, for the lithe, sensual beauty of her body had been marred with dozens of long white lash scars. When she had been a mortal human, she had been whipped with such force it must have been a ferocious cruelty, and yet she moved with the strong, sleek, confident sensuality of a tiger-striped cat. The sight of her had stopped his breath, stopped his thinking, stopped his soul, his everything, so that he needed some kind of cosmic reboot that hadn't happened yet because part of him was still caught frozen in that epiphanic moment.

Snap—he bore witness as an antique gun that both fired and exploded in the forest clearing, killing both a traitor and a good woman. A woman he had liked very much. A strong, funny, fragile human who shouldn't have lost her short, precious life because he and his fellow sentinel Aryal had screwed up and left her to protect Niniane on her own.

Snap—he saw Cameron's face when she had been alive. The human had had the long, strong body of an athlete, her spare features sprinkled with good humor and cinnamon-colored freckles.

Snap—he saw her that final time as the Dark Fae soldiers prepared and wrapped her body for transportation back to her family in Chicago. All the pretty cinnamon color had leached out of her freckles. The exploding gun she had shot to save Niniane's life had taken out a large chunk of her head. It was always so harsh when you saw a friend in that last, saddest state. They were okay. They didn't hurt anymore. At that point you were the one who was wounded.

Every little thing is going to be all right.

Except sometimes it wasn't, Bob. Sometimes things got so fucked up all you could do was send them home in a body bag.

Rune's temper grew short. Normally he was an easygoing kind of Wyr, but he had started snapping off people's heads for no reason. Metaphorically, anyway. At least he hadn't started snapping off people's heads for real. Still, people had started to avoid him.

"What's up your ass, anyway?" Aryal had asked after Niniane's coronation, when they crossed over from Adriyel to Chicago and were en route back to New York.

They took their preferred method of travel, which was flying in their Wyr forms. Aryal was his fellow sentinel and a harpy, which meant she was a right royal bitch ninety percent of the time. Usually her snarky attitude cracked him up. At the moment it almost had him drop-kicking her into the side of a skyscraper.

"I'm being haunted by Marley's ghost," he told her.

Aryal slanted a dark eyebrow at him. When she was in her harpy form, the angles of her face were pronounced, upswept. Her gray-fade-to-black wings beat strongly in the hot summer wind that blew wildly around them. "Which ghost?" the harpy asked. "The past, present or future?"

Huh? It took him a second to click to it. Then the Dickens connection happened in his head. He thought of Jacob Marley's ghost, not Bob. Aryal had gotten the Jacob Marley character all muddled up with the three spirits of Christmas past, present and future.

Time and time and time. What happened, what is and what is to come. He barked out a laugh. The sound was filled with ground glass. "All of them," he said. "I'm being haunted by all of them."

"Dude, give it up," said Aryal in a mild tone that he recognized as a conciliatory one, coming as it was from her. "Believe in Christmas already."

His Wyr form was that of a gryphon. He made the harpy look almost delicate as he flew by her side. He had the body of a lion and the bronze-colored head and wings of a golden eagle. His paws were the size of hubcaps and tipped with long, wicked eagle talons, while his eagle's head had lion-colored eyes. His feline body had breadth and power across the chest, had sleek, strong haunches and was the dun color of hot desert places. In his Wyr form he was immense, easily the size of an SUV, with a correspondingly huge wingspan.

In his human form, Rune stood six-foot-four, and he had the broad shoulders and lean, hard muscles of a swordsman. He had sun-bronzed, fine-grained skin with laugh lines at the corners of lion's eyes that were the color of the sun shining through amber. He knew how to use his even features and rakish white smile to his best advantage, especially with those of the female persuasion, and his tawny mane of sun-streaked hair that fell to his broad shoulders held glints of pale gold, chestnut and burnished copper.

He was one of the four gryphons of the earth, an ancient Wyr who came into being at the birth of the world. Time and space had buckled when the Earth was formed. The buckling created dimensional pockets of Other land where magic pooled, time moved differently, modern technologies didn't work and the sun shone with a different light. What came to be known as the Elder Races—the Wyrkind and the Elves, the Light and Dark Fae, the Demonkind, the Goblins and the Djinn and all other manner of monstrous creatures—tended to cluster in or around the Other lands.

Most of the Elder creatures came into being either in the dimensional pockets of Other land or on the Earth itself. A few, a very few, came into existence in those crossover points between the places, where time and space were fluid and changeable, and at the time of creation, Power was an unformed, immense force.

Revered in ancient India and Persia, Rune and his fellow gryphons were the quintessential liminal beings. They were born at the cusp between two creatures, on the threshold of changing time and space. Lion and eagle, they learned, as the other ancient Wyr had learned, to shapeshift and walk amongst humankind, and so they also became Wyr form and man. There would be no others like them. Creation's inchoate time had passed, and all things, even the crossover points between places, had become fixed in their definitions.

The past, behind him. The future, the unknown thing that waited ahead of him and smiled its Mona Lisa smile. And the ever-fleeting now that was continually born and continually died, but was never, ever anything you could get your hands on and hold on to, as it always pushed you on to some other place.

Yeah, he knew a thing or two about liminality.

He and Aryal had returned to Cuelebre Tower in New York. There were seven demesnes of Elder Races that overlaid the human geography of the continental United States. The seat of the Wyrkind demesne was in New York City. The seat of Elven power was based in Charleston, South Carolina. The Dark Fae's demesne was centered in Chicago, and the Light Fae in Los Angeles. The Nightkind, which included all vampyric forms, controlled the San Francisco Bay Area and the Pacific Northwest, and the human witches, considered part of the Elder Races due to their command of magical Power, were based in Louisville. Demonkind, like the Wyr and the Vampyres, consisted of several different types that included Goblins and Djinn, and their seat was based in Houston.

Upon their return, the first thing Rune and Aryal had done was debrief the Lord of the Wyr, Dragos Cuelebre. A massive dark man with gold eyes, Dragos's Wyr form was a dragon the size of a private jet. He had ruled over the Wyrkind demesne for centuries with seven immortal Wyr as his sentinels. Rune was Dragos's First sentinel, and among his other duties, he and the other three gryphons—Bayne, Constantine and Graydon—worked to keep the peace in the demesne. Aryal was the sentinel in charge of investigations, and the gargoyle Grym was head of corporate security.

They had just lost their seventh sentinel, who had not yet been replaced. Tiago—Wyr, thunderbird and long-time warlord sentinel—had walked away from his life and position in the Wyr demesne in order to be with his newfound mate, Niniane.

Dragos's temper was not the most even at the best of times. At first he had not been pleased with the debriefing. He had not been pleased at all.

"You promised her *what*?" The dragon's deep roar rattled the windows as they stood in his office. Dragos planted his hands on his hips, his dark, machete-edged face sharp with incredulity.

Rune set his mouth in the taut lines of someone struggling to hold on to his own temper. He said between his teeth, "I promised to go to Carling in one week and do a favor of her choosing."

"Un-fricking-believable," the Wyr Lord growled. "Do you have any idea what you gave away?"

"Yes, actually," Rune bit out. "I believe I might have a clue."

"She could ask you to do anything, and now you are bound by the laws of magic to do it. You could be gone for HUNDREDS OF YEARS just trying to complete that one fucking favor." The dragon's hot glare flared into incandescence as he paced. "I've already lost my warlord sentinel, and now we have no idea how long I will have to do without my First. Could you not have come up with something else to bargain? Anything else. Anything at all."

"Apparently not, Dragos," Rune snapped, as his already shortened temper torched.

Dragos fell silent as he swung around to face Rune. It had to be in part, no doubt, from surprise, as Rune was normally the even-keeled one in their relationship. But Dragos was also taking a deep breath before releasing a blast of wrath. The dragon's Power compressed in the room.

Then Aryal, of all people, stepped in to play her version of peacemaker. "What the hell, Dragos?" the harpy said. "It was life or death, and Tiago was bleeding out right in front of us. None of us actually had the time to consult our attorneys about the best bargaining terms to use with the Wicked Witch of the West. We brought you a present. Here." She threw a leather pack at Dragos, who lifted a reflexive hand to catch it.

Dragos opened the pack and pulled out two sets of black shackles that radiated a menacing Power. "Oh, now, there's finally a good piece of news," he said.

The three Wyr stared at the chains in revulsion. Fashioned by Dragos's old enemy, the late Dark Fae King Urien Lorelle, the chains had the ability to imprison Dragos himself, the most Powerful Wyr of them all. Dragos listened, his outburst of anger derailed, as Rune and Aryal finished telling the story of how Naida Riordan, wife of one of the most powerful figures in the Dark Fae government, had used Urien's old tools in her attempts to kill Niniane and Tiago.

"The shackles prevented Tiago from healing," Rune said.

"We nearly lost him while we were figuring how to get them off. That's when I had to bargain with Carling."

The dragon gave him a grim look. "All right," he said. "Use the week to get your affairs in order and delegate your duties. And when you get to San Francisco, try like hell to persuade Carling to let you do something quick."

So that's what Rune did, while Bob and the images in his head kept him company at night. He was supposed to coax Carling into letting him do something for her that was quick, huh? Maybe he could ask if he could take out her trash or do her dishes. He wondered how well that would go over.

Did the Wicked Witch have a sense of humor? Rune had seen her at many inter-demesne affairs over the last couple centuries. While once or twice he might have heard her say something that seemed laden with a double entendre, or he might have thought he'd seen a sparkle lurking at the back of those fabulous dark eyes, it seemed highly doubtful.

On Thursday, the sixth day, his iPhone pinged. He dragged it out of his jeans pocket and checked it. It was an email from Duncan Turner at Turner & Braeburn, Attorneys at Law, headquartered in San Francisco.

Who the hell?

Oh riiight, Duncan Turner was Duncan the Vampyre. He had been one of Carling's entourage as she traveled to Adriyel for Niniane's coronation. Carling had been in her position as Councillor of the Elder tribunal. The tribunal acted as a sort of United Nations for the Elder Races. It was made up of seven Councillors that represented the seven Elder demesnes in the continental United States, and it had certain legal and judicial powers over inter-demesne affairs. Their main charter was to keep the current balance of Power stable and work to prevent war.

Among other things, the Councillors had the authority to command the attendance of residents of their demesne when they were called to act in their official capacity as representative of the Elder tribunal. Rune wondered how many billable hours Duncan had lost for the privilege of attending Carling at Adriyel. Not only had the Vampyre proven to be an asset on the trip, he never showed a hint of frustration or resentment.

Rune clicked the email open and read through it.

RE: Per verbal contract enacted 23.4.3205, Adriyel date.

Dear Rune:

    As payment for services rendered by Councillor Carling Severan, please present yourself at sundown tomorrow to my office at Suite 7500, 500 Market Street, San Francisco, CA 94105. Further instructions will be given to you at that time.
    I hope you have had a good week and look forward to seeing you in due course.

Best regards,
Duncan Turner
Senior Partner
Turner & Braeburn, Attorneys at Law

Rune rubbed his mouth as he read through it again, and his already grim mood darkened. Ask Carling if he could do something quick, huh? Take out the trash. Do the dishes.

Bloody hell.

He said his good-byes, packed a duffle and fought a nasty, short battle with the pride of Wyr-lions, Cuelebre Enterprises's army of attorneys, for the use of the corporate jet. Despite their vociferous objections, the argument was over the moment he pulled rank. He sent the group of pissed-off cats scrambling to book first-class tickets for their corporate meeting in Brussels.

He could have flown in his gryphon form from New York to San Francisco, but that would mean he would arrive at the law offices tired and hungry, which did not seem to be the best strategic option. Besides, as he told the cats, he had some important things he had to take care of during the flight.

And he did. Soon as the Learjet had left the tarmac, he stretched out on a couch with pillows propped at his back and a pile of beef sandwiches at his elbow. He punched a button that opened shutters that concealed a fifty-two-inch plasma widescreen, settled a wireless keyboard on his upraised knees and a wireless mouse on the back of the couch, and logged into the game *World of Warcraft: Wrath of the Lich King* via the jet's satellite connection.

After all, he didn't know when he was going to get the chance to play again. And it was damn important to do his bit to save all life on Azeroth while he could. Booyah.

He played WoW, ate and napped while the Learjet shot westward through the sky.

Then the pilot's voice overrode the game on the Lear's sound system. "Sir, we've begun our descent. It should be a smooth one. We'll reach SFO within the half hour, and we're already cleared for landing. San Francisco is currently at a balmy seventy-four degrees, and the skies are clear. It looks like we're in for a beautiful sunset."

Rune rolled his eyes at the travelogue, logged out of his game, stretched and stood. He stepped into the luxuriously appointed bathroom, shaved and took a five-minute shower, dressed again in his favorite jeans, Jerry Garcia T-shirt and steel-toed boots, and went to check out the scenic action in the cockpit.

Pilot and copilot were a mated Wyr pair of ravens. They sat relaxed and chatting, a slender, dark-haired, quick-witted couple who straightened in their seats as he appeared. "Dudes," he said in a mild tone, resting one elbow on the back of the copilot's chair. "Chill."

"Yes, sir." Alex, the pilot, gave him a quick sidelong smile. Alex was the younger and the more aggressive of the two males. More often than not, his partner, Daniel, the more laid-back of the pair, was content to play backup. For the longer flights they tended to switch hats, one flying pilot for the flight out and the other piloting the return trip.

The jet would be serviced and refueled overnight, and they were headed back to New York first thing in the morning. Rune asked, "What are you guys going to do with your evening—have dinner out, take in a show?"

As they chatted about restaurants and touring Broadway shows, Rune gazed out at the panorama spreading out underneath the plane.

The San Francisco Bay Area was awash in gigantic sweeps of color, the bluish grays of distant landmarks dotted with bright sparks of electric color, all of it crowned with the fiery brilliance of the oncoming cloudless sunset. All five of the Bay Area's major bridges—the Golden Gate Bridge, San Francisco-Oakland Bay Bridge, Richmond-San Rafael Bridge, Hayward-San Mateo

Bridge and the Dumbarton Bridge—were etched in perfect miniature in the watercolor distance. The southern San Francisco Peninsula sprouted skyscrapers like flowers in some gigantic god's back garden. At the other end of the Golden Gate lay the North Bay area, which included Marin, Sonoma and Napa counties.

Sometimes there was another land in the distance, sketched in lines of palest transparent blue. One of the Bay Area's Other lands had started appearing on the horizon around a century ago. It seemed to sit due west of the Golden Gate. The first sighting had caused major consternation and a remapping of shipping lanes. Much research and speculation had gone into the singular phenomenon, sparking ideas such as a Power fault that might be linked to California's earthquake faults, but no one really understood why the island appeared at times and disappeared at others. Eventually an adventurous soul discovered that the island disappeared once ocean-faring vessels sailed close enough. After that the traffic in the shipping lanes returned to normal.

Soon the island became another Bay Area tourist attraction. Sightseeing cruises increased exponentially whenever the Other land was visible. People began calling it Avalon, the shining land of myth and fable.

But there was another population in the Bay Area. It was not the population that took cruises, ate in restaurants or took in a touring Broadway show. It lived in the corners of old abandoned buildings and hid in the shadows when the night came. The crack addicts and the homeless didn't call the land Avalon.

They called it Blood Alley.

The island was visible now in the distance, the immense orange-red ball of the setting sun shining through its silhouette. Rune watched it thoughtfully, shifting his stance to take in the change in gravity as the Learjet tilted into a wide circle that would bring it into a landing pattern for SFO.

Alex the pilot heaved a sigh and said, "I am required by FAA regulations . . . blah blah . . . seat belt . . . blah . . ."

Rune burst out laughing. "If we wouldn't lose all the shit that's not anchored down in the cabin, I'd be tempted to just pop open a door and hop out."

Daniel shot him a look. "Thank you, sir, for refraining from that action."

"You're welcome." Rune clapped the copilot on the shoulder and left the cabin.

Truth was, he wasn't in all that big of a hurry, and they were setting down soon enough. When Daniel opened up the Learjet, Rune thanked him and took off. He shifted just outside the jet and cloaking his Wyr form from scrutiny, launched into the air and flew into the city.

He was undecided about where to land, since he wasn't familiar with the location of 500 Market Street. Finally he chose to set down near the west end of the Golden Gate Park. As he spiraled down toward a paved path, his shadow flickered over a slender furtive figure that stood in front of a sign and shook a can of spray paint.

Rune landed, changed back into his human form and let his cloak of concealment drop away. He slung his duffle bag onto one shoulder and watched as the figure tagged the sign. The brown creature looked like an anorexic humanoid female, with a skeletal frame and long spidery hands and feet. Her dripping hair had strands of seaweed in it.

She glanced over her shoulder, caught sight of him and scowled. "What are you staring at, ass-wipe?"

He said in a mild tone, "Not a thing, my good woman."

"Keep it that way." She darted to a nearby trash can, tossed away the spray-paint can and dashed across the path to dive into a nearby pond. Soon the quiet sound of brokenhearted sobbing came from underneath a weeping willow at the pond's edge.

Rune walked over to the sign. It was one of the myriad signs that were posted throughout the Bay Area ponds, lakes and rivers that warned tourists: PLEASE DO NOT FEED THE WATER HAUNTS.

This particular sign had one word blacked out with spray paint. It now read: PLEASE DO FEED THE WATER HAUNTS.

Welcome to the Nightkind demesne, the home of water haunts, night Elves, aswang ghouls, trolls and Vampyres. He strolled over to the willow tree and cocked his head to look underneath the dripping leaves. The water haunt sat in the water, her bony, thin shoulders hunched. She caught sight of him and sobbed harder.

He dug in his duffle bag. The water haunt gave a piteous whimper, her lips trembling, as she tracked his movements with a mud-colored gaze. He pulled out a PowerBar and held it up. The haunt's eyes fixed on it. She wailed as she crept close. He raised a finger. Her wailing sailed upward on a questioning note and hitched to a stop.

He told her, "I'm on to your tricks, young lady. You try to bite me and I'll kick your face in."

The water haunt gave him a crafty grin that had far too many teeth. He indicated the PowerBar and raised his eyebrows. She gave him an eager nod. He tossed her the bar, and she snatched it out of the air. With a whirl and a splash, she dived to the other side of the tree to devour her prize.

He shook his head and checked his watch. He had about a half hour to sunset. Plenty of time to walk west, connect to Market Street and find out if he needed to hook either a left or right.

Bob started up in his head again as he headed out of the park. *Every little thing is going to be all right.*

Oh no. Not again. He wanted to at least start out this venture with some semblance of sanity. As he strode down the street, he unzipped a side pocket on his duffle and fished around inside until he nabbed his iPod. He popped in the ear buds and scrolled through his extensive playlists for something else. Anything else. Anything at all.

"Born to Be Wild." Yeah, that'll do. He punched play.

Steppenwolf's strong, raw voice sang in his ears.

Fire all of your guns at once and explode into space.

It was twilight, one of the world's threshold places, the crossover time between day and night. The dying sunshine caught in his lion's eyes. They flared with lambent amber as Rune smiled.

THE FIRST IN A NEW PARANORMAL ROMANCE SERIES FROM

THEA HARRISON

DRAGON BOUND

⇒▪◆▪⇐

A Novel of the Elder Races

Half human and half wyr, Pia Giovanni spent her life keeping a low profile among the Wyrkind and avoiding the continuing conflict between them and their Dark Fae enemies. But after being blackmailed into stealing a coin from the hoard of a dragon, Pia finds herself targeted by one of the most powerful—and passionate—of the Elder races.

As the most feared and respected of the Wyrkind, Dragos Cuelebre cannot believe someone had the audacity to steal from him, much less succeed. And when he catches the thief, Dragos spares her life, claiming her as his own to further explore the desire they've ignited in each other.

Pia knows she must repay Dragos for her trespass, but refuses to become his slave—although she cannot deny wanting him, body and soul . . .

penguin.com

ALYSSA DAY

VAMPIRE IN ATLANTIS
The Warriors of Poseidon

A vampire's oath, a maiden's quest . . .

Daniel, vampire and ally of the Warriors of Poseidon, has fought on the side of humanity—even against his fellow creatures of the night—for more than eleven thousand years. But the crushing weight of futility and the reality of always being starkly, utterly alone has forced him to finally give in to despair. He took the first step into the sunlight that would destroy him—and instead walked into Atlantis.

And the blackest of magic that could consume them both . . .

Eleven thousand years ago, Serai was one of a group who agreed to be placed into magical stasis to ensure the future of the Atlantean race. When the gemstone that protects her sleeping sisters is stolen, she awakens to a vastly changed world—and the one man she could never, ever forget. And with an ancient evil tracking their every step, the long-lost lovers must battle both the darkest of magic and the treacheries of their own hearts.

M13G061(

P.O. 0003494972